the ghost OCEAN

the ghost OCEAN

a novel

richard BENKE

UNIVERSITY OF NEW MEXICO PRESS
ALBUQUERQUE

Library of Congress Cataloging-in-Publication Data

Benke, Richard, 1942–
The ghost ocean : a novel / Richard Benke.— 1st ed.
p. cm.
ISBN 0-8263-3194-7 (alk. paper)
1. Police—New Mexico—Fiction.
2. Mexican-American Border Region—Fiction.
3. Drug traffic—Fiction.
4. New Mexico—Fiction.
5. Mexico—Fiction.
I. Title.
PS3602.E6643G48 2004
813'.6—dc22

2003023786

Printed and bound in the U.S.A. by Thomson-Shore, Inc.
Typeset in Janson Text 11/14
Display type set in Amoebia Rain
Design and composition by Maya Allen-Gallegos

Foreword

*A brief introduction to wolves, drug lords, murders,
wars of contrition, love, and hate.*

All of the above are in the area of Ghost Ocean in abundance, but it is
the land that replaced the water so many eons ago that dominates and
challenges all.

Last year I was on a little scouting expedition into the Black Range
with a friend at the helm of a four-wheel drive. I was amazed that we
had attained an altitude of around nine thousand feet, then suddenly
discovered a plateau not unlike those found in the lower foothills of the
mighty mountains.

We came to a barren spot with a game trail running through it. Out
of habit, we stopped to read sign. There had been seventeen elk, four
buck deer, and a coyote along the trail that morning. By nature I looked
around hoping to sight any of these creatures. I didn't, but suddenly I
realized from this spot on the globe, at that magic moment, there was
not a single item to be seen—other than our own vehicle—made by the
hands of man. What made this such a revelation of wonder was that in
that 360 degrees of my vision, I thought I could see at least two million acres of this earth, but my friend pointed out that to the north we
looked down on most of Ted Turner's famed buffalo ranch known as
the Ladder, and it was 250 thousand acres itself, I realized I'd under-
estimated the acreage. So, from the perspective of a high flying eagle,
we were surveying several million acres of greatly varied terrain. It had
all been part of the Ghost Ocean.

To the east we could see far beyond the Rio Grande. At least forty
miles distant to the west, the seemingly endless Gila Wilderness
stretched all the way to Arizona. To the south we could discern the
desert mountains leading past the border of Mexico and the boot-heel
of New Mexico.

For a moment, I could imagine hearing the eternal, lapping hum of
the great body of water so many tens of millions of years back in time,
before the angry magma had, at intervals, shoved the Black Range into
the sky and formed great islands. The fiery upheaval created the immense
mountains of the Gila Wilderness. On the tops of these are found fos-
sils from their birthplace. Billions of them. As far as seventy miles to the
east, past the space age town of Alamogordo, seashells can be found atop

the Sacramento Mountains. Now, millions of years after the main geo-
logical rearrangements were over, there were other forms of increasing
violence that came from the guns and minds of the widely varied and
scattered human inhabitants. These people have such powerfully different ambitions, desires, and backgrounds that a cauldron of dangerous
confusion has been created. Amazingly, Benke puts the tangled mysteries together in his book for me and others to better understand.

Some three thousand years back, the Mogollon Indians farmed a
few of the valleys. Later, the Mimbres settled all over the foothills of
the now dry ocean and made love and their unique black and white pot-
tery. They lasted a long but unknown time and vanished as mysteriously as they had come.

Then about four hundred years ago, Oñate came up from south of
the border. He and his soldiers, merchants, horses, cattle, and sheep
came to stay. They settled in valleys of spring water and either conquered or joined the pueblos on the big river's northern banks and surrounding areas. Then the gringos came along the Santa Fe and other
trails and the violent wars for control began.

The Apaches ranged across a wide area and dominated for a few cen-
turies. In the realm of the Ghost Ocean, Geronimo, Victorio, Nana, and
the worshipped warrior-medicine woman, Lozen, fought all comers to
the vanishing point. The gringo Cavalry and foot soldiers, the Buffalo
Soldiers, groups of miners, and the Mexican militia all engaged the
Apache valiantly. It would seem that the upheaval from the primeval
waters were for nothing but the drainage and smearing of blood.

At last a sort of peace came. The deer, bear, hawks, mountain lions,
wolves, coyotes, and countless other wild creatures still survived here
even today—all except the wolves who are now being reintroduced and
are an integral part of this book.

As I feasted my old eyesight across this historical—and at the
moment—blessedly empty vastness, I felt a oneness, a sameness with
this land. It was a supreme moment of peace. It was only for an instant
because I knew how deceiving this vision of peaceful grandeur was.

Pockets of chaos reign from the southeast at El Paso/Juarez, across
the border into Mexico, then back southwest to Palomas, Deming,
Ascencion, and Tucson. From the widespread spaces of the north to
the boot-heel that borders Arizona and Mexico, there were murders
and maimings. The Colombian and Mexican drug cartels penetrate and
invade America ready to kill on either side of the border to get their

destructive goods deep into the country and return with billions of dollars in greenbacks.

A different kind of trouble surges—verbal, printed, and sometimes physical battles—between the livestock ranchers and the multiple environmental groups. Endless conflict it seems. However, at this moment of perpetual history always being made or activated, I felt this parallel world of quietude and its consoling aloneness. How could this exist in a land of forever war? Then . . . I realized that the land of the Ghost Ocean was so vast that way up here on the mountain top, the uncountable little wars below were silent.

Author Richard Benke heard and saw all the disagreements over years of special assignments with the Associated Press. Most of the citizens of this huge territory are naturally so concerned with what affects them directly and daily, they are unaware of the boiling, roiling whole. It is an amazing feat for a single writer to see and attempt to understand such a complicated and gorgeous part of our world. Benke has made a struggle almost as great as the Apaches to show both sides of all the unceasing little wars. Of course, little wars are big wars when you are in the center of them. From the killings in battle of the "Cali" and Mexican "bangers" to the uncanny murder of the lovely teenage child, dubbed the "Wolf Girl," to the amazing friendships amidst the carnage on the border, Benke has achieved as honest and fair a representation as I believe possible.

In *Ghost Ocean*, there are totally fascinating adventures and revelations told in page after page of quick, precise prose that would have made Hemingway proud. In its wonderfully convoluted mysteries, the plot— or plots—converges in moments of revelation that shake the reader into a tingling awareness. To become acquainted with this massive landscape is a worthy trip across the pages. The multiple battles of the wild animal and human inhabitants are an added bonus. Here you find a microcosm of the world in a single book. One can choose and absorb what fits. Benke has left plenty to ponder, even after the mysteries are solved and personal and private conclusions are reached. The Ghost Ocean grows wider and deeper with each breath of the new, wild wolf.

—MAX EVANS,
author of *Madam Millie, Now and Forever,*
The Rounders, Hi Lo Country, and others

Author's Note

But fictive things wink as they will; wink most
when widows wince.

—WALLACE STEVENS

Trouble with fiction: T'isn't real. But people want it to seem real.
So they can live it. Trick's to make a reader believe it. See it. Taste
it. Smell it. But let's not get carried away. I know a goodly number
of ranchers. Dozens, let's say. I'm not picking on any one in particular for the characters of Sid and Marlie Braden, William and Alice
Sandrine, Ellie and Clifford and Clayton Endicott, Martin Blye or
any rancher in what I call the Heel of New Mexico or the fictitious
Apache Wilderness or the fictitious Hidalgo National Forest, or the
fictitious towns of Concha, Rio Santo, Gila Wells or Redsleeve, or
any scientist, lawman, environmentalist, physician, innkeeper, criminal or child. And that goes double for the wolves.

—RICHARD BENKE

Chapter One

Wilderness

Tracking a tracker on the trail of wolves, Will Mann rode the Gila Divide brim down to keep the spiraling snow from his eyes.

The first winter of the wolves was fading. Four wolves shot. Four rangers shot *at*.

The winter was colder than anyone expected. And longer.

No matter, Mann kept earflaps up. So he could hear.

Crossed the wolf pack's tracks just north of Gila Wells, and followed them. Surprisingly close to the town. In less than a mile, the tracker's sign cut in. Big horse, lightly ridden. Bent nail in one shoe. Somebody sloppy. Somebody in a hurry. But now they were slow, following the Mexican grays.

Out of a less than clear blue sky, his cloud-gray horse pulled hard right. Caught wind of something. Mann suspected water since she was owed a drink. So he let her take them off their trail a hundred yards up a draw, thinking there'd be water.

A place known for its confusion of rivers flowing all directions. Where the Black Range mingles with the Mimbres and Mogollons, where the Gila turns west, looking for the Colorado. Other rivers scatter east or north, vanish underground or dry up and die.

Mann rode along one of the rocky ribs buttressing the river-silted bedrock table land that overlooks the ghost ocean, where it fans out into Mexico: The green-edged mesa was one of the sacred places, not his jurisdiction, and he knew it.

And the draw turned out dry except for a little snow. Whatever Lady smelled wasn't wet. The pale dapple gray almost-white horse stopped, edged backward uneasily.

Mann scanned the bluffs. Had Lady misread the land or had he misread her?

Above them was Cerro Verde, the green-topped bluff where Mangas Coloradas routed Colonel Oreste Madrid's territorial militia in 1860. The lost colonel had followed the wrong river in the wrong direction. Bones and ammunition still littered the canyon under a shroud of sand. The battleground had a marker, placed by the Museum of New Mexico, Office of Cultural Affairs. No marker needed from the Apache point of view. The Apache knew every drop of water, every eddy, every trout.

While Mann looked up at green-edged Cerro Verde, a bullet came down *zshhhhhhung!* in the dust close to his foot.

"Aw, people!" Mann said aloud. "When will it end? When will it end? *¡Esta es nuestra tierra, todos!* Mann got to thinking if anyone had a right to be inhospitable, it was himself, but the US Bureau of Land Management strictured him always as guest, servant, the *ranger*; the public are the owners, the bosses, the royal pains in the asses.

Hunkered behind a rock three feet tall he peered at the ridge. Another bullet came with that withering sound cut short by snowy dust. The *crack* of the brush gun echoed from the ridge, lever-action cocking the next round. Wind hissed and rasped in the trees.

He supposed he could rest safely behind the rock, but he released Lady. Grabbed his thirty-thirty and saddlebag, then sat with his back against the rock, listening to Lady chuff down the draw. He wondered who he'd run up against: Bandits, enviros, migras, mules or coyotes—the smugglers—or the ranchers, miners, loggers or the Neighbors, any one of them might be crazy-mad enough. Didn't even rule out migras if they were dirty.

No more bullets came, but the wind did, lashing him with leathery pellets of snow. Scallops of white began to cover his tracks and everybody else's. Beside his footprints was a little crater in the snow with a bullet in the middle of it. He dropped it in a zip-seal plastic bag from the big canvas saddlebag, and there it was—a plastic water bottle; yep, had water all along. Forgot about it. Wasted trip up this draw. *Wasn't it?*

Mann called: "Lady, girl!" Sloshed the water bottle. She came to him quick then.

Gave her everything left in the bottle and held it up empty for her to see. Then she let him climb into the saddle and they rode up the old elk trail that led into the mountain.

Probably not smugglers up so high, he was thinking. *They'd never find the way.*

No, maybe not smugglers. Maybe war, like what Jack Felix told him. Just yesterday. Over at Dolly's Cafe. Eating chorizo and beans. Sat there in the padded booth, Jack in his threadbare fatigues, his brass-top cane across his lap. "It's just simply war." The scarred-up, gimpy Felix, who'd tried to pacify half of Vietnam, knew about war. Felix the spook. Cuban hat jaunty on the elk antler behind them. Told Mann he was up from El Paso looking for a missing Mexican. Mann had known Felix since he got back from 'Nam. *Pacify* meant something else back then—meant beat someone so bad that everyone wakes up smelling Agent Orange. This looked like maybe three or four wars. "Like that pipe bomb they found up in the wilderness," Jack said. Footlong. Stupid. No prayer of going off. Message bomb, that's all. Like a phone call in the night. Some thought a ranch hand, Bertie Williams, put it there for himself to find.

Mann gave Bertie both more credit than that—and less. One, he wouldn't. Too straight. Bertie worked part-time for the sheriff. Two, couldn't. Didn't know how.

That left: *Who? Why?*

And which war?

They overlapped.

Yeah, he smiled. Bureau of Land Management. Somebody always asked him: What's this B-L-M? They'd point at his shoulder patch. What's that? *Bombs and Land Mines*, he thought. That's us now. United States Bureau of Bombs and Land Mines.

Lady swayed up the rocky switchback, walking steady and sure. Mann kept his head down, looking for sign. It took about twenty minutes to reach the top. He tethered Lady on the trail. *Some scurrying up on the ridge, for sure.* They had departed in a hurry. Left their spent Dow-Winchester thirty-thirty shells. He picked them up and put them in the plastic bag with their perfectly matched slugs. And they left tracks, boots, and two horses, one of them mounted, the other maybe not, and a mule, no doubt. *Was somebody left behind?* There was a smaller set of oddly placed footprints, like jogging shoes. The wind was rapidly degrading the tracks. *Maybe a jogger.* He knew about the mountain runners. They run fifty, a hundred miles. *This wasn't that, either. Joggers don't shoot at you.* He was getting disgusted with himself. Off the track, off the scent. But . . .

The stampede of tracks channeled into a line leading down the backside. He photographed them, then climbed a tree and used his binoculars to scan for movement down where the tracks appeared to lead, but whoever was down there wasn't moving.

He started a checkerboard search of the ridge, pausing to view. The town of Gila Wells spread out below, a little jewel on the edge of the foothills. The smoke from the adobe kiva fireplaces and wood-burning stoves smudged the sky down in the distance.

Up here, loose earth, recent. *Too high for prairie dogs.* Nine-thousand feet here at Cerro Verde summit. He used his rifle butt as a hoe. Had nothing else but bare hands to sweep away the loose dirt. *Yeah*, he nodded to himself, *yeah*, there's something here. Then that sick feeling. *It's a girl, oh, God.* Had to be eleven or twelve, dead a few hours. *Backshot. Brought up here on a horse, backshot, and buried. Backshot, maybe running away. Not jogging, but running, all right. They shot her running. Running away.*

Mann unfolded a plastic tarpaulin, rolled her up inside it, slung her over Lady's back behind the saddle and tied her solid with his catch rope. Back on his grid, he photographed more of the boot prints, found a piece of torn cardboard, maybe from a matchbook, maybe from God knows what. Also, he found an eyeglass lens, oval. And he went down the trail to check and see if the girl wore glasses; he doubted that she did. He pulled back the plastic. No glasses. He sighed, and he stewed about it for a minute, until he realized the time. He laid her on the trail, untied her, unrolled the plastic, looked in her pockets and looked under her and in the dirt that had fallen from her. Dirt had covered and filled her half-opened eyes. No glasses. But there was something familiar, a little girl he had seen on one of the ranches. She was almost. . . . He knew this girl—why couldn't he say her name? He repacked her on Lady's back and returned to the search, pestered by the dying sun. He would have maybe an hour to finish digging out that grave and to checkerboard the rest of the ridge. Winter hours. Early March. He sighed. Maybe he'd get lucky in the low sunlight coming under the clouds. He positioned himself at right angles with that sun. Something shiny did catch a sunbeam. Brass-framed glasses, one lens missing. Right about there he also found two unspent Winchester rounds and a twenty-five-cent piece. Sloppy, all right. This stuff went into a second baggie. White tuft waving in the wind on a broken-off pine bough, shoulder high. Mann checked his down jacket, thinking it might have torn. It hadn't. Another Zip-Loc and he was finished. Marked off the perimeter with yellow tape. It looked incongruous as he glanced back, riding away.

It was dark and sleeting hard, with unusual winter lightning, by the time he reached his SUV and trailer on Highway 35. He radioed the sheriff, loaded Lady in the trailer and put the dead child on the back seat of his BLM four-wheel.

Sheriff Corona met him halfway up the road from Gila Wells and took custody of the body. Mann gave Corona the crime-scene coordinates. Turned over the bagged evidence. Then Corona squared up on him, and Mann thought: "Here it comes."

"Shoulda contacted us before disturbing the scene," Corona said.

"Not doable. The shooters were still out there. If I'd left, they'd've come back and got rid of all the evidence, including the body. I interrupted them. They ran off. But I know they were nearby."

"Yeah, how?"

"Nothing moved out there but the wind in the trees. I could see three-sixty for twenty, thirty miles. They were out there, waiting for me to clear out."

"Who'd do this?" the sheriff asked, directing the question at himself as much as at Mann.

"Well, sir, wish I knew. Wish I did. But I don't. Any idea who she may be?"

The sheriff hesitated. "We do have a girl missing, twelve years old, off the Two Square. Out riding, was it yesterday? Never came back."

"Lord, that's who she is," Mann said. "Millie Braden, the Bradens' girl."

"You're sure," Corona said.

"Well, yeah, I remember. Saw her a few times. She wore glasses. This time her glasses fell off, got trampled. Plus, you know . . ." testing words . . . "the usual distortion."

Sheriff Corona acknowledged the depredation of death with a single, grim nod.

"Bertie Williams' niece," Mann added.

"My Bertie?" Corona said.

Bertie, the sheriff's radio dispatcher. Mann nodded.

"A quarter in the bag plus some gun shells might have prints on 'em," Mann said.

"Okay, we'll tag it all," the sheriff said.

"That tuft of stuff came from someone's coat," Mann said. "About shoulder high."

"Okay, we'll tag that too," Corona said.

"You might just seal off the wilderness," Mann suggested.

"Gates are shut," Corona said. "Anyone comin' from out that way, we got 'em."

"They had two horses and a mule," Mann said.

"You saw them?"

"I saw the tracks," Mann said. "We need to get a team out there and track it."

"It's night, and it's snowing," the sheriff said, pulling his sheep collar tight around his neck and snapping it shut.

"Tracks won't be there tomorrow," Mann said. "I'm going back out. Alone if necessary. A team would be better."

"I don't have any team. Call your feds. Maybe they have," Corona said.

But he agreed to be at the scene next morning with his Gila County detectives.

"Somebody needs to notify the parents, Sid and Marlie," Mann said.

"See what the coroner says. Maybe get an answer tonight," Corona said.

"Won't ever happen. Ought to notify the parents now, anyway," Will said.

The sheriff stared back with dead eyes. "We'll handle notification, like always."

Mann accepted it. But Corona could see something additional in Mann's eyes. It wasn't anger. That wouldn't be Mann. Funny thing about Mann.

"What is it?" Corona said.

"I thought I was tracking a wolf killer. Someone tracking a wolf. Not this," he said.

"You're a good man, Will. Work for me. Give you a ten percent raise for doing exactly the same thing y'already do. Ten percent, full benefits. Get paid your overtime."

Mann shook his head. He'd been through this before with Corona.

"It would be too much desk," Mann said. "Too much crime. Too much politics."

"I handle the politics," Corona said with the sour smile of a man who knew how. "With us you got backup when you need it. With your guys, *never.*"

"I still get backup from you, either way, right?" Mann said.

Like tonight? he was thinking.

"Everybody's got a budget," Corona said.

"Goodnight, Elias," Mann said, getting in his SUV. Corona watched and wondered as Mann drove back into the mountains. *Ten percent plus overtime.* Surely, surely, he thought, Mann couldn't have just turned down an additional five grand a year.

Chapter Two

Quinceañera

The land was a databank for Pete Alderete, and he could see it all. See it the way it was back when the grass stretched from the Peloncillos north of him to the Sierra Madres below him—and the gravelly expanse it had become. Sometimes it got better, but sometimes wind or water roared through and ripped it all apart. And the scrubby little *pinos* grew thick as an army on the plains that climbed into the Madres.

All quiet now, the predawn fog curling up along the base of his one remaining mesa. He was there, on Isla Mesa, so he could be at the heart of it all when the sun rose.

His six-hundred-square-mile ranch in northern Mexico, wrapped around the corner of New Mexico, had been established more than a century before the so-called Mexican War and the zigzag boundary that grew from it in 1848. It cost the Alderetes the pie-wedge of desert that contained their other mesa. Rancho Dos Mesas had extended across that empty place that became the *frontera*. His mesa was called Isla because it once had been an island. And in that morning fog, as with the mists of ancient places trying to reach up and reclaim human memory, it seemed an island again.

Then the sun edged over the Hermanos Peaks up on the border by Concha, New Mexico, and sprayed light through openings in the clouds. Pete kept the two-mesa name even though the other mesa, Dolor, now belonged to his friend, William Sandrine, the neighbor on the US side. From Isla, Pete saw the border monuments all in a row from the south corner up to the Heel's north corner, then east to the monument below Concha at Rio Santo, Mexico, where his four-hundred-year-old hacienda was built as a fortress against Apaches. He also could see the truck lights on the highway above his western headquarters at Llanos—and beyond, to where the Cali, the Colombians, were camped.

With the monuments as reference points, he mapped every protrusion in the mist. This morning they included a few stray cattle, encroaching volunteer trees that needed to be cut to keep his grasslands intact, and two Cali riders, carrying automatic weapons and their contraband across the border into New Mexico. He saw they had ropes on their saddles, and he knew more of his or Sandrine's beef would go missing by day's end.

Alderete was fifty-eight, and all his old *charro* friends were gone. He made this pilgrimage to Isla for perspective at those times when he saw how totally he was alone.

His wife gone. Cancer. Three years now. He talked to her spirit here, even though she was buried at the cemetery in town. His son gone. Missing. Believed shot. Now his daughter. Fifteen. She didn't know yet that he would send her away to finish school in Colorado. She would fight it. He was unwilling, too, but he had to do it.

He'd picked the Arabian because he was fast and strong and knew the uneven path back from Isla. Needed to be back before ten. Preparing for Blanquita's quinceañera.

The horse was ready. Pete could feel the Arabian's muscles twitching.

"*Sí, bueno, amigo, ándale, vamanos!*" he whispered.

Didn't need a nudge. Just a whisper and they were off.

Until Mann rang her doorbell in the woods near the hamlet of Redsleeve early in the morning, nervous, with granules of snow sparkling on his hat, Doctor Sara Armstrong had never met him. She knew who he was. Last fall he'd brought in a child nipped by a bear cub for stitches . But Mann had disappeared before Doc came out. A deputy sheriff was with the girl's parents. No Mann. Never saw him till today, asking her to carry a birthday present to Blanca Alderete. He'd meant to ask earlier. Now he was mid-tragedy, tracking a wide-bed pickup and horse trailer that had gone west from Cerro Verde.

"Wish I could repay you this favor," he told her. "Rude of me to call so early."

"I'm already back from my run," she said. "You're a ranger. Show me the range."

He thought a moment. "You mean ride? Horses?"

"Sure, ask me to go riding," she said.

"I will, later this week. I'll call," he said, holding his hat until the door had closed.

Blanca Alderete, in curlers, flannel pajamas and a pink chenille robe, saw the tiny dusty speck like a little twister coming in from the west, and she knew it was her dad.

He came fast and direct and vaulted off the horse when it reached the corral. Hector, her cousin, had a wide smile as he took the Arabian into the stable, and her dad ran for the back door of the bunkhouse, billows of dust trailing after him like an aura that could not quite keep up, and he pushed through to the main house. Blanca had to laugh.

Her dad was like some kid when he was late. Wanting to prove he could still do it.

He burst into the house, still dusty, swatting the dust with his hat.

"Oh, great, let's pile it all up on the rug," Blanca said to him. "I'll just get the vacuum cleaner. Unless you'd like to bring the horse in, too. I'll wait, in that case."

"What a morning!" he said. "I saw two Cali mules with AK-47s on their backs carrying huge packs of something across the line."

"You're lucky they didn't shoot you," she said.

"They were miles away, never knew I was there. What a glorious day. Happy birthday, chiquita."

"Thanks, daddy," she said.

"What time is it?"

"Ten o'clock," she said. "You made it in record time."

"Not record time," he said, "but pretty good time."

"When are you going to take me with you?"

"Never," he said. "A darn rough ride for a little girl. You couldn't keep up."

"I'm big now," she said. "I can keep up with anybody."

"Fifteen, yeah. Meaning to talk to you . . . about your education."

"Yes?" she said.

"Yeah, we'll talk about it. Later. Just doing the party today."

"Don't send me away," she said. "This is home. You need me. I need you."

He gave her a hug: "Got to get ready for your party."

"Yeah," she said. "Take a shower."

He started for the stairs.

"The bunkhouse," she said. "Maria vacuumed upstairs already. Vacuumed down here, too. And now I have to do it again, which I don't have time for!"

"How long can it take to vacuum a four-square-foot patch of dust?"

"Just take your shower and don't be coming in here till you have," she said.

"You're bossy," he said, "like, like . . ."

"*She* told me how I need to be," she said. Fists on hips, elbows sticking out.

"How can you talk like that and not . . . ?" Choked him up.

She choked too. "Just trying to hang *on*," she said, "till you tell me what happened to Juanito. Been waiting for you to get back. You said you'd tell me after I was fifteen."

He'd been letting her believe her brother might come back.

Two months since he vanished. New Year's at the Jalisco Bar in Rio Santo.

Pete Alderete sat through the first month of silence waiting for the police to tell him something. They never did. So he drove the sixty miles east into El Paso to see Felix the Fixer in February, wrote him a check. Now another month gone. No word from Felix, either. Frustrating. Pay and get nothing. But Felix was expected at Blanca's party.

Pete thought Felix knew the full story. He'd been at the Jalisco on New Year's. The three-story bar was the tallest building in town. Third floor recently added as bedrooms for the girls. Fancy iron balconies on their windows. Twinkle lights for New Year's Eve. Twinkle lights but no whiskey. "They ran out of whiskey," Felix told Pete. But the boys just switched to tequila, often jump-started by dustings of meth and coke that gave tabletops a wintry look. One *ski trail* blurred another.

The bar wanted it all. White-nosed gangs, *pistoleros, turistas.* The Jalisco wanted people to park in the Concha municipal parking lot, a patch of dirt next to the border, and walk across into little Rio Santo, Concha's twin town. Get what you want no matter what.

To walk in it, Rio Santo seemed normal, peaceful. Workers lined up waiting for buses. Old men played cards under streetlamps in the Parque Central. Police slowly, quietly cruised the streets. Visitors would never know they were in a war. Unless they looked someplace like the Jalisco and heard fighting words . . . like *quinceañera.*

The bar mirror, through which Jack Felix had watched hostilities unfold, had been shattered twenty-four times in five years by flying bottles, mugs, bullets, farm implements, and the bar bat, widely swung. Glass was glued twenty-four times. The mosaic distorted all reflection. Everything seen through it qualified as surreal.

Felix, the quiet man in the back corner with the Cuban hat, had been seated in an unpadded hardwood booth, unnoticed, but noticing. The numbing hardness of the seat made his fragged leg ache so that he had to get up and walk it off. *Mariachi New Year* pumped from the neon jukebox. Mostly happy people dancing, drinking. Some unhappy. Edgy. Getting pissed, again, about one side of the border or the other. *Norteños* swaggering, snarling about the drugs, wanting to pick a fight, or see one.

Didn't take much to start it—an idle glance. Didn't dare daydream, staring off in someone's space. "Lookin' at somethin?" The phrase could be etched on headstones.

Over by the pool table, two *vatos* squabbled over a girl too pure to mention there.

Felix knew war when he saw it. Five armies in place now. Showing off, getting drunk, doing what armies do. Always, women around them in the low-hanging smoke. Jack made his way to the men's room and barely heard the final crescendo, a few distinct words: "You little bastard prick!" People shuffling, falling back on the worn board floor. Boots skidding. Was Juanito dragged out the door? *Bam . . . blam . . . bl-blam . . . bl-am!* Four shots? Muffled but no silencer. Echoey. Outdoors. Felix missed it. Nobody noted who said what. Knew not to. Torpedos rose, cool silvery question marks unholstered.

That's how the war and the year started, and by the time the shooting ended in the spring, there was a body count. David Belknap, a neighboring sheriff, told Jack six died.

There were skeptics to the north. Concha Chamber of Commerce executive director Mona Fleance complained: What right did Belknap have painting Frontera County some kind of war zone? "Few enough people stop'n'shop as is," Mona said. "And when they do, they're harassed by the Border Patrol." Then Dave insists it's war, with armies, casualties. No way to get re-elected. Mona told him once: "Don't care if you use cluster bombs. Just shut up about it. Don't want to know unless my girls are in it."

"Already are, Mona," he said. "Already are."

Mona had three daughters.

War and peace coexist. Felix said it in February: War. The Cali, the Cortes, the Costilla. And the ranchers, easy targets, were in somebody's crosshairs, too.

The Cali moved up from Miami when the Feds got thick as old paint. Octavio Cortes found ways to work it out, avoid confrontation, for a year. Enrique Costilla stayed on the Concha side running distribution. Heroin, cocaine, marijuana. Cortes just got it across. The Cali were his pupils but had their own distribution and their own pistolero army. Cortes' pistoleros were feared before the Cali arrived, then both the Cortes and Cali were feared. The Colombians were faceless, remote-controlled from Bogota.

Costillas did not shoot much. They telephoned. Planted figurative land mines, just seeds of information. Juanito was the only one at the Jalisco working for Costilla.

"A very brave soul," Felix said, "to have gone to the Jalisco."

"He shouldn't have gone there," Pete said. "I don't know why he did."

And while the *guerreros*, the pistoleros, the gang babies wore their dark uniform, dark glasses, Blanca Alderete wore white. Lacy dress, snowy stockings, shiny black pats. Tortoise-shell combs in her hair. She was ready. She looked out the window at the rocky, pale, ochre hills, bare, that blocked her view of America.

Looking there for her brother Juanito to come over those hills with a white package tied with lace ribbon, the way police said he would. She'd been waiting weeks. Now the vague sick feeling focused to a hard painful point. It was her birthday. Clock struck two. Now she had to believe the talk. Zero news from her father. She told him a schoolmate, Miguelito Cortes, had caught her outside the five-and-dime in Rio Santo and told her Juanito was drinking *there*—pointing to the Jalisco.

"Regrettably the subject of *you* came up," he said. "Don't think we've seen Juanito since." But he added: "Whatever they tell you, I had nothing to do with it."

That wasn't the news she had in mind.

Ramos, the torpedo, shifted his tiny eyes. They were like turrets bulging out from the middle of craterlike eye sockets. Stepped back. Readjusted his holster harness with a shrug, rotating just the one shoulder. In case a fourteener threatened. Then sagged both shoulders. Seemed to physically shrink, like a toad exhaling. Back to rolling his cigarette. One-handed. Badly.

Blanca shoved Miguel away and strode across the road to the Parque Central. She looked back and saw Miguel had grabbed Ramos' arm. Stopped him following her.

She could not *wait* to get home and tell her father that Miguelito and his creepy bodyguard Lizard Eyes had stepped so out of line on the eve of her fiesta. By the time she got home, she'd changed her mind. *Let it ride*, she thought she heard Juanito say.

Juanito never drank at the Jalisco, she was sure. Prostitutes worked that bar and sometimes danced there and slept upstairs. Men with tinted glasses and heavy firepower hidden in their black suit coats sat nightly at the teak bar, around the stage and at tables just large enough for a girl to dance on. Sometimes something happened. But nobody would expect it to spoil a quinceañera. Yet here, first to the party, was the bandaged Diego McFee, one of Alderete's neighbor ranchers who'd been shot by the Cali when he failed to move out of his house. He hadn't really refused them. He just thought about it too long. His *ejido* homestead was gone, Cali installed, deeds recorded, by the time he left the hospital. Pete gave him a job.

So at the party they tried to entertain. Tried to empty their eyes of pain. Never could. Blanquita was twelve when her mom died.

Pete had to be Dad and Mom and party-giver.

Quinceañera, the Spanish-Indio puberty rite, seemed a year or two late for most girls. The white formal wear—meant to convey the threshold of adulthood—actually notched Blanca's appearance farther back into childhood. Her legs seemed skinnier in snow-white nylons, her hands smaller in white gloves. It all only served to underscore her innocence. And her brown eyes were wide when her father presented the keys to the customized Oldsmobile that belonged to Uncle Harry Olean, former mayor of Concha.

"Happy quinceañera, hita. Now all you got to do is pass driver's ed," Pete said.

Harry, now wheelchair-ridden, couldn't drive. Vern Laughlin had taken his Olds, pulled off the chrome strips, filled the holes and painted it an orange-flake maroon that changed colors whenever it turned a corner, clouds blew in or the sun climbed the sky.

Sandrine, a friend of her dad's since long before she was born, had bought the tires. Pete pointed to a southern window. Down below she saw the orange-flake chalupa.

"Oh, Daddy."

"You like it," he said with a pleased chuckle.

"Yeah," she said. "I promise to be the girl you want me to be."

"The caterers are all ready," he added, guiding her toward the door.

"Caterers? You mean my cousins, right? The caterers," she laughed. That was Dad.

He smiled. "I'm not Don Octavio."

"Thank *God!*" she said. She was more American than any Rio Santo girl ever. Uninterested in ranching. But she did honor important traditions. She was beautiful, but it was too soon to say just how beautiful she would be. Pete was always thinking, worrying. They say true beauty shows through. And if true beauty dies, that shows through, too. He was proud of her, but there was work to be done. He'd do what he could to save her *tranquilidad*, the serenity of truly beautiful women. For that, he felt sure, she must never know exactly what happened at the Jalisco, what was said. If anyone tried to tell her, he'd stop it. He'd know it. He'd step in. Never let her believe it. Of course she guessed some of it. But nothing he couldn't soften or deny. But he knew the reality, except the one fact—where Juanito ended up. *Ah, God, Juanito.* Focus on your daughter, he told himself. It's her day.

"You have to buy your own gas, remember," he told her, "and you have to pay half the cost of adding you to the insurance. No Daddy's credit card for you, *princesa*."

"I know," she said, and then it was time to go downstairs.

Music was starting. Aunt Gussie's country-and-western mariachi called Familia was tuning up. Gussie's uncommon common-law husband, Johnny Red Horse Garcia, with waist-length gray hair, sang backup, danced wildly on stage and played guitar. Blanca's mom, Maya, had been the pianist—when real pianos were available and properly tuned. Now they did without piano. They'd been breaking Juanito in on drums. Now the drums sat in boxes in the room he had shared with Hector, his cousin, and a classified ad in the Deming, New Mexico, Headlight said: "Drums for sale." Harry's electric bass was all the beat they had. He played it sit-down. Could no longer play the upright.

And here came McFee, who knew better than any of the guests what Pete was going through. When he went to thank Pete for the invitation, both men wept.

To kill someone's son and for everyone to know it, even though it was well covered up, demanded some kind of action. With or without that action, Juanito's disappearance brought severe dishonor to the family, but especially without. Alderete kept saying he would "see to it." But doing the wrong thing would bring even more dishonor, maybe disaster. Worse than doing nothing. Pete had to be patient. *Keep looking.* Find the body. Then at least he could rub police noses in their words. *Oh, you can't be sure. He just ran away. Crossed at Concha, looking for work.* Like a million other boys.

Alderete was sure he knew which three young men—coked up, black-suited—had dragged his son out of the Jalisco. Two were from the countryside outside Llanos, where the cartel had combined several old ejido homesteads as a staging area and airstrip.

Now the guests were arriving in clusters. Sandrine, Mitchell Barnes from the Bootheel settlement of Sunflower, the Karajans, the onion and chile farmers. About thirty guests from the surrounding farms and ranches. All duded up, hats off, hair slicked.

Sipping Mazatlan champagne in Juarez stemware, they clustered in the sala, seated on the bancos that Pete's great-grandfather had hand-carved. They sat on the carpeted staircase. The women each formally greeted Blanca and handed her cards and small gifts, books or decorative candles, earrings, a charm bracelet. The hatless men bowed, filing through the reception line. The mariachi music was low-key, husky-voiced. The punch was tangy. A tinge of *sangria*. Dancers' skirts swirled, boots tapped. Blanca beamed like one of the halogen lamps placed on the border to detect incursions.

Will Mann sent regrets through Doc Sara Armstrong, who handed his present to Blanca, explaining there was trouble up at Gila Wells. Sara thought about Mann, compact, wiry, twitchy. Contrasting all the six-footers at the party, all at ease in their white Western shirts with ma-pearl buttons. Mann, who couldn't sit still, couldn't finish a cup of coffee, was better off in the hills. After conveying Mann's congratulations, Sara watched over Pete and his not-very-well-masked grief. After the dad-daughter dance, she saw Pete carefully work his way back through the guests, stopping along the way to talk with the cousins and his own brothers and sisters, his ancient aunt who was blind in one eye and had sagging socks, and to Sandrine, who hugged him and shook him like a rag doll. Finally he got to the back of the room and turned around, twice, like a dog priming his bed. Except he looked lost. In his own house. He met Sandrine again, coming back.

"What's wrong? Looking for someone?" Sandrine asked him.

"Guy with a cane. Felix. S'posed to be here but isn't."

"Jack Felix?" Sandrine said, then nodded. "You called him to find Juanito."

"Been months now since he's been gone, Juanito. We keep hearing rumors . . . why he's gone . . . why he isn't gone . . . why he would be coming home . . . or not. We guess we know what happened . . . to Juanito . . . *right?*"

Sandrine nodded, and Pete noticed Doc looking at him. He raised his right hand and thinly smiled a weak, belated greeting.

"Just wanted Juanito's body back, to prove it . . . prove murder, then bury him."

Doc could see him struggling. Sandrine saw it, too, and they squinted at each other, trying to think what they could do.

"So we can *accept* it," Pete went on, "so the police will know they're ignoring *murder!* Not just some runaway." Doc came over and tried to put healing hands on him.

"Missing persons," Sandrine said, "where the long arm of the law foreshortens."

"Felix was going to find him, bribe the *rurales*, the *pistoleros*, whatever. He was going to *find my boy*. Report to me here, today," Alderete said.

He told how he pushed a check across the desk in Felix's El Paso office. February, with the gray sleet slanting to the window. They talked about the *mordida*, how much it would take here compared with Michoacan, Juan Feliz-Abreu's home state.

Feliz-Abreu. Forgotten name. There seemed barely a trace of Michoacan left in him, but Felix used what he remembered, even though he spoke West Texan. The ranchers in San Angelo had changed his name to Felix, since the Spanish language was a special renovation project for Texans. They saw it as their duty.

As a kid, really no more than that, Felix did a couple big, dirty cleanup favors for Waylon Sydney, largest of the San Angelo cattlemen, and that got Felix citizenship. Next thing, he was the youngest man on the San Angelo City Council. Then, in a strange political twist, somebody else's sun rose back east and Felix was sent to Vietnam.

Naval intelligence . . . wounded on his first ground mission with a squad of Marines. Shrapnel. Right leg. Once his strong leg. Knee cartilage like shredded cheese. Felix did not move well for a man of action. Felix told Alderete he was transferred to the Philippines because he spoke Spanish.

"First time bein' Mexican did me any good," he'd said, closing the window.

Mustered out a captain, set up shop in El Paso, made an art of "fixing things." Not rigging them but *correcting* them. The methods scared people. But jobs got done, whatever, however. Knew the convolutions of the maze, how to get in, get out. Did some Mexican and Cuban skip-tracing for the United States government. On contract. There were rumors. Pete had known about him and the rumors for a long time. Had seen him around Rio Santo before. But sitting there in his El Paso office still made him nervous.

"Who do you think should we approach?" Felix asked him. "Relax. I'll simply show 'em there's no profit in keeping your son's body hidden."

"I told him, 'Don Octavio doesn't take bribes, he *gives* them,'" Alderete said.

"That changed the picture. There was nothing Felix didn't know about Octavio."

But that was February. Now it was March, end of the party, and no Felix.

Chapter Three

City of Stone

L ight as a breeze it brushed Bryce Weeks on the shoulder. Then something similar seemed to breathe in his ear. Fine gray hairs rippled on the back of his neck.

Moonlit, near Concha. Satellite locator on the dashboard indicated he was sixty miles west of El Paso, six miles north of the Mexico frontier outside the Concha city line.

The flawless black car idled in front of him with a deep gargling sound. Chrome exhaust pipes blurred in their vibration. The car was trembling, ready to spring.

Weeks could see the boy's slicked-back hair glistening in the moonlight. A boy. Just a boy. Maybe not yet fifteen years old. Sixteen, tops.

The car was customized beyond recognition. Could be Chevy. Could be Pontiac, Buick. Olds? No way to tell. Chihuahua plates. *How'd this get past Customs?*

Should be somebody else in the car old enough to drive. Or . . .

Well, he'd pulled the kid over so Weeks couldn't very well just walk away. Weeks' Tec-Nine dangled about thigh-high off his trigger finger.

The whole situation called for margin. He had parked an extra car length away. Trudged the soft, sandy shoulder. Footing awkward. He slowly approached, keeping eyes zeroed on the windows and the rear-view mirrors. But he couldn't see the boy's eyes or any reflection of eyes, just a silhouette with moonbeams bouncing off pomaded hair.

Weeks reached out to touch the polished left rear fender.

The car lurched backward at him, and the dust that millennia had mixed with the sand and sea salt rose up in clouds from under the wheels. The fender brushed his legs and bumped his gun, which began a kind of crazy firedance in his right hand.

It *brrraaapped* for several seconds. Enough to put a hundred holes in the side of the kid's pride and joy. A *clunk* came from the car's epicenter—transmission going from reverse to forward. The black arrow flung itself into the night, leaving Weeks coughing the dust. Took off his hat. Rubbed his forehead. Found a gritty film of sweat and sand.

The moon surrendered to a bank of clouds moving up from Mexico.

Never find the kid now. Unless he found him dead. Suppose a bullet nicked the boy. *Can't rule it out.* Weeks climbed into his tan cruiser. He followed the dust and the melted rubber to the edge of Karajan's cornfield, where a swath of flattened corn showed just where the car had left the road.

No, he would not be getting stuck tonight in a cornfield. He parked. And he followed the fallen corn on foot toward the dark entity ahead. It was the kid's car.

Weeks stepped quietly to the side and squatted amid the still standing cornstalks. He waited, watching and listening for any sound or shadow of motion.

The angle of the car, relative to his position among the cornstalks, brought it all back to him a second time that night—the haunted stretch of road north of Lordsburg, the drug corridor where he had found Mikey's body still behind the wheel of their patrol car.

It had been eleven years, seven months, twenty-two nights, six hours, and a scattering of minutes. But it was still new every time he made a stop. Mikey at his side again, whispering to him. Tonight, twice over.

The stopped car became Mikey's car, the driver became Mikey, staring up at him with infinite patience, the pale wisps of grama grass bent down like hairs slicked flat on a dead man's head. The cactus and yuccas waited like pallbearers in the background.

In twelve years, maybe fifteen thousand stops, everything from speeders to burned-out tail lights, to suspicious driving within the hundred-mile zone that allowed discriminatory stops, singling out drivers by race. Three stops a day. They add up.

Yeah, they had the bagpipes for Mikey, *Amazing Grace*, the white gloves, the seven guns firing three volleys, but that really didn't help

Sybil, Mike's widow, or his boys. Weeks knew it would have been pointless to promise resolution or closure for them. The boys, then four and five, were now sixteen and seventeen. They were about the age of the phantom lowrider now off in the corn, waiting as Weeks waited. How could anyone promise anything? Whoever did Mikey was already somebody else.

Weeks realized: Probably lose his job over this one. *No witnesses?* Just a bunch of bullet holes. And bullet holes do not lie. Plus he's five miles out of town and in Sheriff Belknap's territory. Weeks shrugged. *You do what you got to. Everybody's alive. The night's a success. Tomorrow's another day.* He went home and wrote that report.

Home was a forty-year-old, single-wide trailer in a trailer park across from what used to be a Mexican restaurant. Parabolic arches made of fake adobe brick. The brick painted the diarrheic brown of refried beans. The restaurant once had belonged to Octavio Cortes of neighboring Rio Santo, Mexico.

The restaurant was closed because Octavio's American assets had been seized under drug-trafficking laws, although his Mexican assets were untouched. The town of Concha inherited the building, designed to seem architecturally menacing, to bespeak corruption and dispassionate murder. The Conchans wanted to make it a public library.

Weeks would look out his window nightly at the restaurant's arches with satisfaction. He had taken so much away from Octavio, whom he had tracked ten years. Weeks took the jobs that put him closer and closer to the don of drugs in Rio Santo.

When he got to the office-jail Saturday morning, the bullet-riddled car was parked out front, right next to a tank-like, all-weather Border Patrol Excursion SUV deluxe.

Octavio's lawyer, Juan Reilly, sat inside Miguelito's car, arm on the driver-side window rest, staring out at Weeks. Border Patrol district agent-in-charge Robert Frey leaned against the yellow brick wall, just below the barred windows of the jail. From those south windows, inmates could see the *aduana*, the customs checkpoint, on Mexico's side. Frey looked down the road to the aduana at Rio Santo. Not a soul; not a light bulb.

"Weeks."

"Bobby."

"Weeks, this here lawyer has some issues."

"I got some issues, me," Weeks said. "Where's the driver? And where's Dave?"

"Dave is coming. Had a thing he had to do."

"The driver?"

"You and him—the driver, the kid—you were in Dave's jurisdiction last night," Frey said. "Mister Reilly has surrendered the young man's driver's license." He waved the little white card with the photo in the corner.

"What's this got to do with you?" Weeks asked the fed.

"We like to keep jurisdictional things straight, like to keep 'em neat and tidy."

"I didn't recall that, Bobby."

"New attorney general, she wants it that way in the hundred-mile *frontera*."

Weeks nodded.

"She can sure assert that," he agreed. "Course, if I'm in hot pursuit, the law requires us to continue into county territory and make the stop. You can check the state constitution on that."

"You ought to read the part about illegal search and seizure," Reilly said.

Frey looked coldly at him, and Reilly said no more for the moment.

"I don't think I'm going to be discussing our case with you just yet, counselor," Weeks said. "I will, however, arrest your client."

"That's why I'm offering to bring him in. Surrender him safely to the law. And Mister Frey is here at our request until Dave gets here to take charge of him, when I make my phone call, and books him and releases him on bond, which I have in my pocket all green and crisp. For the record, I've explained to Mister Frey that the only law that Miguelito broke was driving without a valid New Mexico license."

"*Fascinating*," Weeks said. "He has a valid Chihuahua license, and obviously he came across, so I can sure stop him inside the hundred-mile frontera."

He looked beseechingly at Frey, who stood silent.

"Well, if Dave's coming to handle it, I'll just get busy with my chores. No need me hanging around. I'll be inside," Weeks said.

Weeks unlocked his office and went inside. Helen had Saturdays off. Frey followed him in. The desks, tables, shelves—all the dark gray of a stormy, charcoal sky. Only the bars on the cells were different. They were rusty.

"Maybe you *should* put that boy in a cell and not wait for Dave. Kid's obviously a hardened criminal," Frey said with a smirk. "It is procedure."

"That little piss-ant tried to flatten me with his car last night," Weeks said.

"So you opened fire?"

"Backed his car right into my gun hand. Dang thing went off for several seconds."

"Why'd you have the gun drawn?" Frey asked.

"Well, okay, the truth? Don't have a holster for it," said Weeks. "Look, whole thing's a setup. Octavio's been trying to set me up ever since eighty-seven, when they got my partner. He knows I'm coming for him. The kid drives like a bat out of hell for two-point-four miles, just across the city line into county turf. Then he stops. I walk up on him. He guns it in reverse. Right into me. Not straight into, but kind of brushes my legs. I'm sure he didn't mean to hit my gun hand. If he'd've seen the gun, he never would've."

Dave Belknap opened the door and walked in. Belknap was rail thin, tall as the door. Sat on an oak bench against the wall, legs stretched out halfway into the room.

"Octavio's gonna win this round, son," Belknap said. "Gonna paint it so every mom sees little Miguelito as her own. And you, my friend, will be gone. *Are* gone."

"He doesn't have a holster for his Tec-Nine," Frey said.

"Well, he better get one. And he better keep that dang thing in it. Christ, are we lucky nobody got killed," Belknap said.

"He says the kid backed into him, set off the gun," Frey said.

"I saw where the car jumped back, saw the Tec-Nine shells. I saw all that in the dirt. Just came from there," Belknap said. "And I saw the little scratches on the left rear fender. I assume there is paint on your gun; can I see it?"

Weeks unlocked his arsenal, pulled out the Tec-Nine and handed it to Belknap, who looked it over while talking: "I know we could go after Miguelito for assaulting a peace officer, and you might have had a valid argument for self-defense. Problem is, you ain't saying you fired in self-defense. You're saying you fired by accident because the car bumped your hand. That makes you the dangerous, not the endangered."

"Well, I . . ."

"Weeks, the commission's going to end our mutual-aid deal," Belknap said. "They won't allow you to ever pull a gun in Frontera County again. I'll back your story, but it won't help. See? It hurts you no matter how you tell it. And, yeah, there's a filament of shiny black paint stuck to your gun barrel, buddy. Your story's straight," he said, "for all the good it does you."

"Set up by Don Octavio," Weeks said. Shook his head. "He got me. Got me, too."

"Very likely. But don't call him *Don*. It's respect he don't deserve," Belknap said.

Reilly poked his head in.

"Do you want the young man to come in and surrender, or shall I go?"

"Sure, bring him in, absolutely," Weeks said. "Get out there, do your job and shut up. Just get out of my office—and stay out of that car. You can't use it. It's evidence. We'll get with you when you bring your client in. By the way, how old is your client?"

"Why?" Reilly demanded. "You don't think you're trying him as an adult?"

"There's no date of birth on his Chihuahua license."

"Almost seventeen. Like in a month. Okay?"

Miguelito sat on a bench in the Cortes courtyard three miles south, waiting for the car to come for him. Octavio, silvery haired, sat next to him. The boy's hair was slick and straight, cut short in back. He wore a shirt imported from France, sleeves rolled up two turns. A gray shirt, black slacks, polished black shoes. The boy chipped with his right toe at a rock embedded in the packed clay of the courtyard. He chipped patiently for over a minute, and finally the little rock hopped out of its hole, and the boy kicked it and it sailed across the court yard, dribbling to a halt underneath Octavio's car. The boy frankly did not understand why the old man had to be so old.

Old enough to be *presidente*. Wearing old-man clothes, string-tied peon pants and huaraches. Old like a stone left by God when he created it all.

The old man sat quietly watching the boy from the corner of his eye.

Finally Octavio spoke to him with typical sarcasm but rare restraint.

"Want to explain what you thought you were doing over there?"

"I had to try," the boy said. "Don't owe nobody no explanations."

The old man's eyes flashed a split second of anger, then welled like dark ponds.

"I know," he said hoarsely. "But now you know that was stupid, what you did."

The boy simply nodded.

"Trust family. If you can't trust family, then there's nothing," Octavio said.

The boy said nothing.

"You understand that by now, don't you?" Octavio said. "Trust family?"

The boy sat silent for quite a long spell. His eyes seemed to blink inordinately, as if re-watching a movie.

"I know I . . ." Too strong. He stopped himself. "I know," he said finally.

Reilly was gone. Belknap sat as if dozing. Frey looked at Weeks apologetically.

"If we'd sat on this kid last night like we should've, you'd be in the clear," he said.

"Until the next setup," Weeks said.

Belknap's shoulders bucked a quarter-inch and a short little laugh puffed out from his nose almost silently, but they heard it.

"You look for solo, like Tommy," Frey said. He meant Tom Hartley, a Border Patrol agent and tracker down in the 'Heel.

"One day I'll find that Glock Nine with that funny little twist that got Mikey. Some kid'll be carrying it. Then we'll be into international law," Weeks said.

Weeks ran his fingers across the top of his ballistics rack, behind his desk, a long narrow rack with a couple hundred layers of cotton-felt webbing for test-firing seized weapons. Both Frey and Belknap knew Weeks must have test-fired at least four thousand guns into the rack in those twelve years. The rack traveled with him. It looked like it was about to resume its trek.

"We'll back you all the way," Frey said, but Bryce Weeks knew that particular *way* stopped way short of Washington, or even Santa Fe.

"Understand ol' Elias Corona needs a hand up on the Gila. You know 'Lias?" Belknap said.

Weeks looked sadly back at Belknap.

"Ever hear of the City of Stone?"

"City of *Stones*. Lovely place. Boulders like tenpins from here to Huntley. God's bowling alley."

"That's where Corona and I parted company."

"Because of your late partner," Frey said.

"My dead partner, who was shot in our patrol car. I found Corona down in the City of Stone, what I call it now, tracking some coyote and about fifteen quails, and he wouldn't clear on that to help on a *deputy down*. Know why?" Weeks said.

"I know why," Belknap said.

Frey emphasized, and it sounded like an official warning: "We don't say it."

"Unless," Belknap said.

"That's right," Frey snapped. "Unless you're who we ain't."

Chapter Four

Cobwebs

The patchwork ranch house in Wells River Canyon in the mountains above Gila Wells had been added on to seven times, starting with the original peak-roofed log cabin in 1885. Now the roof, as seen from the road above, was a parquet of surfaces and angles. The cabin at the center was still the warmest part of the house.

Except for the phone line, nothing connected the Two Square with the world. It was all self-contained. Propane got filled two, three times a year. Sid Braden brought in his own gasoline for the generator and kept a supply for the trucks and chainsaw in beat-up fifty-gallon barrels out behind the barn and tool shed. A rusty old Sears Roebuck hand pump stuck out from the top of one barrel.

Wells River flowed down from the Black Range headed for the Gila. Leafless willows, sycamores, aspens, cottonwoods lined the trickle of a river. Ponderosa, spruce, and white fir lived upslope about a hundred yards into the forest. The rest was grass.

Braden leased more than three-fourths of his range from the federal government. Nearly everyone in Gila County had federal pasture. Braden had a mixture of his own acreage plus BLM, state and Forest Service lands that fit together jigsaw-like, each with different rules and fees. It made puzzle sense, he said, but nonsense for range management.

On this overcast morning in March, Braden got an early call saying Mann, the BLM—Bureau of Land Management—agent was coming to see him. No *why* offered, none asked. Always happy to see Mann, a fellow hunter, less happy to see Margaret Carton, the Forest Service district ranger who controlled most of his allotments and who now was arriving unannounced in her lime-green Suburban. No sign of Mann.

Braden's grass was getting uneven. Along the river it was ragged. Up below the trees it was in better shape. So Braden, Ed Marquez, and Marlie's brother, Bertie, were stringing fence to keep cattle away from the river. Braden ran about eight hundred head all over allotments that totaled more than two hundred square miles.

Carton, sliding down from her Suburban, looked nervous, as though forcing herself to do something scary or distasteful, depending how one read her face and the halting sidewinding way she approached the men on the fence line.

With her deputy ranger, Wiley Willabaugh, tagging along, she stopped several yards from Braden and informed them all coolly that she was being forced to jack up Sid's fees and impose new rules preventing him from protecting the river.

Sid, Ed and Bertie stopped unspooling the wire and twisted it off with the big cutter-pliers, then ratcheted it tight. Had they heard her?

"You know, Sid, we're not supposed to fence the rivers anymore," she said.

One year they want you to fence a river, keep cattle and elk away; next year not.

The new order meant Sid couldn't use areas near the river for grazing at all. It was a long river, and the amount of adequate pasture where Carton would allow him to graze cattle was suddenly cut just about in half.

And so, with a light drizzle beginning to mix with some snowflakes, Carton stood there with Willabaugh and told Braden he would have to cut his herd by half, as well, to about four hundred. Willabaugh stood behind her like a bodyguard and witness, just so there'd be more than one of them to stand up against the Two Square three.

"Did someone complain, is that it?" Braden asked.

"Not the issue, not the issue," she said in her abbreviated but repetitive way. "The issue is the rules from Washington."

"But somebody did complain," Braden said. "You know I know it. Just admit it, since it's the truth."

"Sure, there have been complaints. We've had hikers complain."

"Hikers? The only hikers we've seen up here is Raylinda Wells and her boyfriends. They like to skinny dip up in the Hot Creek," said Bertie, who worked as a sheriff's dispatcher when he wasn't helping Sid run the Two Square.

"They didn't appreciate your fencing it," Carton said. "Raylinda's lived here all her life. Not like she's some *interloper.*"

"They tore down the fence," Braden said. "Loosed about a hundred head, and I'm still searching for about ten. Gone all the way, maybe, to Arizona. I get calls, 'Come get your cows.' If these fence-wreckers weren't vegetarians I'd suspect they ate my herd."

Carton looked a young thirty-five, and either she'd lost weight or believed she needed to conceal an attractive figure because her puffy uniform was easily two sizes too big. Her flat-brimmed "Smokey" hat was also oversized. So all her wavy, rusty hair fit inside.

"You have until June fifteenth to cut your herd, give or take a few days and a few strays. Three and a half months. We're not unreasonable," Carton said.

"I can't make it on four hundred head," Braden said. "How's that reasonable?"

"Sorry," she said. "Wish we could sometimes look the other way. But rules exist, and we've got to enforce 'em. You know the pressure we're under. Everybody's lawyer is watching. We don't have budget for a legal rodeo. Can't give preferential treatment."

Braden slammed the brakes on his speeding mind. It produced a silence that seemed to unnerve Carton. She waited for Braden to break the silence. "Well, you *are* enforcing preferentially," he said. "Going after wilderness ranchers hardest of all. Law says you can't. This ranch predates the wilderness area. Supposed to be grandfathered."

"We hashed out this theory before. I've got no authority to change or even debate the rules. Sorry. And I'm *so* sorry to hear about your daughter, too. It's just terrible."

"Don't worry about Millie. She'll be fine. We're thinking she's over at the Endicotts'. Just about to head over there when you pulled in," Braden said. "She'll be back soon. She knows the country. She's fine. You'll see."

Carton must have looked as if her breakfast had caught up with her.

"What is it, Margaret?"

Carton shook her head, looking pale enough to write on with a ballpoint. She started backing away, and backed into Willabaugh.

"Well, what about you, Wiley?" Braden said.

"I'm just a witness," Willabaugh said.

"Well, be a true witness, then."

"I will." He tried to sound matter-of-fact, but he still felt threatened and it showed.

Carton's eyes, for that matter, started to water.

"What the blazes is goin' on?" Braden said.

Then they saw his face go pale, just like theirs.

"You *know* something," he said. "But you ain't s'posed to say. You've got to tell us, and you better damn well tell us now. We'll get Marlie out here, and you look us in the eye and tell us both. No, wait, that isn't right. You'd better come inside. Yes, come inside."

Bertie was at a loss. "What's goin' on, Sid? What happened?"

Carton and Willabaugh followed them inside, through the mud room that was added five years ago, the year they bought the ranch from Texas Bank and Trust. They settled in the family room that was added just the year before they moved in. The old wood stove from the barn had been transplanted in the family room. It was throwing off some fair heat, and the coffeepot was still hot on top of it.

"You all sit down while I get Marlie," Braden said, pointing at two armchairs.

Carton asked to use the phone. Braden handed it to her, then went to fetch Marlie.

It took ten rings for Clyde Tristano to answer Carton's call down at forest headquarters because Clyde was down the hall photocopying. Once he did answer, Clyde could barely hear who was on the line and asked: "Why are you whispering?"

"Look, just get Angie, get her now. *Do it!* Don't care if she's in the ladies' room."

"She's right here," Clyde said, and handed the receiver to Angie, the Hidalgo National Forest supervisor. Hearing Carton's story, Angie could only sputter: "Oh, no, no, God, no. Please say you didn't."

Angela Archuleta was in her late fifties, looking to retire late the next year. She used a rinse to cover her gray. Didn't look quite right.

Now she was joining the ranks of the suddenly ill. Long-established stress lines in her face creased deeper.

"We can't wait for Will Mann or any deputies Elias may have sent," she told Carton. "So now *you're* going to have to tell them. What on earth possessed you going up there today, of all days, knowing what you know, to talk about cutting their herd?"

"Today's the deadline," Carton said. "Should've come yesterday, but it snowed."

Carton could hear Angie breathing on the other end. After a few seconds, Angie answered: "Oh, Miss Margaret. You tell 'em, then you stay until Will and the sheriff arrive. Don't leave the Bradens alone with this. Dig in your heels if they try to push you away. Once Will gets there, you pull out, then come straight back here. I want a report on every word that's said."

When Carton hung up, the Bradens were standing next to her. They came in too late to hear anything but "yes," "yes," "uh-huh," and "yes." But from watching, they were prepared for the worst.

Marlie Braden's knuckles were gnarled from roping, hard-riding, and the same ranch chores that her husband's hands survived unscathed. Hers were uneven, scarred. And now they knotted together. Her eyes wide, blinking dry, blinking in search of moisture to keep eyelids from sticking. Wide and empty as the great inland sea that once covered this part of New Mexico. And as blue. Now thirsty-dry, heartsick to the point of heart-dead. Tried the imagining, the anguish of remembering, picturing, touching, tried them all, trying to cry. Couldn't. Not a single tear would wet her wind-dried face. So she cocked her jaw like a lever action brush gun and growled: "Where's my little Millie? Speak up now. *Speak up!*"

Carton stammered: "She's been found. God, I'm so sorry, but she's dead."

Marlie, focusing on Carton, shook her head in disbelief that quickly set like concrete. Bertie Williams stood behind her, holding empty coffee cups, nodding his silent support, his graying hair flopping over on his scarred forehead with each nod.

"You don't know what you're talking about, as usual," Marlie said. "Millie's up to the Endicotts'. Don't call Angie. She doesn't know a thing. Call *them*. Call the Endicotts."

Carton took off her hat, and her russet hair fell first to her shoulders and then slid the rest of the way to her waist. She looked Marlo Williams Braden in the eye and said: "I'm sorrier than you'll ever know, but she *is* dead. Will Mann found her on Cerro Verde. Shot in the back with a thirty-thirty. Will found some tracks. And he's on his way here."

"Green Ridge is the wrong way. She never goes that way—no reason to. She's over at the Endicotts. You have the wrong girl," Marlie said. Edgy. But lacking the confidence that usually bulldozed an audience. Marlo W. Braden, county commissioner, state cattle growers chair, Senator Albert Settles' county campaign co-manager. Meant *nada*.

The last couple days compressed into one. That phone call: *"Your daughter home?"* All night awake. A man's voice. Touch of Texas. "Who was that?" Sid asked. She'd concluded he was from the school or the Science Fair. Didn't worry. At first. Now wondering.

Now Carton pushing that *not-me* face at her again, trying to wriggle off.

"You wouldn't be the one to notify, anyway!" Marlie snapped. "You didn't even come up here to tell us that, anyway, did you? That isn't even why you're here."

"Are you saying—Millie's dead?" said Bertie, finally taking his guess.

"Shhh, Bertie," his sister said.

"No, no, I couldn't do that, not ever," Carton said, and now her words ran together. "I thought you already knew. I didn't know they hadn't. The sheriff, he's on his way. Angie says he and Will are on their way. I thought you'd been told. They told me Will called. I just assumed." Then she took a breath and added, again: "I am so, so sorry."

Sid Braden's face softened some. He'd started breathing in even strokes, but he didn't realize how fragile easy-breathing was.

"It ain't your fault, Margaret," he said. "They should've sent up deputies to do this duty. You had every right to expect that had been done, as it should've, by now."

"Thank you, sir, for saying that," she said.

"One thing, though," Braden said slowly as it dawned on him. "You may have thought we'd been told, like you say, but that only makes your intentions coming up here all the worse. You thought you'd break us with some new ad-order, drive us off, and we wouldn't never fight," he said, "because—*oh, my Millie?*" His voice went up the scale.

Caught himself. What was he *doing?* His daughter, was, was . . . where? He refused to say it. Couldn't think. Sat down on the floor next to the wood stove, knocking over fire irons.

Bertie stood in the background, shifting his weight left foot to right, mind spinning.

Marlie was frozen. Emotions fused. *Anger-fear-panic-grief.* Blurred. But she saw Sid coming apart. Trying to get the fire irons to stand. They kept falling. Marlie sat beside him, hugged him, held tight a minute to let him take hold of himself, which he finally did, because he was realizing: Maybe the fight would pull them through.

"This is Millie's place," Sid said. "Fact this place and Millicent, they're one in the same. This place *is* our daughter, and she *is* the land."

He stopped. Groped for words the way a pump sucks air in a dry well. That was it.

Marlie didn't cave, though. "You owe us truth," she said. "Everything you know. Don't hold back like some lawyer. Say where and how they found her."

"Up on the green ridge, in the trees, the clearing up there. Someone opened fire on Will—two, three shots, missed him. Will waited. They . . . they left. Then Will went up there and found her . . . found her . . . buried. Only dead a little while. Found tracks."

"And someone told you all this and they never told us a *word?*" Marlie said.

Carton dug her fingers into the arms of the chair, just trying to ride it out.

"You couldn't wait to come up here and slap us with your papers," Marlie went on. Braden put his hands on Marlie's arms, trying to steady her.

"Well, they should've sent someone," Marlie said, "should've . . ."

"I'm sure two deputies are stuck down below the pass," he said. "River of mud. Will's coming from around Cerro Verde. He'll be here."

"Should've been here yesterday," Marlie repeated, and Braden agreed.

Within minutes, Mann's SUV clattered to a halt outside and they heard Corona's high-pitched, edgy voice followed by Mann's deep, muffled response—the sheriff telling Mann to remain silent. Marlie believed it was clear as a hawk's cry echoing over Wall Lake.

Marlie sat down on the sofa against the far wall. Tried to take herself through the process of crying: Let carefully woven defenses unravel. With the sheriff arriving she sagged. Sid saw. Sat down next to her, put his arm around her. She buried her face in his shoulder and took deep breaths. But rage beat the tears. Then Corona knocked.

"Come on in, sheriff—you, too, Will," Bertie said.

The sheriff strode in and stared around the room.

"You got your down jacket around here somewhere?" Elias Corona said.

"Sure," Braden said. "Right there on the peg. Why?"

"Get it," Corona said.

"Real sorry we don't have more chairs," Braden mumbled, ignoring the jacket.

"We found your daughter's horse by the corral," Corona said, grabbing the jacket and examining it. "Her horse, your horse, your mule."

Braden looked confused, then asked his wife: "Did Millie's horse come home?"

Marlie sat up cold, like she had been slapped awake.

"What are you saying?"

"Her horse is out there by the corral. Know when she came home?" Corona said.

"Sugar came home?" Marlie said. "She's home?"

Millie's mom got up and ran down the hall to her daughter's bedroom. Bertie followed, whisper-shouting *Marlie, Sis! Hold on.* He'd forgotten to say the horse was back. Ed Marquez stood by the door, ready to leave the unresolvable to play itself out.

"Did you send deputies up to notify us, Elias?" Braden said. "'Cause they never got here. Margaret unintentionally broke the news we should have had yesterday."

Corona was in no mood to relinquish control. His eyes burned at Braden, but Braden's burned right back. Mann kept silent.

"They're good people, sheriff," Carton said. "They didn't—I was the one to break the news. Angie told me to. It just worked out that way."

"I want you and Wiley outside. You, too, Ed. And don' touch nothin'," the sheriff said. "This was a real bad day for you and Wiley to come up here, Margaret. If I didn't know you from church I'd see evil in the decision to come here."

Margaret and Wiley hurried off, leaving the door to swing shut on its own. Ed caught it, stepped outside and quietly closed it behind him.

"Will *was* here to fill you in," Corona said, "about what he found. I originally thought it would be only right and proper. Now we're unsure, frankly, with them fresh-rode horses in the corral, that mule."

Braden looked to Mann for help. Mann said nothing but kept his eye on Corona.

"Millie went out for a ride. We never saw her again," Sid said. "We didn't know Sugar came back. But the horse would come back, wouldn't she? It's Sugar's corral. She likes to hang out with Fred, Elvis, and Charlie."

"Fred and Charlie?"

"Our horses, Marlie's and mine, and you know Elvis, our mule."

"Mind if we look around?" Corona said.

Braden studied Corona carefully. He'd never had a problem with Corona before, but obvious liberties had already been taken. Braden was suddenly uncertain.

"Here's what I think ought to happen, sheriff, okay?" Braden said.

"I frankly don' care a hoot in the holler what you think should happen. I can have a warrant up here in half an hour by helicopter," the sheriff said.

"I'd like everything back to normal," Braden said.

"That's not going to happen," Corona said. "Either let us search or wait out the warrant. Your call."

Marlie came out of the bedroom, saying, "No need for a warrant, Elias. My commission hired you. Do your job."

Corona nodded his thanks, then turned to Bertie. "We need you on dispatch tonight, pardner. John's out on a case. Can you handle it?"

"Sure, Elias, sure can. Be there at five."

"When . . . can . . . we . . . see our . . . girl?" Braden asked—words battling past a chestnut-sized knot in his windpipe.

"Tonight, this afternoon, we'll take you down there," Elias said, "just as soon as we wrap up here, that is, if you're done fighting us."

Corona wanted unconditional assent from *both* Bradens. Corona had her body. He had control. Sid fought to hide tears, slight overflow, a drop or two, just enough to whet Corona's predatory instinct. Sid was only forty but sounded much older when his voice shook. Their daughter was their only child. Braden forced himself to nod and step aside.

Mann tried to picture Sid Braden shooting his daughter in the back. *Unimaginable.* Even if there might be a rip in Sid's coat—which maybe there wasn't. Didn't want to look. Might never. Couldn't imagine anyone, least of all Sid, doing what was done. Here lately so many mad people. Mad in different ways.

"That your gun on the wall there, Sid?" Corona said. "Mind if I . . .?"

Braden just looked numbly at him.

"Go ahead," Marlie said.

Corona looked into the gun-mounted barrel, then sat down again. No sniffing, no nothing.

It would be a long, unrewarding case.

Mann, sighing, got up and looked into the gun barrel as well. Spiderwebs.

Chapter Five

Wonderland

The two-by-four was twelve feet long, heavy with weights from an old barbell set bolted to it, chains on either end. Between weights and chains, Border Patrol agent Tom Hartley had to gear himself up to lift it. That's what he hated most about Jackrabbit Wells down at the bottom of the Heel of New Mexico.

With this primitive thing, he'd drag the sandy road that ran along the border.

He hooked those chains to the tow bar on his half-wrecked Ford Excursion. About four-thirty every afternoon, and four-fifteen this afternoon because he was early, he smoothed the surface of the road starting at Jackrabbit Wells, *good ol' Jay-Dub.*

Half the time, Hartley went west to Arizona and circled back through a place of vast prospect too small to be a village, called Sunflower.

From the porch of the Sunflower post office and store, he could see the remnant ruts of the ancient road that led to the sandstone-adobe ruins at Casas Grandes, a pueblo located one hundred miles into Mexico.

Other times, like this time, he went east to the corner of the Heel, where the Mexico–New Mexico borderline begins its north-ward stretch to the instep. Tonight, he turned that corner again, heading north at the white obelisk.

The concrete monument stood twelve feet tall, fat at the bottom, pointy at the top, sticker weeds sprouting in the dust along its base. The base was chipped by gunfire.

Completing the loop, Hartley drove southwest through Martin Blye's Boothills Ranch to Highway 118. Slid the dragger beam into the back of the Excursion.

He began to retrace. Back across the Heel of New Mexico. Looking for the tracks of anything that had crossed his newly smoothed-out surface.

Hartley wore a Border Patrol baseball cap, his only concession to uniform. Otherwise, it was T-shirt and jeans, sometimes a leather vest over the T-shirt. Wal-Mart sunglasses. Tex-Mex boots. Stood a muscular six-two. Crewcut. Tennessee drawl. Called it *Tinnessee*. Occasionally laid a store-bought fly on the waters of the Gila. But mostly, spent a lot of time watching. Claimed that was how he managed to never get shot at.

Far as anyone knew, 'cause they were too busy ducking to check, he was the only one claiming that distinction.

Opposite a paneless, roofless, abandoned building on the Mexico side, right along Blye's much-repaired border fence, he found about a dozen tracks mostly concentrated midway on the north-south boundary.

They seemed to have stepped across from the gray-flake shell of the farmhouse, next to a Mexican cornfield, where the barbed wire hung like rags on a Juarez street kid. People could just walk in, and did. Hartley had no idea who they were, what they were doing, where they were going or why. They could have been assassins or acrobats, drug mules, smugglers, refugees, job-hunters. Anyone, anything, from anywhere.

He made a quick inventory. Picked a set of tracks. Followed them. With the halogen flashlight wired to a battery pack carried on his belt, he found two sets of footprints, one a little smaller than the other, that seemed to be traveling together. A half-hour later, he found the people whose sneakers matched the tracks. Huddled behind a yucca. He wished he'd picked another set. She was thirty. Looked like forty. Wanted her twelve-year-old daughter raised in America.

"Can you not just let us go?" the mother asked.

Where would it end if he did? He shook his head, no.

He took them back to his port. That's what they called his dusty one-man gate—P-O-E, port of entry. He, too, had a semi-abandoned building, since he was only in it about an hour and a half per day, but it did have a roof, and most broken windowpanes under the steel grid got replaced. He left one unrepaired for ventilation.

The woman stood too close beside him as he typed their info into his computer.

"Sit down here, please, the two of you," he said, pointing at the banco on the wall.

He made photographs of them, individually, and ran their data, including the photos, through the national crime computer. No hits. It was their first time. But, he sensed, probably not their last. Next time they would be in the database. Unless someone made a mistake. Maria Teresa Algeciras and Reyana Maria Torres.

Algeciras set off a whole network of survival alarms. Reminders of the unreal woman who threw him off his feed two years back. Hadn't thought about her in months.

"I have a job," the real woman said. "I start work in Deming tomorrow. Whistle Clean Incorporated. Cleaning houses. My daughter's supposed to be at Deming Middle School."

But Hartley felt the unreal woman beside him. Tugging at his sleeve. Sometimes he wished she'd come back, the way she had in that little red car. Apply the coolness of her white skin to his burning brow. Yeah, that'd be nice. But by now, she'd graduated to the realm of dreams. Dangerous dreams, but he never could call them nightmares exactly. It's just that he knew where she led.

Next time, he wondered idly, might he not pass up that yucca and look under an ocotillo instead? Shook his head at himself. *That would be stupid.*

"Take me back across, but let my daughter stay," the woman begged as Hartley raised the crossing arm, decorated with peeling reflector tape, and walked them through.

He led them down the little driveway that connected 118 with Highway 2, curving within a few feet of the borderline on the Mexico side.

The part-time *aduanero*, the customs officer with his little black military cap, slouched against the unpainted wall of the customs house, a cinderblock cube, peering in through car windows at women's legs, little girls' legs.

Crumpled uniform, never pressed. Short sleeve shirt, blue epaulets. Loosened tie. Put his skinny arm around the twelve-year-old in the guise of protection. The girl recoiled. So did Hartley, inwardly. He watched—making sure the customs officer knew he saw him usher her into the building. The mother trailed, helpless, behind. She waited outside. Until the child came out and ran to her, and clung to her.

The girl was changed. Moved stiffly. As if reassembled. Poorly.

Hartley felt ill. Jotted an entry in his log book that he knew would go nowhere. He no longer felt righteous, as when he first reported it. Four years ago. First day on the job. Reported it for most of those four years. The black cap was still there.

Borderlands desert wildlife, he called it. Tagged for observation. Hartley always said he patrolled an area inhabited by all the critters of the West, including manmade breeds—dope runners who were also cattle rustlers or people smugglers, depending on which way they were headed. The cartel also sent along enforcers. *Torpedos.* Pistoleros. One of those now slouched fifty feet from the customs house. Leaning against the fender of a black Infiniti with black windows. Mother and child walked slowly up the road toward the car. The torpedo spoke to the woman. Offered her a stick of gum. She gave it to her daughter. The aduanero looked out his dark door at the little girl.

The torpedo wore black. His black tie and his black hair fluttered in the breeze. Kept trying to call someone on a tiny cell phone cupped like a pebble in his large hand. Hartley knew he wasn't getting through. No reception out here. Finally, the mother and daughter got in the Infiniti. The car drove quietly east on Highway 2 headed for Santito. Octavio ran a hostelry there for hopeful émigrés. Next to the Jalisco, it sustained itself mainly as a brothel, but that depended, Octavio always said, on the willingness of the girls. They're free agents, he said, and he had nothing to do with it. "If she wants to, I'm not going to stand in the way." He did take a cut of their income, though.

Hartley drove back along the bladed road, picking off one or two more "quails."

More of his wildlife. He also kept watch over several breeds of cattleman—and the ghosts of ancient medicine men who ate the little button cactus and etched the rocks.

Hartley had known Martin Blye forever—from those days of child-hood when Hartley's daddy took little Tommy in his old Bronco down past the playas at Seguro, foraging for snakes in the Mormon Mountains, named for the Mormon troops who battled the Mexicans in 1846.

Even the snakes, it was evident, hated it down here. Hartley guessed they were trapped by their own terrain. Tommy felt a little trapped, himself. They found three rattlers on that excursion. One got loose in the Bronc. Dad skirled to a stop. Tommy dove out a window. They stood around waiting, till finally the snake peered out and dropped down into the dust. It looked cross-eyed at them, then slithered off.

"I said don't let that snake in here!" yelled the half-deaf Gringo Horn, manager of the trading post in Sunflower, just up the road ten miles from Jackrabbit Wells. "Don't bring them others in here, either." He didn't want to see any snakes in wire cages. "That other guy escaped, didn't he? How d'ya know these won't squeeze out, too?" Horn recalled it every time Hartley came in. Gringo was eighty-three. He'd lived in the trading post, which doubled as post office, fifty years.

Hartley, now visiting in Horn's trading post once again after finishing his dusky rounds, remembered that first day: Blye had come in to fetch a parcel for his daddy. Blye was a skinny kid, just thirteen. He looked at the rattlers sullenly shaking their rear ends. "You *could* always eat a snake," he said, "but we raise cattle." He looked at Tommy and raised his eyebrows and his hands, palms up. Like, *why?* Why bother with snakes?

Born to ranching, Blye ran about five-thousand head of steers and heifers in his corner of the Heel and sometimes beat hell out of his range until he needed hay. Blye's daddy still owned the Sunflower Ranch in the southwest corner, and when Boothills Realty listed the other corner of the Heel, Martin grabbed it before Sandrine could.

Sandrine's huge Diamond S grassland, stood between the Blyes, dwarfing both. The S, as everybody called Sandrine's spread, was too big to be called an oasis but was green enough. They also said the S inside the diamond brand should be a dollar sign.

"Think Blye'll go along with all this stuff Sandrine's doin'?"

"Don't think *you* need to worry," Hartley said.

Horn was worried. He imagined business dwindling if the ranchers made good their plan to band together and protect the land from spotlight hunters, off-roaders and most everybody else. But Horn's business was imaginary already. Hardly anyone came in. His merchandise moved so slowly that folks, when they did come in, just wanted to look at it for nostalgia's sake. He still had stuff sitting there from the fifties. Some tourist just a few years ago had bought up everything he once had from the forties.

Sandrine had a problem with spotlight hunters. Wanted to gate them out. He'd found a bullet hole in his Cessna. It missed the fuel tank, missed the hydraulics, and was easy to patch. *But.* Hitting a Cessna instead of a javelina? Something to think about.

"Blye's a lot different than ol' Sandrine," Hartley told Horn, munching on the pork rinds Horn kept in a big glass pickle jar. "Martin was raised here."

"Ranchers is ranchers," Horn said. "Only the grasses is different, and of course you don't find much of that black-leg down here—too dry. Blye's not the crazy kid he was. Getting gray like his daddy. 'Portant man. Big spread. Serious, tough. Got to be!"

Earl Westerfield came in, and he was angry.

"Fifteen head of my cattle were shot."

Then Blye came in for a parcel that Danielle, the mail driver, hadn't delivered.

Horn's store was the place Westy came to complain. Some of the old hands who remembered the range war of '29 hung out around the post office potbelly and played tiddly winks, checkers or chess. Poker wasn't allowed since one fellow got shot.

"Fifteen? That's a lot. Anybody else's herd get hit?" Hartley asked.

Nobody knew of any. Blye was intrigued.

"Why'd these boys hate you?" he asked Westerfield.

"I don't know that hate's the right word," Westerfield said. "I just have no idea."

"Were they shot dead or just wounded?"

"Dead," Westy said gloomily.

"Bet they don't muck around with Sandrine's herd," Hartley said.

"I'll call Sandrine," said Blye. He called. Sandrine answered. He wasn't shocked. He said Westy was desperate, owed Karajan several hundred dollars for hay. He thought Westy'd done it himself. But since Westy was standing right there, Blye didn't say it.

"Sandrine had no cows shot," Blye muttered with a shrug.

"Were your cattle ill?" Hartley asked Westerfield.

Westy just shook his head.

"Ought to get a vet, get a necropsy," Blye said, "in case they weren't shot."

"Oh, they were shot," Westy said, then nodded. "Guess I'd better."

"You might jest check your own weapons, too, Westy," Blye said, "just in case those enviro bastards used your guns on them cows."

Westerfield looked awhile silently at the pork rind jar on the counter.

"Go ahead and help yourself," Horn said.

"Me?" Westy said. "I don't need nothing. I'm a regular Sandrine."

William Sandrine grazed but eight hundred cattle. Born to money, he could afford the luxury of grass over the necessity of cattle. Loved grass. Loved to see it waving in the wind beyond any limit of vision, to know wherever he stood, there'd be no end to it.

Sandrine sat in his rocker under his portal with his morning coffee watching the blue grama and the bushy sacaton ripple out across his savannah, one of the biggest, wildest ranches in all the wild history of the West. Wilder, he was sure, than anything in old Arizona—Clanton or Brosius. Wilder than anything Chisum or Goodnight ever ran in Texas or New Mexico.

A lost pronghorn antelope trotted up close and stared at him and his wife for nearly ten seconds, took a few steps closer, paused again, then rocketed out into the field with parabolic leaps when Sandrine lifted his coffee cup.

"Alice, *Alice*," he told his wife standing barefoot beside him in her robe, "it's Wonderland."

The S had two mountain ranges. Sandrine had a report that told him he had more than a thousand plant and animal species. He had people to help count the odd rabbits, turkeys, hawks, quails, cougars, bobcats, what all. Plus he was bringing in ferrets, prairie dogs, condors. He would tell Blye one afternoon in a Mexican jail that ranching was his salvation, his only chance to see the land whole. Blye thought he overstated it. There were bigger issues. Like getting out of jail.

South of both Blye and Sandrine, Pete Alderete ran a ranch bigger than either of theirs. Raised a small family—small for Llanos or Santito. Held famous dances. Sang his notorious *corridos*. Faithfully attended every church event, every fiesta, and fought the same battle with the smugglers that his northern neighbors did.

Alderete had given Sandrine his first cow-pushing job. Sandrine was good at it, but it was a lot easier juggling Sandrine's eight hundred head than Blye's five thousand.

Blye, growing up cowboy, would never have escaped his fate, just like those generations of Blye before him. As a concession to his parents, he studied ranch management at Western New Mexico University, but he didn't need it. The instructors were fine, and they had nice long talks, but none of them could tell Blye anything about ranching the Heel, the kind that went on without measurable grass or water, where the cows just mostly ate dirt and drank air. This brand of ranching was in his blood.

March morning: "Dang if I'm not good." Blye smiled at himself, knowing fate would make him pay for that little joke. With two hundred square miles of desert, about a hundred thousand acres, Blye owned eight and a half ranch houses, including three grungy, leaky-roofed fence-rider shacks strung along the border where Mexican bandit-smuggler-dope growers spent many a night. He approached his houses with great care.

Waterholes, spaced properly, kept his herds alive. Windmills sucked the water up from the mysterious aquifers and spilled it into galvanized tanks, and despite the barren look of the place, scattered little pastures sprouted in unlikely locations, in the lee of small cone-shaped mountains and a few larger ragged ones. He had to move his herds a lot more than even his daddy did.

Blye and his *vaquero*, Inigo Gonzales from Llanos, and a few borrowed hands from both sides of the border, were moving three-hundred-ninety head, a large group, across from the snaggle-toothed Mormon Mountains to the Hermanos.

Gonzales was standing in his stirrups.

"Somebody coming," he said.

"Hartley," Blye said. "Expected him."

"Because of all the sign you been seeing."

"That's right, amigo. All the sign."

Hartley's tail of dust drew near. Blye had e-mailed him: That's how Blye stayed in touch with the distant world—it was a hundred miles to either Lordsburg or Concha—hunched over his keyboard, keeping tabs on e-mail and watching satellite TV.

Blye reported mucho sign, tracks, discarded matchboxes, crumpled cigarette packs, beer cans. Lots of traffic.

"*Hola*, Humphrey," Hartley said. He meant Inigo.

"*Hola, capitán*," Inigo replied.

"Will you tell this dude I am not a captain?" Hartley asked Blye.

Blye waved him off. "Don't mess with him, Tom. He's jest bein' amable."

"You tell him I am no Humphrey," Inigo threw in.

"Got to get you boys to Berlitz," Blye said. "I can't be translating you forever."

"How's Jane?" Hartley asked.

Blye's brow notched a niche. He was unmarried, some said unmarriable. The nearest single American woman who wasn't related lived seventy-two miles away.

Every six months or so he'd call on her. She'd stare him down like a cougar. "Don't see how a man keeps so thin. Only a fool forgets to eat," she'd say.

She had no use for him, nor he for her.

"Haven't seen her, wouldn't know," he told Hartley.

Blye gazed south, thinking, thinking of a certain unattainable, then he pointed down at the full plastic quart bottle of water under the yucca next to Hartley's foot.

"Some poor sumbitch probly gonna die of thirst," he said.

Prescott, Arizona: The young Sandrine had come knocking one evening in the rain. The girl's father answered. A drenched derelict was found upon the doorstep. How could Darius Marks have known not to slam the door? Sandrine bided a bit. Ultimately he carried the girl off. Brought her to the Heel, which he tried to portray as pure, utopian, a dream. But it was a hard washboard-road dream, sharp-edged as the Mormon Range, running grass-fed cattle. The morning they came back from their honeymoon in France, the road was running free and wild with water, and frogs were jumping all over the place. Pete Alderete was standing at the gate in green rubber waders, holding a shovel.

Sandrine left the luggage in the Land Rover and trotted back to the wellhead. The chain that held the cap in place had finally rusted through, and she was a gusher all over again. Water was geysering out the pumphouse roof through a vent, through all three windows and under the door. He opened the door and the water blasted him.

"Give me a hand, please, Pete," he said. "Still enough chain left to re-establish."

"You sure?" Alderete said.

Sandrine got down on his hands and knees. Told Alice he needed the black rubber washer to reseal it.

"What's it look like?" Alice said.

"Like a Kerr-Mason jar seal, only this big," he said, cupping hands football-size.

"Like this?" she said, picking the floppy ring up from the submerged floor.

Bridegroom folded the well cap down onto the seal and bride stood on it—on one foot—bracing on the two men. The best man hooked one side of the chain, the groom the other. Frogs sprang in all directions around the inside of the pumphouse like sparks from a bottle rocket. When the water quit, the frogs vanished as mysteriously as they'd come.

"They come from all over when they hear about the water," Alderete said.

"Hear about it—what, they watch Eyewitness News?" Alice asked.

"They know water when they hear it. They're *frogs*."

Eighteen years fixing wells and pumps and generators. Eighteen years of blading and grading, snowplowing, shoeing and branding and birthing, setting posts, stringing wire—even helping string neighbors' wire. She tightened barbwire right along with him.

Then she said: "Can we *please* do some entertaining?"

"Who'd come see us?" Sandrine said.

"Invite a whole bunch, then if only a few come we still have a party," she said.

Everyone came. The purpose, Sandrine patiently told any pilgrim off Highway 118, was bringing the battlers together, to reconcile enviro with rancher. The two Sandrines loved both, although Alice mainly wanted people to come over and visit.

Sandrine had learned more than a trade at Alderete's Dos Mesas, where he had gone as a teenager on summer break, carrying his saddle down the dirt road to Llanos.

Alderete at breakfast: "Sandrine, ride the border fence. Know it from both sides."

"Same either way—gone," Sandrine remarked.

"Well, put it back up. Your job."

The fifty-mile fence was fantasy. He was supposed to make it reality. He hated fences anyway. Used 'em. But hated 'em.

"Why can't the government of the United States put this fence up?" the young man asked.

"They can," Alderete said, flashing a *you-know-nothing* eye, "is why they don't."

That actual night, one of Pete's Llanos fiestas—the friends, the neighbors, all their families from the very old inching along behind walkers to the little ones with lightning-bright and lightning-quick eyes, spinning and somersaulting and running full throttle—tested the limits of control and of sobriety. Alderete always pushing that edge, just to see, just to see. And then, *wham*, he's preaching sermons. He's up there, glass in hand, spilling a little red, sudden guru—giving advice, advice without anyone's consent.

"Have many friends," Alderete recommended. "Be wary in all directions."

He disregarded the inherent contradiction and plowed on: "Look under everything, behind everything, around everything and be careful picking anything up."

"*No hay tiempo en el dia para esto,*" Sandrine scolded. "Life is risk."

And anyway, he said, "*You* don't live that way."

Alderetes had been on this ancient seabed four-hundred-fifty years. Some had owned land on the side ceded to the United States after the

Mexican War, and they never had been properly compensated. *Fortunes of war*, Pete Alderete always said. His great-great-great *abuelito* had opposed that war. And, too, his spread was on the Mexico side, and he still owned it—he could afford to be magnanimous, which he was.

But then that shadow crossed Pete's eyes. They went dull. The drogueros. The tide of guns, drug- and immigrant-smuggling. The land-grabbing, the disappearance of his son—and, too, the little ejido or homestead farmers. Their only safety lay in humility. Stand up macho and expect to die, like McFee almost did. Rodrigo Camacho and Paco Corrales both disappeared and were presumed dead. And, of course, they did find one body, which the constables labeled a suicide because the victim's own gun was the apparent instrument of death, and the cops found it next to him. Along with footprints.

But there was no note, and there was nothing anyone could do about it.

Sandrine, because of his power, was now powerless. Too big to just climb through the fence and walk into Mexico as he once did—everyone, both sides, would notice.

His focus had to stay on his own lands and those of his neighbors, who were nearly done in by drought. What would happen if his neighbors lost their lands? New neighbors. Maybe some with capital N's. Ones you might not want. Wilbur Dove said it first, about sticking together. Wasn't but a year or so ago Sandrine threw his own fiesta, observing the second year of the "dust harvest," as his parchment party invitations put it.

Announcing the Grama Group

About a hundred-fifty people, from about twenty ranches, came just to find out what the blazes he was thinking. They gasped: *He's letting our cattle graze his range.*

"You're opening the S to our herds? Just based on what I said?" asked Wilbur Dove, who had been talking about such an idea for a year or so. Sandrine thought it was a good idea. Decided to do it. Bang. It was done. The stipulation on the invitation: That they protect their land from subdivision and share pasture when needed, when available.

"When you can," Sandrine. "Wilbur figures we can all do it, and do it easily, if we work it out together, but we can't do it if we aren't together."

Wilbur looked around, and everybody was looking at each other.

They talked it over. Most, including Blye's daddy, but not Blye, signed that day as mariachis strolled, strumming, under the canvas canopies rented in Tucson. Even with only a dozen of the ranches signed, a vast amount of land was suddenly blocked together.

And when the sky clouded up, the canvas party tents were more than sufficient for the group, who watched the lightning strike at a gnarled oak lonely on the pasture just south of them. Limbs shattered and flew off the tree, smoldering. The old oak burned about fifteen minutes before the rain snuffed it. Then the *Gramaros*, named for the grass, had another round, and another, until the rain let up. Well along toward dawn, several men led by Sandrine hiked down through the mud to toast the oak's survival—one year ago.

Blye the Younger went that year without the "rich guy's" help but was now thinking he just might join in Sandrine's grand solidarity adventure.

"Hey, y'all heard?" Blye joked to Hartley, "Sandrine's goin' to pump in seawater from the Gulf of California and refill the ghost ocean. He's bringing back ancient tunas and dolphins and giant squids. I'm buildin' me a boat."

Blye probably needed something like a boat, something to seek refuge in.

Like Pete and other borderland ranchers, Blye saw the horsemen on the Mexico side, two by two, carbines strapped on their backs. Lighted by the moon. When morning popped up like a slice of toast, more cattle had vanished.

The ranchers, the Gramaros, at least, went high-tech, called up rocket scientists from White Sands. That got Blye's attention. They started painting their cattle's hooves with radio-isotopes and implanted GPS chips in their best bulls to track them by satellite.

They could tell right where those cattle had been trucked. Some went deep into Mexico. But technology still couldn't breach the tradition that required they pay ransom to retrieve the animals. It was the same old *mordida*—"the bite," the payoff.

Now cattle were being shot. *How does that make sense?* Blye asked himself as he rode down to check on Westerfield. Will Mann dropped by, too. He got there just as Blye was leaving, so Blye turned around and went back in for more.

The old rancher, Westy, looked threadbare in ragged jeans, long-sleeve long john top under a grease-stained sport coat. Sleeves with holes in the elbows, cuffs frayed.

"Don't know how they got shot," he told the two visitors, waving a hand at the carcasses of fifteen cattle strewn before them. "Maybe them aliens or them enviros."

Mann took a ballistics sample from one of the carcasses. Blye noticed something else. The Westerfield range was hammered, yet no hay that he could see anywhere.

"Those cows were malnourished," he told Mann later after they drove out. "Lay you odds ol' Westy shot those cattle himself."

Mann acknowledged with a nod.

"At least those *drogueros* won't be kidnapping any of Westy's cows," Blye said.

"That's one way around it," Mann said.

Sandrine had retained a law firm in Mexico City, and he let those lawyers handle the problem. His focus was always the land first, the cattle second.

The idea, he told the Grama Group in its monthly newsletter, "is to preserve the land, the traditions associated with the land, and to, by God, have a good time."

Blye read about their junkets. They'd gone drinking, hunting, fishing together. But they also toured a couple days in Egypt on the way to an eight-day photo-safari in Africa. Sandrine told Blye he couldn't wait to get home and make some comparisons.

Said he liked his own savannah better than the Serengeti.

Fewer tourists.

The group planned marketing campaigns with people in Italian suits from New York, Chicago and Kansas City, selling environ-mentally honorable beef. Blye read about the presentation they made. And Sandrine sat back enjoying the working cowboys in their string ties and Stetsons, some of the toughest and smartest people he knew, as they matched up against this unsuspecting Armani army. To Sandrine—and Blye had to agree—it appeared the ranchers mowed the brokers like alfalfa. They came, they saw, they were conquered, dumbstruck by the vastness of the land.

Time was, the likes of Blye and Sandrine might've shot each other on the streets of Lordsburg, Mesilla, or Tombstone. Now, instead, Blye's compadres gathered with Sandrine around polished maple tables surrounded by potted palm trees and computers. Blye would like to have seen that Tucson meeting, instead of just reading about it. He wanted into the biweekly truck/Jeep convoys to Tucson/El Paso, Sandrine in his Cessna.

El Paso, last summer: By custom, they ended up in Charley-O's, a bar teeming with stranded cowhands wanting a ride, a drink, a job. Sometimes just respect. If one couldn't find a girl, he'd settle for a fight. Gramaros, barely able to walk, laughed hard enough and looked so prosperous that every ranch lizard crawling out of the wainscoting wanted retribution. Gramaros always saw people they knew and wished they didn't.

Like Lupe "the Fizz" Ramos, pale-eyed sociopath from Santito. Couldn't leave a pleasant evening alone. Had too much drink, too much meth, and he had too much hair on the sides of his head and not enough on top. Ramos, one of Octavio's pistoleros, showing off at Charley-O's, twirled a pool cue like a drum major baton. Tried unsuccessfully to light the tip-ends. They wouldn't burn. The barkeep refused to allot him cognac for fuel.

"Hey, ain't that a *girl's* activity?" someone well back in the crowd finally yelled.

Ramos stopped cold. Twitchy about gender due to his first name, Guadalupe. *Who?* Question on his face. Ramos jumped up on the pool table to survey the crowd. His boot edged the thirteen ball and chipped it off into Sandrine's quick hands. Then Lupe toppled off the table, crashing into Sandrine.

The rancher, just turned fifty, and with the first traces of gray in his beard, had begun working on a beer-and-sausage gut that added a couple of years. The older the better, far as the balding Ramos was concerned. Ideal would be an opponent of eighty or ninety. The Fizz had a little gray, too, but he plucked it out every morning. He was old enough, fortyish as close as he knew, to recognize that the days of potentiality were gone, forever replaced by the *who-you-are*, like it or not. Most folks did not like who Ramos was. He used that. But he didn't relish it.

"I see in the Fizz an angry carbonation," Sandrine said to the gathered Gramaros, "that sparkles and dances like tiny bubbles when he looks at you."

The Fizz didn't like the comment and zoomed his sparkling eyes at Sandrine—and also swung his pool cue. Sandrine caught it in his left hand and twisted it instantly from Ramos' grasp. Some of Ramos' pistolero buddies stepped forward, but then they stepped back when they saw Ramos fizzle. They also noted a couple Border Patrol boys at a back table. They quickly calculated how long it would take the Patrol to descend en masse and round up the entire bunch—and how long before Octavio exacted his own penalties. Sandrine patted Ramos on the back, said no harm intended. Ramos shrugged, grinned and staggered away as if he'd been touched by an angel.

Sandrine always prevailed in his quiet way. He'd hoisted as many bales of hay in his adult life as most cowpokes. A big man who worked out regularly, sometimes with a weight-training coach from Las Cruces. Most necessary muscles in his upper body were solid. He didn't worry much about lower body. He figured he'd keep the skinny legs, let the horse do the work: "Cowboys ought to have skinny legs," he told his trainer.

Not Blye: Skinny everywhere. Weighed under one-fifty, standing just six feet, most of it muscle, but without any layers of insulation. He got most of his weight training by chasing and lifting cattle, one way or another—and then tracking them into Mexico. Blye got worked up about that, and about news in general—*a news junky*. Had to drive thirty-two miles round trip to his newspaper drop box on Highway 118. There most mornings were his newspapers with a twelve-pound rock on top, the *Albuquerque Journal*, *El Paso Times*, *Deming Headlight*, *Silver City Daily Press*, *Lordsburg Liberal*, *Heel Bull-a-tin* and *El Gramaro*, Sandrine's newsletter. Blye'd scan the headlines as he drove home, the papers arrayed on the passenger seat of his muddy pickup.

And coming home on a wintry breezy Highway 118, sure enough—one morning in March, Blye hit a ditch. A headline caught his eye.

"Heel Ranchers Accused of Abusing Public Lands"

Why, hell, he said to nobody, *there probly ain't even twenty Heel ranchers have public lands that are more than just rocks and dirt.* Blye dealt minimally with Will Mann, who oversaw his three-thousand acres of BLM allotments, mostly inaccessible islands rising from Blye's deeded sea of dust. Some ranchers west of Sandrine had forest allotments. But so far, everybody had been getting on just fine, even ol' Sandrine and his son and his buddies from the National Wildlands Coalition, which furnished a biologist, Bert Hackett, to help him run the ranch. This particular report quoted some woman named Wells from up on the Gila. *Well, hell, she ain't even from here.* Heel folks would never say such things. Blye got to reading the fine print, not just the headline. That's how he hit the ditch, busted an axle, and got a concussion off his steering wheel.

He bent the wheel to where it couldn't turn a full circle. He'd need a new one.

Hartley, doubling back on regular patrol, found Blye wandering dazed about a mile from his truck, heading the wrong direction. He took him to Doc Ruelas in Lordsburg.

"Damn fool left your keys in the ignition."

"Well, it ain't going nowheres on a busted axle," Blye said.

"Yeah, your house keys? You want to leave them laying around?"

"Hell, they ain't nothing to steal. It ain't locked."

"Your electronics? Sensors, radar scanners, your motorbike, whatever and whatnot?" Hartley said. "You don't want it, give it to me, I'll find a use for it, sell it at a swap meet."

The doc, Roland Ruelas, took Blye ahead of weeping, whining ones on account of he was too quiet, Hartley said on the drive back.

"Too quiet. You had that doc worried."

The doc flashed some tiny little flashlight right in his eyeball. Blye pulled back so fast he cracked the doctor's aquarium with what was left of his head. The nurse, Anamarie, had to come in and put a swatch of packing tape right across the front of that fish tank to keep it from leaking.

It kept leaking anyway.

"You have a concussion," the doc said.

"From the wreck or from your gol-dinged fish tank?"

"Well, it's sure gol-dinged now," the doc said. "It sure didn't help any. I guess we're going to have to hogtie cowboys from now on. Make a note, Anamarie."

Ruelas was a little out of focus, but he assured Blye that would pass in a day or so. "Won't be long before I'm just as sharp as a Sony TV," he said.

He let Hartley take Blye away, but he looked doubtful about it. Blye walked with one shoulder dipped, and it shifted his balance.

"Don't worry, Doc," Hartley said, noticing. "He looks this way all the time."

They got back in the Border Patrol Excursion, and Blye suddenly lit up like he'd remembered he was mad.

"Who're the enviros up in Gila Wells who want to shut down ranching?" he said.

"What are you talking about?" Hartley said.

"Wilderness Wack-o's," he said. "The National Wilderness Wack-o Alliance. They want to gol-dinged shut down ranching."

"Now, don't get too hot. Doc said take it easy, Martin."

"Ain't takin' it back. They're craven *dunno-whats*, attacking us from some office in town with a f-f-freakin' fax machine."

"You talk this over with Sandrine? He's got some pretty good contacts in the enviro community. People with some good ideas. They're helping him," Hartley said.

"Enviro community, *shee*," said Blye. "This woman said Sandrine was a gol-dinged turncoat traitor, right here in this paper. She put a bounty out on him, big type, big as you please."

"Bounty? To, you mean, to . . . "

"You got to read between the lines. They said something like for information leading to something or other, some such. That's when I plumb hit the ditch, didn't quite finish, but I see what they're *at*. Out to git him. Plain as potatoes."

"You're nuts," Hartley said. He got him back home by nightfall, a whole day shot. "God knows how many drug mules got through or how many tons of marijuana or cocaine went north or how many cattle got driven south," Hartley said.

"Just be thankful you had some company for a day," Blye said.

"A half-vegetized rancher delirious from brain damage ain't what I call company," Hartley said. "Frey won't see why I didn't just leave you roadside, call a tow."

"I'll call Billy straightaway for the tow," Blye yawned. "You don't need to."

"Hear he's backlogged."

"No matter. Be laid up days the way I feel. Jeez, I hate this. Those gol-dinged enviros. Hey, ought to teach ol' Sandrine who his friends are. Teach him what friends are all about. Going to call him straight-away, straightaway . . ." Then Martin Blye conked out in the front seat of Hartley's overhauled Excursion.

Hartley carried him into his old adobe over his shoulder, dropped the keys on the dining table. On his way driving back to Jackrabbit Wells, Hartley stopped by the gimpy truck, half nose-dived into a dry gulch, and pulled out the Heel Bull-a-tin to read about this bounty on Sandrine.

Raylinda Wells, it said, was offering bounties up to $5,000 for information about environmental violations in the New Mexico Heel. Didn't mention Sandrine by name. The intent seemed to be to turn one rancher against another, divide and conquer. Just the opposite of what Sandrine was trying to do. There had been grum-bling for years among ranchers resentful of Sandrine ever since he bought the Diamond S.

"Wild West is preparing a lawsuit against Heel ranchers, alleg-ing habitat degradation, which has caused a decline in nesting by the Southwest gray-flecked starling," the article said. And there was a nugget that made Hartley drive a little faster as he headed back for his evening shift at Jackrabbit Wells. He clocked in, picked up the phone and pushed his speed-dial button.

"Hi, yeah. Let me read you something. This group says it wants to purchase the Two Square Ranch, and here's the quote, 'once the ranchers set an auction date.' I didn't think those ranchers wanted to sell. But you asked about that, so I'm letting you know."

Hartley listened a moment, said, "OK," then hung up.

Chapter Six

Outcaste

The medical examiner wept. Tears fell on his sky blue paper mask. He dabbed at his eyes with the powdery backs of Latex gloves. Suddenly face-to-face with locked-up feelings about death. A ticking time capsule had been cracked open.

He let his hand rest on the scalpel—to see if it was steady. It wasn't.

Horror. Grief. Blamed on tribal tradition. As though something were wrong in it, instead of right. *What if it came straight from the undiscovered human heart?* Sarkisian, torn by conflicting tribal traditions, ransacked himself. Didn't like what he found.

Outcaste. He'd expected to be called that. Always there near the surface. Somewhere Sam Sarkisian had crossed a line. No shaman would see him. Called Irwin Sanostee in Chinle, got the shaman's voicemail, left a message, weeks ago. The shaman did not call him back. Sam called his mother in Fence Lake, and she clucked her tongue. "Why do you torment the *hataali?* They know what's right," she said. "Come to you if you're ready."

She practically told him to heal himself, get himself in harmony.

"If a person were in harmony they wouldn't need Sanostee," he said.

Sark found it difficult to speak of *himself* consulting a shaman. It was always "a person" or "they" who accepted Navajo tradition. He'd fought it since childhood. Just as his father, the Baluchi rug merchant, had fought it. Maybe why the haatali hesitated.

Now, alone with it again, Sarkisian had to hesitate. *Ghosts.*

He frowned at himself. He'd mastered death. Hadn't he? Or should he find a new profession? He was half Baluchi. He *looked* Baluchi. Maybe he should just *be* Baluchi.

Stoic acceptance of death is the honored way in the deserts of Baluchistan. You never dwell on it. His late father, Irag Sarkisian, had told his story about coming to America. Hidden from the Savak, the secret police. He'd left Tehran at midnight on Ramadan after the coup that restored the shah to the Peacock Throne. Made it home to Zahedan on the Pakistan frontier. The proud Baluchi tribesmen, their Pashtun ammo belts crisscrossed, their long rifles inlaid with scrimshaw and spangles, helped Irag smoothly flow to Pakistan. The tallest, the turbaned Mohammed Abdur Shahnawaz Khan with the gray handlebar mustache, stayed with him as chowkidar through Mexico, then New Mexico. All easy, illegal crossings. Now the son of Irag was crossing another border. Into the realm of *ghosts*. Bad spirits, trapped spirits. How did they get there? How did *he* get there? Friends who knew him as a scientist presumed him free of superstition. None believed he could be saddled with conflicting tribalisms. But the coroner decided Sark was into a new dimension and simply knew more about death.

Now this helpless grief. Sarkisian tried to shake it off. But it hung there as he made his midsaggital incision, sternum to pubis, avoiding the edge of a huge exit wound, which he described as seventeen centimeters in diameter, about seven inches, obliterating her left breast. Carefully, he removed the entrails, noting any interaction with bullet fragments. Small heart, even for a twelve-year-old. He noted many diagonal lacerations. The bullet had broken apart as it struck the heart. He set it aside. One heart, set aside.

He examined her feet. *Mud.* Fragments of vegetation trapped in clay. He bagged a sample for biotyping, left it with Sheilah Ryne. She specialized in plant tissue.

Then Sarkisian pried open the fingers on her left and right fists. "Hey, George. Better have a look."

Glenwaller stepped over from his own stainless steel alcove and observed as Sark removed a small golden locket from the girl's right fist, and then opened it. "A woman's picture," he said into the microphone. "Antique photograph. Printed on metal with an engraved inscription. Odd. 'For Our Bride.' *Our* bride?" Glenwaller shrugged.

The photograph showed a woman with grayish-seeming hair, shoulders back, chin high. Gaze rising at about a fifteen-degree angle.

Pearly looking earrings. Pendant around her long, slender neck. Apparently the same locket. Her hair was piled high on her head.

"Prematurely gray, mid-thirties," Sarkisian said. "We'll isotope it. Need to show it to the family. They may know who this woman is."

"But Corona said not to show the family anything; they're suspects," George said.

Sark paused the taping. "He said that? Probably said to keep an eye on me, then."

"Yeah, he did," George said with a smile.

"He the one who started the *wolf girl* thing, or was it you?"

"That's what they're calling her, the newspapers, TV, everybody," he said. "They say she adopted a wolf. Why, you don't think it's true?"

"There's good reason to doubt it," Sark said, switching the recorder back on.

The light was low in the examination room, except for focused lamps over each table giving the impression of a stainless steel pool hall. Sark stood, folding and refolding the flap of skin back and forth to check the broken bullet's scattered trajectories. The pieces had taken a slightly upward path. The shooter was ten degrees lower than she was.

"Hey, George?"

Glenwaller stepped over once again.

"Help me double-check," Sark said. Flapped skin back and forth over the cavity.

"Shot by a someone in a hole," George said.

"The gun was a little below the entry wound," Sark said.

"In a hole or prone, on the ground."

"Well, what if she was on horseback, maybe on a hill?" Sarkisian said. "The shooter could've been standing on a ladder if the hill was high enough. Look how the exit wound spreads. Seventeen centimeters, George. *Seventeen.*"

"Range?"

"Not especially close. Not a speck of powder residue."

It was four o'clock. Sark looked at his watch at four every afternoon. He needed to allow time for transcribing. That now would have to wait. He had a meeting.

Glenwaller was already all packed up for the day, just kibitzing.

"This seems to be hitting you hard," he said.

"The Braden girl?" Sark said. "I knew her family. Her mom and I are the same age. She was a Williams. My mom's a weaver. Up at Fence Lake. Mom's family ran a feed store, just off the Ramah rez. The Williamses stopped at our store, sometimes. I'd see them coming, full of energy, especially Marlie. And now, *this* is her child."

He pulled off his face mask and angrily slid the girl into the cooler.

"Can't finish today," he said, hands shaking. "Got a meeting. Where's Sheilah?"

"Over here," Sheilah said from behind a lab partition, "Got a good clear answer."

"Just stuff it in a folder," Sark said. "I'll read it on the fly. I'm late."

George gave a last bit of input: "Take the janitor's exit. A reporter's out front."

Sark was ten minutes late for his racetrack meet. Mann was waiting in his Bureau of Land Management SUV. Sark got in. "About time they gave you a case," Sark said. "Nobody knows the land like you. The land was a *witness*."

"They didn't give this to me," Mann said. "The FBI just sent their guy back to Quantico for a couple weeks. I'm a stand-in. Very interim. So the bullets were carved?"

"Seventy to eighty percent likely. I've got four clearly separate trajectories and three less clear. No doubt about fragmentation," Sark said. "Ever do this before?"

"A long time ago in Arizona," Mann said.

"Any thoughts about *where* she was killed?" Sark said.

"Elsewhere." Mann didn't hesitate. He'd been thinking about it. "Why?"

"You know the one about the tree falling out where nobody can hear it. Well, I was there. Didn't hear it, and I would have. Also, no track older than forty-five minutes, and you placed time of death one to two hours before the first bullet."

Sark nodded. "Her shoes weren't tied. Notice that? But there were striations on her feet from laces. Shoes were initially tied, then later untied post-mortem."

"Probably searched her, looking for something, who knows what," Mann said.

"I got a very interesting thing," Sarkisian said. Opened the folder. Showed Mann the gold locket. "Maybe they were looking for *this*."

Mann puffed. Half-whistled. "What is it; where was it?"

"In her hand. Open it."

Mann popped it open. "Prematurely gray woman with antique locket—this one?" Sark nodded. Mann looked closer. "*For Our Bride?* What the heck does that mean?"

Sarkisian shrugged, then read Sheila's one-paragraph report. "And we've got mud with sycamore mulch on her hands and feet," he said.

"Well, everyone said she was going to Endicott's. Maybe she was," Mann mused.

"Cliff Endicott was gone all morning, along with Clay Endicott and their hand Jaime, rounding up strays, according to Endicott."

"You want to drive up there and talk to them again?" Sark asked. "I could go along, visit my mom, check the plant life on the E-Bar-E. By the way, what d'you want me to tell reporters? I've been dodging them."

"Don't dodge 'em. Send 'em to me."

Eighty minutes later they turned off Interstate 25 at Socorro. Headed west. The huge white dish antennae of the Very Large Array radio-telescope turned deep pink-magenta in the shadows. The sun stretched long, then winked out between two peaks in the Apache Wilderness. They turned south onto an unlit dirt road that led to Beaver Wells. But the E-Bar-E came first. Marked by a gate tall enough for the trucks.

Driveway took another fifteen minutes. A herd of antelope thundered past in Mann's headlights. He estimated about a hundred pronghorns, leaping, running flat out.

"They hunt 'em out here," he said, and Sark nodded.

The SUV pulled up in front of Endicott's ranch house. Ellie Endicott came out to say "Hi." She wiped her hands on her apron. "Jest bakin'," she said, inviting them in.

Mann introduced Sarkisian, said he was from over by Fence Lake and was helping with the investigation. "Like to retrace a little of your range tomorrow. Okay?"

"Sure," she said, handing each man a slice of pie on a plastic plate.

"Have any sycamores up here?" Sark asked.

"Sure, why?"

"We'd like to eat some of your pie under a sycamore."

Ellie beamed, "Oh, well, then, sure, gentlemen. Need horses? Philly'll drag a pair out for you. He's in the barn. I'll call him, and I'll pack you some pie."

"Who's Philly?"

"New kid. He replaced Jaime."

"Jaime Garza?" he asked. "Where'd he go?"

"Who knows. They come, they go. Heard he went back to Zacatecas or such."

"Who said Zacatecas, and when did he go?" Mann asked.

"Somebody told Clay," she said, "back about the time that Millie died."

"We'll want to talk to Clay. Don't bother about the horses until tomorrow . . . if that's okay," Mann said.

"Clay's with his uncle in Springerville."

"Arizona? He shouldn't have left the state while this investigation's ongoing. Have him come home," Mann said. "Believe me it's better if he does it voluntarily."

Sarkisian asked where the trees are, and Ellie told him five miles south and added: "Five miles is a long way to ride to eat a piece of pie you can have right now."

"Excellent point," Sarkisian said.

"We still want to talk with Philly tonight," Mann added.

Felipe Mondragon opened the stable door reluctantly. Lately he'd felt beset by the law. Philly was norteño. Law didn't pester up north the way it did here. But he needed a job, and the Endicotts offered one: Wrangler. Sounded good, but it was mainly a glorified stable hand, moving horses around, making sure they were saddled for the Endicotts, that the saddles were soaped, the horses curried, the stalls cleaned, and everything in place. A day's work every day. If not, there was fence to string. Grunge work. Similar to ranching.

"Well, son, d'you know that Jaime who had your job before you?" Mann asked.

"I know he did a lousy job."

"Uh-oh, lousy, eh? How so?" Mann said. "We'd like to talk to him."

The kid volunteered: "I think he's dead, actually."

Mann weighed that. Sarkisian looked back with a doubtful frown.

Mann asked Philly: "What makes you think so?"

"That shooting. He disappeared then the way people who are shot disappear."

"That shooting . . . where?" Mann raised eyebrows.

"The girl."

"You know about that? Hear something, a shot?"

"I wasn't working here yet, remember? I was up in Pojoaque."

"You heard talk?"

"Everybody's heard talk, but I wasn't here."

Mann was frustrated. Preoccupied. Mann had expected Garza. Had Garza questions ready. Now, no Garza and no *nada* about Garza. Had Garza skipped?

Sarkisian wandered farther back into the stable, poked around the tack room, inspected a few stalls, while Mann toyed with Philly.

"Tell me what was so lousy about the job ol' Garza did. Was that his name?"

"He left things like he hadn't been around for days."

"And had he been?"

"Well, no, he hadn't been. He just disappeared. Left things in a mess."

"How long had he been gone when you arrived. Are you sure Garza's his name?"

"Don't know. They called him Garza."

"How old are you, son?"

"Sixteen."

"You should be in school."

"Got a work permit. I'm going to raise cattle." The kid reached in several pockets.

"Skip the permit," Mann said. "I believe you. Find anything of Jaime's worth bothering with? Maybe something you wanted to send back to him or his family?"

"No," Philly said. "Anything he left got tossed. Wasn't much."

"Show me where he slept."

"Same place I sleep," he said, pointing at a day bed in the corner of a spotlessly clean stall, concrete floor, a reading lamp, a radio, and a CD Walkman with headphones.

"Give me where I might find Jaime, if he isn't dead."

"They said a little Baja village near Ensenada. But I don't buy it."

"Why not and who said so?"

"Mister Endicott. I heard him guessing. I think they were talking about Jaime to an old guy, kinda rich looking. Mexican. And then I heard Mrs. Endicott say Zacatecas."

"She told Sheriff Corona," Mann said. "How do you get along with the sheriff?"

"Oh, pretty well."

"He hassle you about your shoes?"

"What about them?"

"Mexican shoes," Mann said. "He thinks you're an illegal, doesn't he."

"I'm from Española. I'm norteño. My great-great-great et cetera came from Spain with Oñate. I ain't no wet. Bought the shoes from a road vendor. Guess he was Mexican."

"Here's my home number," Mann said, scrawling on one of his cards. "Call me if Corona gives you any trouble. Or if *anybody* does. Keep in touch."

Fence Lake was another hour-plus. Mann spent the night in a ten-dollar room behind the cantina. It had a toilet and a hot-water shower. He took a shower, and lay back to write and review notes and call Doc, but his cell phone was stranded out there, pay phone by the Chevron dead. He'd had to postpone their ride out into the wilderness. Sara seemed to understand. "Call when you get clear, or any time," she said. Out the window, stars intimidated all electronics. Somebody played a mariachi accordion in the cantina.

He found his notes folded oddly under him when he woke the next morning.

Mann picked up Sarkisian at eight a.m. They had eggs at the Highway 60 crossroads and were back at the E-Bar-E by ten. Philly had two horses ready. They headed south with saddlebags carrying sandwiches and more baked goods.

"Doubt Miss Millicent made it up this far," Sarkisian said.

Mann agreed. "She never made it up here. I rode this the day after. No tracks, but it had snowed, just a little. I'm sure there were no tracks."

"You rode it from which end?"

"Rode down from Endicotts'."

"All the way to the Braden line?"

"Not quite. Just far enough to satisfy myself she hadn't been to the Endicotts'."

"What about the backside of Cerro Verde?"

"Yeah, the Mangas trail. The killers rode out about a mile to an old mining road. They met a vehicle, probably a Silverado judging by the wheelbase. Pulling a four-horse trailer. They loaded some horses. They let Millie's horse loose so she'd head home."

"Did you get as far as these sycamores?" Sark said.

Mann shook his head at the cluster of trees with newly budded pale green leaves huddled against the base of a small, solitary foothill known as La Rondita.

"I was up here a long time ago, but not recently. Sure you can recognize this dirt when you see it?" Mann said.

"Doesn't matter. We'll test whatever's there."

Mann nodded: "You already had the mud analyzed and it's got sycamore."

"That's true. It's what made me late yesterday, matter of fact."

They rode silently to the edge of the grove and tied the horses to a low branch.

"Here's that mulch," Sark said. "This is the stuff I found on her fist and her feet."

"Bag a sample," Mann said.

"Here's her footprint in the clay," Sarkisian said.

"Here's her horse's print; see where she mounted," Mann said, turning slowly and following the hoof prints upslope. The pinkish clay could hold the tracks forever.

He found some darker discoloration preserved in the hardened mud and bagged it.

"Could be some blood here," he said, handing it to Sarkisian.

"I'll run it," Sark said, "unless you'd rather the feds do it."

Mann paced down from the point of entry just a few steps, to get the angle approximately correct, and found stationary boot prints. *Tex-Mex Saddlery.* Juarez.

"Any *idea* who owns this land?" he said sourly because he already knew.

"You know this spot?" Sark said.

"BLM land," Mann said. "Tradeable land. Between the Bradens, the Endicotts, and the wilderness. Sam, our uncle, wanted to get rid of it. Nobody wanted it because—no access. Well, Sid almost did. He backed out. Somebody else came in to bid on it."

"Endicott?" Sarkisian said.

"Some corporation. The land includes this little foothill and that's about it. You could say it was overlooked when they created the wilderness. Because there were so many allotments, Two Square and E-Bar-E, Braden and Endicott, Watanabe, Brody all interlocking as well as a couple others nearby. They just missed it, too small. Too much trouble to go back and fix it. They'd rather just get rid of it."

The two men rode up to the crest of the little hill and did a quick survey. There were signs of test-boring and surveying, little stakes with little day-glo flags. And there were pylons to support some platform-like structure on the hilltop.

"This construction wasn't permitted by the escrow. I'm getting an evidence team out here," Mann said. "Freezing the land transfer. See what crawls out."

"And the wolves?" Sark said.

Mann frowned: "Just don't call her the wolf girl, OK?"

"You heard about the sale where, up in Albuquerque or here?"

"Ellie made mention of it."

"They goin' to buy?" Mann asked.

"She said they don't see how they can, with the wolves threatening the pronghorns, it's just too much. Why? You keepin' track?" Sark asked.

"Yep, trying to. I'd have to work with whoever it was."

Chapter Seven

The Wolves

The gray wolf named Bob came to the end of the chain-link fence and stopped. He knew every square inch of the square-mile pen, the big trees, the broken ones, the dead ones, the burrows where the snakes, mice, and possums hid from owls, hawks, and eagles, the dry creek that cut diagonally across, and he knew this fence had never before just ended the way it did today. He was wary. The fence had four sides and corners. Right about here—he circled, emphasizing annoyance—was where he and his family usually found a dead elk that, as far as they could tell, had fallen from the sky.

Instead, today, the fence was gone, and there was no elk. The wolf stopped, retraced, sniffed. Yes, here were the smells of dead elk.

It made him hungry. It made him angry. Why would elk stop falling from the sky? Tentatively, the wolf named Bob, whose real name was One-Fifty-Six, ventured out into the great Apache Wilderness hoping to smell more elk.

There were a lot of other smells, but no elk.

Here, about fifteen feet outside the fence, Bob stopped again. He was thinking dimly about his mate, One-Fifty-Seven, and their pups, One-Fifty-Eight through One-Sixty-One. Maybe he'd bring them along and show them what he found and maybe he wouldn't. He turned back. But then he thought again. Maybe he'd better . . . *Mmmmf.*

Micah Walton focused huge binoculars from a blind about one-hundred-forty yards up slope. Six wolves. Other than Bob One-Fifty-Six, he didn't know which was which. But it looked like Bob caught a whiff of something, maybe him.

"He's turning back. Why's Bob turning back?" Walton asked Donald Badderly, the Brit who headed this division of the wolf project for the US Fish and Wildlife Service.

"Retracing," Badderly said. "They do it all the time."

"I think Bob's looking for his family. He never strays far from Romy," said Michelle Westover, wildlife biologist with the privately funded Wolf USA Project.

"Which one's Millie?" asked Walton. He was a graduate student interning with the Forest Service. "The one the wolf girl adopted." He zoomed in on the pups.

"One-Sixty-One," Westover said. "The youngest. Standing next to Romy, the mom. Then in back, sis Alice, Marky, the youngest male, and Milo, prince of the litter."

Millie's attention was outside the pen. Walton scanned and saw a fat chipmunk on a log. Millie's ears were straight up. She was ready to go. But she waited. The other pups hung back behind Romy, who tried to pry Millie off her flank. The pup wouldn't budge.

"It's absurd to suppose One-Fifty-Six would turn back because of his wife and kiddies," Badderly said. "He's simply retracing. Now, look, he's turned 'round again. He's just making sure. And *Wolf Girl's* a public relations nightmare. Don't go near that."

"What do I call her?" Walton said.

"Call her the latest victim of a trigger-happy land," Badderly said.

"Ridiculous," Westover said. "Evidence points to Colombia-Mexico drug cartels."

"What evidence? There is no evidence. There is no investigation," Badderly said.

"Did you know the girl? I did. A sweet kid," she said.

"I'm sure she was. If she'd lived in England, she'd still be alive," he said. "But I do not recall her being closely associated with us, at all, before March. We were in a terrific big hurry to squeeze her interest for every drop of publicity we could because she was a Juliet in Sid Braden's house. And now she is dead. I pray—do you?—I pray it had nothing to do with wolves, *but* you drag her into this and now she's dead. How long—"

"That's crap, Badly. Crap."

"I have to agree with her," Walton said to Badderly.

"How long before somebody starts asking questions?" Badderly said. "They call her the *wolf girl.* You've overplayed this thing, you and Wells. It'll blow up in our faces."

"Well, don't you play it up, then," she said.

"I'm not. Wells was on *television*, for pity's sake. Talking about a child's great sacrifice for the environment."

"Well, it was a great sacrifice," Westover said.

"It was murder," Badderly said. "They're blazing away at everything we release."

"They are not. Six of thirty-six. That's all. Help me out, here, Walton."

"Don't know what I'd add. Someone had a gun. Everyone had a gun?" he said.

Bob finally turned around and headed back for Romy and her pups.

These were still the first days of a monitoring program that was supposed to keep the wolf team for a full month in the wilderness just west of the Two Square, tracking Bob and his pack. Walton wondered if they would make it. Wolf USA had been the bitterest critics of the government's Fish and Wildlife biologists. Too political, they said.

"And where do you get off calling the federal government political?" Badderly yelled after her with a broad British grin. "Amazing to be here," he added to Walton.

The idea of wolfists in "pup" tents amused him. But really only Micah Walton had a true pup tent. Badderly and Westover were in separate dome tents, as far apart as they could manage and still be in camp. A large, low-spreading piñon between them.

Their dinners were all prepared in advance. They merely removed them from a propane refrigerator and cooked them over a propane stove. Each tent had a propane heater. And Westover had her own shower, a black plastic bladder she filled with hot water and hung on a tree. Nozzle on a hose, and a circle of pipe to hang a shower curtain.

"Ingenious," said Badderly. "I'd like to try it."

She let Micah use the shower, then told Badderly, simply, "Go to hell, Badly." Another time when he asked, she told him, "Drop dead, Badly," then added later when he merely looked in her direction, "Screw yourself, Badly." Badderly took sponge baths in Braden's hot creek. He asked the Bradens' permission, and they cordially gave it.

That night, dinner was linguini, then they crawled into their tents and switched off their propane lanterns and went to sleep.

They slept bundled up in the best that Abercrombie, Fitch, and REI could offer the well-heeled. They dreamed rustic dreams in which they restored some small part of nature. And they were getting paid for it. They had not only God, but the law, on their side. Baddlerly refused to play the God game. "We've been playing God with wolves for five thousand years, maybe more. Three hundred years in this country."

"Who's we, white man?" Westover had demanded. That was the night before.

"The human race," said Badderly, who had worked in Eastern European wolf recovery. That was a tough assignment. "Don't get me started on the biblical end."

During the night, Westover believed she heard a wolf howl. It made her feel warmer in the twelve-degree darkness.

But to the figure on the ridge overlooking the camp and the chain-link and the field beyond, the howl was the beacon he needed.

The grease-smeared man used a directional microphone and laptop computer, state-of-the-art US Army issue, and peered through an infra-red scope that was not quite state-of-the-art but good enough to put cross-hairs on Bob's neck. He also used a silencer. *Zhuuuumpf.* The bullet hit Bob in the neck. Bob fell over on his side, twitching. Then Bob died silently, less than one hundred yards from the enclosure.

The carcass lay about two-hundred-fifty yards from where the painted man had been watching. The man had to fire over the sleeping camp to hit Bob. Nobody stirred.

Then the man broke apart his gun, scope, microphone, and silencer and concealed the pieces in the framework of his backpack, which innocently contained a change of clothes, a canteen, and ten packs of trail mix. His laptop looked right at home in there.

He hiked back toward the highway, away from the camp, away from the dead wolf. He unlocked his truck, an old navy-blue Chevy with bogus plates, and he emptied the backpack. He put the clothing into a plain, unaltered backpack, tossed the trail mix into his glove compartment and slung the canteen behind the seat. Then, he locked the deadly backpack in a hard-to-find compartment under the shortbed, behind the spare tire, next to the gas tank. And he drove quietly back into eastern Arizona, toward Springerville. It was three-forty-five in the morning, mountain standard time.

The mountains above the sleeping biologists were edged with early light when the whimpering of the alpha's mate, Romy, awakened Westover, the lightest sleeper of the group. She was first to hear the sounds Romy made. She also heard the pups cavorting, impatient, unaware. Quietly, Westover bundled up and went out to see what was causing the disturbance. She found Bob's body. The other wolves had withdrawn a safe distance away, disappearing back into the enclosure, by the time she arrived.

She verified that he was dead, finding a clean shot through the neck that dropped Bob where he stood. Assuming that was correct, she could only conclude the shot came from the direction of the camp, or the ridge beyond. She popped open her cellular phone but found it was out of range and could not connect with anywhere. "Shit," she said.

"What's wrong?" Badderly asked, startling her.

"Jesus H, don't do that."

"I don't mind the love names when it's just you and me," he said, "but I wish you'd use restraint in front of the Bambino."

At the moment Walton the Bambino was asleep in his pup tent.

"Christ, you think I'm joking. Get lost, Badly," Westover said.

"Not possible," he said. "I've crossed the Sahara, the Gobi, the rainforests of Brazil, and the Yucatan. Never could get lost. Tried. Failed. Sorry."

"Bob is dead," she said.

"I see that," he said.

"You don't sound worried."

"I'm not. I'm *disgusted*. It will cost us another wolf pack that we will have to put at risk down here. But I knew when I took this job there would be shootings. It's Americker, after all," he said. "And in Americker, people go out and shoot things."

"Ever read '*The Hunting Party*'?" she asked him.

"Oh, for God's sakes. Don't bring that up. Not the same at all. Sound like a college sophomore. No matter your lot sued us. We're in it together, regardless."

Westover always clammed up when Badderly brought up the lawsuit. Wolf USA claimed USFWS didn't protect habitat. The judge had been avalanched with affidavits and legal briefs. Badderly kept it all neatly straight in his head. Westover walked on eggs. She'd debated him before and been caught short when he presented documents.

The sky was brightening, and Walton, who heard their voices, climbed out of his pup tent and surveilled three-sixty with his Bushnells, then came down barefoot in his briefs, rubbing his eyes and breathing steam.

"What the hey?" he said. "Bob? Oh, no, Bobby."

"Yeah, Bobby gave his life for his mates," Badderly said. "Damned annoying."

"Oh, God, Donald, act as if," Westover said. "We've got to round up the rest of the pack and restore the enclosure—until Washington makes a decision."

"If they're loose, we need clearance *first*," said Badderly.

"The wolves are already back in the enclosure," Walton said. "I scoped it a second ago. Spotted them up against the fence on the other end. If we put the fence panels back up right here, we'll have them, and we won't have to recapture them."

"I think that's best," Westover said. "This release is compromised. We can try the radio, but not for a few hours."

Badderly urged immediate radio contact with Washington, but then agreed it was more important to get the fence back up, then call.

The three of them unstacked the eight-by-eight-foot sections of chainlink fencing and bolted them back onto the still-standing panels.

Badderly whistled while he worked. *The Woody Woodpecker Song.*

"When we get back, I'm asking for your replacement," Westover told him.

"Go right ahead, dear. Why wait? Radio it in. I hope it goes through because I'm tired of your anthropomorphic fantasizing. Sad thing is, since I'm in charge of this operation, it will probably be you gets sacked. We'll all try to carry on."

"I'll ask that you be deported as well," she said.

Badderly laughed. "Oh, that's ripe," he said. "Jolly good. The judge will get a giggle out of that."

"I liked what you said before about us all being in it together," Walton said.

"Yeah, sorry, Micah. You didn't bargain for this. But you could do a thesis entitled: 'Flaw in Wolf Recovery: Wolves Will Be Wolves and People Will Be People.'"

Chapter Eight

A Silent Bell

Blye woke up on the sofa. Television pulsed subliminal sound at him, and he woke with a craving for Excedrin. Noon, Sunday, March fifteenth, *the Ides*. Dusting of new snow was beginning to melt in the clear sunlight out on the desert chaparral. Blye kicked off the comforter and tried sit up. It was as if somebody turned up the rheostat on a pain machine. He slumped back on the couch, mulling whether he could move at all. He wanted passionately to shut off the TV. Saw the remote on the coffee table but couldn't reach it. Pushed his boot at it. Hartley hadn't even pulled off his boots. Did Hartley really believe he slept with his boots on? Blye hooked his boot on the remote and pulled it along the edge of the table toward his outreached hand. Almost, but . . . *clack*, knocked the gol-dinged thing on the floor. It lay, all unfocused, an inch beyond his fingertips.

Slid gingerly toward the edge of the sofa. Leaned down. Picked up the remote. Shut off the TV. Scrunched back onto the velvet pillow that said "Chihuahua" on it.

Silence. He dozed a while longer.

Then there came a transmission-like whining from outside, and Blye knew it was Billy's truck. He hoped Hartley hadn't locked the old adobe's front door.

Billy Neergard knocked, and Blye tried again to sit up, but he still couldn't. His head felt split down the middle, and he ran his fingers along the ridge left diagonally on his forehead by the steering wheel. It felt hot. It felt like a large worm had crawled under his skin, died there, and petrified.

His skin was hot, he reasoned, because his body was trying to eject this worm, and the worm was dead and did not give a damn.

"Just come on in, Billy," he yelled. The pain arrow went up with those resonating words inside his skull.

Couldn't y'all just speak, did you have to yell? He said this to himself.

Better one yell than two whispers, he answered. Least ways the yell did get to Billy. He came in, Stetson in hand, because it was a low-bridge doorway, typical of a lot of Mexican adobes, and Billy wanted no dented hat.

"I got yer truck hitched up out there," Billy said.

"Can you fix it?" Blye said.

"Sure can. You want to sign for it, or I can tell Vern to jest put it on yer account."

"Either way," Blye whispered.

"Wha—?"

"Either way," he said. "Hurts to talk, see?" He pointed at his forehead.

"Oh, my lord," Billy said. "You're the one bent the steering wheel. You can see them little finger knobs on your forehead, plumb imprinted."

"Look bad?"

"Bad? Makes you look like something from out there in space, or at least not from here. You want me to hold up a mirror?"

"Don't have a mirror, and now I for-sure know why," Blye said, quiet as he could without whispering. "Just fix my truck. I'll ride the motorbike in, pick it up next week."

"Where is yer motorcycle? It ain't out front."

"In the barn. I moved it cause snow was coming."

"Yeah, snow. You had visitors leaving tracks in it," Billy said. "Looks like maybe four, five. In mountain boots. Probably mules or coyotes. Want me to check your barn?"

"Yeah, would you, Billy? See if everything's all right."

"Can rustle you up some chow. Could send Janey, maybe cook for a day or two?"

"Real kind offer, but I don't want to impose, not the way she feels about me."

"Well, heck, she treats ever-one the same," Billy said. "But she can cook. It ain't like I'm sending you a belly dancer. You cain't move yet. That's purty plain. She can help you. You helped us last winter. We all help each other. That Canadian fellow, Sandrine, lets you use his range. It's like we was some a them communists, only we ain't."

"Yeah, just ask. Don't tell her. If she don't want to, that's more than OK with me."

"You don't like her much, I know."

"Goes way back, with Janie," Blye said, "to when we were kids. We get on okay. We just don't tend to pair up. You wouldn't want us pairing up, now, would you?"

Billy thought a moment, then said: "No, s'pose not." He didn't sound sure.

"Preacher'll come around to visit," Billy said. "If Janey won't come, preacher'll bring you some chow. We'll give him a bunch a chicken to bring."

"Preacher'll eat half before it gets here," Blye said.

"Naw, he's on a diet."

"The drive down'll sure kill that, smellin' yer ma's chicken."

"Yeah, well, I'll jest check the barn."

The boot prints in the snow did lead to the barn, and Billy Neergard noted the trackable tread patterns, including those of one guy wearing two different brands of shoe—left and right didn't match.

He opened the barn door. Light spilled in, framing his shadow. Particles of dust were caught swirling in the sudden sunlight. The barn was silent. The motorcycle was in one of the stalls, one wheel missing, the hub hitched up on an oil-stained cinder block. *Explains why they didn't steal the bike,* Billy thought.

Out back was a different deal. He spun around and returned to the house.

"Yer horses is gone," he said. "They're *gone.* All of 'em. How many was there?"

"A dozen."

"They took 'em. Didn't even leave us one to track 'em with."

"That's kind of nasty," Blye said. "Do me a favor, call Tom, tell him I need him to come back out here and have a look around so he and Frey can make a report to the Gol-dinged Mexicans."

"Hartley's kinda got himself hung up today," Billy said.

"How so? He was fine yesterday. Hell, he drove me all the way to Lordsburg and back."

"He's got a meeting with the BLM up to Gila Wells. About a little girl got killed. He asked me not to say, but, heck, now I figure I got to."

"What a world," Blye said.

"Tommy says he'll be back dragging the roads tomorrow."

"I'll notify the coyotes it's okay to come across," Blye growled.

"They'd be coming anyway," Billy said.

Hartley sat at Dolly's corner table, where he could look out windows in two directions. It had been nine months since he'd been in Gila Wells. Last summer. Fishing with Belknap. Place never changes. Knew Mann only slightly. Knew him by sight. Knew he was from Arizona, and that's about all he knew. Hartley'd got in early. Road crews he'd expected were gone, leaving their equipment and their orange plastic barrels and pylons lined up roadside. *Maybe on strike,* he thought brightly.

Down the street, he could see the compact form of Willard Mann coming toward Dolly's, which doubled as a cafe in the mornings, serving eggs and flapjacks. Mann walked like a mountain lion, muscles always ready to spring. Wore his BLM jacket with the fake fur collar. Had to give Mann credit, Hartley thought, being assigned to run this case, even temporarily. When was the last time a BLM agent got assigned a murder case, let alone led one? Obviously Mann had done things properly in the past. Hartley answered Mann's call as much out of curiosity as anything.

Mann raised one hand, greeting him as he reached the middle of Brown Street, after crossing at the corner of German and Brown. Hartley raised two fingers. Mann opened the door, reaching up to grab the bell-on-a-spring, to keep it from ringing. He did it so familiarly. His fingers went right to it, knew right where it was. The bell did not ring. Funny habit. And Mann sat down across from him with a nod. No smile. Just a nod.

"Thanks for coming," Mann said. "Get right to it. I asked for you as backup. They told me I could have anyone so I asked for you."

"Why?" Hartley said, sounding genuinely mystified. "I can't just pull up stakes. I got patrols, port duty. I got a life."

Mann smiled. "They can put someone else down there to drag the roads."

"Yeah, but why me?"

"Because you're a tracker, because you enter a room and nobody remembers seeing you, and because Sandrine recommended it."

"I've got some bad habits," Hartley said. "I drink. I can't hang onto a woman. All my friends are some Bootheel cowboys. You know Sandrine?"

"Yep, it's why you're here. I always thought you did a good job down on the border, Tom. Not much slides through to here, like it used to. Until now, that is."

"Yeah, and you've got the wolves."

"Yes, I do. And now this. You heard?"

"Yeah," Hartley said. "Corona don't like you stealing his case. We all heard."

"Didn't steal it, never asked for it. Assigned, like every job I get," Mann said.

"I haven't worked a murder case in four years," Hartley said.

"The last case was one reason I picked you—you had it solved, but no arrest."

"I had to pull out after that. Dave understood."

"But you stayed on the border, like Weeks," Mann said.

"Yeah, I figured something would come my way."

"Maybe it has," Mann said.

"You mean *this* case?" Hartley said with voice-cracking disbelief.

"Four years ago. Pancho Villa Day in Concha. Kids with Uzis grab Fred Archibald's pickup. Fred starts to give 'em a tongue-lashing. He gets about three words out before one kid ventilates him with about fifteen rounds. The Mexicans said they never could decide which kid it was. They wouldn't surrender any of 'em. They all scattered back across the border. But you had it figured for one in particular," Mann said.

"That's right, except for the scattering. They were already in Mexico, and they mostly stayed there," Hartley corrected.

"And you know this kid almost got arrested a couple days ago."

"On a driving infraction."

"With asterisk," Mann said.

"Yeah, a definite asterisk. It cost Weeks his job, and the kid stays free," said Hartley.

"Weeks is taking your spot at the JW crossing for awhile."

"I've worked with Weeks. It's . . . *interesting*."

"We're going to construct this from scratch. You in?"

"I'm a skeptic," Hartley said. "Got to be honest. Don't see it. FBI should run it."

"They are. Fertig, the supervisory agent, checks in. Their guy's in Quantico, but he'll be back. They and you will help keep me on track," Mann said. "But if I'm right . . ."

"Okay, show me what you've got."

Mann reached into his accordion file and pulled out a plastic bag with a gold locket. Laid it on the table. Locket open inside the bag. Hartley saw the woman's image.

"Ever seen one of these?" Mann asked.

Hartley frowned. "You, son-of-a . . . Is this a joke? Where'd you get this?"

"In a little girl's fist."

"It's . . . Doña Marianna."

"Your missing evidence," Mann said.

"How'd you—?"

"When they did the autopsy," Mann said.

"But how'd the girl get it?" he said.

"Need you to think about that," Mann said, "for when we talk to Mrs. Braden."

"Four years gone, I have no way of knowing. Could be anything," Hartley said.

"But?" Mann said.

Hartley looked at him. "Yeah? But? But what?"

"It's no coincidence," Mann said. "Maybe if we talk to her, it's clearer. You in?"

Hartley rubbed moist hands together.

"Hate dredging up old cases. Bad memories. Don't want to," he said, "but I will."

"Well, you shouldn't unless . . ."

"Feel I got to."

Chapter Nine

Late Snow

nowy, snowy day in Redsleeve, on the western edge of New Mexico's great Apache Wilderness. Herman Wells, who should have been plowing snow, sat in the rear of the dark saloon under the elk rack and the flickering, neon Schlitz-Miller-Bud signs. Wells had his back to the pulsing neon because the glare gave him a headache, but he still saw the blinking red reflected in Ted Franks' eyeglasses and in the buildup of beer bottles between them. Franks sat opposite Wells, facing the bar—with just one afternoon customer over on a distant stool. Franks kept pushing a hundred-dollar bill over to Wells, who kept pushing it back. Wells was drunk and starting to sweat. He took his hat off. Hated sweaty sweatbands. With his fingertips he furrowed the flattened hair on both sides of his head, and then he flicked his fingers to get rid of the moisture.

He was about to become a drunken snowplow operator.

"Look," he told Franks in a hushed voice. "I never did no work for you, and I never would."

"You provided information. We *pay* for that," Franks said. "C'mon, take it."

"Never gave you nothing. Never would."

"That mine they're planning up on the Gila," Franks reminded.

The C-note that Franks kept folding, unfolding, rolling, unrolling, was starting to take on some scale until Wells realized the *third man*, the solitary customer at the bar, was Henry Benton, founder-chairman of the gun-toting group called Neighbors. Franks was more than aware of Henry, he was playing to him. And that was clear to Wells.

"I was drinkin' here a week ago," Wells said. "I asked Wiley if he heard about the copper sulfide cores. Went down eleven-hundred feet, hit some color. You overheard me. Ain't the same as informing. You planning a lawsuit to stop 'em or something?"

Franks just sat there silent like a neon Sphynx. Wells' daughter and Franks' wife, Raylinda, wanted Ted to help her dad, but it wasn't working. Wells, for his part, was trying to guide Ted but had the feeling Ted was looking down his nose not just at Wells but at the entire county and every rancher, logger, miner, or cowhand in it. He had no sense of the humiliation, the loss of standing, if Wells ever accepted his money.

"Life's too short," Wells said. "Why shorten it worrying about wolves, owls, flycatchers, or goshawks—and Benton? What kind of threat did y'all receive?"

"Just a voice on our answering machine. 'Tick, tick, tick, *boom*,' was all it said."

Wells knew about this. Not from his daughter. She'd never tell him. He heard it from the clinic, that Raylinda had come up asking Dr. Sara Armstrong to X-ray a parcel.

"Don't call me informant—and if Raylinda's hurt, you'll X-ray packages in hell."

Franks, eyes narrowing, folded the C-note, got up and wordlessly left.

Henry Benton slid off his barstool and moved in.

"Heard that. Liked it," Benton said. The reddish light shone in his eyes, too.

"Another eavesdropper," Wells sighed.

Redsleeve had changed, constricted, pulled in its horns. It was a town that used to have a sawmill—Wells' sawmill—once the biggest timber producer in the state. It had spirit, it had dances, it won football championships. Now the mill was closed, in receivership, taken over by the bank, padlocked by the IRS, and there hadn't been a timber sale in three years. One hundred of the town's six hundred people hadn't worked a day logging in three years, not even for Christmas trees. At least eight ranchers big and small in Gila County had been served notices about their fences and told to cut their herds, rest their allotments. That didn't even count the Heel or Arizona.

"Doc Armstrong told me somebody came in yesterday and wanted to use her *X-ray* on a package they'd received. They wanted to know if there was a bomb in it," Wells said, not mentioning it was Raylinda. "I found almost forty spikes on the last few timber sales before I went out of business. Knew a guy over in Snowflake who got hit right above the eye—got a scar in his forehead—from where a sawtooth busted off from a timber spike. Me, it cost me about twenty blades, a couple thousand bucks."

Benton's eyebrows knotted together like two little pieces of rope. And his eyes were squinting as he scanned his memory for some childhood example of imaginary battles to the death, some useful pleading for the killer instinct in us all, perfectly normal, nothing wrong with it. But most people stay under control. Like Herman Wells when his sawmill failed and when his daughter turned against him and became a virulent 'viro.

Benton, horsefly looking for a vein, had a question all prepared and prefaced it by saying, "This is only a question," looking dead into Wells' eyes. Then he asked how it felt to have Raylinda betray him, go against all he stood for, his livelihood, his beliefs, when she and her boyfriend Franks bought that fax machine and created Wild West. Raylinda turned bitter, brittle, harsh.

"You know, some people *need* to have their packages X-rayed," Benton said.

He just had to work that in. To let Wells know he knew.

"People listen and watch. Ever do that?" Benton said. "Set up on a ridge with a scope and just watch for movement—see who goes whither and who comes hither?"

"Nope, never did. Mind my business," Wells said.

Wells, with his snowplow parked, his daughter in need of a fatherly chat, was immobilized. Franks would say it's that Wells is a drunk. Benton would say it's because of rage in need of release. But Wells just saw it as pain. He was immobilized by pain.

"Your family's blood is in the soil here, Mister Wells," Benton said.

"I figure we bled enough," he said. Sounded like he might go on, but he didn't.

"Want a beer?" asked Benton, who was in town to buy a bull from Sid Braden.

"Not a beer from you," Wells said.

Benton, adjusting his sore neck, set his Stetson beside Wells' on the Naugahyde.

"You're looking at me like you think I want something from you," Benton said.

"I know you do," Wells said.

"Well, I don't," Benton said, "What I want you can't give. I want to run my herds the way my daddy did, but that'll never happen again. They're telling us how to ranch like it was something new on Earth. We'll be run off like they ran the buffalo off the cliffs."

Wells got up to leave.

"C'mon, sit down. We're just talking."

"You're talking. Nobody's listening." He picked up his hat.

"Aw, sit down."

Aimee, co-owner of the Red Elk, came over and scrawled out a bar tab for Wells. Benton grabbed it.

"I got this," he said.

"I will hand Aimee a tenspot and walk right out of here," Wells said.

"It's fifteen," Aimee said.

"Okay, I hand her a twenty," Wells said.

"If Aimee were to pick up the tab, though, you wouldn't squawk," said Benton.

"That's different, different, different. Different," Wells said.

"We're neighbors," Benton said.

"You live in Arizona," Wells said.

"Not when I own the Two Square. And even if I stayed in Arizona, we'd still be neighbors. Everybody knows everything about everybody, El Paso to Tucson. We *are* neighbors. Grew up together, got in fights together, fell down in the street, and went to jail together. What stops you from accepting a friendly gesture from a neighbor? Pride?"

"Cussedness," Wells said. "Pissed-offedness. You're like one a them Colorado condos tryin' to offer me a weekend—only it's buying me *for* a weekend."

"Neighbors should stick together," Benton said. "You going to drink or not?"

"Not," Wells said, and walked out of the Red Elk.

Wells was shocked there was still daylight left. Then he heard the door slam.

"Wells! Talk to that daughter of yours. An X-ray machine maybe ain't enough."

Wells looked at his snowplow like an old friend. Something soothing about plowing. Yeah, time to plow.

A chill descended, and with it, a low haze slunk down in the trees, between trunks. Snow hardened. Most wolves could not have walked on the brittle surface without scrunching it like dry cornflakes. But the young wolf named Millie made her way daintily across the crust without breaking it. She snagged her collar on a low branch and stopped to twist and pry the collar off, left it hanging on the branch, then crept on like the haze.

She wondered now and then whatever had become of her mother, her pack.

The snow was knee-deep from Mann's garage down the drive to the mailbox.

He didn't get the chance to use the snowshoes much, so he strapped them on. If they saved five minutes they'd be worth it. Time was falling away. Ironic, on such a late and heavy snow day, he'd be forced to fly out for the interview with Marlie Braden. She had meetings with the senator's campaign, and she wanted her lawyer present for the Mann interview. Mann was having to pay for Hartley's plane ticket as well as his own. It would take him almost as long driving to the airport as the flight would. The snowshoes were aluminum with canvas webbing, BLM issue.

The snow and sleet had not kept Judy the mail driver from her rounds. Mann snow-shoed duck-like down the drive, learning with each step, then had to excavate his mailbox from the six-foot-high snowbank left by the plow. He peered into the box and saw a thick stack of papers, including a postcard from mom, buried in pizza coupons.

He read her card as he crunched back through the drifts. Written in her small, hard-to-read hand, it was laid down straight and hard. His father, Willard Mann II was losing his battle with cancer. His time was measured and mapped.

Mann walked back to the small adobe bungalow he rented from Henry and Helen Fleck just outside Gila Wells, on the road to Redsleeve. He clunked in, stomping off the snow. It was snowing so hard that he could not see out his office window. The snow had coated the windowpanes one-half–inch thick on that side of the house.

He tried to call Mom. No answer. Called her neighbors. No answer. Called Dad's office. Busy. Tried again. Busy again.

Then he got through on the third try. Persistence pays off, he thought.

"How are you?" Mann asked the old man.

"I'm fine," he said in a gravelly, unsteady voice. "Doin' fine."

"Mom said you had a report from the doctor."

"The usual," his father said. "Same old."

"I want to come for a visit next month."

"That would be great," the old man said. "Your mom misses you."

"Okay, I will, then," the younger man said.

He had the television going as he sorted the bills—phone, credit cards, gasoline, utilities. Sometimes, he ran the TV at a murmur to blur the day and preserve a feeling of home—the years in the Arizona mountains, the year and a half spent in Washington, D.C. He picked up the phone and called Doc. She was with a patient, the nurse said. He got ready to hang up the receiver, but the nurse said, "Hold on." Doc wanted to talk to him.

Doc came on the phone, and Mann lost the ability to speak.

"What is it?" she said.

Mann shrugged, oblivious to the fact the shrug didn't make it over the phone.

"Do you eat?" she asked him.

He nodded, started to say, "Yeah," but then coughed.

"I can't hear you," she said.

"Yeah, *yes*, in fact I would like to take you to dinner," Mann said.

"That's more like it. I was afraid you were going to make me ask you," she said.

"Well, I just mean I would like to take you to dinner, so that's what I said."

"I see," she said. "When would this happen? Tonight?"

"I hope so," he said.

"I hope so too," she said.

"Okay, then," he said, but he was distracted by looking out the window.

"What time?" she said.

Mann rubbed off the film of fog that had condensed on the windowpane.

"Hello?" she said.

"Um, sorry, got something wrong out here. Could you hang on—no, I, let me call you right back."

"Promise?"

"Just a few minutes," he said.

From the back of the house, the side that was sheltered from the snow-spattering wind, he saw that Lady was in distress down in the corral, snorting steam as though she had the startings of a cold. *What was she doing away from her stall?*

"Oh, lord," Mann said. He had to go back out.

Mann threw the sheepskin coat back over his shoulders and trotted out to the corral with a woolen horse blanket, which he threw over Lady's back, then put his ear up against her long gray and white neck.

A slight gurgle, the first hint of a wheeze and he hurried back inside to the kitchen.

Mann mixed an oat mash with vitamins and electrolytes, bean sprouts and molasses to mask the chemicals. Then he disappeared back inside the oversize coat, which he had requisitioned from the Border Patrol's unclaimed evidence locker.

Lady looked up with that bemused smirk the bullet scar on her chin gave her. She was a classic though smallish warhorse, bullet-wounded three times in her eighteen years. She moved slowly these days. Her focus on Mann kept her alive. Without that focus, what Mann put her through would surely have killed her.

"Now, girl," he said, trying to coax. She was skittish.

"Something hanging around?"

The horse looked back toward the barn. Then she looked back at Mann.

Then Mann also looked—bird tracks, a bunny, deer sign frozen overnight.

He rubbed her neck with camphor, hoping that would edge her back in the stable.

It didn't. So he went inside the stable, intending to call her from there. But there was a quick *click* just off to the right, and Mann instinctively went down flat. But nothing happened except another click, then another, and another.

Rolling over he could see the sound was from a taut rope hanging from a hook in the rafters. The ten-foot rope held the dangling body of a wolf yearling, female, twisting three feet off the ground in the half light of the eave vents.

He cut her down carefully. She slid into his arms. She still wore her collar. Number One-Sixty. Then his belt pager went off, and he was glad Lady was still outside.

She hated the pager. Once she'd crashed through a plaster wall when it chirped. He ordered one of those vibrating ones, but the company got merged out of business and it never arrived. The number self-identified as "USFWS Regional Office, Albuquerque," although not an extension he recognized. He slogged back to the house and telephoned.

It was a federal interagency bio-hotline, manned twenty-four hours a day all year. Mann didn't know the biologist on the other end. He heard her name, but it was mush.

Wolf telemetry—the word the biologist used—indicated Alice had moved rapidly in his direction. Possibly by airplane.

"She's here," Mann said. "I've got her."

He listened awhile, amazed at how little information he was getting out of her.

"The wolf's dead," he said. "No idea what killed her, or who. I'll bring her in."

As it happened he was flying. The biologist offered to have someone from Washington clear it with the airline. Scheduled airlines, she said, might disallow it. They'd refused them before when cause of death was unknown—what if it were disease?

"No, I'll handle it. This isn't cargo. It's carry-on. Nobody but me has to touch it."

Mann put Lady, blanketed, back in the stable and turned on the baseboard thermostat in her stall. Then he wrapped Alice in plastic and packed her into a gym bag. At Gila International Airport—international meaning short hops along the border—Hartley greeted Mann in front of the New MexAirCo ticket counter.

"They're holding the plane for you," Hartley said. "What's going on?"

"Alice One-Sixty is dead."

His smile quit. "Where?"

"Right here," Mann said, pointing at his bag.

"You're carrying a dead wolf onto a plane?"

Mann held up a finger and turned to the counter supervisor, who had an expectant look on his face. Mann looked him over. He uncrinkled his neck and thought about it. No. No way to explain. He just handed the man his credentials and apologized for the delay.

"Oh, you're not even late," the counter man said cheerfully. "We could hold that plane another fifteen minutes and not be considered late."

Hartley poked curiously at the gym bag as they moved to the gate.

Alice One-Sixty was not supposed to have been outside the wolf enclosure.

Did she dig out? Did she just not get back in when they closed it up? Weren't they watching, or were they blind? Did someone take her out or let her out? Mann had tracked it just last week. He'd noted for the record that he saw only two pups, not four. But the intern, Walton, swore they were in there, so Mann accepted it.

"You should see the muscle structure in these babies. The bone mass is amazing. I know a dentist who says their teeth are the hardest of any mammal. Never lose a tooth."

"Unless somebody shoots one off," Mann said. "The Apache say the wolf's a brother. Brother Smoke."

Mann, holding the door, waited while Sark put Alice in the refrigerator.

"I've got my files in my car," Sarkisian said.

"*Refrigerator!*" Mann gasped, his jaw dropping.

"Yeah, that's what we call 'em," Sark said quizzically.

"Oh, lord," Mann said. "I forgot to call Doc."

Hartley persuaded the floor maid to let them have fifteen minutes in an upstairs conference room not yet cleaned from a morning meeting of the state bar board. Butter rolls and croissants were still fresh in the bun warmer, but the Sterno had burned out.

Marlie Braden didn't much like that touch. She lifted an unfolded napkin and found biscuit crumbs underneath it.

Hartley smiled and reminded her that they'd all driven though snowdrifts to fly some wheezing little Cessna over freezing mountains to get here.

"You understand, Mann's got the tiller now, not Corona," Hartley said. Corona would have booked a whole suite of rooms.

"Who d'you think got Mann the job?" she asked.

Hartley looked at her crinkly eyes. She enjoyed power.

Sarkisian and Mann found the room a few minutes later, followed by the Bradens' lawyer, Selwyn Osteen. The lawyer slapped his soft leather folder on the red maple table, tossed his coat on the buffet table against the wall and slid into the chair next to Marlie. Mann could see Osteen was ready and raring, nostrils flared. It was clear in his fired-up eyes that he was all set to take hold of the meeting and clamp a lid on.

Mann held up both hands. "Let's just smooth out here a second. Everybody rushed here. But the rush is over."

"Agent Mann," Osteen said.

"Just a second. See what I mean about rushing."

Osteen looked at Marlie for support.

"Yes, but . . ." he said, but Marlie cut him off.

"Easy, Sel," Marlie said. "I know these guys." She beamed at Sark like he was her lost twin. "Sammy." The name melted like chocolate in her mouth. Sarkisian grinned.

"Mrs. Braden will be in Albuquerque, working with the senator until the ranch is sold," Osteen informed them.

Mann and Sarkisian were surprised.

"Sold? I thought Sid was going to fight, not sell," Mann said.

"Thought better of it," she said

"But why sell?" Mann said.

"Had it," she said.

"Anybody pressure you?" Mann said, then instantly regretted it.

Marlie laughed. They all waited about eight seconds until she finished laughing.

"Who'd pressure us?" she said. "Just everybody. They all wanted us to quit. They wanted our land. The Forest Service, Raylinda's bunch, the so-called Neighbors, that other bunch—they all offered to buy us out. Wells said he'd buy our private parcels for the timber. Can you imagine? He couldn't afford that. Where would he get the capital? And anyway how would he get back into his padlocked sawmill? Somebody got to him. Three different enviro groups sent us written offers. If we look in the mailbox today probably five, six more. Sandrine's letting us graze most of our herd until we sell."

She looked around at each individually. "So now there's just one thing left to do."

Mann nodded and lifted a cardboard accordion file and set it on the table.

"Still a mystery—I've got to caution you," he said.

First he pulled out the ZipLoc with bullet casings from Cerro Verde.

"Clean," he said. "Not a hair's width of a print fragment. Anyway, she was shot with another gun. These bullet shells aren't it."

Then he pulled out the bagged twenty-five-cent piece.

"Partial print, unidentifiable yet. A young person's print size, I'd say."

Then he laid the gold locket in front of her. "Recognize this?"

"No," she said. "Should I?"

"This was found in her fist," Mann said. "We think maybe she wanted to hide it, that it was something important to her. What was most important to your daughter?"

"Oh, schoolwork, I suppose," she said. "Church. Four-H, FFA, Junior Rodeo."

"Favorite school subjects?"

Biology was always the heart of Millie's science projects. One year it was mosquitoes breeding on stock ponds, last year *The Meaning of Dragonflies*, she said.

"This year?"

"Frogs, I think. She and Clayton collected frogs."

"She say why?"

"Something called a basic, a . . . basis study?"

"Baseline? Not for this year, was it?" Sarkisian said.

"Thought it was," she said.

"A baseline study is meaningless by itself," Sark said, "meaningless in the first years. Nothing to compare with."

"Don't know," she shrugged.

"So—if not frogs, what?" Mann asked. "You mentioned rodeo. It wasn't boys, was it?"

Rodeo's *all* hormones. Marlie gave him an icy stare.

"It's an investigation, ma'am. We ask questions."

"She's a *girl*." Her eyes gazed off toward the mountains as she remembered what that meant. "No," she said, "not boys very much. Too young, although she and the girls at school would giggle about one boy or another. She did have strong feelings for Clayton. She said that boy was just not catching on. She worried over him. Said he was caught in the Apache Wilderness trap, how it lures you, lulls you, grabs you, and bullies you. But it grabs different folks in different ways. They were both stubborn about it—their way of seeing it. They were going to prove something to each other. If she proved it, Clayton was supposed to change his mind," Marlie said.

"Prove *what?*"

"Ah, you know, global, uh, enviro stuff, big stuff, big as the land, maybe the universe, big, like *frogs*." Marlie laughed. Then she stopped to collect the tears she was about to let loose. "Well, *she* felt frogs were important. But anyway, without proof, she loses. That was the deal. We figured it would be good for her to lose. Nothing's ever conclusive, and frogs aren't big. If they were, scientists would already be here doing it."

Sarkisian put up his right index finger, and she stopped.

"Not in this country," he said with a smile. "The academics wouldn't know where to begin. They'd back off a cliff."

"Well, she did know the land," she said.

"Whatever she found was going to be at least damned interesting," Sark said. "I'd like to see her syllabus, her papers. I bet she had a bunch of them."

Marlie nodded. "Sure, we'll get 'em to you."

"So when she wasn't with Clayton, who *was* she with?" Mann said.

Marlie looked at the ill-at-ease Osteen loosening his collar. Osteen, who spoke oddly, generically, in muffled legalese, replied that nobody knew what Millie was up to. If it wasn't the frogs, her folks had no idea.

"Wolves?" Mann prompted.

"No," she said. "I don't—"

She broke off. This was why she had her lawyer. She looked at him. This was where she didn't want to go. Osteen looked back at her with frustration in his eyes and shook his head almost imperceptibly.

"The wolf from the Gila pack is named after Millie," Mann said.

"Oh, *that*. She entered an essay contest," Marlie said.

"She didn't adopt that wolf?"

"They . . . she wrote the essay, showing both sides, oh, my God." Something caught Marlie Braden off guard, and her hands started to shake. She thought she was about to cry. Osteen thought so too. He put an arm around her. She grabbed Osteen's shoulders and closed her eyes tight. The moment passed. She reopened them.

"The little girl never wanted to adopt a wolf," Osteen said. "The wildlifers, the wolfists—they wanted her to."

Marlie almost went along, again, but this time she stood.

"No, no, that's not right," Marlie said; reclaiming a balance of sorts, gaining another false footing. "Sorry, sorry. We told Selwyn wrong. She . . . came around to their side. She agreed to it. They showed her the wolves. We were crushed, betrayed—it was betrayal. I admit we didn't want her betraying the trust of our neighbors."

"You mean neighbors or *Neighbors?*"

"No matter. We weren't with any group. Everybody else—*they* were in groups. And *she* wasn't with any group, either. Saw both sides . . . the wolves caught in the middle. She felt sorry for them, for the wolves."

"Was Sid fighting with his daughter over the wolves?" Mann asked.

"They argued non-stop," and now she almost started crying again, then stopped herself, again. "Thing was, he felt sorry for the wolves as well."

Mann looked doubtful.

She answered it: "Well, it isn't the *wolves'* fault. Sid said he wouldn't fight the wolves if they'd let us graze six-fifty. We could make it on six-hundred-fifty head."

The letter went to the Forest Service, Fish and Wildlife, BLM. No reply.

Mann remembered the letter. He'd recommended six-fifty before the letter. Sid mentioned Mann's recommendation in the letter.

"Could she have had a wolf project?" Sarkisian asked.

"Maybe. She didn't say. She talked to audio-visual about a video camera. But she never told anyone what it was for. Her teacher claims he doesn't know. Maybe she just felt it would be easier if nobody knew. I don't think she wanted her dad to know. But she told me: '*Wouldn't it be neat if I could see them just when they ran free?*'"

The camera—empty—was in her saddlebag when the horse came home.

"She *was* heading for the Endicotts that day. You were right about that," Mann told her. "Sark and I found the hillside where it happened, just below Endicott's south pasture. Then, somebody moved her up to the green ridge, but the actual shooting was on that hill. They call it La Rondita. You know the spot?"

"A mining claim," she said. "Sid wanted to buy that parcel at one time. We had an option. Sold it to some lawyers—or to their clients."

"When was this—who'd they represent?" Hartley said.

"Four years ago," she said. "Whoever. The only letterhead I saw was a lawyer's."

"Four years?" Sarkisian said. "They can't get that done in four years?"

"Someone possibly slowed the process," Mann said, pointing at himself. "The Connecticut investors, EightCorp, say they want a copper sulfide mine. Never made sense, price of copper where it is. Shutting down smelters nearby. But they still want it."

Osteen poured coffee from a thermos carafe left from the bar board meeting, asking Marlie with a gesture whether she wanted any; she didn't, so he sipped it. Still warm.

"Don't you have some sense of what happened to Millie or why? You ask about frogs, then wolves, then mines. You aren't too far along, seems to me," Osteen said.

Hartley held up the gold locket. Turned it over and over in his hands, then popped the cover so Marlie could see the tintype inside.

"Marianna Abreu-Cortes," he said, holding the image up. "Great lady, wife of Don Octavio Cortes Rivera. Her father was a lawyer, and consul general for Mexico in El Paso. The family had a great deal of money and influence. They were from Michoacan. In El Paso right before the war they were just kids. Octavio came across the river as a vato to court her. He wasn't rich. Not like her family. He was like a young torpedo is today, *macho-guapo*. In his twenties, about ten years older than Marianna. Young Tavio Cortes smuggled wax, you know, *car wax*, across the frontera for the Aguilars. Then he grew up, got into the *drogues*. They caught him in Concha in Sixty-Three, selling a kilo of Mexican brown. That's heroin, Mrs. Braden. Lately he's been into cocaine, racehorses, real estate, really rather curious real estate, all starting with her money."

Osteen, unhappy, drummed his fingers. Marlie reached over and stopped his hand.

"This locket—when Mann showed this to me, I didn't believe it," Hartley said. "This item was key evidence in a case I worked four years ago. Nasty child called Miguelito. And then it disappeared. Right out of the evidence locker."

"You guys have any idea," Osteen said, "what you're getting these folks into?"

"No, we figure we're maybe gettin' someone out of somethin'," Hartley said.

"The worst has already happened," Marlie said. "Go on with it—your old case."

"It was in Mexico," Hartley said. "We had no jurisdiction, though we solved it."

"Tom did," Mann said.

Hartley shook his head emphatically but stayed on track with his case-study of what not to do and where not to go:

"Fred Archibald was a farmer. Neighbor of the Karajans."

"I remember Fred—and, I think, how he died," she said.

"Down checking his ditches," Hartley said, "down near one of his boundary markers. Three boys with guns, including Miguel with a new Uzi, came across the line, wanted Fred's truck. While he's over checking his onions, they hop in and roar off toward the border with it, crash it right through a spot where the fence was down. There's only about seven, eight thousand spots like that in our hundred-eighty miles of border. Fred ran after them. They got stuck in the soft sand. When it looked like Fred was going to catch up with them, the boys shot him. All of them were in Mexico, including Fred. Eleven bullets in him. Fell right under a sign that said, '*Peligro,*' Spanish for danger. One of them signs showing pictures of rattlesnakes. I heard the gunshots on my scanner—like *pop, pop, braaap!*—from Fred's open mike. I headed down there. A couple campesinos dragged Fred back across the line. They got on his CB—yelling, '*¡Ayudenos!*' and calling out the location, over and over again. We drove him up to Deming.

Unfortunately Fred died in the hospital there. The campesinos testified at a grand jury. They described which kid had which gun. Only one Uzi. Miguel's. The campesinos were pretty brave to come forward, but they called Fred amigo. He'd let them fish his ditches. The bullets we found scattered on our side we took to the lab. We worked it out that, really, only Miguelito's Uzi got Fred. But the federales didn't buy. Their ballistics didn't show anything that conclusive. 'Course, they didn't have the body. They didn't have the gun. Chain of evidence—they called it *tampered.* They said the campesinos would likely disappear, and it wasn't clear they were the only ones there. They seemed to hold something back. So we gave 'em sanctuary, asylum, and then the federales called that tampering, too. They maintained that the *wetes*—their word—always hated these boys and would say anything to get 'em. Seems the boys had been terrorizing the campo. So if we leave our witnesses alone out there, they disappear, but if we protect 'em, they're tampered.

"The result," he said, "was Mexico didn't arrest or prosecute Tavio's grandson. We put juvenile car-theft warrants out for Guelito, but those are two-bit charges. They're old, and the computer dumps old warrants. Maybe the warrants are why he gunned his car on Weeks the other night, or maybe it's like Weeks says—a setup. Anyway, that's Weeks' intro to Guelito Cortes, that Friday night traffic stop. In Weeks' defense, he never knew who the kid was until it was all over. I'd been at JW four years by then."

Osteen looked furious. Hartley, realizing he had not tied any of this together, paused, expecting another lawyerly onslaught. Marlie simply said, "Finish the story."

"Miguel pawned the locket. Traded it for that Uzi. Back when he was all of thirteen."

"No gunseller's going to—" Osteen stopped himself this time.

"It was a pawn," Hartley said. "He had help from one of the local torpedoes, name of Lupe Ramos. They went in together. We got the records of that transaction, got the videotape surveillance, everything. 'Course, the diamond's gone now."

Marlie's jaw set, her mouth a thin, straight line. No way was Millie involved with these characters. Her daughter would never, *never* even speak to such men, Marlie knew.

"Were there witnesses to my daughter's death?" she said evenly.

"Tracking shows someone tailed this young man, someone investigated him," Hartley said.

"Someone investigated," Osteen said, "but not you. You're offering multiple choice. Either she got in the way of the wolves, or the ranchers, or the enviros, or the miners, and now the *drogueros*. Who'd you leave out?"

"We *have* eliminated the family as suspects," Mann said, "or we wouldn't be here laying it all out for you."

"Well, it's a pretty pathetic smorgasbord. Why isn't the FBI here?" he said.

"No," Marlie said firmly. "These gentlemen will get it done. No FBI."

"Mrs. Braden," Osteen said.

"Actually, the FBI is in charge" Mann said. "Agent Moore's in charge of this case. Fertig, the supervisory agent, is expected here this morning."

"Sheriff Corona wanted Sid the easy way. Mann's going to see this through. It's good the Feds are working with him this way. It's Mann's jurisdiction all the way."

"Thank you, ma'am," Mann said.

"He hasn't done anything," Osteen said.

"He hasn't done anything *wrong*," Marlie said, giving Osteen some silent guidance with her eyes.

Hartley and Sarkisian nodded their allegiance to Mann.

"Where next?" she asked them.

"Still a lot of areas unresolved," Mann said. "Endicott, wolf killers, the mining group, Miguel, maybe more. We just have to work through it all. I warned you. Big country, no known witnesses, international, cross-border issues."

"But if that locket is connected with the drogueros," Osteen said.

"That locket has been in circulation four years," Hartley said. "Who knows what it means? May be someone—a witness—sending us or me a message. May be anything."

"It's more than nothing, though," Osteen said.

"I looked at her hands," Sarkisian said. "Tendons stretched post-mortem, really stretched. Either she held on while someone tried to take the locket—or someone pried her fingers apart to place it in her hand post-mortem. I can't rule out the latter."

"Now why would someone do that?" Osteen said. He looked at Marlie. She shook her head. "Why would someone plant a locket on a—" Osteen stopped short.

"Can't speculate why," Sark said. "I just know if they'd pried her fingers open that far to get the thing out, they would have gotten it. So maybe it's the other way."

One last coincidence lay in the bottom of the file. Mann pulled out a photograph, enlarged from a snapshot furnished by the Endicotts, of the missing Jaime Garza.

She looked a long time, at first skeptically, it seemed, and then closely, maybe half a minute, before setting it down. "Actually I think I might have seen him," she said. "Could he have been riding with Millie? Who is he? How old is he? He seems young."

"That's how he looks. The picture was taken last fall," Mann said. "In a couple months he'll be seventeen."

Marlie picked up the picture and looked again.

"He sort of looks like him," she said, "like that Jimmy. He's too old for Millie."

The men could see her dismay. She just looked down and said nothing.

"Could she have discovered who he was?" Mann asked. "She say anything?"

"Who is he?" she asked. "Another criminal?"

"Well, maybe, I'd say. Vanished just when Millie died. We're looking for him."

Mann had seen Jaime Garza, but Hartley hadn't. The photo was grainy-fuzzy. But something in the angle of it caught Hartley's eye.

"This is Garza?" Hartley said.

"That's him," Mann said.

Hartley stood up and looked over Marlie's shoulder at the print.

"You recognize him?" Mann said.

"I think it's Jimmy," Marlie said.

"No, I meant Mister Hartley."

"Something about him," Hartley said. He seemed suddenly lost in thought.

"What is it?" Marlie asked. Hartley just shrugged her off.

Out the window as they left the room, cars poured off the interstate and puddled downtown, inching around the convention center and civic center plaza and under the railroad trestle. The traffic was emptying out of a massive DeMille-o-scope construction zone where thousands of workers erected a twisting, twirling monument to fluidity. Marlie surged out of the hotel onto the noisy street. She and Osteen turned the corner en route to another meeting. Mann watched her square her shoulders as she disappeared.

Then, back into the hotel for a quick phone call to Doc.

Doc was the only person waiting at the gate when the ten-seat Cessna worked its way across the Redsleeve runway to the quonset hut that served as hangar and terminal.

Mann stepped down. Doc held the gate open for him.

"The restaurants are closed," she said, "but I put something in the oven. Should be done in a few minutes."

Mann looked into her eyes. Discovered he and she were the same height.

"Right nice of you to do that," he said.

"A girl's got to eat," she said with a shrug. "So does a guy."

"That would be me," Mann said.

"Yes, it would," she said.

Chapter Ten

Ojorito

The wolf's yellow eyes widened like lemons. Lightning had illuminated an array of cattle sandwiched in a barbwire circle as if shrink-wrapped.

And right there on the outside edge were two calves. Easy . . . Easy!

It was clear to both adult wolves they'd arrived in the promised land—that is, the land that was promised to them when elk fell miraculously from the sky.

This was just like that.

And now they were about to take their yearlings to Sunday school. Teach them a lesson that would remain with them in their dreams, their paws quivering with excitement in their sleep: Penned cattle are easy. But if these cattle get loose, if they get crazy, well . . . Let's say it's just better this penned-up way. Simple lessons. Be selective, not greedy.

But man, these calves . . . right where Braden had corralled them for his auction.

The Mexican grays came down on them like missiles. Their jaws clamped into the little calves' necks and bellies and twisted until the calves were down—dragged from the pen before either cow knew much of anything at all.

Just over the hill, Raylinda Wells lay on the hard-rock banks of Ojorito, a volcano-heated creek usually suitable for bathing. Clayton Endicott watched her through a small brass field glass as he clung to the right side of an outcropping that, on the left side, also overlooked the latest wolf release enclosure.

Clayton wasn't interested in wolves. But as he gazed at Raylinda, knowing she was looking at him kind of sideways, he was beginning to believe that shortness of breath was a good thing. So it paid to have an open mind.

Raylinda lay on her side, back to Clay, running her fingers through the white-gold grama that crept from fissures in the sandstone. Her right knee was bent, pointing straight up, so that her foot caressed the inside of her left thigh. Her sandstone-colored hair fell among the grama and interwove the thin buckwheat-like stems. In the pale grass on the pinkish-tan stone shelf she sunned like a chameleon, camouflaged.

The Adelita of the enviro movement had been keeping her eye on Clayton for awhile, although her sunning was not intended for his recruitment. But Clayton already had shown a weakness or two. Raylinda saw in Clay a needy vulnerability.

And he carefully began his descent while clouds put an overcoat on the sun.

Raylinda smiled and watched the churning white and gray cumulus outline the azure through heavy-lidded eyes, the dark green ponderosas swaying like a Greek chorus, and the waving grass tickling her all over. But the cold wind raised goosebumps all over her while drying her skin—she didn't like a coarse towel scraping her. She watched from the corner of her eye as Clay sought footholds and handholds on the tooth-shaped spur.

He had chosen the quickest of three possible routes down to her. But it meant he would have to drop twelve feet from the final ledge— or be stranded on it. When he got to the ledge, Raylinda sat up and watched him consider his options. He hung off the edge and dug with his boot toes, feeling for some indentation. While his back was toward her, Raylinda sat up to get dressed. Her cantilevered breasts swung forward and pointed at him. She quickly tied her halter back on. When he had given up and started pacing the fifteen-foot-long ledge, she raised a hand in acknowledgement—and farewell.

Clayton kept looking for a shorter fall with a softer landing, or at least a level landing where he could be assured of not busting a leg. There were no assurances.

It rapidly became clear that Clayton wouldn't decide. Raylinda got up, threw on a loose cotton sun dress of yellow flowers over her bikini, shouldered a loden parka, then started up the trail. It led over a hump and down to the forest road on Braden land where her Outback was parked. At the rise, before descending, she looked back at Clayton.

"Can I call someone for you, Clay?" she said. He heard only the sarcasm. He wasn't old enough to hear six or seven shadings of disappointment, hope, wistfulness.

"Could you just come around behind me on the tooth, and throw me a rope?"

"You going to climb back up?"

"I would if you were up there," he said. "I'd climb down if you were below."

"I don't have a rope," she said. "I'll call your dad for you."

"No, don't call him," he said, insistent. "Could you maybe come back up with a rope? God, I sure would appreciate it. I'd owe you."

"Yes, you would."

"Well, I would. I'd do *whatever* to pay y'all back."

"I will, then," she said. "But it might take awhile. I'm late for a party."

Hours gone. The waiting interminable. Clayton tried dangling from various points along the ledge and searching with his boots for toeholds, but the ledge was undercut, and he would have to commit before he could be sure of getting back safely—he might end up falling straight down on his back. Finally he gave up and put his trust in Raylinda. He took his knit cap out of his coat pocket and pulled it down over his ears. No doubt about it. It was freezing out. Midtwenties, he'd guess. And then he fell asleep, pressed against the rock for whatever heat his body and the rock might share. The rock was stingy. It was a one-sided affair. Every time his eyes blinked open, he was cold. Once he awakened with a start and nearly fell off the edge. Probably the cold woke him. What else? Maybe footsteps on the rock above? Clay caught movement in the moonshadows below, the silhouette of someone in a Stetson and greatcoat climbing steadily up the crag, carrying something long and narrow on his back.

He thought about calling out to whoever was there because they were probably sent to rescue him. But he kept silent. Unsure about the shadow rifle or about what a sharpshooter's priorities would be if confronted with someone like himself. He kept back against the sandstone wall so the shadow man couldn't see him or his shadow.

The boy heard a whirring and clicking that sounded like a brainy camera. Then he heard the unmistakable sound of a bolt shoving a bullet into a rifle chamber, the click of the bolt, then the ringing of the brass scraping into the chamber.

Then he heard the thing Millie always wanted him to hear.

It started low, like a singer in the shower, tentative, embarrassed to be heard. Then it took on some steam, like a teakettle, only more baritone. And finally it hit its groove, a full-blown howl, followed by a couple of enthusiastic yips to sign off.

Then there was a single *chumpf* that sounded like a punctured tire. But Clay knew the sound of a silencer, and this was no flat.

He turned over on his back and scooted toward the edge, so that his head and shoulders extended over the ledge into the black night air. And then he saw the hat itself and the rifle barrel. He guessed a two-forty-three, judging by its narrowness.

He couldn't see a face to go with the hat. But the hat—as deciphered in moonlight —was an almost luminescent white with some sort of turquoise-studded hatband and something shiny on its crest, like a souvenir pin or official emblem of some sort.

Suddenly Clay realized he was hanging out in thin air, visible if the person above so much as stretched. They'd see each other. And he, Clayton Endicott, could be in the worst trouble of his life. Maybe already was. He rolled back against the stone face of the mountain. Tried to plaster himself against it. Stayed there silently 'til almost morning.

Raylinda Wells had not forgotten about Clayton. She just moved him back into the shadows a little. She picked up Franks and the rest of her stable, Harlan Utterboeck, Phil Walsh, Milt Everett, as well as their equipment and piled into their 4-x-4 for a quick drive up to Redsleeve. *Pot Luck.* They'd seen the fliers. *Live Music.* Harlan tore a handbill off the screen door of the general store. Gave it to

Raylinda, hoping for favors. Raylinda gave him a one-arm hug that compressed his larynx and set him coughing.

Ranchers Only, Please. That challenge could not go unanswered.

While the sun set on Clay Endicott east of the Mogollons, it was still up strong shining in Raylinda's eyes as she drove the west side to Redsleeve.

"I called the three TV stations," Franks said.

"What about the papers, what about the wires?" Raylinda said. "These are no altar boys. Already killed four wolves; you might be next. It's news, and it's happening."

"You don't seriously believe they'd shoot anyone," Utterboeck said.

"Sure might if it would save them going to jail."

The ponderosa and white fir flew past as they roared through the tunnel of trees. In Homewood they stopped for gas, and the Forest Service ranger, Todd Markie, came out of the convenience store to talk to them. It was a cold evening, and his breath billowed steam. He held a coffee cup that also billowed in the steady breeze.

"Just a word to the wise," he said. "Even I'm staying away from that meeting. Somebody scrawled: 'greenpants go home' across the poster I saw. We're unwelcome."

"Well, maybe we'll get some pix of some Neighbors," Raylinda said. "Any TV?"

"Not here," the ranger said. "They'd probably come down Highway Sixty."

Raylinda gestured to Harlan and Walsh, on the opposite side of the guardrail peeing into the weeds, to get back in the four-wheeler. Their movements were lethargic, clumsy. Raylinda concluded they were exhaling more than steam.

"C'mon, guys!" she snapped.

The four-wheeler moved quite a lot faster than what got her ticketed the last time.

"Gotta break eggs," Benton, leader of Neighbors and national vice president of Common Sense Comitatus, wrapped up just as Raylinda's SUV pulled in.

Raylinda's group finally located the dangerous people, and they were drinking punch and having pie. Sitting at long tables borrowed from the Baptist church. Sharing quiet conversation. Soon somebody else was probably going to get up, speak and ask for money. And some of them might chip in a few bucks. Most probably not. Most didn't have money to fritter away on "causes." They only had money for feed and seed.

Raylinda was ready to record the event on videotape. She had her tripod set up, and Franks, wearing headphones to monitor the mike, was at the lens. The directional mike stuck out like a lance from its mounting under the camera. Some potential Neighbor recruits thought Raylinda was from Channel Six or Five or Eleven, one of the local stations, if you could call El Paso or Albuquerque local when they're a hundred-fifty, two hundred miles away. Down on the Gila, local was a relative term.

Dressed for combat, wearing her trademark olive drab, Raylinda was ready to do the missing TV guys' jobs for them, to ask tough questions, demand answers, challenge assertions, and then produce the true facts and figures. She even had the questions ready. Then Henry Benton quietly stopped off at their vantage point behind the card table chairs in the Redsleeve Community Center. Politely he reintroduced himself. Raylinda nodded.

"See, Miss Wells, this a private meeting, and we want everyone to feel at ease. You are no friend to most of these folks," Benton said.

"But I *am* friend to everybody else," she said, "who own the lands you'd ruin."

"That's the debate, isn't it?" Benton said. "We've stated it rather well, you and I. Now we'd like you to leave so all our friends and neighbors can enjoy the evening."

"We're neighbors, too," she said. "You posted public handbills inviting us all."

"Not everybody," Benton said. "Just ranchers, if you'll notice."

"You invited the TV stations," she said.

"They aren't coming," he said. "You're no rancher, not since years."

"This is a public facility," she said.

"Which we rented," he said. "You're no journalist. We can have the sheriff come up here and throw you out, but we don't want to. We'd just ask you nicely to leave and let us have our evening. We'd do the same for you."

"Well, thanks, Henry. I appreciate that. I just think the public has a right to know what y'all are up to, what your plan is for taxpayers' property. You want to be secret."

Henry walked away from her shaking his head. He saw Clifford Endicott walk in. Told him about the situation, then headed to the kitchen, where the wall phone was.

Benton knew the sheriff himself wouldn't come. Undersheriff John Olson would. The dispatcher refused to put him through but offered to forward a message.

Benton was furious, but he bottled it. He couldn't let on that things suddenly weren't apple pie. He could see Raylinda enjoying her guerrilla theater, dressed in battle fatigues. He should enjoy his kabuki, too. So he fumed: *Raylinda was going to have to retire. That's all there is to it.* Franks was easier. He could almost talk to Franks.

Benton made another run at her, insisting she leave. She refused, jaw set.

Endicott came over with a couple ranchers, Ron Lee Singlebest and Bobby Walston, to back him up. Utterboeck, Milt, and Walsh stepped forward. They were younger than Singlebest and Walston, but they did not underestimate either man. Both had consistently slaughtered the boys at bronc and bull riding. The boys had studied their skills and long ago concluded Bobby and Ronny were just plain stronger and meaner than them and never quit. But with Raylinda on the line, they had to make a stand even if it put 'em in a hospital—or in jail. Franks, Endicott, and Benton stepped aside.

"This isn't our style," Franks said.

"*We* might have an advantage," Benton suggested. "That's what you're saying."

Then Raylinda's camera got bumped and fell over with a crash, the side panel popped open and the video cartridge clattered out. Walston scrambled for it and got kicked in the head by Milt, who was also coming over to retrieve the tape. He lay there on the floor rubbing the dent he felt just above his ear. Until the dent became a big lump.

Singlebest stomped the cartridge a few times. It appeared to crack. But that wasn't enough. He reached down to grab it and pull out the tape. Utterboeck grabbed his head and wrenched it, as in steer wrestling. Singlebest ran his feet fast on the wood floor to keep his angle, but his leather soles slid. Finally, he flopped over amazingly like a lanky calf, but he reached up and grabbed Utterboeck by the belt buckle with his right hand and by the shirt front with his left, and he dragged the footballer down prone under him.

Utterboeck looked up into Singlebest's eyes with amusement. Singlebest only wondered a second what the amusement was for. Walsh brought down one of those folding chairs on Singlebest's back. He hardly felt it, but it made him mad. He gained traction planting his right heel on Utterboeck's chest. He took the chair away from Walsh and fitted it over Walsh's skinny head and shoulders. Grabbed the chairlegs and started spinning Walsh. He spun and twirled Walsh around three, four times, until he was centrifugally facing the door, then let him go.

Well, he missed the door. But he did crash through the plate glass window next to the door. Which Singlebest felt was close enough.

"We're going to need an ambulance," Singlebest said to Utterboeck, under foot.

"That's right," said Milt, bringing down another chair on Singlebest, this time on his head. A long crescent ribbon of red formed where his hair met his face. Singlebest went down, eyes fluttering.

Then Walston recovered enough to half-blind Milt with a chair swung horizontally. It caught Milt right across the bridge of his nose, where it met his brow. The lights winked out for Milt, who wandered screaming, "He blinded me! He blinded me!"

Maybe Corona might show up in person, after all, Benton decided. He made another couple of calls, first for the ambulance, second for the sheriff.

Raylinda came over to him with that crooked smile of hers.

"We've decided to accept your offer and leave," she said. "Enjoy your evening."

Benton thought about detaining her under comitatus until the sheriff arrived or about suggesting she wait for Corona. Then he decided he'd rather just sort it out himself.

"Don't come back. It t'isn't safe and I'd feel terrible if you were hurt."

Endicott added: "A person could end up dead over something like this."

"You threatening me, Cliff?" she snapped.

"No, I mean Singlebest. He's in convulsions." Singlebest was twitching on the floor. "Your guy hit him in the head with a metal chair."

"Your guy started it," she said.

Endicott looked her close in the eye for any flicker of anything familiar. He had wiped her nose, carried her piggyback, when Wellses and Endicotts were friends a long, long time ago. There was no incandescence of any kind today. A wall is what he saw.

"You're something, Raylin," he said. "You ain't who you're supposed to be."

"Yeah, well, a lot of things ain't how they're s'posed to be," she said. "Like that peeping-tom son of yours, stranded on that cliff up above the Hot Creek. He's been there since before sunset with his spyglass. Better see to him, while you reshape the land."

Endicott accepted this information without comment, but his eyes showed some urgent concern. He conveyed that concern silently to Benton. With a look, a jerk of his head, he left. His Silverado revved like a slow-cranked Gatling gun. Then he was gone.

Benton watched him roar out of town, then turned to Raylinda. "Ought to slap you or shoot you. But I don't want to dirty my hands, and I forgot my gun," he said.

"You should be hauled off to jail for that, shouldn't you?" she said. "That's what tonight's meeting was all about, wasn't it—your little initiative *requiring* citizens to have guns at the ready, loaded, for when duty calls. Known you all my life. Never knew."

"Well, move, for God's sake. *Move.* We'll pay the movers and provide your deposit and cleaning. Glad to. Ask your daddy. Hell, Raylin, even your own people—I mean the enviros—are turning against you. Nobody approves of your methods. Go."

Sid Braden was in Texas talking to the bank. Marlie was in Albuquerque talking to lawyers and politicians. Bertie came down from his trailer in the hills and Ed came up from his apartment in town to try to get the Two Square ready for its new life.

Sid was in a Motel 6 in Amarillo that smelled of sweat and cigarettes. The caulking around the tub had flaked away and water migrated from somewhere inside the wall into a puddle along the back wall, behind the toilet.

Marlie had an apartment on the west side of the Rio Grande, up on a hillside with a hundred condos all done in brown stucco with white trim, a little balcony from which she could see the river, actual water, when the sunlight hit it a certain way.

Braden called her and left a message. She called him and left a message.

Ed and Bertie had a fire in the wood stove back at the ranch. They had their boots up to keep them warm. They were playing checkers as the snow fell outside the windows.

"Tell me again why they're selling and who they're selling to?" Bertie demanded.

"We don't know," Ed said. "We don't know either answer, *any* answers. And what the hell yew askin' me for—she's yore sister. Ask her."

The wolves, after feeding through the afternoon on the two calves, climbed the rocks to a point where the great moon signaled down to them the message only they understood. They howled back code in reply.

Chapter Eleven

Pinwheel

Corona couldn't believe his eyes. Starting with the shattered front window greeting him in the entry of the Redsleeve Community Center, blood on the shards and puddled on the floor. Five chairs, two tables, and a dozen plates and glasses broken, five people seriously injured. And where was Raylinda Wells?

Her online buddies, stretched across the country from Bryn Mawr, Pennsylvania, to Mills College in California, had been calling her the Hero of the Hidalgo. She had, they said, single-handedly forced Hidalgo National Forest wilderness ranchers to cut their herds, to stop fencing the streams and, in more than one instance, to clear out entirely. She had stood up to some of the toughest men in the West and survived. She stood on the brink of fund-raising nirvana. Where was she? Home throwing up. Pregnant.

"I want an abortion," she snapped, "*now!*"

"But, babe," Franks said.

"Don't *but* me, don't *babe* me."

"We want a family," Franks said. "That's what saving the land's for—*family, future generations*. What's the point if we don't generate?"

"The flippin' earth is bigger than a freakin' family," Raylinda said. "I can't do it."

"Raylin, you're . . ." The phone rang.

"I'm what?" she said as Franks picked up the phone.

He cupped the mouthpiece. "It's Westover, wolf woman, the biologist."

Westover, whose idea it was to make Millie the *wolf girl*, was camped out at a new wolf enclosure on the Hidalgo forest's Apache Wilderness, where the adult wolves—One-Ninety and Ninety-one—

and two pups were penned. "Another wolf shot," Westover said. "Wounded, not dead." Her voice was breaking with rage.

"Cool down, Mike," Raylinda told Michelle Westover. "How are the cows those other wolves hit?"

"Dead," Westover said.

"Well, good, then," Raylinda said. "Wolves two, cows nothing."

She hung up. It rang again. She picked up while the ring was just a truncated chirp. "Yeah?" she growled, thinking Westover. But it was Corona.

So she sat down and listened, it seemed to Franks, for quite a long while. Then she said, "OK," and hung up. Elias, who had bought Girl Scout cookies from her, had a six-count warrant for her arrest. Inciting. Property damage. Attempted mayhem. Assault and battery. Attempted murder. Conspiracy. He said them slowly, individually, hypnotically. And when he had her drowsy and weak, he told her: He hadn't filed it in court. He'd held it. She agreed to meet him in fifteen minutes at sheriff's headquarters about a mile and a half from her own headquarters and home.

"Guess we better go," she told Franks.

"Michelle says the wolf should survive," Franks said.

"Not in the wild. Don' count if he isn't in the wild. Might as well be dead."

Franks started the car and backed out. The road was slushy turning icy. He was silent almost the whole way driving, then he turned a little to see her eyes. She was looking at her watch.

"Taking us fifteen minutes to go eight blocks," she said. Then they skidded into Corona's parking lot. "Take it a bit slower. It won't kill you—or us," she said.

"You wanted speed. Think they'd de-ice their parking lot?" Franks muttered.

Corona would never notice. He parked around in front. His own private space. Isolated behind myrtle hedges. Shoveled by cadets. Marked with a large bronze sign: *Elias Corona, Sheriff, Gila County, Unauthorized Vehicles Will Be Towed.*

The new public safety complex was testimony to Corona's political clout and skill. The state and the feds, acting within the hundred-mile border intensity area, paid half-and-half to build it. Gila County only had to furnish and decorate it. Corona delayed hiring one deputy for a year. That paid for the wood paneling and leather furniture in his office. He'd pretended he was going to hire Weeks, but he never did. He strung Weeks along, securing an FBI background check. By the time it was done, Frey was using the FBI report to hire Weeks, temporarily replacing Hartley. Better for all.

Raylinda waited, fogging up the windows in the truck while Franks cleared a path with one of the shovels leaning against the wall. She rolled down the window furiously.

"Christ's sake, Teddy. They're not sending a photog. Won't be judged on points."

"I don't want you slipping," he said.

"Can we just park this toad and get going? Please?"

Franks gave it one more shove. Left a ridge in the middle of the parking lot. They walked in through the back entrance with the overhead night light. Entrance to the jail. Had to surrender keys, nail files, clippers, ballpoints, and other sharp objects.

"You want my shoelaces?" Raylinda yelled through the heavy wire grid.

"Maybe later," the booking sergeant said.

He buzzed them through directly to Corona's hallway. No transition. Sudden elegance. Antiqued bronze lighting fixtures with cut crystal chimneys. Passageway led to his hand-hewn Mexican door, heavily lacquered. Bronze plaque with his name.

"Does he love bronze or what?" Raylinda said.

"Let's remain civil and respectful so as to avoid jail," Franks said.

"Okay, okay," she said.

Franks knocked respectfully, and Corona opened the door with a broad, grandiose wave of hospitality. He wore a black silk shirt with matching tie and a gold Gila County tie clip. He had a gold bracelet on one wrist, gold watch on the other—real gold, not Kmart gold—given him upon retirement as captain from the state police ten years earlier. His charcoal jodhpurs had gold braided stripes tucked into polished brown riding boots. He looked fresh as a spring afternoon, clean-shaven, at 1:15 a.m.

"Would you care for some coffee?" he said.

"That would be nice, Elias, thank you," Raylinda purred.

Corona flicked his intercom and yelled: "*¡Lupita, tres cafes, por favor!*"

He got up and started to wander around the room.

"You should both be in jail," he said. "I know your father."

"Everybody does."

"Fine man. I remember how he cried when the mill closed, but never mind. Singlebest has not regained consciousness. Self-defense, that's your story," Corona said.

"Not my story," she said, "their story. I had absolutely nothing to do with it. I gave no instructions to anyone except to videotape the meeting. That's all I said. 'Videotape this hearing.' End Quote. They started running people at us. We thought we were within our rights to be there. Nobody in authority came forward to tell us different. We were waiting for the undersheriff to show. Henry called, and we were waiting. I guess Henry's boys didn't want to wait. My camera was smashed, the videotape ruined."

Corona held up a hand to halt the proceedings.

"We're unclear on a point," he said. "How did the camera get knocked over?"

"Well, I believe it was Singlebest," she said.

Corona smiled. "Unfortunately—or handily, as the case may be—we can't question him right now, if ever."

"Oh, he'll be fine," she said.

"He was in convulsions when they admitted him this morning," the sheriff said.

"Very sorry to hear that," she said, sounding sober and sincere.

The sheriff straightened his tie, reclipping it.

"We're concerned about your intent in crashing this party uninvited," he said.

She cut him off: "Fliers all over town. We've got a dozen copies."

"We can subpoena your copy machine—do you believe this? We can test it to prove you made the copies."

"If I only have one copy I'm invited. I'm as much a rancher as anyone here."

"Asked to leave: You defied that request," he said. "Brought goons with you."

"Camera crew. Videographer, sound man, tech, standard crew," she said.

"Goons," Corona said.

"God, we can argue that easy enough. But that was certainly not my intent."

"Sheriff, we want to cooperate. Incidents get out of hand. Emotions are high," Franks said. "There was some pushing and shoving. Some people fell or were thrown to the floor. Was I guess a fight but was over quickly. Just tried to protect our equipment."

"But you left the scene."

"We were told to leave," Raylinda said. "We left."

Corona was drumming his fingers.

"Don't want a lawyer," Raylinda said. "Look, wish we'd never gone. Wanted to show them pushing for guns in our town. Just who would those guns hurt? Law officers could be hurt, I could be, Ted could be. Did you know Ted and I are having a baby?"

"No, I didn't. Are you? Congratulations!"

Corona slapped the desk.

"Have a cigar," he said, opening an oak mosaic box and offering one to the amazed Franks, who was thinking: *So this is the fulcrum on which a new life turns.*

"No, thanks," Franks said. "Don't smoke."

Raylinda reached for one, but Corona pulled the box away from her.

"Uh-uh," he said, pointing at her belly. "None for you."

Down the street from Public Safety, there barely stood a crumbling one-room adobe office in need of plaster inside and stucco outside with two desks and a plywood sign with simple lettering, US Bureau of Land Management, Gila Wells HQ.

The lights were on, the door was open, and Raylinda Wells walked right in.

"Hey, Mann," she said.

"Hello, Miss Wells," Mann replied digging through records for references to Wolf One-Ninety-One. So far, he'd put together a list of more than one hundred people, still growing, who'd had contact with that wolf or who knew what the plan for it was.

The longer the list grew, the more absurdly incompetent he felt. He wished the list could be shorter, but he'd checked and double-checked, and there was no way to remove anyone from it. After his hello, he basically forgot the couple was there.

"You can call me RL," Raylinda said after awhile. "I believe we have a witness for you."

Mann looked up.

"To what?" he said, putting down his pencil at 2:00 a.m.

Hartley's phone went off in bursts, like mortar rounds somewhere nearby. He'd forgotten where exactly. He found it when he stepped on it. Held it to his ear.

"Yeah," he said, "yeah, yes."

Set it down. Slowly groped his way to the toilet. Been asleep an hour and a half.

Sky was a snowy gray like Lady when Mann and Hartley got to Piedra Colorada. They had the two-horse trailer with Lady and Joe, a stalwart BLM roan, tall gelding. Good lines, long legs, strong shoulders, large brain, amiable.

They rode their horses in opposite arcs, curving back around the little toothy mountain to meet at the top.

Quickly they found boot prints in the dirt and rope marks around one of the thicker piñons, frayed-off hemp, rasped-off bark on the red rock spur overlooking Ojorito.

Down below on the ledge they could see more tracks, scuffing, and there was a rope burn on the rim that led down to the ledge where Clay Endicott had been stranded.

"Tell you what, they're sloppy if they think they're covering anything," Hartley said. "I don't think they are."

Mann pointed to three places on the top of the tooth where the dust had been brushed aside, it appeared, with a saddle blanket or the like. Coarse cloth.

"A little extra housekeeping, it seems," he said. "Mm-mmm, look at this view."

Hartley followed him up to the top of the rock for a straight-line view of the new wolf pen and the Mogollon Mountains beyond. Then even father off, past the Mogollons, they could see the hazy Blue Range of Arizona. Mann felt something warm on his neck and turned around. A hump-backed edge of sun beamed a deep vermilion laser into his eyes, which snapped shut automatically. He saw orange spots for a couple minutes.

Five-thirty. As Mann loaded his horses back in the trailer, he could see across the ancient seabed the Fish and Wildlife investigators arriving in their Jeeps and Explorers down the Ojo Pass over by Braden's Hot Creek. He and Hartley passed them with a wave on their way out. One of them, Michael Ivers, had been a surveyor on the Diamond S. Both Mann and Hartley knew him. Mann wondered if Weeks knew him, or anybody, down there in the southwest corner.

"How's ol' Weeks doing down in the Heel?" he asked.

"Everybody likes him, not like it was in Concha," Ivers said.

"Maybe this'll work out for him," Mann said.

"Hope not," Hartley said. "I'm kinda like wanting my old job back."

"Thought you had a mission," Mann said.

"You're the one who's so all-fired mission-oriented."

"Solve the case, move on," Mann said. "Hardly a mission. Just a job."

Hartley, like many a cop, believed he knew when a man was lying. Built-in polygraph, or the like.

"You have a mission," Hartley said. "You just don't want to say it."

Mann shrugged and said nothing.

"What's the agenda?" Hartley said. "You takin' sides on this wolf thing?"

"No," Mann said. "Just the side of the law. Popular causes don't interest me."

"A lot of lawmen don't want the wolves. They feel it's a lot of bio-crap and a lot of extra, unnecessary trouble."

"Well, I just see it as law," Mann said, turning up onto the road to Beaver Wells. A red-tailed hawk circled overhead looking for early-morning mice. The sun, by now, was warm and full on the Gila River Valley. Six-thirty. They could see the pronghorn herd laid up off in the distance against the northern toe of the Black Range.

Hartley nudged his horse over closer to Mann to get a better look at his eyes. Mann was holding back. That was evident. But what?

"Guys like Endicott running these prong herds, they've got to hate the idea of wolves," Hartley said. "One wolf could cause serious economic damage in just a month or two on a prong herd. Should that be legal?"

"Civil matter," Mann said. "Not for us to say."

"Civil? Who do you sue?" Hartley said.

"Ask a lawyer, I don't know." *Ease off*, he seemed to say.

"Just talking, buddy." Whatever it was, it wasn't wolf-related. It made Hartley a little nervous, not knowing.

They drove north in silence past the Beaver Wells work station to the entrance of the E-Bar-E and turned east through the gate.

The truck and trailer vibrated on the wet washboard dirt. Mud splattered up on windows all around the SUV. Neither Mann nor Hartley could see out until the wiper-washers eventually cleaned up the mess. And then they saw a similar flume of brown soup coming at them from the direction of the E-bar-E, where the thaw had taken hold again by midday. By evening it would be freezing hard again.

"Welcoming committee," Hartley said. "Don't look friendly."

"Won't be pie this time," Mann said, "unless it's mud pie."

In less than a minute the two vehicles stopped nose to nose. Endicott was out, rifle in hand. Two hands, including young Philly Mondragon, were behind him, also holding rifles, but Philly's gun was backwards, the butt in the damp dirt, the barrel up, the trigger pointing away from him and toward the two officers.

Mann nodded amiably at Endicott, who merely seemed nervous.

"Dragging kids out here with guns, Cliff?" Mann said.

"Philly's a hand. Works for me. Helps me protect the range."

"Good, that's my job, too," Mann said, "helping you protect our range."

"Don't want your help today," Endicott said.

"Yeah, I'm sure of that, but I still got to talk to your son," Mann said.

"Ain't here," Endicott said.

"Please, don't play games. I can see he's not *here*. Wherever he is, the federal government needs to talk to him. I don't know where you think he can go that we can't reach, Cliff. Now, produce him. He's a material witness, and we need him now, or we'll be holding you for witness tampering, contempt, obstruction, illegal stuff," Mann said.

"Well, he's gone," Endicott said. "Don't have to say where. I didn't send him there."

"Think about how this would sound: 'Clifford Endicott I'm arresting you for obstructing justice.' That was just a test run so you could hear what it sounds like. Think it over while we all drive back to your house."

"No warrant, no drive," Endicott said.

Mann clicked on his base radio several times and finally got Margie.

"Margie, I want you to go to Judge Miller and get me a warrant to search every inch of Cliff and Ellie's place for any evidence of their son's whereabouts or anything pertaining to wolves or firearms. Have one of the rangers, whoever's available, fly it up here in a chopper. I need it now. Tell the judge we have a witness says the boy saw the whole thing. The break Judge Miller's been waiting for."

Actually, Judge Woodrow Miller wasn't waiting for anything, but it sounded good. Mann knew the judge was on the bench this morning. He'd seen the docket.

"We're going to have a warrant in less than half an hour. Shall we wait at the ranch house or shall we wait here?" Mann asked.

"Aw, hell, might as well come on back," Endicott said, shoulders sagging. "I don't mean to cause trouble for the law. Last thing I want to do."

"Ride back with us. We can talk," Mann said.

He opened the back door to his SUV, and Cliff got in.

"Why all the trouble, Cliff?" Mann said. "Just doing our jobs. Never gave you a problem. Never told you to cut your herds."

"No, I know, Will. This county quagmire has us all cross-wise. Look what we're losing. Feds shut down six ranches, de facto. *Two* schools'll have to close. Two. An elementary school and a middle school. It was the middle school Clay attended."

"I understand. You know Tom Hartley from down in the Heel?"
Hartley touched his hat brim. Endicott brimmed him back.

"This gun issue that rose up last night: That's a bad thing," Mann said. "That's something you ought to slam your brakes on, turn it around and drive it back where it came from."

"It's a citizen's right," Endicott said. "My right, your right, everybody's."

"That don't *make* it right."

"We can't have federal troops seizing our land and assets," Endicott said.

"What federal troops? It's just me and Tom. I've known you since seventy-two. I was at Clay's christening. House-sat for you that one time. Fixed your barn roof, too."

Endicott sputtered a little getting restarted: "You made the choice being a fed. Feds don't do what's right, not for the people, not for the land, not for the animals, nothing. You got it all screwed up, bass-ackwards, flipping on somebody's political whim, somebody trying to raise funds, make a change for change's sake, some cockeyed idea gets started in Hollywood so they can get themselves photographed doing stuff, half of it won't never work. Why should the freakin' government go along?"

"Whoa, Clifford. We don't hurt you. Tom tracks the frontera down in the Heel. I track jobbers up here in the hills. All we see are people on both sides of the line cutting corners to suit themselves, devil take the rest. That's not the way it works—nor ought to. We don't make the rules. But when they do get made, it's just automatically our job."

He pulled into the courtyard. Four vehicles were parked there, all bearing the E-Bar-E logo of two E's facing each other with a bar between them. Ellie did not come out of the kitchen. Nobody came out. Who was in there?

"You say you didn't send Clayton off to wherever he went—well, who did?" Mann wrapped it up. "Think about that while the warrant's arriving."

Everybody walked into the main house, carrying their own guns. Nobody made an issue. It all went fine. Philly felt uneasy holding a gun, tried to hand his gun to Mann, and Mann waved it off. Only Hoss Atwood, a neighbor, didn't feel guilty just being there. Hoss was new. Just got in this year from southwest Kansas, near the Colorado line.

Hoss was playing it by ear, but the tune kept changing. It changed key, changed melody, changed tempo, to where a person just wouldn't recognize it. This place down in southwest New Mexico had to be the most screwed up in the entire country for confusion, for people not knowing one minute to the next what they were going to do, where they were headed, what was right and what was wrong.

"Hell, bet if you helt up a compass, the danged thing would jest spin like a blasted pinwheel on the Fourth of JU-ly."

Marlie Braden separated herself from the crowd in Senator Albert Settles' ballroom-sized parlor and stepped through the French doors onto the flagstone veranda. The moon shone on the Rio Grande down in the valley below, and the Albuquerque lights twinkled back at the stars. She squinted a hundred miles. Was that Magdalena Peak down there to the southwest? Just on the other side of it, she thought, used to be home.

Chapter Twelve

Shakey

William Sandrine sat his horse like an English gentleman, as he had been taught starting from the age of three at the Strongs Riding Academy in Salaberry-de-Valleyfields, Quebec, on the St. Lawrence just south of Montreal and just north of New York. He'd gone riding in New Mexico as a Boy Scout. Stayed with one of his mother's five sisters in Santa Fe. And now his manor, like hers, was toasted brown adobe, newly built by artisans who came up from Ascención, Mexico. White trim rescued the house from the equally brown horizon, and the blue door with just a hint of violet referenced the cloak worn by the Virgin Mary. This blue was her color somehow. Stables matched the main house, which had three stories. So the stables had three stories, too. The ground floor was for horses, the second floor served as part hayloft, part storehouse and the rarely used third floor was all bunkhouse, all connected like a cloister.

Cowboys were as much like monks as they were like wolves—and for the same reasons. Sandrine, like an abbot, led them in citizenship but also in revelry. He led them hunting, and in abstaining from hunting. When he explained why they must protect thousands of long-eared white jackrabbits tearing crazily around his north-central pasture, it made sense if they thought about it. Living with it made it clearer: These were the only ones left on earth. They did pretty well, considering, but . . .

"They need our help," Sandrine said. "We help them, they help us."

"How are three-thousand midget jackrabbits going to help us?" Weeks asked him during one of his daily patrol stops.

"If we save them, their existence elevates us," Sandrine replied.

Weeks stopped in as he made his Border Patrol rounds from Jackrabbit Wells, named for those self-same bunnies. He'd come in, have a coffee or a soda or a twist of tobacco or one of Sandrine's cigars. Sandrine sometimes asked him to stay to dinner, maybe share a story or two with the hands, offering a spare bunk if the time got away.

Weeks wasn't much for stories. He'd lived a story that frightened him. He never talked about it. When he did tell a story, people's eyelids started fluttering like castanets.

This one morning in late March, Sandrine rode down with Weeks to the frontier, pulling the Border Patrol trailer with their horses inside. Then, Sandrine horse-backed down from the Peloncillos above the international boundary, watching how the Mexico-side traffic was on Highway 2—how often vehicles peeled off, either for the port or for the tattered, sagging fence strung down along the sand east and west of it. He was preparing to testify before a suddenly security-conscious Congress about border traffic, and he didn't mean drugs. He meant comings and goings. A nonexistent barrier.

Sometimes a car, or a van full of illegals, just crashed the fence and kept driving. Sometimes they got stuck, and the Border Patrol—right now that was just Weeks, solo again—came along and unstuck them and directed them back across.

Sandrine kept a helpless eye on it. His mother in Montreal worried over her grandson, Pete Sandrine, who lived south of the Diamond S, close to the border. She'd done her diligence. Knew the story of Shakey Bill White, a Texas ranger who founded ranch in 1866 after returning from the Civil War. He'd been a deputy US marshal as well. Helped track down the Robin Hood-like stagecoach bandit, Javier Pedroza, after he'd caught Pedroza and seen him hanged. Unbeknownst to White, a mortician signed a deal with Bartz's Pharmacy in San Antonio to display the open casket containing Pedroza's body in front of the store. After his burial, a body believed to be Pedroza's, was dug up and taken away by a traveling circus that displayed it in the major cities of the West, from Vancouver, British Columbia, all the way down to Matamoros.

One day, a solitary horseman came up from Mexico covered with the dust of a dozen states, from Quintana-Roo, down in that corner where the Rio Azul crosses from Guatemala to Belize, having ridden north the full length of Mexico to Sonora. Tough, impatient, in need of a bath and a shave after six months asaddle, he rode into Ascención. Said his name was Angel. Said he'd come north to take someone to heaven. White's oldest son, Vick, named for the hell that was Vicksburg.

It was 1872. Vick was twenty. Lived in Tombstone, working for the ranch by proxy. Determined either to improve his father's water rights or to sell the ranch. And he said as much during a visit with Wilfred Blake from the territorial water office.

The day after that conversation, Vick White's body was found in the Guadalupe Pass. Vick, checking the waters, was murdered. Left propped against a rock clutching a tarot card—the hanged man. His boots, hat, chaps, cigarettes, spurs, saddle, and horse were gone. His watch had been stolen from his pants and then his pants were stolen. The silver studs and buckles were pried from his saddlebags. All that remained were his denim shirt and his long johns. Ants had moved into those. His father hired Pinkertons. They got a line on who killed Vick, name of Angel Pedroza. Others stripped or robbed him.

The watch turned up in a Nogales pawn shop, the ticket signed with a flourish by Angel, brother of Javier, the notorious Barranca Bandit. White understood the retribution. It was like a pilgrimage. And it set White on a pilgrimage of his own. The example of the Whites and the Pedrozas was the one cited by Pete Alderete when he told prospective border dwellers: *Watch all sides.*

"There's more than two sides to the border," Pete said.

White's Ranch became the Diamond K for awhile after White, riding off to meet his fate in Mexico, sold out to US Senator George Kane of California. White never returned. Some said he was killed down there somewhere. A few said he fell in love—with a bit of land and a woman that came with it. Senator Kane, when he toted up his ranching and mining interests, owned nearly one-tenth of New Mexico.

Sandrine's mother, who lived an urban existence in a large apartment overlooking the St. Lawrence—needed constant reassurance that her grandson was safe. Called every afternoon. Sandrine was glad she had found that excuse to check in. He liked trying to explain New Mexico to an English baroness in Canada.

Like today. This afternoon, he told her about the burgundy van that tried to crash the fence and got stuck. Weeks had backed his truck up to the van and pushed it back across the line, then radioed back to Concha to get Jose Arias' towing service to come haul them the rest of the way to wherever. A dozen bewildered people who spilled out of the van stood in the sand and looked hopelessly around. They saw the trucks roaring by on Mexico's Highway 2. Nobody gave any hint of slowing down. Weeks took the names and home-towns of each prospective immigrant and entered them into the database when he got back to Jackrabbit Wells. He'd looked them over pretty carefully. They included a young mother and twelve-year-old daughter named Algeciras. He figured the group might just try to walk in. It would be the last likely chance until the fall. So he kept an eye on them all day long, on and off, and they kept an eye on him. They sat on roadside boulders that marked the shoulders and waited. Someone told them a bus would come. But none did. Instead there came a flatbed truck, and all of them piled onto it, and it took them back to Juarez. Sandrine, heading back from a loop that brought him once again to the marker Bill White erected for his son in Guadalupe Pass, saw the flatbed heading in. He stopped to watch it load, then watched it carry off its human cargo.

The ride home, he told Mom, was always glorious in the after-noons, with the grama gathering sunlight and radiating milky gold. Those stupid whiskered cows standing around the pasture staring at him as he rode by. The rabbits covering their chaos with sheer athletic speed and enthusiasm. The occasional mouse sniffing snacks moments before fate crashed down with talons. He heard his mother gasp. So he did not tell her that after every ride, though exhilarated, he felt weak on the eastern flank.

Missing only one thing in his grassy empire—Blye.

"Gonna go reel me in a whopper," Sandrine told Hackett, his wildlands biologist.

Blye was still a little fuzzy. The bruises on his forehead hadn't dis-appeared the way they were supposed to. And the headaches, something he hadn't anticipated, had begun—and with them the nausea. Hector Alderete and Jimmy Olean had come over and moved some cattle to new pastures for him, and he paid them out of the insurance settlement, so he was still ahead for the moment. But it was eating at him that every time he tried to walk across the room, he'd start weaving. The air in front of him seemed to fog up, as though there were some translucent entity between him and whatever he happened to be looking at.

Just keep up with the walking, Doc Ruelas said over and over in his monotone.

Well, hell, I ain't going to walk around the entire gol-dinged day, he thought and sat down in front of the tube.

Of course, there's nothing on, he said to himself. He watched with fascination as an aging Brit in a bright green shirt and orange tie sliced vegetables without once looking at what he was doing—his eyes steadfastly on the camera. He was sure this Brit would lose a finger or two. And so he watched closely, and by the end of the hour, with all Brit fingers intact, Blye felt he'd been bilked. So he turned it off. He'd begun to doze when something new screeched to a halt outside.

An out-of-focus cowboy was sitting behind the wheel of an Iwo Jima Jeep.

"Hey, Blye, want to go for a ride?"

Blye approached the vehicle doubting his eyes.

"Is this real or is it one of those kits? My daddy had a real one. Left over from the war. We bought it at the Army base in El Paso as surplus."

"Got this Jeep from your daddy," Sandrine said. "Wondered if you'd recognize it."

Blye settled back in the leather-covered passenger-side seat as Sandrine gunned it. It spat out dirt and rocks that sent Blye's old golden retriever retreating under the porch. Blye's hands jumped around looking for something to hold onto. There wasn't a door, so there weren't handles. There was no roof, so there were no ceiling straps. He pulled down his Stetson 'til his ears winged out and grabbed onto the bottom of the seat, while the machine skidded around several corners. And Blye, with his head swimming, took stock of his insides. So far, so good. Sandrine floored it, and they were gone.

The Jeep was olive drab with "US Army" stenciled on it. The tilt of the windshield could be adjusted with pressure screws at either end of the brackets that held it. It could be laid flat on the flat hood. Blye tested the screw nearest him.

"Don't mess with those screws," Sandrine said. "One bump, the damn thing falls down. Already broke one. Why have a droppable windscreen, anyhow? I mean, what's the military advantage of having wind in your face?"

"It was so they could stack them," Blye said, "you know, for shipping. And some had gun mounts on the hood, where the windshield was in the way."

The Jeep putt-putted and every now and then *brraaaaapped* like a go-cart down the dirt road that led to the border.

"Show me your famous corner monument," Sandrine said. "Does it really stand taller than the other obelisks?"

"Until somebody blows its head off," Blye said. "Take a right turn at the fork. Follow the cattle tracks."

The road was rutted, badly eroded from rains two years ago. It had not rained appreciably since then. And Blye had done nothing to blade it.

"If you swore not to read while driving I'd lend you a road-grader," Sandrine said.

"You got your own road-grader?"

"Absolutely. Always wanted one ever since I was a kid."

Cattle tracks scattered over a hill, then regathered and focused toward the corner. In the distance the men saw the wedge of concrete, like a mini-Washington Monument.

"I can show you right where they cut the fence, pulled a truck up, and loaded my cows into Mexico," Blye said.

"Fences are useless," Sandrine said. "Mine get cut all the time. Hunters, wets."

Blye looked at him in astonishment. "You call 'em wets? That ain't PC, pal."

"Go on, mock me, but I'm not the one who bent his steering wheel with his head."

"Ain't mockin', swear to God. Just wonder if I need a tutor to understand *enviro*."

Sandrine, grinning, followed the tracks across a once-muddy field that had been hard-baked by the sun. Its fallowness swept north on the border as far as could be seen.

"You're hammered beyond all recognition," Sandrine said. "Not a blade of grass."

"I've got other pastures. Feed 'em hay if they need it."

"Don't use hay. Drive 'em over to my south pasture," Sandrine said. "It's just over that little pass, you know. It used to be the road up from Llanos. It's not far, and it's no worse, smuggler-wise, than this is. We need to reseed you."

"How many head can that pasture take?"

"More than you've got left," Sandrine said.

The monument loomed before them. Both men could see the fence was down.

"I'll be dipped," Blye said. "These new tracks go right through the fence just like the old ones. Second time in a month, third time this year. Must be twenty or so cows."

"I'd say you're feeding the cartel," Sandrine said, pulling the Jeep up to the wire.

"No, they put 'em in a feedlot down in Ascension, and they charge me an arm and a leg for board," Blye said, dismounting. "It's a racket. I have to pay 'em to get my stock back, and even if I don't get 'em back, I still owe them for the board."

Blye had a short length of culvert set vertically in the ground as a tool cache. It was covered with a slab of flagstone. He pulled out a spool of barbed wire. "Always keep a stash down here. They hit the corner more than anyplace else."

"It's an easy landmark. If you want, I can talk to Pete Alderete," Sandrine said.

"He don't want into this, and I wouldn't, neither," Blye said. "Get him killed."

"He's got his own pistoleros," Sandrine said. "They're good."

Blye took wire-cutters off his left boot. Pulled the wire taut. A gap remained.

"Looks like we're missing about an eighteen-inch section. Lately they take a section of fence with them aways into Mexico and drop it, so I'd have to go in after it and find it," Blye said, "or I have to bring wire with me. So I set this little cache."

"An idea," Sandrine said. "I'm gn'a do it, too. Fact, I think I'll put a bunch of 'em in, spaced out along the line, covered up just the way you have. We put a fence up, they just tear it down. How many ejidos butt up to you out here?"

"Oh, a dozen, maybe ten. They been consolidating 'em. Why?"

"That seems like a lot."

"They're small," Blye said.

"They'd be glad to help you, I bet," Sandrine said.

"Shoot me, more like," Blye said. "They put out a contract on me. One of these boys up here said I'd reported their pot plantation. Fact it's right up here about five miles."

The dirt road went due north from the corner, straight, and flat and uneventful.

A twelve-foot stock tank stood beside a windmill pumping groundwater that trickled from a pipe into the tank. Behind it a stream ran off into a weed-choked ditch.

"Fact I've got to pick up a generator up ahead here at the next tank," Blye said.

"Hope it's still there," Sandrine said.

"So do I. It's right opposite that cornfield where they're growing the grass."

"Pot, you mean?"

"Yeah, marijuana. Growing it right in the middle of the corn, so nobody can see it except by air. That's how they spotted it. Crop just didn't look right, kind of husky dusky around the edges and bright green in the middle. Come on up the road. I'll show you."

"Let's stop at this little ejido first. I want to talk to these boys," Sandrine said.

The young men were drinking Coronas, and he asked them if the beer was cold.

"*Sí, señor.* You want one?" one young man said, showing off his English.

"Sure, how much?" Sandrine asked.

"Thirty cents, U-S," the boy said.

"We'll take two if you got 'em," Sandrine said.

"Nah, Doc Ruelas says I can't cause I'm medicated," Blye said.

"I'll drink 'em both," Sandrine said, handing the boy two dollars.

"Don't have change, *siento.*"

"Doesn't matter. You weren't charging enough anyway," Sandrine said.

"Okay," the boy said.

"What do they call this ejido, son?" the rancher asked.

"San Tomas."

"How many of you work it?"

"Twenty or thirty on busy days. It will feed thirty families, plus pay us a little bit. We stay about even," he said.

Sandrine got his vital statistics. He was sixteen. He got one day off every second week. He worked on the equipment. He had a vocational degree from Chihuahua City, which helped him get a job in Ascension. They sent him up here to the ejidos. He serviced equipment of four ejidos, loosely federated because of their family ties.

And these were the profitable ejidos.

"You know about this *grife* they found up the road—that your ejido?" Blye asked.

The youngster was taken aback. It sounded like a hostile line of questioning.

"I don't know about it," he said. "It's not one of mine. I go from here down to your beautiful monument, and I work sometimes for Alderete."

"What's your name?" Blye said.

"I rather not say. You get us in trouble," he said.

"Hell, no, I won't."

"I hear you already did."

"Well, where the hell'd'you get a story like that?"

"That bar in Llanos. You been in there. I seen you," the lad said.

"Yeah, I used to go in there before I busted up my head. But I never ratted no one. I don't care what they say in the Pinto Bar. You know what I think?" he told Sandrine. "I think someone's trying to run us off, get us to quit."

Sandrine waved at the teen-ager and continued up the road.

"How much farther?"

"About a mile. Slow down a little ways in advance."

Sandrine looked a little worried.

"Just in case they're working it or defending it or whatever. I don't know what to expect with the cartel all moved in south of here. Say, I meant to ask you—you have a gun?"

Sandrine showed him the WWII-vintage Army forty-five he had in the glove box.

"You are one amazing bundle of nostalgia, you know that?" Blye said.

"When I saw this Jeep in your daddy's yard, I had to have it. I loved rebuilding it. Working on this machine gave me more joy than anything I've done since I closed the deal on the Diamond S . . . except my granddaughter being born."

"How old is she?"

"She's two. My son Pete's girl."

"Hold up here. Here's where . . . Uh-oh. Wait a minute, wait a minute, they're coming across. Stop the Jeep, stop the Jeep. Don't say a thing, not a word, let me handle this, William, if you don't mind."

Five Mexicans with rifles spilled onto US soil, fanning out like a U.S.-trained combat reconnaissance team. Sandrine and Blye sat patiently in the Jeep as the men trotted toward them from five different angles. A pickup truck with half a dozen other men shifted gears with a loud grind and lurched across the border as well.

"Who'd they think they are, Pancho-freakin'-Villa?" Blye whispered.

The lead Mexican was in uniform, sort of. He wore the black shirt of the federal judicial police, the federales, and blue jeans with tattered sneakers.

His rolled-up shirtsleeves had three chevrons. Unless he stole the shirt, he was a sergeant. And he looked to be in charge. Blye wondered if he'd taken it upon himself to cross into *los Estados Unidos*. If so, it took guts. He seemed to have weighed the odds. And it looked like he was going to get away with it. He waved an old chrome-plated thirty-two at Sandrine, motioning him and Blye away from the Jeep. The sergeant and another black-shirted officer searched the Jeep and found the forty-five. They looked it up and down and considered stealing it, then put it back in the glove box after removing the clip and removing the bullets from the clip. They threw the bullets away and handed the clip to Blye.

There was another whole box of bullets in the glove compartment, but they left that alone.

"*Es mi tierra*," Blye told the crew, trying without success to convey some weight of authority.

"We don't want no shooting," the sergeant said, waving while turning his back and leaving the arena. "Have a nice day."

"*That* was a moment," Sandrine said, watching the crew return to stacking the sheaves of marijuana. "Are they going to burn this stuff right here?"

"No," said Blye. "They're going to truck it off to a dump someplace and burn it."

"How do we know they won't just package it and push it on across?"

"I don't know. I thought maybe you'd know."

"Why would I know?" Sandrine said, turning his Jeep around to drive back south.

"Enviros all love this stuff," he said.

"Bullshit."

They drove in silence until they came upon the turnoff that led back diagonally to the ranch house along beside Las Cuevas, a set of cave-eaten desert peaks.

"You want to see my archaeology?" Blye asked.

Sandrine looked skeptical.

"How long a detour?" he said.

"It's right here, up the hill," Blye said, looking up to the top of the closest mesa.

"Well . . ."

They parked at the bottom of the mesa, and Blye led Sandrine to an upward trail.

"This ain't no national park," Blye said. "This is reality, just you and this old bean pot that is worth about fifty-thousand, sixty-thousand."

Sandrine made the climb while the still-woozy Blye stayed below.

After fifteen minutes or so visiting with the pot and several snakes, he came back down to the truck and just shook his head.

"That is the most beautiful Casas Grandes bean pot I've ever seen. It looks so damn smooth, like a baby's skin."

The pot was about eighteen inches round with a slight lip around the opening. The parrot clan was represented in the black, white, and iron-red designs, and the parrot's round belly followed the line of the pot.

Blye nodded proudly. "You protectionists probably need to add that to your inventory. Me, I'd like to just leave it where it is and never lay a finger on it."

"That would be my plan, too," Sandrine said. "I didn't touch it."

"Thought you'd be all over this, wanting to see it stored in Plexiglass in a museum."

"There is no museum as good as this one," Sandrine said. "It would be a crime to ever tell a soul about this place. A crime."

"Well, it's just between us chickens," Blye said.

"You mind if we stick with the border?" Sandrine said. "Just curious."

So they backtracked.

The ejido of San Tomas was empty now.

"Quitting time," Blye said. "The truck comes for them, they go."

"It's a little early," Sandrine said, "isn't it?"

"They start real early, beat the sun. They don't want to miss their ride. *Wait*."

They stopped.

"You hear something?"

They listened and decided that they were hearing the *pop-pop-pop* and *brrraaap* of gunfire just up the road, possibly from the cornfield where they were harvesting the pot.

"Maybe the inland route is better after all," Sandrine said.

"Yeah, maybe."

Sandrine backed the Jeep around and started to proceed, when a whiny little thing like a gnat-cycle sped across the line and cut him off. The sweat-shirted young man on the Yamaha had a gun pointed at them.

Bert Hackett drove the hundred miles to Gila Wells to chat with a fellow enviro.

Bert had taken his turn as North American director of the Wildlands Coalition and had been instrumental in getting Donald Badderly to head up the wolf recovery program because of Badderly's experience with wolves in Eastern Europe. Badderly had established an education program in Macedonia that served as a model in Bulgaria, Romania and all through the Balkans. Wolves were starting to be accepted there. Because Badderly did not moralize or try to get warm and fuzzy with wolves, make pets of them, live with them, dance with them or talk baby talk to them. Wolves kept their distance from him, and he liked it that way, because that's the way wolves are built. They are distant. And now Badderly wanted Hackett to come quiet the partisans.

Braden had received a note in his mailbox: "This might have been a bomb."

"They thinking since they screwed Braden the worst, he'd be the one making the *tick-tick-boom* phone calls? So they should retaliate against him?" Hackett asked.

Badderly let a long few seconds pass before saying: "'Tisn't easy being me. Obviously, Sid made no threats. He lost his daughter. If he was going to do anything, no threat, he'd do it. Wrong how they done him." Cockney twang caught static on the phone.

The national office called Badderly and also Bert, so Hackett got both calls, urging a consultation with Raylinda. She'd gone over the line with videography. Franks answered the phone and then, a few minutes later, the door. Bert was a guy Ted liked talking to.

"Suffragettes gonna come in here with axes and bust up your fax machine," Bert said. "I'd hide it or move to a new location."

"Yeah, been thinking of it," Ted said.

"Can I see Raylin?"

"No, turns out she won't see you," Ted said. "Under the weather." He gestured, making a balloon-like arc over the stomach area.

"I heard. Great, congrats and all. But I drove all this way. After calling first."

"Yeah, 'fraid so, 'fraid so," Ted said. "She disapproves of you and Badly."

"Donald lives in the city. Scarcely know him. It's crazy," Hackett said. "She's become part of the problem."

"Y'know Raylin," Franks said quietly. "Never could play team ball. Gets benched."

"Well, otherwise she'd be in the game," Hackett said. "Lemme talk to you, then."

"Okay," Ted said. And they sat in understuffed chairs and spoke of issues.

Chapter Thirteen

Roundup

I t was dry, but it was about to be wet. Snow seemed like too much effort. Old man winter was huffing and puffing, and the grounded earth coaxed lightning up to tickle the belly of the black cloud overhead. Wind broke the white clouds apart.

Cattle vans were lined up half a mile on the highway waiting to get to the turnoff for Braden's Two Square corrals, which were about halfway up the road from Gila Wells in an area clogged by spectator traffic, so the trucks were bottlenecked trying to turn.

Television crews and photographers as well as environmental warriors wanted to share the "downfall of defiance," as one placard called it. Also, ranchers bowed their heads, ashamed to let go. There was unfathomable bitterness. Not about punishment or crime, just in-your-face politics pretending to be science, *using* science as a prop.

Thunder shook them all like God's words, water pouring off their hats, sparks flying off the cottonwood that took the hit. In a moment, the smoldering branch fell smoking about halfway down. Got hung up somewhere in mid-tree and became invisible.

It just stayed there forever, unquestioned, undisputed.

Just as the rain began to cascade in vertical sheets, the yellow-slickered cowboys started bringing in the cattle from their scattered high-meadow pens. The men pulled and pushed, breaking the trance that immobilized the cattle—had to move now. No more stalling. "*Mrrrnnnggghh.*" The general response. Some cattle were down, and the men had to dismount and physically tail them up. One or two did not get up. One cow had pneumonia. Wanted to die. The other got up, then sank back down. Braden rode over.

"What's wrong with her?" he asked.

"She's the one whose calves got et," Bertie said.

"Spank her. She'll move." And she did, finally.

The rest of the animals were cajoled into the pens. They milled about until they realized they were being squeezed into a "V", like geese. A narrow wooden pathway appeared before them, and the chute had them. They tried to look backward, trapped. Most panicked and let go of whatever bodily wastes were available. The runny green stuff flowed onto the chute and made it slick so that the next forty or fifty cattle found no footing. Moonwalked the chute. Seemed to be going up but were really going down.

About three hands worked the chute. Should have had extra pay but were volunteers. The rest were on horseback, driving the herd down from high-country pens the big trucks couldn't reach. The lightning was even more prevalent in the high country, and would have started a dozen fires except for the heavy rain. One horse passing under a tree was electrified and burned by a bolt. The cowhand had to carry his saddle down to the horse corrals for another mount. The comatose horse had to be shot.

"Steer clear of trees!" yelled Endicott, who was supervising the upper pens.

Braden sat his horse mainly at a point along the trail where he had a clear view of the corrals but also where he could help keep the cattle turned away from the crowds. He'd called Mann and the sheriff because of crowd concerns. Corona, after conferring with county commissioners, sent four deputies on overtime.

Once the high-country cattle were cleared down to the corrals, seven hours later, Endicott and his hands eventually rode down the slope to help round up horses. They set up a temporary remuda on the wilderness. Just an interim, one-day pen for the roundup, but it was illegal. A Santa Fe enviro group filed a protest. The Bradens were fined.

Robert Sapello, the state livestock board chairman, came down in person from Albuquerque to observe the herd. The cattle looked fit. But he also had to ride up to the high pasture on the west slope of Willy's Peak to see about the earlier wolf attack. The alpha One-Ninety, nicknamed Charlie, and three other wolves attacked the flank of the penned cattle, held together by a two-strand fence. Sapello concluded the two calves had been killed. He signed an affidavit that would qualify Braden for compensation from the enviros. The compensation equaled the fine. But Braden never knew it. He didn't care to get an accounting. He saw his task as move 'em out and sell 'em.

Slowly the semi trailers filled with cattle. One by one, each scrunched into gear, heaved a few times before the clutch plate meshed, and then eased out onto the road toward Sunflower. Not a long ride. Just over a hundred miles. The cattle would still graze the pastures of New Mexico until time rolled around for the slaughtering. Under normal circumstances what happened this day would be routine—rancher loads cattle, moves herds. But this time it marked the end of a period that sparkled in human imagination. Death of a fantasy. Camping trips. Horseback riding. Cowboy movies. Barbecues. C&W. All took a hit in their sleep.

"It don't take much to kill a dream," Braden, who had few illusions left, told Will Mann at the corral gate. "All you need do is prove it's real. Even if you don't prove it; if you can just get people to think it might be real, it's dead."

"That's the difference with Sandrine," Mann said. "For him it stays a dream."

"Well, it's good somebody has the dream," Braden said, nodding. He felt no twinge of bitterness. Sandrine had come riding in to save his saddle-worn butt when it seemed all the world was against him. "Look at 'em," Braden said, leveling his arm across the panorama like a symphony conductor.

The scene was like a cross between a wedding and a funeral. The enviros had their used Saabs and bestickered VWs festooned with white crepe streamers, parading in front, in back, alongside the cattle vans, honking at the cattle, waving placards that said, "Two Square Equals Green," "Bye Bye Braden," "Cattle Call," "The Cows Have Come Home." There were others. They were brandished one in front of the other, so that none could be read. Yet, except for the procession, it was pretty near subdued. There was chanting, now and then—but no mooning, no flashing, no streaking, and no explosives.

And, they could almost brag, no rudeness, no violence.

Hatred had its edge knocked off. People were tired of the whole sad affair, rolling their eyes. Feeling for the humans. They could no longer sit and listen to the scrabbling.

Photos of Raylinda were on several protest signs. Franks, concerned the posters might help some *solitary stranger* recognize her on the street someday, walked over to every protester with such a sign and quietly asked each to remove or cover up her image.

She was not present for the final demolition derby. Her doctor guaranteed the trucks thundering out to Interstate 10 would make her physically ill. It wasn't as if she hadn't seen trucks before. They were only driving one hour to the spooky Ghost Mountains of the Heel, the misty valleys, the smoky spirits. The trucks—they were real. Shaking dust down into cellars. The horns blaring, lights flashing, placards waving through the sunroofs in the now-steady, heavy rain.

Fourteen semi-tractor trailers modified for livestock crossed the Gila that Sunday in early April, arriving while the sun still shone at Sandrine's southeast pasture. Each truck unloaded negligibly farther north, until five hundred cattle, all that was left of the great Two Square, were strung along the humpback of the Ghost Mountains, once White's, then Kane's, now Sandrine's. But where was Sandrine?

Raylinda was missing, Sandrine was missing, Mikey, Miguelito, Juanito, Millicent, Marlie. All missing.

Sandrine's absence went unnoticed only briefly. The party shifted to Sunflower. There were more people than cows, all of them bent on revelry. Alice Sandrine ordered up a dining hall table with tortillas, beans, chips, and salsa. But the little trickle of people who asked, "Where's Sandrine?" became a river. They had to wait awhile for an answer.

Marlie sat at her desk on the phone in Albuquerque, checking her bank account. She got that blipping that indicated another call trying to get through. Waiting to get hooked up with the bank, she just let the other line ring. The bank account was bottoming out, and the last deposit hadn't cleared yet.

Senator Settles said he planned to move Marlie to Washington as part of the capital staff. She would have to sublet her condo, renegotiate, or break a just-signed lease.

A photo of Sid and Millie on horseback crossing Wells River at a shallow ford hung behind the desk. Marlie did not look at it. Or at the wall mirror between the doors.

Instead she looked out the window at a fragment of a view of the river, with the wall of the neighboring condominium complex occupying two-thirds of the viewframe.

"Rio Solano," the condo complex was called. *Sunny River.*

But it was gray out, not sunny at all. And it was gray inside, too. And except for a pencil-thin wedge of water, half obscured by salt cedars and olive trees, the only river she could see was the gray one, the one made of concrete leading east.

Chapter Fourteen

Jail

Pete Sandrine, now alone with both his father and Bert Hackett gone, kept watch on the electronic monitor and tracking alarms for Dad. Diamond S had tracking chips implanted in one percent of their steers and all their vehicles. But Pete wasn't sure about the vintage Jeep. Might not have been fitted yet. And that Jeep was gone.

Pete did what his father told him if anything like this happened. Call Hartley.

But Hartley was gone too. So he called Weeks and then Mann, who called Hartley.

"I've got to clear," Hartley told Mann. "Weeks is all alone down there."

"Go ahead and clear," Mann told him. "I'll meet you down there in an hour."

Hartley was already rolling. He'd started the motor as soon as he heard Weeks had checked out extra guns from the Port of Entry arsenal.

And he was already turning off onto Highway 35 by the time his conversation with Mann was finished. Even full-bore with sirens and lights, it would take him well over an hour to reach the border.

The yellow sunburst exploded without warning behind Blye's seemingly fused eyelids, accompanied by the kind of sudden pain that was intended. The guard, using the butt of Sandrine's forty-five as the peen, hammered Blye a second time.

Blye was unprepared, undefended. He took both blows straight and unimpeded on his left ear. The second one especially was savage, all-out, emphatic, meant to do worse damage than it did. Blye's pudgy ear cushioned the impact. But the gun barrel did split the ear open like a papaya, and it made a total of three head traumas in two weeks. He bled awhile, and he lay on the floor unconscious.

After hammering Blye, the guard looked ferociously at Sandrine, daring him any excuse to do worse. But Sandrine, surrounded by the three federales, including the biker in the cutoff sweatshirt who intercepted them on the border, simply raised his hands and backed away, bowing just slightly enough to cool the killer instinct. "*Por favor, señor, por favor, padrón. No nos matas.* Please don't kill us." Sandrine kept his eyes down. He controlled the amount of light that emanated from them. He controlled his body language. He shrank. The guard was curious. He stepped over Blye's hulking form and took Sandrine's face like a *pelota* in his cracked and calloused right hand. He put his Glock between Sandrine's eyes, on the bridge of his nose. He pressed until the barrel left a little round imprint. Pressed his whiskers against him, looked him in the eye.

"Eh? eh?" the guard said.

"*Por favor, padrón,*" Sandrine half-whispered, lowering his head even farther.

"*Quién es esto?*" the guard asked him.

"*Soy nadie,*" Sandrine said. "*Soy nadie.* I'm nobody."

The guard flung him down on the bunk and left, shaking his head. At the door, before closing it, he looked back at Sandrine again, and shook his head again.

The door closed. Sandrine sat just a moment on the flat little thing he imagined they called a mattress. But he refrained from asking or commenting on it, either in Spanish or in English, because he figured they were listening.

"*Nous sommes fichés,*" he said. "Know that? *Nous sommes absolument foutus.*"

Blye did not understand French, but he couldn't hear him anyway. Sandrine knelt down and lifted Blye onto the bunk, the only bunk. It seemed reasonably clean. He'd seen worse jails in bigger towns. This was budgetless Llanos, nowhereville. This was the town where migrants coming across Highway 2 from Mexicali could get their farm papers.

The rumor was that the new guy dragging the roads was crafty as a skink. The new guy, Weeks, would drag just a small section of road, proceed over a rise, then stop and run back and look down to see who crossed, where they headed. Then he'd circle ahead of them and wait behind a yucca, cholla, or agave. They'd walk right up to him. He'd offer a cigarette and ask for a light. It was vulnerable to deception. Once they caught on, word among hands was Weeks was a thorn; somebody'd have to do something.

Some of it Sandrine heard in the jail. Much of it to do with the whore in the cell outside. The guards all wanted her. Even though, they said, she was the ugliest whore in northern Mexico, from Baja to Chihuahua. She had lost some important teeth, in front. But the guards wanted her not because of how she looked but how she seemed.

Sandrine was curious. They had no inkling why they wanted her. Yet they seemed to want her all the more for not knowing. He could hear them snorting outside his window as they leered at her. She was cold, he heard them say. Colder the better, they said. Then she would want them. Get her a blanket, one of them said. No, then she would not be cold anymore. She would not want them. Sandrine found the discussion horrible but fascinating. Terrible for her. The woman could develop pneumonia. He'd seen this jail before. Pete had shown it to him during orientation twenty-five or twenty-seven years before, and it had not changed. If Sandrine pulled himself up to the clerestory, he could see her huddled on the ground in the front of her cell, hoping for a therm of sunlight.

The guards talked endlessly. Even at night, it turned out. Sandrine awakened with a start. The woman was crying. The guard who wanted her was entreating. *Let me comfort you*, he said to her. Sandrine heard this and awakened. The woman did not answer with words, but Sandrine heard her cell door open, then he heard her moaning and the guard calling her his *little dove*, his *little love*. A shaft of light hit Sandrine's window as the night commandant interrupted them with a halogen floodlamp. Sandrine jumped to the window, clutched the sill with his fingers and pulled himself up to where he could see the guard and the woman, en flagrant, in the open cell, the commandant standing over them. Sandrine held as long as he could, until his fingers weakened and he dropped back to the floor. Blye stirred in the sudden light as well.

"Is that you, Sandrine? Where are we?" he said.

"The Llanos jail," Sandrine reminded him.

"Oh, God, no. I thought I was dreaming."

"You need a better class of dream."

"Sorry," Blye said, then realized he was in pain.

Llanos was the town where Pedro Alderete had his western headquarters, including half a dozen barns and bunkhouses and five corrals. But since Juanito Alderete's disappearance and supposed death on New Year's Eve, Pete had been staying at the Rio Santo hacienda. Unavailable for this particular emergency.

"No way to get word to Don Pedro?" Blye asked him.

"Pete's got problems of his own right now," Sandrine said. "He needs us. Worse than we need him. That boy dragged him somewhere he didn't want to be."

Sandrine never said it aloud: Pete had become obsessive in ways he'd always warned everyone else against. He wanted to watch Don Octavio, and he wanted Don Octavio to know it—even if Pete was mistaken for a Costilla partisan.

When Octavio drove by in his midnight black Chrysler Imperial, Alderete stepped out from the shadows of his portal and watched with steady eyes. Just watched. Octavio usually didn't notice, but once or twice he'd tap Rico on the shoulder: "Who's that?" Rico would reply: "Pepe Alderete, padrón—Nito's father, Pepe senior."

"Oh, yes, Juanito's father. Isn't he with the Costillas?"

"So they say, padrón," Rico told the old man.

"What's Pete's problem?" Blye asked.

"He needed one of the blows you took, and you needed one less," Sandrine said.

"I wish . . ." Blye paused and looked up through the clerestory at the stars, as though seeking counsel. "I wish Octavio had some problems for a change."

"Pete says never wish harm on anyone," Sandrine said. "It comes back to you."

"I already had mine," Blye said.

The crows clustered in the barely budding fig-cottonwood copse in the Parque Central as Octavio went hatless into the church of San Jimino and confessed to Padre Villareal that he had wished some men dead—and then was not sorry when they died.

"Did you have anything to do with their deaths?" the priest asked.

"Oh, no, padre. I could never do that. But I might have said something to a very bad man I knew and, you know, made a comment."

"What sort of comment, Don Octavio?"

"Like what a worthless person, how much better the world would be without him. But that was years ago that I said that, years ago."

"And the man did disappear?"

"Yes, padre."

"The man did not simply catch a train to Guaymas?"

"I hear they found his body, so I suppose not, although he could have taken a train there and then come back."

"It's good you feel contrition, my son. Say fifty Ave Marias and beg for God's forgiveness."

"I do that every day, padre."

Enough bull, *enough already*, Villareal thought, then said: "Know what else?"

"No, what?"

"You make peace with Don Pedro Alderete. You show him a kindness."

"That could hurt my business, padre. Word gets around."

Padre Villareal seldom raised his voice, but now he did, and pounded on the wall for emphasis. The confessional shook, and old women in the back row of the santuario stood up halfway, crossed themselves, bowed and left, so as not to hear any more.

Of course, there's always one to stay and listen.

"You *will* make peace with Don Pedro Alderete no matter what it costs—if it costs you your *life*," he said. "Or else it costs you *eternal* life."

"I never expected eternal life, padre."

"Well, then your mediocre expectations can be realized. Why come to me? Why come to confession? You hoped I'd give you the easy ride everyone else does, didn't you? You believe based on what you want, not on what's true."

Octavio did not like this. The unfolding of these thoughts made him nervous and vaguely ill. He was unclear where these voices came from. Did they come from within him? Or did they come from the spirit of loss felt by the old woman? Or did they come from the spirit of malevolence that seemed to spread out like spilled ink around Octavio.

"Now see here," Octavio said, a phrase perfect in its meaninglessness.

"It would kill you to have Alderete over for dinner one night?" the padre said.

So Octavio answered: "No, I don't think so, I hope not. Why would Alderete want to come to dinner? He thinks I killed his son. But I had nothing to do with it."

"Why not eat with him, then, if that's true? Is it? You have so much in common."

"No, I mean, yes, I didn't do it."

"But you killed somebody's boy, didn't you."

"Not personally."

A long silence.

"Not personally," Octavio repeated.

A longer silence.

"Padre? You there?"

Octavio felt he was being asked to remember a little boy whose father every Sunday took him up to the padre in the front of the church for his weekly Bible lesson.

"The padre instructed you then: 'Remember that little boy.' That was you, yes?"

"Yes, padre."

"What happened to him?"

Octavio said: "Oh-ho, well! He got introduced around, y'know, padre? Grew up."

"Is he dead?"

"Pretty much, yes, I'd say."

"I'd say so, too. Good day." The wood panel slid shut.

Octavio tapped on the panel but got no answer. "I'm pretty busy, too, padre," he said. Then he stepped outside and looked behind the drapes on the priest's side of the confessional, and the priest was gone. He looked at the floor—maybe there was a trap door. But no, just floor. He came out and looked around the *santuario*. One old woman, three rows back, was knitting.

"Why are you knitting?" Octavio said.

"Making a sweater," she said.

"A sweater, why? This is the desert, summer is coming. By the time the sweater is done it will be . . ."

"Summer," she said.

"Did you see the padre?"

"I saw the padre and I heard the padre," she said.

"I mean did you see where he went?"

"Straight out the door, with wings on his shoulders," she said. "He looked like San Miguel, the archangel."

Octavio shook his head in disbelief. "Are you Señora Buscarenas?"

"Guess again."

He was not used to being addressed in this way. "I don't want to guess," he said. "I want you to simply tell me what is your name?"

"Bustamante," she said. "You never did know our name."

"Bustamante, oh, yes," he said. "Your husband ran the pharmacy."

"That's right, and what happened to him?" she said.

"Well, I was about to ask you that question. How is he? Is he still a pharmacist?"

"They don't need pharmacists in heaven. He's dead, Octavio."

"I'm sorry to hear it," Octavio said.

"You came to call one day forty years ago. Maybe you don't remember."

Octavio blinked several times. The recall images he saw were silent.

"You wanted us to stop carrying Linea Corso medicines. You wanted us to carry the Gutierrez brand instead, to please your sponsors in Juarez and Agua Prieta."

The young pharmacist, Xavier Bustamante, who had just received his diploma, politely declined, saying Gutierrez was inferior, unreliable, and Corso was better.

"But you want to stay in business, right?" the young Octavio asked him.

"I don't think of it as a business," the pharmacist said. "I think of it as service."

"Other pharmacists can serve the public better, in my opinion," Octavio said.

"You're entitled to that opinion, sir," the pharmacist said with a smile, turning his back on Octavio and returning to his task of funneling pills into a small glass bottle for a patient.

Octavio left the store and crossed the street to a cafe. He ordered tamales and a bottle of tequila. He ate the tamales quickly, then nursed the tequila all afternoon. Occasionally the bar man came by and asked if he could get anything for him. Octavio got angry. He didn't want to be bothered. The bar man returned to the bar.

At sundown, Octavio went to his car, opened the trunk and pulled out a gasoline can. He walked down to the gasoline pump in front of the Hotel Guadalupe. He pumped gasoline into the five-gallon can. Then he walked back to his car and poured a few cupfuls into his tank and set the gas can in the trunk.

"Ran out of gas, eh?" said Mrs. Bustamante, who had been watching him relive it.

He looked at Bustamante's widow and said, "Is that you, Mrs. Bustamante? I am very sorry about your husband."

But suddenly he and Mrs. Bustamante were standing in front of the pharmacy. They were young again. And her husband was behind the counter again. Ghosts.

"Why, nothing's happened to him. He's fine," Octavio said. "I see him working in his shop." But then Octavio's skin seemed to stretch tight over his facial bones, black hair receding, turning silver, disdain percolating up into his carefully cultivated voice. "Take a good, long look," the menacing voice said. Seemed to come from beneath his feet.

The last traces of sun disappeared from the sky, and it was black as crude oil in a forty-gallon drum. Mrs. Bustamante took a last, fond, dreamy look at her husband filling pill bottles. And Octavio, whistling, removed the gasoline can from his trunk, unscrewed the cap, and poured the contents against the base of the pharmacy. The liquid ran down the street toward the end of Bustamante's building, and Octavio knew he would have to light the match immediately or all the gasoline would flow down into the town, and everything would burn.

That was his public-safety thought as he lit the match, but he had second thoughts about dropping it. It would mean the well-meaning Mister Bustamante could be hurt, and it would mean that Octavio knew it and dropped the match anyway. *Ow!* The match burned Octavio's thumb and forefinger, then it fell from his grasp. It landed in the liquid and for a moment it appeared that the fuel would drown it.

Instead, maybe one second, maybe two, after the match seemed out, the entire puddle leapt with fire against the building and quickly ate into it. Hundreds of thousands of doses of medicine were destroyed.

There was another pharmacy in town, and that pharmacy was fortunately able to serve the needs of the town. But Bustamante burned to death, as history duly recorded.

Although Octavio Cortes, in his dream life, always insists he didn't mean to—and denies the deed—the words of the widow, the gasoline seller and the firefighters filter back to him. They all know what happened: Don Octavio threatened the pharmacist, bought the gas, poured it on the building, lit the match and dropped it, burning, into the fuel. Vestiges of Mr. and Mrs. Bustamante were there to remind him forty years later.

"I tried to put the match out," Octavio told her, "but it burned my fingers. I didn't mean to drop it. I meant to put it out, but it burned me."

"That burn was just a sample," she said, "a preview of what's to come."

"Who's the sweater for?" he then asked again, beginning to understand.

"I'm thinking I'll give it to you, in case you aren't warm enough."

Summer suddenly seemed to be starting, in April.

Sandrine dropped off to sleep again on the floor of the cell, and Blye fell back asleep on the cot.

At around 1 a.m., a guard woke them all over again, bringing them dinner. One plate. They would have to share. Blye could only open one eye. Sandrine fed him two bites of gruel—the two with chicken in them. Then Sandrine drank the rest.

Blye threw up a few minutes later, and the chicken flew across the cell as if it had wings again. Sandrine put the chunks back in the bowl and left it next to the door.

When the guard came in at 7 a.m., he stepped in it.

"¡*Chingá!*"

Sandrine looked up at him with one eye open, one shut.

"Visitor," the guard said in English.

"Thank you, son," Sandrine said, stepping forward with his hands out in front to be cuffed.

"No, behind," the guard said. So he turned around and got cuffed behind.

The guard also fixed him up with leg irons, so that he could not step forward more than about eight inches without rasping his ankles.

At the barred gate which separated the jail office from the penal end of the building, Roberto Salazar stood waiting.

The tall, elegant Salazar, foreman of Alderete's ranch, held his white Stetson over his chest with two hands.

"Don Guillermo," he said with a small nod of his head.

"Bobby!"

"Are you okay?"

"Sure. Blye's hurt, though. We need to get him back across the border."

"We need to get you back, too," Roberto said. "Why don't you just let me post your bail, the mordida?"

"That would be a lot simpler than taxing the judicial system, but then down the road when we're in Ascension buying cattle, or retrieving them, we get to be rearrested," Sandrine said. "But getting Mister Blye to the hospital in Lordsburg is the first order of business. I, on the other hand, am fine. Can you get me the American consul at Juarez? Have him come over to see me? If you can't get Blye released immediately, try to get us both transferred to Juarez."

"Don't do that, señor," Salazar said. "Best you stay here, nice and quiet so nobody knows what you are up to. I will have Don Pedro notify your authorities, and I believe your consul will be able to do some good."

"For a change," Sandrine said.

"I didn't say that," Salazar said.

"Could you also stop at the commandant's. Ask if I may meet with him."

"He's not a bad sort," Salazar said. "I sat next to him at a chamber of commerce luncheon a couple of years ago. He believes in keeping the peace so there is never a disturbance at all, not even anyone singing too loud at night."

"Tell him it would be my honor to talk to him if he would allow it," Sandrine said. "But don't quit on the other thing. Call Bryce Weeks at Jackrabbit Wells. Let him know where we are. Weeks will take care of the rest. Oh, yeah, better steer clear of here for awhile afterward. It might get . . . colorful."

Marlie went into Office Plus and ordered new business cards with the name changed to Marlo, not Marlie, with her new address and phone in Washington.

Clearing out. Down on the floor behind her desk, cleaning out the bottom drawer. Two executive secretaries who could not see her discussed her early return to work. She was back two days after the much-delayed burial. And people noticed her hard, cold anger.

"Brrrr," said Angie Fairweal.

"Yeah, creepy," Bama Miller said. "My girl died, don't think I'd be back for *months*. Oh, God, it must be so hard. Poor, poor soul. She's like in Kevlar."

"Don't think I've ever seen her cry," Angelina said.

"Me neither," Bama replied, then paused. "Her father's funeral. Years ago."

It would take far worse to break Marlo W. Braden, not to crush but *uncrush* her.

Blye sat up, a clean dressing on his ear, when the commandant himself, Oswaldo Rodarte, came back to see Sandrine.

Rodarte seemed very gracious, apologetic. He bowed, as to royalty.

"Until Mister Salazar informed me, I did not even know you were in here," he said. "Allow me to introduce myself, Oswaldo Rodarte." The cellblock noticed.

"Please let me pour you each a drink in my office," Rodarte said.

"I can't drink," Blye said, "and I sure can't walk."

"Blye, he's had a bad run of late," Sandrine said. "You might have someone call his pharmacy up in Lordsburg. You got that number, hoss? Blye needs his prescription."

Blye mumbled: "It's in my wallet, which they took."

"We'll get it, we'll find it," Rodarte said. "Better than that, we'll release you."

He motioned Sandrine to follow him out of the cell and across a grassy courtyard to his office. They sat. Rodarte poured a tequila for Sandrine, who waited for Rodarte to get his own drink up to his lips before tossing his own shot back.

"I tell you señor Sandrine, the charges against you are most serious," Rodarte said. "In fact, they are amazing: Resisting arrest, assaulting a police officer, destruction of public property, attempted murder, three counts, arson, let's see, conspiracy. Those line up with your memory of events?"

"First of all, my memory is crystal clear. I had not had one drink," Sandrine said. "This my first one today."

"Ha-ha-ha," Rodarte said quietly, so no one outside the room could hear.

"I'd love to read the report, find out how they came up with all this. Could I?"

"Certainly," Rodarte said, handing him the report, written in Spanish.

Sandrine read it quickly, then handed it back to him. "Very interesting. Could I have a copy of that for my own? I might need it if the case goes to court."

"Court?" the commandant laughed. "Why would you want to do that?"

"Clear the record. I wasn't in any bar—I was driving my Jeep. I wasn't even in Mexico. They came across and got us on Martin's ranch, as we were driving along that border road, on the US side of the fence. They did not identify themselves as police. They were not in uniform. We were unarmed. And we never set fire to anything."

"Yes, but you should never resist an officer. Why don't you just pay the bail like everybody else and go back home? I can give you reasonable assurances that nobody would ever reassert any of these excessive charges against you or Mister Blye."

"Can't we simply drop the charges if they're excessive?" Sandrine asked no one.

"I'd consider it," he said, "but the prosecutor would have to agree."

"You like coffee. Fifty pounds of coffee a year. Tires. You need new ones."

"Yeah, well, no, not now." Rodarte now was sounding a little guarded.

"A set of new tires in eighteen months. This is not bribery. It's not considered bribery, and it isn't bribery. Our compact provides for dignitaries exchanging gifts within a certain limit."

"Is this within the limit?" Rodarte wondered.

"Absolutely."

"What shall I give you?"

"That's a nice Casas Grandes replica you've got there under glass."

"How'd you know it's a replica?"

"Made with manufactured tools but made by descendants of the same Indians, using the same designs. It's pretty valuable. But if it were real Casas Grandes, you wouldn't have it here. You'd have it someplace with special security, maybe a vault."

"It's still called Casas Grandes."

"Nuevo Casas Grandes," Sandrine said. "Nuevo. Someone should have paid about a hundred-fifty dollars for this pot, which is very nice. And that Tepultepec serape is very nice, as well. You paid about fifty for that, or maybe thirty."

"Twenty-five," he bragged. "In trade."

Sandrine did not ask what got traded.

"Good for you. Very good. Well, that sounds like a very honorable exchange of gifts. You and I have the utmost regard for each other," Sandrine said.

The sergeant was ordered to prepare the release order and write a list of the gifts in case either of them forgot.

When Sandrine returned to the cell, he found Blye trying to walk gingerly around the perimeter of the eight-by-eight cell, holding onto the walls as he shuffled forward.

By the time they made it to the front gate, only one jailer was left on duty. He opened the gate without discussion.

"Where is everybody?" Sandrine asked him, speaking Spanish.

Blye waved both his hands, three four times: "Could we just get going? I can only take about three more steps."

The jailer offered Blye a wheelchair, which the jail kept for emergencies and court appearances by inmates who are no longer ambulatory. "Just return it when you're done."

"Could you call a cab?"

"Your vehicle is parked outside," the jailer said.

"Call us a cab. The Jeep's too rough a ride for Mister Blye."

"The cab is . . . there are no cabs."

"Rental car?"

"No rentals . . . unless maybe over by the airport."

"We'll just have to drive the Jeep, I guess. Where is everybody?"

"On a radio call up near the corner of what you call your Heel," the jailer replied. "Some kind of border violation, or invasion."

Sandrine looked at Blye with a warning in his eyes.

"Well, okay, good luck, then, bye."

The two men girded themselves for a rough ride in the Jeep.

"Wartime vintage sadly lacking," Blye said. "Not a gol-dinged thang to hang onto."

The beeper on his belt buzzed. The initials ONA 150-82 appeared on the display panel. It meant Weeks was pinned down inside Mexico, twenty miles southwest of Concha and northeast of Blye's boundary, about the same time that Sandrine was told. Only they had farther to come.

Weeks and Braden had crossed in at Jackrabbit Wells at about eleven in the morning. Weeks simply closed the gate and tacked up a note saying "Drive east to Concha." Then they headed east on Highway 2 toward the Llanos cutoff. Weeks knew the lay of the land as well as anyone. He'd driven it many times, clandestinely, as a "tourist." Weeks deputized Braden.

Belknap, sheriff of Frontera County, met Mann and Hartley at Playas. They left Hartley's Explorer behind the post office. They rode together in Mann's four-wheeler.

"You're sure you have clearance for this?" Belknap said.

"Renewed just six months ago. Only deal is, you will notice I'm not wearing a gun."

"Oh, *jeez*," Belknap said. "What do I do with mine?"

"Yeah, me, too," Hartley said.

"I'm not carrying any iron," Braden said.

"There's a lock box in the trunk, under the spare tire."

"You want to call the governor, or shall I?" Belknap said.

"You or Corona—where is Elias? Was he notified?"

"As much as any of us was," Belknap said. "He got the code alert."

Belknap left a recorded message with the governor's office. Somebody listened to it three days later.

The SUV stopped within sight of the border, and the officers dumped their every gun into the safe, and locked it.

Within fifteen minutes they were chasing along Highway 2, noticing a filament of smoke rising from an ejido up ahead.

The inside of an adobe was burning, and flames were venting up through the ceiling, burning so hot, they noted, that the straw in the bricks had burned through, opening little pinholes and fissures in the earthen walls, which generated an ear-piercing whistle and a much hotter fire. The adobe walls were crumbling, popping and toppling.

They could see a Border Patrol SUV parked at the base of a knoll and Bryce Weeks at the top, firing over and over again at federales who were hiding behind logs, fenceposts and scrawny cactuses scattered around the burning adobe. They had been hiding behind the adobe until it got too hot. A field of about one hundred feet separated the combatants.

The three lawmen and the rancher all looked to each other for a quick decision on who was to extricate Weeks from his heroic but untenable position behind a railroad tie atop the knoll.

Belknap was the youngest. He was elected. And he flew. Some of the federales started shooting at Belknap as soon as they saw his long, bony legs churning up the hill to where Weeks was dug in. But they all missed. One bullet shattered the timber in front of Weeks, though, and peppered him with little creosoted wood splinters.

Belknap knelt beside Weeks and said, "Look, Weeks, fun's fun. We got to pull back across the border."

Weeks, open-mouthed, was in shock. Defibrillating. Staring back at Belknap. Uncomprehending.

"Weeks, have you gone and got yourself shot?" he said.

Weeks kept staring.

Another shot crashed into the railroad tie.

"Nice little blind you got here," he said.

Weeks started nodding, as though agreeing with Belknap, and then he slumped over. Belknap dragged him down the back of the knoll, bullets flying overhead, then hoisted him onto his back, so the weight was pretty much centered.

The Mexicans seemed content to let the wounded *yanquis* retreat, particularly since none of the federales had been hit. That was an acceptable ratio. The invaders had been repelled or, at least, had returned to their side of the line.

Mann took the old dirt Mormon road that cut diagonally up from Llanos to Jackrabbit Wells. And halfway along it the four of them found the body of Guadalupe Ramos, nicknamed the Fizz.

He had been shot seven or eight times, his feet, knees and other places intended to deliver separate and distinct messages to the observer. The body was left to rot in an area where rotting occurred very rapidly, aided by insects, reptiles, amphibians and rodents, working their way up the food chain to cougars.

"Do we know this guy?" Mann said.

"I know him," Sandrine said. "It's Ramos. He once tried to take my head off with a pool cue in El Paso. We had an adult discussion and he agreed to sit down and behave himself. He belongs to Octavio Cortes. Or so I was told."

"Seems he offended someone grievously," Belknap said. "I've seen this degree of retaliation before. In warfare."

They took a bullet from the body for analysis and a Glock Nine found under him.

The wounded Weeks started the paperwork for early retirement. Had a ranch in southern Utah. Sandrine said he would set him up with a dozen cattle, and everybody else took up a collection and bought him a six pack, which they drank.

They ate stuffed chiles from the Karajan brothers' farm west of Concha. The farm sat on the border and was surrounded by bur-bling irrigation ditches that flowed coolly, beckoning entry. The canals were stocked with perch and trout. And the citizens of Carmelo, a small settlement near the northern corner of the Heel, came across through a convenience gate to go fishing. The BP would routinely stop them, question them and then leave them to their angling.

Nobody the agents spoke to knew a thing about the death of Guadalupe Ramos.

Give it a few days, he'd been told, and so Alderete was sitting on the banco looking out on the camposanto, with its colorful array of crosses and plastic flowers. Stone monuments of every size and degree of refinement, from smooth and professional-carved to coarse, homemade.

He was thinking about Juanito's funeral, how it would be, when the telephone rang on the bench beside him. He picked up on the second ring. The voice on the other end asked, *"What are you doing today, Don Pedro? Are you sitting on your porch feeling the pain of injustice? I've decided you have been wronged, after all. Let's make it right."*

Let's: As though it were partly Don Pedro's responsibility so he owed some favor.

"Who's this?" Alderete said, though he knew. He just wanted Octavio to admit it.

"Never mind who. Just look down, straight down from where you are."

"The camposanto."

"Specifically."

"The big cross. Red marble."

"Look right next to it."

"A grave," Alderete said.

There was no reply. There was not even the sound of hanging up. Pedro Alderete called Sandrine.

"I couldn't think of anyone else," he said, "so I called you."

Sandrine flew down with two cowhands and helped Alderete dig up the unmarked grave that had existed in the shadow of his house since New Year's. They found a body in such disrepair. But the color of the few remaining strands of hair, the alignment of the smile, now leering out, the still-small, boyish hands, told the grieving father

more than he needed to know. He looked tearfully across the rocky
hole to his friend leaning on a shovel. Sandrine tossed the shovel
aside and walked around the grave to wrap old Pepe in his arms.
"Going to start getting better now," Sandrine said.

They moved the body to the Juarez morgue for an autopsy. Five
gunshots. Nine millimeter and three-fifty-seven. At least two guns.

Now police had a mystery to deal with. Detectives asked Octavio
about his son, Miguel, who had vanished. Octavio told them the boy
was out of the country.

"What country is he in, Don Octavio?" one investigator asked
him.

"Not sure," Octavio said. "Maybe *Francia, España* or *los Estados
Unidos.*"

"You must know how to get in touch with him."

"Well, no, he's traveling. I may get a postcard from Rome, Italy.
But if I try to call him there, he's already off to Zaragosa or Malaga.
But he will be back."

"When?"

"I will let you know."

No clue who the guns belonged to. A shrug.

And then they moved Juanito's body back to within twenty feet
of where it had been found. The Alderete plot was ready. The priest
was ready to say kind things about a boy. The polished stone gave
the boy's name and age. It said only: "Gone too soon."

Marlo W. Braden got on the Metro at Green Belt and rode down
to Union Station. Grabbed a cappuccino. Walked to the Senate
Office Building, a sunny block south.

Deep-bending branches laden with cherry apple peach pear blos-
soms did calisthenics outside her window, bending low to the
ground—low enough if they'd had fruit, she could have picked it.
On her desk, a letter from Sid. She held it awhile, looking at the
scrawled return address, then dropped it, unopened, into her purse.
Not now, she thought. *Can't right now.* Back of her hand to her mouth.

Chapter Fifteen

Gila Sunset

The river sliced through the rocks like the silver blade it was forged to be. Then, it moved the pieces downstream. It did whatever was necessary to make a home for itself. For now, it formed a pool. That the rock was no more than solidified volcanic froth, lightweight, porous, helped the superheated water, invade, fracture and erode it away. The only real weight these rocks had was the water that soaked into them, the same water that then expanded or contracted or condensed or turned to steam.

Winter was a real rock breaker, cold on the outer shell of the rocks, hot inside. Sometimes pebbles would explode in the confusion, and pieces of them would fly around like shrapnel. Sometimes three or four would go off at a time. *Pop-pop-p-pop.*

No warm days yet, just warm water. The snow was glazed with ice where the steam had melted it and it had refrozen. A little wind blowing the steam away was enough to let the ice re-form. There were also patches of volcanically heated sandstone where snow never accumulated. There, the icy edge of the snowdrift was shiny white, like milk glass. It was treacherous—too slick-fragile to step on, razor-sharp when broken.

Raylinda, Todd Walker, Harlan, the battered Milt Everett, Phil Walsh and a muscular blond stranger whom Todd brought along from Gila Bend—Todd's boss—all had to walk almost all the way around the hot pool to a ledge just wide enough for one person to stand. There they could jump into the pool four feet below. She watched them walk, far enough away from the river's edge that the snow was still fluffy, wearing their boots. Except Walker. He was barefoot. He followed in their footsteps. And they lined the boots up at the foot of the ledge. Milt's body, especially his face, showed deep blue-black bruises from the brawl in Redsleeve. The bruise around his nose and eyes took the shape of lopsided goggles. And he limped. Utterboeck, too. He still had a bandage where somebody's signet ring initialed his jaw with an S. And Ted was absent today.

Only the stranger seemed to respond in those ways the others knew to avoid. He was attentive, solicitous, gentle, kind. She'd helped keep him from falling when he appeared to lose his balance slipping on the icy trail. Some wore swimsuits, some undies, some nothing. All six eco-warriors jumped into the water.

The current sent Raylinda sliding past the stranger like an eel, brushing him underwater. He stepped back. He was tall enough he didn't need to tread water.

"Sorry," she said.

"I see rocks over here," he suggested, pointing off to his left near the shore. She moved over to the sulfurous rocks and sat down at tub depth.

"Here's a warm spot," she said. "It's normally our stairway in and out when the ice isn't piled up like it is."

Currents shifted the warm and cold.

The blond man followed her. He sat beside her, hanging onto the rocks on either side of him to keep from slipping down to where he would begin siphoning nitrates. She arched her back, and her large belly broke the water's surface.

"So you're Todd's boss?" she said.

He nodded. "Chris Belleran."

She extended a graceful hand, which he grasped, she thought, sensually.

"I wanted to see the situation," Belleran said.

"The lay of the land?" she said. "Is that French, your name?"

"It once was," he said. "Grandpa came over before the nastiness." He was referring to World War II.

"I'm Raylinda."

A wind shear rippled the pines and showered the pool with dead needles, a few baby cones and some rabbit and rat droppings.

Utterboeck rose from beneath the water with a thatch of freshwater seaweed covering his head.

"I am Neptune!" he shouted, loud enough that a scattering of early-arriving finches left the overhead tree limbs. "I rule the waves!"

"Ain't no waves to rule. Sit down. Giving me a headache," Milt said.

"I'll give you some waves," Utterboeck said, submerging full force.

"Cut it out," Walsh muttered, but Harlan was under water, out of earshot.

These were her team, she thought, too embarrassed to say anything in front of their ranking visitor.

Another blast of wind crushed a corner of the milk glass and sprayed ice shards into the pool like little MIRV warheads, where they instantly melted leaving a slight oily scum on the surface. Utterboeck resurfaced, shivered in the wind, sank back in the soup.

"It's that time of year," Raylinda said, looking deep in Belleran's eyes. "It's trying to get warm, but the winter keeps fighting back. It's a turf war."

Belleran seemed happy to talk about the weather and himself, which Raylinda saw as a good sign. He worked for Raymond Feuerstein, founder of Southwest Eco-Net, the umbrella group that oversaw and mostly funded Wild West, Raylinda's local group. The wealthy Feuerstein would never appear in the flesh in New Mexico unless he had to, and then only under compulsively tight security—bodyguards for the bodyguards, bulletproof stuff, electronics everywhere, microcams hidden in jewelry, satellite tracking. There had been lots of threats, most of them spoken bravely in saloons. But occasionally one hit close to home. Feuerstein's four-year-old son came chauffeured to his doorstep from preschool just weeks earlier with an unsigned note pinned to his shirt: "I want to go far, far away." Even Belleran was cautious, but as long as Miss Wells traveled in such robust company, he felt safe enough.

"Speaking of wars," he began.

This has got to be it, Raylinda figured. She scooted over closer to him, so that her thigh touched his and her hand brushed his. But danged if Belleran did not, in turn, scoot away, leaving her hand resting on a pile of rocks.

Oh, she thought. *Oh-oh*. She wasn't getting through. It wasn't working. She looked at his pupils. Not dilated *at all*.

"It's really all about heat," she said. "Hot versus cold."

"Well, I'm talking about a smaller war, a lower profile," Belleran said. "I'm talking about your battle with these ranchers."

"We've got 'em on the run," she said. "We've abso-freakin'-lutely kicked their butts. They've packed up their herd. Next sound you hear will be the auction gavel."

"What I'm saying is I will hear that sound, but you won't," Belleran said.

She shifted her bottom, looking for a foothold, trying to stand, but there was none.

"After all I did?" she said. "You're . . . serious? I mean, um, you're n-not serious?"

"No, I *am* serious," he said so quietly nobody else could hear. "Time for Raylinda Wells to step back."

"Why?"

"It turns out to be time for a change. Things change. Missions are accomplished. Yours are. We all know the great job you did . . . the group you created . . . and named—"

"Blah-blah-blah," she said. "What about all the twenty-five-hour days, the confrontations, the threats, the *risks?* You weren't at Redsleeve when Milt got hurt."

"I was getting to that. It *is* like a war. Sometimes you attack. Sometimes you fall back. Sometimes you send in fresh troops. That deal at Redsleeve. That was ugly. Not what we want. *¿Comprendes?*"

"We never wanted violence. Somebody else did the same thing a while back and got away with it," Raylinda said.

"With no violence," he replied.

"Yeah, peaceful. So we figured . . . we . . . could. . . . It's Sandrine, isn't it," she said. "All the years I worked here, he never sent a dime. Him and his *cowboys.*"

Belleran faced her. His job was to ensure she understood. He had some doubts.

"Key difference," he said. "Sandrine *was* invited to that potluck in Redsleeve. Nearly went. Finally decided not to. Time wasn't right. Things take time—something Sandrine understands. He stayed away, as did every other environmental group but yours. But Sandrine did contribute large sums of money to the Wildlife Federation, which sent you a stipend last year. You may have noticed it sent you nothing this year," Belleran said, placing his hand upon her arm cautiously, so as not to inflame anything.

She turned away from him, looking for a shortcut to her clothes. The wind came up and raised goose bumps on her shoulders, and she slid down to where her shoulders were submerged and warm. She couldn't escape. She realized she had to face him.

"All Sandrine ever did was get in the way," she said. "Except for him, we could have driven every rancher off the wilderness by now. That grass would be growing tall. They ran to him with their Prayer of Intercession every time we had 'em on the ropes. They'd all be gone. The Bradens, the Endicotts, the Wellses, Greens, Brodys, Watanabes and all the rest of the Dirty Dozen."

Belleran tightened his grip on her forearm just a little. In his briefcase, back on the trail, there was a letter received that morning in Flag. From Sandrine. It told what happened to eight of twelve highly targeted ranchers scattered around the Apache Wilderness. Two sold out for less than they paid and moved to California. They went to work, coincidentally, in the aerospace industry, one as a security guard, the other as a fence contractor. One went to Gettysburg, Pennsylvania, and bought a motel.

"Five moved to Albuquerque, but one couldn't take it. Alonso Brody. He went in for a job interview at one of those HMO's. 'What can you do?' they asked him. 'Run cattle,' he said. They said they *never* treated patients like cattle. Obviously, Brody hasn't worked out his problem. He's back in Redsleeve, living upstairs over Maybelle Foliard's convenience store, still looking for work," Sandrine's letter said. "Most of those five live in mobile home parks and apartments. One moved in with his daughter and her family, promising to build them a thousand-square-foot addition onto their home so they wouldn't all be so crowded. That was a year ago. They still haven't got that addition started, although they have done some measuring."

Belleran wasn't actually interested in one-by-one examples of humanity huddled in mobile homes or apartments or double-bunked with their adult children, unable to afford the price of gasoline for a drive into the country to visit the rolling hills that used to surround them. *Hello, hills.* He was concerned, though, that the letter also went to every member of the House and Senate Appropriations and Budget Committees and several subcommittees overseeing natural resources.

"Just four ranches left," Belleran said. "You've done a great job. Almost a clean sweep. The rest of them will be gone, too, someday. There will be that season of auctions. And you will get due credit when history's written. There've already been blurbs from every eco-group in the country: *One soul's solitary battle for the land.*

"We want you to step back," he told her, "take some classes, earn a master's, a Ph.D., travel around the country speaking to little groups, like yours, Wild West, what a great name. Grow into the role of senior ecologist, the Jane Goodall of the environment."

"Wild West's copyrighted," Raylinda said.

"And we'd help you defend that copyright as a lasting legacy," he said. "Shoulder to shoulder." He leaned over, smiling, and fraternally rubbed shoulders with her.

But she was past rubbing anything with Chris Belleran. Now she knew who he was. Father Time, a ticking device, a slamming door.

Looking out his favorite window, an old wavy pane in the kitchen, Sid Braden saw the commotion down by the horse corrals and came half-trotting across the draw to get there before it was over.

A cowboy was busting the last of his green-broke mustangs, among the few remaining horses the Two Square crew was able to round up from the high pastures.

A couple horses were left up there above the tree line, a feral mare and a stallion that was also roaming loose. They were working together. As a team. Too smart and too quick for the cowboys and knew the land too well.

The marked-up Milt Everett reported their synergy to Braden at the end of the roundup. It was, Milt said, as if the ghosts of Redsleeves and his woman had come back as a pair of ponies.

"Aw, let 'em go," Braden told him. "Jest let 'em go."

"That's easily four hundred dollars worth of horse at the mustang auction, boss," said Philly Mondragon, whom Endicott sent along to help.

Another thing Philly didn't understand: Why did both the Endicotts and Bradens give work to Utterboeck and Everett, knowing they spied for Raylinda. "They're spies, boss," he said.

"Well, now that you've told me that, so are you," Braden said with a smile.

Philly didn't play football in high school, except out in the pasture with his friends or in gym class. Few norteños knew about the Everett-Utterboeck year, nine-and-oh, at Gila High. Followed by Everett's own greatest season of rodeo. Now Milt was scarred inside and out by some subliminal war they'd all found themselves in. That was something the ranchers could not forgive, although nobody'd ever hear them say it—contaminating those boys. But Braden knew that boys would do the damnedest things to get with a girl, and contamination wasn't usually considered a problem.

The best athletic talents Gila Wells ever produced were now looking to blow the whistle on anyone cutting trees, putting up fences, snowmobiling, taxidermy-ing, overgrazing. Poaching, too—Watanabe asked Sid if that included swatting flies.

If it bugged Raylinda, it did. And those boys got paid for reporting it. And they didn't mind trespassing to do it. Trespassing, to them, was one of those antique laws like *you shall not spit on the boardwalk*. They got cash for wolf *rumors* unless it turned out they made 'em up. And they weren't exactly clear on where it all was leading.

"Who's the fella bustin' this mustang?" Braden asked Philly. "He's good."

Mondragon shrugged. "He never said. He just slapped that saddle on and started ridin'."

Braden could tell the saddle was an antique of some value, but he'd never seen it before. On the back of it, the name *Twister* was tooled into the leather.

After the horse was gentled down, the rider slipped off his gloves and crammed them in his pockets while he walked across the corral to where Braden and Philly were standing.

"You don't remember me, I bet," the rider said, pulling off his big white hat.

"Yeah, I do," Braden said. "It's Theo Wister from the bank, isn't it? You sold us this place. How am I going to forget that?"

"Mister Braden, pleasure to see y'all again. Sorry we missed you last week. You and the boss set up an appointment today to draw up a chart? What's federal, what's state, what's private, how many waters, how many shacks, barns, sheds, *inferstructure?*"

"Pity we all didn't assess a little better *before* we bought, ain't it?" Braden said.

Wister's smile froze, but he understood. "Y'all know we had a *deal* with the Forest Service. It was a done deal. They reneged, not us. You know that," he said.

"Just beating up on myself," Braden said, "because I knew it would happen. I saw it like a TV show: You and the feds backing out on the deal, and nothing for me to do about it. The deal is *done*, all right."

"We just want you to know," Wister said, "how sorry all of us at the bank are about the way things turned out for you. Tragic. You were doing just great until they started pulling down fences. Not much to do when that happens."

"Yeah, but . . ." Braden smiled sourly. "You know the way this is going. I'm just the first in a line. Banks'll have hell to pay. Unless they're willing to renegotiate."

"Did you want to renegotiate? We'd have to see about that. Been making a study. Trying to zero in on the exact moment it all started to go bad. I think it was Vietnam."

Braden's eyes rolled. "I'm sure everybody's heard enough about Vietnam. I believe the book's closed on that chapter."

"Wouldn't it be nice," Wister said, "to put it behind us. I'd like you to reconsider."

"Won't reconsider, won't renegotiate. Want to sell. Let's get on with it. I don't give a good dad-gum about Vietnam."

"You should—you're fightin' that war, and those warriors, all over again and don't even know it. They found how to change the world and figured, 'Why stop?'" he said.

"Mount a horse, let's go take a look at the almighty Apache Wilderness," Braden said, "and best not use that green-broke stud. It's rough country. You might kill us all."

Wister took a bay mare named Sister. He wrenched himself around in the saddle so he could see to spin his yarns and deliver the punch line to each one of his listeners. An anthology of ranching deals gone bad—mostly bad for the bank, to his thinking—of disappearing debtors, co-opted collateral, fake investors and shadow *gangs*, never mind shadow corporations.

Like the time Wister sold a hundred thousand acres worth of federal allotments to a Mexican cartel in which none of the principals was a real person. Or the time he sold allotments to the John Muir Lands Foundation using money Raymond Feuerstein donated specifically for that purchase. The money, instead, bought the group a new office complex in California, and the bank never got the payout. All Wister's work on that one had to be erased, not just cancelled—the New West Museum in El Paso had to give back all the ranching artifacts, guns, the old saddles, tack and his smithy tools from the forge, from the sale that never happened. Feuerstein sued the Muir Foundation. It went to arbitration, and the group agreed to buy half the allotments the following year. By then they'd disbanded, and the office complex sat vacant in Palo Alto.

Wister could have gone on, and on, and on. With just that story alone.

Most of these yarns sure wouldn't entertain Braden—many a rancher simply going bust. Too familiar. Luck delivered the riders at Cerro Verde with a minimum of repetition.

"Can we ride up there? I want to see the wolf pens on the other side," Wister said.

"I'll ride around and meet you," Braden said. "Marquez'll go along."

"No, please, Sid. I don't go up there no more," Marquez said.

Wister had no idea why. Didn't know Braden's daughter had been briefly buried there. He could see Sid's anguish was a thorny thing, and he didn't pry into it. He spurred his bay up slope to the summit, took out his glasses and scanned the seamless sweep of the Apache Wilderness with its network of two hundred springs and streams—give or take a dozen or so that came and went seasonally—its little valleys, with independent grasslands, and the four historical hand-hewn corrals that former Two Squarers had erected eighty years before the wilderness was envisioned. Wister also saw the wolf pens—three of them bolted together in three separate canyons. Each square-mile pen would handle a family of four to six wolves, to be released separately over the next six weeks to six months. Then, he rode back down to intercept Braden, EdMarquez and Bertie Williams before they got too far around the mountain.

"Hey, wait up!" he yelled after them. They stopped. He spurred the bay to catch up.

"Look, we don't have to venture over there. I saw the condition. I could tell with my bi-nocs it ain't hammered, I can see that," Wister said. "And them pens—why, that's just a flat insult to ranching, to place the wolf pens on grassland pasture before they're needed. That in itself has got to be a violation of the Wilderness Act. You can't tell me they didn't use power tools bolting those pens together."

"Battery-powered," Braden said. "I think we should ride over there. I think you should see it close up."

"Long as we get up north," Wister said.

"We don't go up north much anymore, either," Bertie said.

"Bad memories," Marquez mimed to Wister.

Braden read his lips. He said nothing. His jaw line set a little straighter. That was all. He did need the money, or rather, needed to be out from under the debt. But he didn't care about that. Never even thought about it. To him, the ranch and Millie were simply part and parcel, one in the same, *e pluribus unum*. Since he never really talked to his daughter about such things—and it grieved him infinitely that she was afraid to debate with her father, who would have done anything for her, anything, *anything*—but since they hadn't *talked* and now she was *gone*, he had one option and that was to extrapolate.

Fill in imaginary blanks. So he simply had to leave. Tried to close his eyes, grit his teeth, bear down, strike out in one direction or another, flailing. He was blinded. Could no longer see the rough and rambling old place without getting heartsick.

Sometimes real estate can't survive a curse like that.

Wister had never seen so clear an example before.

He saw Sid Braden, of all people, head down, heart down. For the first time, Wister was thinking the bank might very well get stuck with this one. That could be trouble. There were over seven hundred other ranch loans in the Texas-Oklahoma Panhandles, southern Kansas and Colorado and across New Mexico and Arizona that seemed to be going into default. Wister knew that was on Braden's mind if the Two Square didn't sell. If Braden went, there was the danger the belt might snap from the weight of all the others. What, he wondered, would happen to those lands? Other than development, he meant. Banks had to sell to buyers with cash. That likely meant development. Then, who'd take the federal allotments and protect them? That question sort of hung there. He'd asked it again, over and over. It swung in the breeze each time.

"Well, you got to show me the deeded areas on the east and west," Wister said, but his tone had changed.

"That's right where we're heading, on the west," Braden said, sounding far away.

"Yeah, you saw the pens—well two of 'em's on our land, without our permission," Bertie said.

"Well, we'll just get that changed," Wister said.

"No, no, thanks," Braden said. "Leave her be. Millie would've wanted it that way. She would've taken that as an honor, and even though it comes too late and even though they did it dishonestly, without asking, I want it left alone, let it stand. Anyway, it's probably legal."

Wister nodded tentatively. "Well, Sid, all well and fine, but when time comes to sell—"

"Cross that stream if we come to it. I say *if* because streams have a way of disappearing up here," Sid said. "Don't follow a stream unless you know where it's leading. One of Pete Alderete's old expressions. The pens are temporary, short-term."

They rode up to the first of the three wolf pens, the one just occupied by a family of four wolves, two adults that were former Gila yearlings recaptured and then bred in captivity.

"Just circle around this one. You'll see where the survey stakes are marked with orange tape," Braden said, "and you'll see why they were anxious for us to leave, why they built up the elk population."

"Where are the scientists?"

"They're around," Braden said.

"Here and in their hotel," Bertie said. "Monica checked this morning. They're due up here fulltime tomorrow. They come and go. Left a message yesterday. They didn't call back. They're in the Oak Plank Lodge. It's a hundred fifty years old. Run by one family, the Ochoas, for that whole time."

"Maybe I should change my lodgings," Wister said.

"Nah, it ain't that good. Just *old* is all," Bertie said.

Wister got curious and focused on the baseline of the fence, wondering was there any way the animals might escape. The wolves had been placed inside this first enclosure about two weeks earlier. They were supposed to be monitored every day, but the Wolf Project had an illness and a delay in finding a replacement, and they checked it every day. But there were time gaps. He wondered if there were fence gaps, too. He turned and rode fence a bit. The base of the fence was well secured with dirt screws, steel spring-like screws that spiraled into the ground and held against the wind. On some slopes they'd had to cut the earth to fit the fence flush. Hard hand-trenching, he thought.

But . . . what the heck, he wondered, is *that?*

"Is that a pump handle?" he asked. S-shaped laying in the tall grass. At one end it had a square bit to fit over a valve head. And there was a wooden swivel knob at the other. He dismounted and was about to pick it up, but Braden shouted.

"Hold up there! Don't touch nothin'." He rode up. "That's no pump handle. It's a crank. Leave it be. I say it goes to a gasoline-powered generator, maybe war surplus."

"Definitely a crank, but I'm thinkin' a trencher," Wister said. "This forest, BLM, state or private?"

"Forest land, part of the Hidalgo National Forest. Right here's where my private land leaves off," Braden said. "It's the great Apache Wilderness."

"They put it in the wrong place and they used illegal tools to do it," Wister said.

"Yeah, if you wanted to make a fuss about it. I don't," Braden said. "This is how Millie would have wanted it. This is how it'll be."

"We really should protest this," Wister said. "New owner mightn't feel the same."

"What new owner?" Braden said. "You got a buyer?"

"I got a maybe," Wister said. "That's all I can disclose. Just a maybe."

"Sid, *maybe* we've got to take this crank back in to the district ranger, Maggie Carton, *maybe* show her what's *maybe* been goin' on up there," Bertie said.

"You think Margaret's going to cross the US Fish and Wildlife Service over a thing like this? You'd need witnesses, you'd need all the same evidence they'd use against me if it was the other way around. They'd say we planted it—did we?" he asked Bertie, who didn't *get* the question. "Leave it be. We'll report it. But leave it be."

Wister photographed it where it lay, Sid kneeling beside it.

It was dark as they rode into the Wells River corrals and unsaddled. The moon set early in thick black clouds. They could see Marlie in the lighted kitchen window. She'd come back, just for the weekend, just to get some of her things and to meet with Wister.

"I sure hope sis's cooked up something," Bertie said, unhitching his chaps.

"Don't want to make her cook tonight," Wister said, brushing off clouds of dust.

"Oh, yes, we do," Bertie said.

Marlie cooked just like their mom had. The food seduced Bertie's subconscious. Added to the fact that Bertie never understood why Marlie became Marlo, why she left.

The banker offered to take everyone out for dinner. But Sid and Bertie turned him down. Braden already had his boots off. Even Marlie seemed intent on one last go in the old kitchen—for nostalgia's sake.

"I've got these papers y'all need to sign," Wister said, "then I'll leave you."

Marlie emerged regally from the mud room and caught them all de-booting.

"I think you ought to stay to supper," she said.

Braden nodded agreement, grabbed Wister by the arm and shooed him into the chute. He went without digging in his heels—he was in his stocking feet.

"We can always sign the papers on the kitchen table," Wister said, grabbing for his hat that Braden had just plucked off his head.

Chicken-fried veal steak, chile, sautéed *new* potatoes, slaw. Then she set a pie in front of them and a knife and just let them decide how to handle it.

"What happens to this pie if we don't eat it?" Wister asked.

"It goes stale in about four days and gets thrown out. I made it for you, Theo," she said, "since we owe our last five years' livelihood to you. The least I could do—and my last chance to do it, *here*, at home."

Theo picked up the knife and cut himself a wedge. "Anybody else?" he said. Bertie raised his hand. Wister cut him an equal slice, and they ate it wordlessly down to bits of crust and crumb. Wister waited while Bertie finished, then put his plate in the sink and set his briefcase on the table.

"Law says we've got to handle this by sealed-bid auction. Pick a minimum, stick with it and take the best overall bid that exceeds the printing," he said, meaning the published minimum.

"Can we know who's bidding?" Bertie asked.

"No, you can't," Wister said.

"That's the law, Bert," Marlie said.

The out-of-work Bertie knew very little civil law. He even had problems remembering criminal law, for which Corona had fired him, twice. The second time looked permanent. *Failure to transmit a report.* Bertie was responsible for the brawl with the Neighbors, in Corona's opinion. He never notified the undersheriff. Said he *forgot*.

He was lost without his sister. And she was gradually moving out everything she owned. Preoccupied, confused. Bertie was lost.

"But you can know how many bids there are, and that can be a clue about your published minimum, if you ever get the chance to re-offer it later," Wister told him, adding gibberish to fill in the blanks.

"Why can't you just tell us who the 'maybe' is?" Bertie said.

"I'd be in for a world of hurt—you'd be messing with the US Justice Department, the Securities and Exchange Commission, the USDA, Interior Department, FBI, and every enviro lawyer from here to Alaska," he said.

"Don't care," Bertie said.

He grinned: "This auction, folks, will be the gol-dangdest thing yew ever saw."

Sid and Marlo looked across the room at each other. The room had never seemed so large or empty. As if the entire state of New Mexico—mountains, rivers, deserts and dead seabeds—stood between them in this one room. Marlo saw a man threadbare who didn't care if his final years were spare. That he would speak seldom, give little thought to his appearance and prefer the howling, sand-spitting wind to the company of people.

Of course he'd always been that way. He just wore neater clothes for awhile, to please her. She came with her own book of instructions, and he saw her just as clearly as she saw him.

They recognized each other, across the room, deep down into their hidden layers.

Chapter Sixteen

Mirage

They'd waited too long. Bad mistake out there in the sand. Too hot. And with the sudden desert heat the cicadas appeared like extras in the *Wizard of Oz*—flying armor *braaaaapping*, a deafening chorus of smoke-alarm klaxons all surrounding, spattering the sky, darkening the day. Two-hundred-twelve desperate people ducking and swatting. *Hell of a place*, they all thought. And they'd paid every last dime to be there on the border.

Camped between two abandoned buildings on the Mexico side, one of them a roofless bus stop, the other a remnant of jagged walls, they waited, waited. Nine days. Wondering: *Why are we waiting?* Every afternoon the truck that served as a bus came. And some of the people would give up and go back. But others would be dropped off. Two-hundred-twelve remained of three-hundred. For almost a week the truck had brought no food. For days no water. A gray-bearded stranger named Sandrine came finally one morning from the U-S side with bottles of water. By noon that same day, young Ricky Abeyta arrived from Rio Santo to say he was the Moses designated to take them across.

Now on the ground among the lizards and snakes, the teeming anthills, abandoned suitcases, discarded clothing, the human detritus of hasty departure, the refugees took their first steps out of a feudal world.

In threes and fours they stepped over the last strand of wire, the bottom strand, that remained on the border fence. They walked awhile, then they stopped awhile. The women knotted their shirts, ventilating perspiring midriffs, the men just took theirs off and abandoned them on chollas or chamisas for the wind to shred. They moved slowly, trudging in the gravelly sand, avoiding the snake holes and the cactus spines.

And then a murmur of uncertainty passed among them. They stopped and stared, hands shading their eyes from the ninety-three-degree sun, at some strange hologram in the distance. Almost a mile away, they saw the unaccountably tall Dave Belknap, walking across the desert, wafer-thin, blurry-wavy, riding the thermal refractions that rose from the warm sand.

The bad heat was early this year, and they gathered around a cactus to listen to Ricky, who swore he knew the way. Some of them prayed. With good reason.

But when in another moment they saw Belknap's equally disproportionate Suburban *ka-thumping* toward them across the clumps of yucca and chamisa like Pharaoh's chariot, that was sufficiently paranormal for them. They scattered like scarabs. The two-hundred-twelve, dragging backpacks and water bottles, did remind Belknap of the Israelites fleeing Egypt. But here the sea was a different kind of barrier without waves—except waves of heat-distorted light—and with a much larger portion of aimless nothingness. Yes, a Moses was still needed to lead them through.

Whatever the effect, as the multitude fled, Frey's three helicopters and three of his twelve Ford Excursions capped it, clattering in to help Belknap's last big "roundup." After today he was going back to his sheriff's office. Eighteen days of double duty was quite enough, filling in for the wounded Weeks. Frey owed Weeks a favor after helping him lose his job. After the Alamo, as Weeks' solitary stand got to be called, the debt doubled.

And while the crowd had camped along Sandrine's fence, waiting for their Moses, it was Sandrine himself, heading home along the well-bladed Llanos Road, who had noticed the crowd miles away and realized that these people couldn't stay there very long.

They would surely die. They had to move soon or be planted there forever. He brought gallons of water on the back of a flatbed truck, and he called Frey.

The Israelites were dragging those same plastic bottles when Frey and Belknap headed them off.

One of the multitude tried to disappear into a rocky drainage that led back to Mexico. Belknap caught him about twenty feet from making it back across. Ricky Abeyta, one of Octavio's coyotes. Belknap knew him. A sometime pistolero and courier. He normally wasn't this easy to find. Belknap couldn't imagine Ricky agreeing to such a messy decoy operation. Overkill with so many souls. Ricky knew the consequences.

"Gonna have to hold you as a material witness, son," Belknap said. "I know you know what that means."

Abeyta nodded sadly.

Belknap reset the tape recorder on his gadget belt, listened to it whine for a short spurt, then shut it off.

"I really don't know anything about anything," Abeyta said in educated, unaccented English.

"We've got plenty of time to figure out what you *do* know," Belknap said.

"I want Juan Reilly," Abeyta said.

"Don't we have your brother, Nicky, down in La Tuna? Am I right?" Belknap said, ignoring the request for legal representation.

Nicky Abeyta was serving ten at La Tuna Federal Prison in El Paso for smuggling aliens into the country. Weeks had put him there, and Belknap grinned his widest ironic smile.

"I'm going to credit your friend Weeks for this arrest," he said. "Juan *Reilly?* You haven't read immigration law very carefully.."

"I can pay."

"I know you can, Rick. I know it. But we don't have to let you hire a lawyer. How you going to hire him—*hmm?*—if we don't let you?"

"I thought you had to," Ricky said.

"We can just hold you and hold you, son, until you talk."

"What about?"

Belknap liked Ricky. The young man didn't pull a bunch of macho crap, trying to play smartass with agents or inspectors. He dealt straight when caught, his eye ever on the ball. He knew how to deal, when he had something to deal with.

Belknap could see that Frey had the rest of the operation well in hand. He'd separated the migrants into half that were to be turned back immediately to the douana at Santito and half that would be detained in Deming and El Paso for follow up that could end for them in federal prisons or in citizenship classrooms if any were to be granted asylum.

Scattered few had managed to slip through, but they were at serious risk in the dry heat.

"Why'd ol' Octavio set you up like this, son?" Belknap said.

"I have no idea. I do as I'm told."

"Any of your pals have other assignments as part of this op?"

"One of them, I think, was supposed to carry a load across at Four-Wheel."

"Who'd that be?"

"Don't want to say."

"What the hey, kiddo. We catch him we know him, we don't he's outta reach."

"Yeah, it's Albert Ortega."

Belknap, watching as Frey loaded his SUVs with about ten people each, flicked on his hand radio and waited until it stopped crackling. Then he called Frey and the Concha station simultaneously. Frey turned around and acknowledged with a wave.

"Adelberto Ortega is crossing with cargo at Four-Wheel," Belknap advised. "Copy?"

"Yeah, I got it," Frey crackled back at him.

"What's he—or *who* is he taking across?" Belknap asked Abeyta.

"Probly dope. They don't tell us," Abeyta answered.

Four-Wheel was an otherwise nameless crossroads in the sand where really good tire treads were necessary and many tire tracks were visible. Someday, Belknap imagined, somebody, probably Octavio or his heirs, would put a tire store right on that very spot, which had so much traffic it looked like a daily motocross ran there.

The fence at Four-Wheel was peeled back on both sides. There was a road there. Unpaved. But a road.

Albert had probably already driven through and almost certainly by now was on Interstate Ten, halfway to wherever. And both Belknap and Abeyta knew it.

"That's a good-faith gesture," Belknap conceded, "but it really gives us nothing, you know."

Abeyta acknowledged with a nod.

"Why would Octavio sacrifice such a large group, such an easy target?" Belknap asked him. "Why wouldn't he save them, spread them out the way he usually does?"

"I don't know. I've been wondering that, myself," Abeyta said. "Maybe he just ran out of time with the early sunstrokes and all. Maybe he just had to move them and waited too long."

"Heard any rumors about Octavio?"

"Oh, dozens. Half of 'em mistakes. Somebody gossips. And, you know, gossip migrates. It evolves into rumor, then it becomes Don Octavio's rumor."

"That leaves what—a dozen stories or more that aren't misapplied? They could make a TV series," Belknap said. "What about Ramos?"

"We never bother checking them. They're rumors. They're all crap."

"Give us a sample."

Abeyta frowned for a couple of seconds.

"Oh, that Don Octavio's going into the mining business at the worst possible time."

"*Really?*" Belknap said.

"Bought some place in New Mexico. Wants to buy land in the United States. To spend every spare dime on it."

"A dime goes a long way here in the Heel," Belknap said, "'specially in real estate."

"Especially in *mining* real estate," Abeyta said. "He's buying copper leases. They're coming onto the market faster than he can buy."

"Tennessee Copper is closing smelters, mills, mines, closing whole towns," Belknap said. "Why's he buying?"

"Probly isn't. Probly bullshit."

Belknap nodded, opening the door of his Suburban and offering Abeyta a seat.

"Need some water?" Belknap had a cardboard crate full of eight-ounce Poland Water bottles in the back.

"I will in awhile. Thanks." He took one of the bottles.

"Other interesting rumors? Ramos?"

"Where's this all leading?" Abeyta said. Odometer check.

"You know."

Abeyta nodded. "Well, word is Ramos got hit by the Costillas, but nobody believes it."

"Why not?"

"Because there was already a rumor that Octavio shot Ramos himself, personally, half a month before his body turned up."

"Which do you believe?"

"Well, nobody believed Ramos had been shot until the body turned up. Then they believed."

"I guess they would."

"Yeah, shot what, six, seven times?"

"Nine, with a nine."

"Very symmetrical," Abeyta said.

Belknap nodded, and made a circle with his finger that meant *Keep rolling*.

"That sort of gave rise to nobody believing the story that came out later, about the Costillas. And you know about the Costillas."

"You mean you heard they left the area."

"We all heard that, yeah. Haven't seen 'em since last year, actually. Heard they moved to Kansas or Oklahoma."

"They're still around," Belknap said.

Abeyta's eyebrows shot up. Belknap was trading with him. Encouraging.

"Where?" Abeyta said.

"You want their address?"

"Okay."

"Forget it."

"Okay." A little deflated but still interested. "Assume Octo did shoot Ramos, the Fizz."

Ricky nodded.

"Why would he?" Belknap said.

Ricky shrugged.

"C'mon, Ricky."

"I dunno, man."

Belknap gave him the barbed-hook look and rattled his handcuffs on his belt. "Jingle bells," he said.

"Jesus, I dunno."

"Was it for killing Pete Alderete's boy?"

"Doubt it. Nito had just threatened Octavio."

"That right? Walked right in and mouthed at him?" Belknap said.

"I wasn't inside, but I heard about it when Nito came out, yeah. I saw him carried out and dumped. He was laughing, going *'wheee!'* Ramos and a couple other goons didn't think it was so funny. They roughed him up a little before they dumped him."

"So Ramos did kill Nito?"

"Everybody says so."

"And Octavio had Ramos killed?"

"Maybe not. Nito also stood up to Ramos that night in the Jalisco."

"That's *it?* Stood up?"

"They say Nito was connected." The rumors were flowing like the Gila now. *Careful.*

"To who?" Belknap said.

"Whom," Abeyta said.

Belknap nodded patiently. "I talk ungrammatical sometimes, assuming you guys don't understand grammatical, okay?"

"Sure, fine." Abeyta unscrewed the plastic cap from the water bottle and took a swig.

"Who to?" Belknap repeated. "*Quién?*"

"Costilla. Who else?"

"I thought you were gonna tell me about the Cali cartel."

"Old man Costilla himself. He was his godson."

"So Alderete senior is hooked in?"

"No, they were friends. In school. Before."

Belknap gave him a long, impatient stare that finally jogged Abeyta's memory.

"Oh, yeah, and Nito came at Miguel."

"Came at? You mean, with a weapon?"

"No weapon. Unarmed. Just came at him."

"You mean like walked across a room toward him."

"More or less."

"Sheesh."

"There are degrees, dude, you know. Degrees. Ramos believed he was gonna stab Miguelito, only Nito didn't have a knife."

"He walked across the room and Ramos shot him."

"You pretty much nailed it."

"At the Jalisco."

"Sí, señor."

"Don't give me that campesino crap. What the hell are you doing over there—informing for the DEA?"

"Making a living, making a buck."

"I don't buy it."

"What, that I'm making a living?"

"That Ramos shot a guy in a public place for nothing more than walking across the room. Gimme."

"What?"

"The whole freaking Friday. You were there, right?"

Abeyta hesitated. Handcuffs rattled like wind chimes.

"Miguelito laughed. Nito didn't like it. That's all."

"Laughed at Pepe Junior?"

"No, laughed at a joke one of the pistoleros told."

"Which pistolero?"

"Ramos, I think."

Now two large olive drab buses, borrowed from the National Guard, swung in from the highway. The other hundred-twenty immigrants filed onto them, and they left. Abeyta and Belknap paused until the noise of the engines and gears faded a little.

"You were there, right?" Belknap repeated.

"No, I wasn't there."

"Who was there that told you?"

"Nicky."

Belknap turned and faced him, eyeball to eyeball.

"Hear me. You both could walk if you talk," Belknap said.

"Or?"

"Neither."

"I can ask him. You mean a new life and all that?"

Belknap nodded but said nothing.

"I want something more substantial than a nod," Abeyta said. "I'd like it in writing."

"It will be in writing when the time comes, son. When the time comes. In writing with our thanks."

"Why do you care?" Abeyta said. "I don't think Nicky knows anything you need to find out."

"If he was just there, we can leverage the rest of the story from everybody else he saw there, if we have to put a wire on him and send him back to Santito."

"You'll never get him back. He won't do it."

"I know. But he can find out, and he can tell you, and you can tell us."

The sky was starting to fade into the yellow mushroom glow of dusk. Belknap started the Suburban and edged it onto the border road.

"Best clear to the paved road. Just keep in mind, with Nicky, two choices. Both in or both out. In or out."

"No wire."

"Talk to him."

"Walk if we talk."

"Yep."

"Green card."

"Yes."

"Permanent resident."

"Yes."

"Civil service job in Burque."

"No way, kiddo. Dream on. What you want witless protection for? Get your own job."

"But we get some whatcha call it—seed money?"

"An apartment, first and last months paid up. That's it. Okay? That's it."

"For each of us," Abeyta said. "Two apartments."

"One. Just one."

"Why do you want this stuff? What could you *do* with it?"

"Stuff we need to understand, to make the world go round."

"I'll talk to him. But I tell you. This is a crappy deal."

"Listen, Ricky. Your daddy."

"Yeah?" Ricky sounded wary.

"He always wanted something better for you. How come you don't do better?"

"Jesus, bring on Father Freakin' Flanagan. I'm doin' okay," Ricky said. "Really. I am."

"Shit," Belknap said, turning onto the paved highway that got them into Concha right around dinner time.

Belknap turned in his BP hardware, the hand-held radio unit, the cuffs, the Mace belt with its many gadgets, beeper, tape recorder, rubber rounds, all the stuff that Congress dictated. Then he got back in the Suburban and headed north to his own office and lockup. He'd told Eric Grande, the port commandant, "I'm keeping Ricky 'til Will has a shot at him. They're the ones need to talk. Let me borrow that cell phone."

"What for? Boss'll kill me if I run over on minutes."

"What type commandant are you?" he asked Grande, staring

him down. "Afraid to show Frey the bill? Send it over. I'll pay it. You been using it to call your girlfriend, eh?"

Grande gave him the phone. Belknap carried the phone out to the car and handed it through a slightly open window to Ricky Abeyta.

"Call him," Belknap said.

"You can't just call into a federal prison," Abeyta said.

"Give me the freakin' phone." Belknap dialed, nine-one-five, then the number he had for La Tuna. A woman answered.

"Need talk to Nicky Abeyta," he said. "This is Belknap."

In about a minute, somebody was handing the telephone to Nicky inside his cell.

Just up the hill it was still wintry, though. Mann awoke. He was alone. It took a moment. The fire in the potbelly nearly dead. He lay there, focusing the will to pump the bellows onto the coals with sticks of kindling, wondering what time was it—and what an unholy mother of all drags it would be if it were only two or three. Then, he recalled, you face the prospect of trying to get back to sleep. Might as well just stay awake.

Every step he had taken to this day had been manipulated and misled by just about everyone, from his own federal bosses' assurances right on down to the suspects and whoever was in between. Todd Fertig from the FBI telling him what a great job he was doing. Meaning what? Lifting their load? Been chewing on that for days. Reporters calling. A few dropped out of the sky in helicopters wanting to know exactly how the "wolf girl" had died. Are they wolf killers? Did she know too much? Are they terrorists? Child molesters? They always wanted to know if there was sex. And why no information.

Mann groped in the dark for the bellows that hung on the peg behind the stove and for the kindling that he kept in an old washtub beside the stove. Kindling running low. He tossed in a few shavings and topped them with the last of the thin-sliced shakes. Less than a minute fanning the coals got those shims ablaze. He added two logs, then slid back under the quilt his mom had made for him.

Oh, yeah, and carving bullets so they'd fragment: More manipulation. People assume it's cruelty or deadly intent. It's merely more efficient, harder to decipher.

The bullets that killed Mike Samuels were carved, too. Fired at close range. But the salvageable one had been encased in bone. Flattened from the outside in, rather than spread and split. That bullet had held together. Mann had seen it on Weeks' keychain sealed in plastic. A plastic relic dangling from Weeks' ignition.

Mann patted the sides of the potbelly gauging the heat. Not much. The twin "pilot" logs were blazing but would die back soon. Mann added six more logs. Found his watch on the bedstand. Five-thirty. Ought to be a thin red line on the horizon, outlining the Black Range off to his east. He looked out the window. Still black. Give it another half-hour.

Often he had seen Weeks hold that little plastic talisman, look at it, turn it over and over. Waiting in restaurants, in elevators, in Mann's office. The cross sliced into the bullet head, it was surprising it had not broken apart.

None of the slugs fired at Mann up on Cerro Verde had been carved. Nobody carves a thirty-thirty round.

Everything placed on that mountain was fake. Even the footprints.

Mann had to admit he might be OK as a tracker but was really no detective. He was no cop. More like a spy, behind the scenes, behind the lines. He had to ask himself why Marlo Braden wanted him on the case. She'd told him: "I want someone I can trust."

But trust him to do what? Foul up the case? Sara, his doctor lady, had told him more than once. *You're doing fine. It's coming together.* But how could she tell? He had no evidence that wasn't fake, so where was the evidence it was coming together?

It got so when reporters kept referring to Millie as the "wolf girl," Mann just let it pass. He found them, pens ready, recorders whirring, peering in his office door. Then they followed him home. He told them: No evidence connecting Millicent Braden with any wolf shootings. Just coincidence. She'd been *like* the wolves, *like* the land. Isolated, vulnerable, in need of protection. Coincidence not selling. Symbolism moved no newspapers. Stole no viewers from Channel Twelve. He told them and told them, then stopped telling them:

Somebody with a two-forty-three shot two wolves. Somebody with a thirty-aught-six shot a third wolf. A twenty-two dart nicked a fourth one. Poisoned it. And once, no more, a camper shot a wolf with a thirty-eight pistol in the dead of night while taking a leak. Millie seemed to have been shot with a nine-millimeter, the hollow-point slug so badly fragmented the techs never could weigh what was left and get it all the way to nine. Always one tick short. Pieces almost fit, suggesting nine or so.

The FBI sent a team down. He dared hope they'd fire him. But they came not to investigate but to set up perimeter surveillance for the wolves. Cameras covering every approach to the "live" pen, the one with wolves in it. Fertig tried to help Mann. The agency, through its Quantico lab, analyzed and profiled the shooters, echoing what Mann already knew. People shot wolves for political reasons. The wolves, innocent animals, were being sacrificed by both extremes, those willing to shoot and those willing to provide targets. In the middle were very few who cared whether wolves were released, but they really didn't want them shot.

The FBI profile came in a large brown envelope. Thirty-two pages. It offered the view that people, in the name of God or nature, manipulated wolves for human reasons. It was like kidnapping for ransom, the white paper said: *People are killing wolves. We need your help. We need your contribution.* Both sides could use that same brochure.

Also, people circulated the idea of a child's sacrifice—for the wolves. It completed the circle. Felt so good they wanted it to be true. Felt terrible that it might be true.

FBI profilers wanted to look at Clay Endicott. He seemed odd to them, especially considering the gold locket, which, they speculated, Clay might have obtained for Millie. No indication how. Mann got his other ear bent about FBI weirdness. Over-polished shoes, over-pressed under-budget suits. Some wore suits in the forest, knights with shiny seats.

"If they can ban a generator, they sure as Shinola ought to ban suits," Vern Laughlin told Dolly over huevos. A good line like that, originating at Dolly's, would run through town faster than wildfire or CNN.

Clay, a self-conscious and un-athletic teen, had no head like his dad's for managing a hunting ranch but was gifted with horses and cattle. He'd loved Millie but was embarrassed she was two years younger. He took some teasing. He'd turned fourteen. She was twelve. He self-shielded, flinched, turned a shoulder. Copped out. Knew he wasn't smart enough—not for her. Even though older. Someday she'd leave, he knew. She was a friend, patient with him. He felt guilty for the shoulder, the denial. Millie never knew it. He'd get a goofy half-frown, voice trailing off, eyes unfocusing, seemingly lost either far away or deep within. She thought he was funny.

The profile found Garza volatile, dangerous. One day riding in triumphantly like Caesar. Antique silver-studded saddle. Slick hair, black boots polished. Sun beaming. Then sudden departure. Jaime Garza *gone* changed the equation. *He'd* listened with penetrating eyes that didn't wander. *He'd* heard her. Either way, Clay's weird.

He thought: *They get paid for this?*

Mann put a pot of coffee on the potbelly, now clanking with heat, and watched the sun edge the mountains under a canopy of gray. He wanted to quit, and he had his list of reasons to quit always ready. Add FBI. Oh, yeah, and add auction anxiety.

The Neighbors, the enviros, the real and the want-to-be cowpokes, the locals and the faraways, the rich and the wishful, the purported miners all said they wanted to buy out Braden. The Forest Service and Fishy Wildlifers were flustered: What's to become of the trees? Too many trees too thick, all agree. But do we cut them or burn them? And if we cut them, can we make lumber from them? What of stewardship? Will beds-and-breakfasts take bites out of mountainsides? He sighed.

Focus on today, he told himself. It could be good. He had a well worn Glock from a dead pistolero. Mann promised not to get slurped into the widening vortex of speculation. He liked the hardness of that Glock, the cool, burnished actuality of it. When it pointed, it was a line to somewhere certain. You'd be a fool not to look there.

Weeks, recuperating in Gila Memorial, mentally prepared his exodus for Utah. Mann waited politely until six-thirty before calling him. Weeks, tangled in his intravenous tubing, caught the call on the second ring. Mann told him he couldn't leave the jurisdiction carrying evidence from an open homicide. That woke him. They planned ballistics tests. Eyebrows up. *A Glock*, just recovered.

Weeks was awake, alert, ready to drive to Albuquerque and stand over the techs while they fired the gun.

"I've got the bullet they need for comparison," Weeks said, rapid-fire. "I'm taking it to them. Got to. You can see that. Just tell me where you got the gun."

"Know Ramos?" Mann asked.

"Yeah-h-h-h. A little shit, likes to play vicious."

"Put it in the past tense, Weeks. He's dead. Found several days ago. Dead awhile. Just off Highway 2. North of Llanos. Just about when you were nailed. The gun was with him. Little doubt it's his. It has his prints. The bullets have his prints. It fit his shoulder pack, the way the leather formed around it."

"I want that gun," Weeks said.

"Let it go, Weeks," Mann said. "You got *your* life to live, especially if the Ramos gun checks out with that enshrined bullet you're carrying. It's done. Let it go. It's obsessive."

"You weren't there," Weeks said.

"Hartley's leaving this morning to take the gun up to Albuquerque, in person. If you could persuade your doctor to release you, I suppose you might ride along."

"Doctor, my whatever," Weeks said.

"But forget the gun. You can't have it. You won't get it. Why do you want it?"

"I'll call him."

Mann blew steam walking out to the barn, but he sensed the day would be warmer. He checked his latigos to make sure they were still strong enough to hold a rain slicker on the saddle if it rained and to carry his brush coat if he had to take it off. Latigos rot with time, but these were fine. Lady was alert, as she knew survival required. She was sharp.

Mann loaded her into his two-horse trailer and hauled her up the hill to where the paved road ends and the locked gate marks the boundary of the Apache Wilderness. The red-letter Forest Service sign warns against motorized intrusions and lists penalties including prison and fines. He unlocked the gate and backed Lady out of the trailer, then led her through the gate and relocked it. Most people just stepped over or under the single-beam gate or walked through the narrow separation between it and a lopsided ponderosa that was worn smooth by passing hikers. The lower branches had been sheered off. But the opening was still too narrow for Lady.

Just one last look at Cerro Verde, and he spurred the horse up through the place where the rock cracks open, past the place where the sun paints the eagle in shadows, usually in the late afternoon, and up higher still to the place that leads into the mountain. Trails used by Redsleeves, Victorio, Nana and later Jerome, even though Jerome was Mescalero from a hundred miles east.

Misdirection. It was a ploy so old even the Apaches can't remember where they learned it. Ask, and they tell a dozen different versions of who, when and why.

Who, when and why was still the question.

The truth: That's what was really buried on top of Cerro Verde.

This time no gunshots, just an occasional lightning bolt off to the northeast in the Blacks. The wilderness was in an area where the storms cycled up from Mexico on a wheel that geared with the northern wheel cycling storms down from Canada. The storm track in between the two wheels squirted the weather eastward.

He tethered her at the summit, and reversed his initial grid search. Nothing had happened up here but a recent visit by a lone rider. That would be Wister, he imagined.

The auction option made Mann nervous. The whole balance of the border could be thrown into turmoil and chaos. *Somebody needed to step forward.*

Then Mann returned to the place where the earth was still disturbed, where Millicent Braden, budding biologist, had been buried. He took the gardener's hand-cultivator from the saddlebag and began combing through the loose earth where the child had been found.

There were rocks mixed in the powdery, sandy soil. There was another fragment of gold chain, possibly from the locket. There were two pennies, possibly from her pockets. Nobody ever quite finished the search that should have been done. Each of the rocks seemed to match the volcanic uplift called Cerro Verde. They were black basalt, sheered off in the violent mountain-jutting and edged with the red-brown earth they had stabbed through.

They ranged from the size of a sand pebble to a Brink's truck. The tiniest was curved, twisted like the molecule of life. Twisted like metal.

Mann picked it up and looked at it more closely. Those umber-sienna stains were a bit different. They had granulated, separated, unlike iron or any other oxide, he thought, pursing his lips and thinking dark thoughts about his abilities as an investigator.

And he guessed he'd be heading up to Burque tomorrow along with all the rest of his team, once again bringing up the rear. He was looking at blood.

Sid Braden sat down to write a letter to Marlie. But what could he say? He was thinking back again, as he often did, on how they met. Rodeo. Teen-agers competing in a rough and tumble high school rodeo. With sex going on under the bleachers.

She was a barrel racer. He was a calf-roper and bronc and bull rider.

She was a cook. He was an eater.

She was beautiful, wore elegant clothes she'd made, herself. He wore jeans with patches on the seat, patches on the knees, and wrinkled shirts with frayed collar tips, frayed elbows, frayed cuffs. She kept everything spotless. He left socks, underwear, beer cans and paper plates with old pizza crusts scattered.

She listened to Ravel, Sibelius, Mozart, Beethoven, Albinoni, and she rotated it. He, on the counterpoint, kept one CD in his changer for months, always Alan Jackson, over and over and over. He had two Alan Jacksons. Alternated. Half a year each.

For all that, just one thing separated them. They reminded each other of Millie.

Mann drove into Redsleeve to pack. But Doc was gone, the place all locked up. He waited in the unmarked driveway and finally saw the solitary figure in turquoise running sweats come over the last little hill, jogging with a slight shuffle, her feet barely leaving the ground. She turned in at her driveway and passed him. Mann followed her up the four-hundred-yard-long ribbon of gravel to her parking area.

Doc stood at the door bent over, huffing, and motioned Mann inside.

"Where's your car?" he asked.

"My car's over at the Sixty-Six getting rewired," she said. "Come on in."

"You should get a new car," he said.

"I like the one I got," she said. It was an old BMW.

"I've got to get unsweated," she said.

"How far'd you go?" he said.

"The usual 10K. Six miles plus a dot com."

She pulled off her shoes and socks and threw them across the room out the door into the laundry porch, where they bounced off the side of the washing machine with a metallic thump.

"Nice shot," Mann said.

She wiggled her toes. "A drink?" she said.

Mann suddenly felt uncomfortable. He shook his head.

"Look, Mann, you're here because there isn't anybody else out there for you," she said. "Why would you imagine it's any different for me?"

"It's just this case," he said. "They finally give me a case, and I think maybe I screwed it up. Not solving it. Not solving anything. Since I came aboard, more people have died in this one month than in any three-month period of history. All I want to do is go back home and climb a mountain."

"You want to finish it, though, don't you," she said. "Say where home is."

"Yeah," he said. "It's here, home, and I do wish this case would end honorably."

"You couldn't leave it unfinished. I *know* you. You couldn't."

"Yeah."

She threw her sweats into the laundry room and stood there in her undies.

"Want to help out a little around here?" she said, unhooking her bra and pitching it, as well. The bra landed on the kitchen floor. Mann stepped over, picked it up and flipped it into the open Maytag washer.

"What help did you have in mind?" he asked.

"Do my laundry?" she said, peeling off the final garment and handing it to him.

"Later," he said. "Too small a load wastes water."

"Oh, you're always right," she said, stepping toward him.

And he stepped the same distance toward her. Choreographed. Like a mechanical creation, Santa and Mrs. Claus or the Munchenkinder clock.

The collarless wolf worked her way south and then east along the northern rim of the Mogollon Mountains, then north again toward Braden's Hot Creek, called Ojorito.

She ate a rabbit now and then, and found a bighorn sheep up on the eastern slope of Old Granite, right at about eight-thousand feet. Meantime, the radio trackers were reporting that she was a likely fatality based on the fact that her transmitter hadn't moved in more than a week. They'd searched for her, assuming her body would be somewhere near where the signal originated. They hadn't found the body or the collar, and they hadn't reported any of it because they didn't want a stir.

They didn't want to release anything to identify the wolf, and they wished they'd never named her Millie.

Didn't want to have to explain why a wolf they announced would remain forever safe in captivity was loose and probably dead. Wolf USA's Michelle Westover had given assurances Millie was in a holding pen, based on a colleague's incorrect report.

Westy took the splash. "She will always be protected," Westy had said.

Donald Badderly, her British overseer, told her: "Best not get too glib about these wolves. We don't know Jack Flash about them. They just love to make us look idiotic."

"Speak for yourself, Badly," Westover replied.

"I do speak for myself," he said, "because I would not wish to be called upon to do *your* explaining for you."

Chapter Seventeen

Witness to Silence

Nothing funny about it that Ricky Abeyta could see. They kept asking him: "What was the joke that got Ramos killed?" How could that even be called a joke?

Sheriff Dave Belknap and Mann circled around Abeyta in an interrogation room at the Concha Jail. The prospective witness sat on an oak chair pulled up to a metal table with a rubber coating on top. Mann was there as a courtesy in the unlikely event of a break in the unsolved, month-old federal case, and Sid Braden, father of the victim, was stashed behind the observation wall. Belknap had agreed to help, kind of off the record.

There was no one-way mirror window in the wall. *Door* peepholes, a cheap alternative, were stuck in the wall for observers. They were too close together. Observers really had to cozy up to use both. There was plenty of space otherwise, though. Big room. Almost as big as the interrogation room. Frey and Braden watched through the peepholes. Bryce Weeks stood behind them. Braden and Weeks took turns watching.

Braden saw into Abeyta. Saw desperation, fear. Abeyta knew little or nothing, but did know people who might have information. It was a complex negotiation because Abeyta was afraid. He needed to convince others to talk. Couldn't even convince himself.

Frey, Border Patrol agent-in-charge, was waiting to question Ricky about his border diversionary. Because the crew found tracks and talked to people who said they saw Octavio's best coyote, Adelberto Ortega, escort a man in a suit while the two-hundred decoys sweated twenty miles west. The Agency had questions that Frey would ask. Neither Belknap nor Mann knew the migras had requested Agency observers. Then Frey's phone played "Pop Goes The Weasel" behind the wall, and Abeyta snapped around.

Weeks had his right arm in a sling, and his upper body was in a thin molded cast, with his left arm free. But he was walking, for the moment at least, and he was impatient.

"Let me ask him something," Weeks muttered to Frey.

"It's Dave's show," Frey said. Weeks knew that was untrue. It was Frey's show.

Abeyta sat silently for nearly ten minutes looking at the rubber surface of the table and shaking his head. They could see he was chewing on the permutations.

"You'd get me killed," he finally said. "I can never go back. See that? *Never.*"

"Nobody's saying you have to go back," Belknap said soothingly.

"But you ain't no federale, Dave."

"I am," Mann said.

Abeyta blew out a gust of disdain. "Freakin' BLM ranger, I don't *think* so. Anyway, your case has nothing to do with me."

Frey's cue to jump in. He knocked. Mann let him in. He nodded at Abeyta, then drew the two interrogators aside and whispered: "FBI's sending Fertig and a federal prosecutor. Take them another half hour. Suggest we break for lunch now so we're ready for them. Sid's got an appointment with an auctioneer. Probably best he gets going."

Frey said nothing about the case, but Abeyta was starting to dream of a federal payoff, maybe even a monthly stipend. Frey also said nothing about the agency observer he'd been told was coming. That must be Bulwer, the assistant US attorney.

Fertig was coming up on Nutt, a little farming crossroads. Gas station. Convenience store. Farmhouses set back beneath gnarly cottonwoods with tire swings hanging and bicycles leaning. Bus stop. Post office. Usually took Fertig five seconds to clear Nutt, lights flashing. He'd count: One, two, three, four, five. Unless some trucker failed to pull over, he and Bulwer, were through it. From there to Belknap's office it was a straight shot through farmland, pecan orchards, chile, onion, bean and alfalfa fields.

Belknap didn't want to break for lunch.

"Sid came all the way down and deserves whatever we can give," Belknap said.

They didn't know Bulwer's Agency connection. To them, Bulwer seemed interested in Abeyta purely as a prosecutor. Typical, they thought. The US attorney in Albuquerque, Roberto Maes, wanted a free flow of information, especially to him, via Bulwer. Not that he didn't trust cops. He did. His desk-top motto: *Trust But Corroborate.*

Mann suggested Frey stay and help wrap up the questioning. Frey was relieved.

"Appreciate it. Believe I will."

"Good," Belknap said.

Now three of them circled, with Weeks and Braden observing in the next room.

"I'd like to nail this down so Sid, there in the next room, can go home," Mann said calmly to Abeyta. "Won't cost you a thing. Usually you're cooperative. I don't get why suddenly you're not. You're dragging yer heels, son."

"I'm still breathin'. You can see that, can't you?" Abeyta inhaled deeply, then let it out slowly like cigarette smoke. "Is there an offer on the table?" he asked.

"You *sure* this joke got Ramos killed? Sure it wasn't just Ramos being Ramos? That would be enough, on an ordinary day," Frey said. "You ain't sad to see him gone."

"I didn't care one way or another about Ramos," Abeyta said.

"You hated him," Frey said.

"Not always. He could be pretty funny sometimes."

"When he tried to brain Sandrine with a pool cue and fell off the table?" Frey said.

"You know about that?"

"Why would Sandrine be detained on the border just as you ran this decoy show?"

"I'm a spear carrier," Abeyta said. "Ask someone who knows—or cares."

"'Tain't like you, Rick," Mann said. "Who was responsible? What was the point?"

"See, you don't know what you're messing with," Abeyta said. "How many different ways can I say it? My brother and I need some serious frigging consideration. We need signed frigging agreements. Need what we were promised and aren't getting."

"Or what, you won't cooperate?" Frey said.

"Or we won't frigging be alive," he said. "How cooperative is that? Our lives on the frigging line. Jeez. One of you ain't too bad. Two's dense. Three's flat-out stupid."

"I know what you're risking," Mann said. "You'll get your deal, you *and* your brother. But we need a down-payment from each of you. Today's your down-payment."

"You're taking us separately?"

"Absolutely. Procedure," Belknap said, "as you well know. We'd never depart from that. No judge would let us."

Abeyta raised his hands: "Okay, what it was: Ramos made some cryptic comment. I think my brother got it wrong. You better get it from him."

"What'd he say?" Frey insisted. "We'll ask him. We'll get it straight. You're in the clear. Just say it, and we'll all go have lunch. Feel like a hamburger?"

"Sure, sure I do. I'd like it with onions and tomatoes and thousand island dressing. Maybe some Swiss cheese and bacon on there, too. And a lot of french fries."

"I'll have one of those, too," Frey said cheerily.

"Come on, Ricky," Mann said. "There's five of us killing time here."

"Nicky told me he thought—and he wasn't sure—Ramos made a joke about the legitimacy of Miguelito's parentage. You know, questioning his legitimacy," Abeyta said, then added, "in a joking way, a joking way, *joking*."

"His own bodyguard? Hard to believe," Frey said. "But that would do it. That would get Ramos killed. Is that what you're thinking? Octavio got word of it?"

"Thinking nothing cause it probably isn't true and he probably heard it wrong. You know Nicky. Remember? Doin' about forty shots. Amazing he was still standing."

"Maybe if it ain't true, Miguelito does not make such a big fuss."

"And maybe if it ain't true he still makes a fuss. Don't know, OK?" Abeyta said.

"Is it true?"

"How in hell should I know?" Abeyta said. "Don't know why *you* care. I don't."

"Then Juanito laughed, is that it?"

"Yeah, Juanito laughed. Said, 'Finally we get it from the horse's mouth.'"

"Horse's. You mean like Ramos was responsible? Ramos was his—"

Another knock. This time, Weeks. Looking a bit pale.

"Can I ask a question?" Weeks said, dropping his hand in his pocket. "Just one?"

Mann looked at him oddly. "What's that in your pocket, Weeks?"

He pulled out his keys, with the plastic container now empty of its lead cargo.

"What question is that, Weeks?" Belknap asked, giving him the opening.

"Was Miguelito the same kid, this Jaime Garza kid?"

"Oh, hell, yes, you hadn't figured that out?" Abeyta said. "Now there's four of you. You belong in a home. He used that Garza ID all the time. For four years."

But that wasn't the question Weeks really had in mind. That was just a warm-up. He'd have to think about any additional question. Maybe ask it tomorrow or next week.

"See, that wasn't so bad," Belknap said to Abeyta.

The boys then went to lunch. They were in line at the Burger Wagon when they heard the sirens. They ran back, Mann well ahead of the pack. Fertig and Bulwer were out in front of the sheriff's office with the ambulance and the coroner's Land Rover. The two vehicles had run a sort of race, and the coroner, in a sense, had won.

Fertig and Bulwer were talking on cell phones to places like Washington, D.C., and Langley, Virginia, when Ricky Abeyta was wheeled out on an ambulance gurney. But he was placed in the coroner's wagon. He had blood and thousand island dressing all over himself. Somebody else delivered the burger he described during the interrogation.

"Milt," said Belknap, hurrying inside. His deputy, Milt Rubalcava, was sitting on the floor, one leg tucked under, dead with the box of burgers in his lap. Milt apparently took the burgers, then took the bullets from the gun hidden under the burger box.

Outside, Braden looked in despair at the corpse of Abeyta being wheeled past.

"Don't worry, Sid. Ricky gave us all the info he had. Wasn't any more," Frey said.

Nobody, not even Frey, believed that.

Weeks knew he'd missed his best chance. But not his only chance.

Mann was on his phone, finding Hartley over at La Tuna the same time Sid Braden was calling to stop the new auctioneer from coming up from Deming.

"Guys," Mann said after his one-sided prison call ended. "Guys?"

The others turned to face him, and he said: "Nicky's dead too. Caught a shank."

Bryce Weeks went home, sat in his desk chair, folded down his table from the wall of his trailer and spread out his cleaning gear. Ran a cleaning rod through his Nine. Then ran it through again, looking out the window at the violet shadows of the moonlight. Three o'clock in the morning it came to him. Mann's words finally registered: *Witness to the silence.* Mann was queasy about what the Feds were holding back. He was ready to start knocking on doors. Alderete, the Costillas, even Cortes himself. Time would never be right for Weeks to approach Octavio. Even if Octavio gave him information, he couldn't trust it. Octavio would talk to Pete, though. All Mann needed was a solid break. Someone who won't bail out. With memory of past lives. Someone who knew the Cortes family tree and history. A guy who wasn't afraid.

Weeks met Pete Alderete at the Pancho Villa Bar in Concha, where the waitresses wore sombreros and flouncy blouses that slid off one shoulder or the other.

"You know, it's not that I give a damn what happens to any of us," Weeks said.

"That's obvious," Pete said.

"I know."

It was like this: You're watching a game. The game ends on a bad call. Somebody wins. Then a referee wipes away the foul that won the game, declares a new winner, exonerates the villain, demotes the hero. Foul falls fair. Hate becomes love.

"That okay with you, jefe?" Weeks asked Alderete. "That we talk a little?"

"You don't need my permission. What d'you want—to out-tor-pedo the torpedoes?"

"Want information. Somebody's holding back. You may know some of it."

Alderete looked him squarely in the eye.

"We're still two different countries. I tell you something, I can't come hide on your side. And, anyway, I should be talking to Mann, not to you."

"But I don't have to hear it from you," Weeks said. "That's the way the rules have changed. I can hear it from a totally different place. From somebody somewhere else."

"People are dying. It's no game," Pete said. "Nobody cares about the rules, old or new or nonexistent. But you're right. I don't really care what happens to you and me. I care a lot what happens with my daughter. And I want her with me. I don't want to send her off to school in Denver. I just don't want to."

"You ever see this?" Weeks handed him a photograph of the locket, ring and pin.

"Oh, sure. That ol' locket . . . does it exist any more? It was a long familia tradition for *los Cortes*. And Marianna wore it at her wedding. I remember seeing it. Those were different times. Not so much with the drogas. That all came later. When Marianna wore it, it held the picture of her mother, Marisabel Abreu."

"So her son, Octavio's son, would want that locket," Weeks said.

"Not his son," Pete said. "Not Octavio's."

"He wouldn't? Why not?" Weeks wondered.

"Trying to tell you he's not Octavio's son. Forget the jewelry."

"Well, but whose . . . ?"

"Whose? Nobody's. Don't know whose. Just know—" He stopped himself. Needed to take stock of what he knew. Not just spout off. Never really knew much of anything about them. Never wanted to know. But here he was opening his mouth again. Shook his head, thinking, then losing patience. "Come with me," Pete said abruptly.

"Where?"

"The bank in Santa Teresa, New Mexico," Pete said, looking at him with a challenging eye. "My safe deposit. Jack Felix left a collection of his family documents with me, just for safekeeping, easy access. Papers. Documents. Copies of birth certificates. Passports. He showed them to me. Even a copy of Marianna's will."

"Why leave 'em with you?" Weeks asked uneasily. "Why not his El Paso bank?"

"In case," Pete said. "Didn't trust Octavio and said he didn't trust the *spooks*."

"I don't understand why your lockbox is any safer than anybody else's."

"It seems there may be a line they won't cross. I don't understand it, myself."

"They'd cross it if they knew you had them," Weeks said. "If they wanted them."

"Perhaps, perhaps."

"And these documents prove what?"

"Well, you'll figure it out, señor. You will."

"And where's Felix?"

Chapter Eighteen

Spain

Aman in a black suit was washing a black car. Sandrine and Alderete stood at a gate at the Cortes compound in Rio Santo, watching him.

"Ever wear a suit to wash a car?" Sandrine asked his friend.

"I have one suit, and I wear it, let's see. . ."

"Never," Sandrine said.

"Weddings and funerals," Alderete said.

"Not a bad idea—the formal car wash. They could wear tuxedos," Sandrine said.

Their eyes drifted off to the right, where Octavio Cortes was emerging from a sliding glass doorway.

"Here he comes," Alderete said.

"That's good that he's coming out himself," Sandrine said, but he didn't know all that bound these men together while keeping them apart.

Both visitors had been frisked at the motor entrance, where they left Alderete's truck, but Octavio had them frisked again. He had the black-suited car-wash guy do it. His name, Jesus. And it was done before Octavio had crossed the courtyard.

Octavio wore black jeans, alligator boots and cowboy shirt, collar turned up.

He was tan and manicured, his silvery hair pomaded, and he was smiling.

"How fine of my neighbors to come and call," Octavio said. "Please come in. Will you have a drink?"

"Sure," both men said.

They followed him back in through the sliding glass door. It was a kind of den, with a big television, a bar, and a lot of autographed photographs of soccer players and a block of horse pictures that covered almost every inch of the walnut-paneled walls.

"Have a seat," he said, pointing at the leather chairs.

The low sun blasted through the plate glass window silhouetting them on the wall.

They sat, squinting until he turned the vertical blinds. Then he got down two glasses. "Gin and tonic, rum and coke, tequila, beer?"

"Just beer's fine," Sandrine said.

"Yes, beer," said Alderete.

Octavio pulled out two bottles of Corona, popped the caps and handed them to his guests, then handed them glasses to pour if they wanted. Then he sat down opposite them, across a round coffee table strewn with soccer and horse racing and polo magazines.

"I am so pleased you came," Octavio said. "I really should have done it long ago."

Alderete looked down, Sandrine looked up. Both of them scrambled for words. No. Couldn't. Just couldn't.

"Hmmm. Well," Octavio said. "Some serious business must have brought you, so if I can help with something, I'd be happy to."

It was not the response they expected, particularly not after being frisked twice.

"Miguel," Sandrine said. The tip of a verbal iceberg.

"What has he done now?" Octavio said with a sigh.

"We have no idea, señor," Alderete said. "We don't even know where he is."

"You call me Octavio. The boy is in Spain. I have sent him to school there."

"Spain," Alderete mused.

"What's wrong with Spain?" Octavio said.

"Bit of back to Square One," Sandrine said. "You giving up on the New World?"

"No, it's for convenience," Octavio said, "so I don't have to deal with any of this stuff he always got into. Girls, trouble."

Alderete knotted his hands and wrung them until his knuckles turned white.

Sandrine looked at the knot. "You know Sid Braden, I believe," he told Octavio.

"Yes, he was good enough to allow us to bid on a piece of land that he also wanted," Octavio said. "We did have to pay him a small consideration."

"And we are also here for our friends Willard Mann and Tom Hartley, who are investigators and cannot come to see you."

"Why not?"

"You know—all the many layers of protection, international law," Alderete said.

"So we'll ask their questions," Sandrine said.

"Sure, sure. Anything. *Fuego.*"

Alderete half smiled, then turned aside so Octavio wouldn't see the smile fade to an almost skeletal mask. He never thought for a moment that he might like Octavio Cortes. But the man was at ease with people who he knew had been his enemies and very likely still were. He didn't want to get ahead of himself. They were just beginning.

"And then we also have some questions of our own," Alderete said.

Octavio allowed his face to harden a little, but he brightened again, and said, "Sure, why not?"

"Tell us about Miguel."

"Named for the archangel, the destroyer of Satan, the hero of heaven. A good boy. It's hard growing up down here, with these," he said, pointing out the sliding window at the man washing the car.

"Pistoleros?" Sandrine said.

"Yes, the pistoleros. What a tragic tradition," Octavio said. "Your country has, what is it—*innovated*—a very workable way of dealing with people who try to rob you. But unfortunately here we have to deal with them ourselves, and that is a very imperfect way. We have so many children who want to play with guns."

"For example," Sandrine picked up the thread, "take my friend, Braden, who yesterday was to have held an auction on the courthouse steps in Gila Wells less than a month after the funeral of his daughter."

"I thought about bidding," Octavio said, nodding. "Yes. I came close. If I'd known my two new friends were coming to call, I think I would have done it. But there are so many misunderstandings between our peoples, our two nations, cultures. So many differences. I decided against it."

"They postponed the auction," Sandrine said. "They will reschedule."

"Even then, though, it might not be safe for you," Alderete said.

"Exactly," Octavio said, refusing to take offense. "The world will not change so fast. A shame. Something I regret, because I know there were things I could have done that might have avoided this. Such as protecting *your* son, my friend. Protecting him from harm. We had our . . . differences." He could see Pete wasn't buying. "Okay, hate, maybe, but that hate grew out of love and the love never dies. I now wish more than anything that I had done that, protected him." Octavio had a trace of unlikely moisture in his eyes.

Alderete dropped his focus down onto his hands, just to see if his rage would pulse out of his fingertips in some form. Not a tremor betrayed him.

Sandrine sat back and watched the two men metamorphose for a moment.

"We've all done harm that we regretted," Sandrine said, marginally aware of the understatement.

"Believe me, I understand your very grave concerns," Octavio said. "I understand what effort it is to come here, and to use the word 'harm,' a mild word to describe the excesses I have found necessary to. . . . I know that is not easy for you. Your politeness paves the way of friendship. You will see. You shall see."

Sandrine nodded patiently, then finished his beer.

"Braden had a daughter. Your boy knew her. They were friends," he said.

Octavio looked Sandrine in the eye and said, "Really?"

"Almost sweethearts, except the girl was too young," Alderete said.

"And now she's dead," Sandrine said.

"The wolf girl," Octavio said.

"Some people did call her that, but Mister Mann and Mister Hartley don't believe that's appropriate," Sandrine said.

Octavio shrugged. "I certainly don't know. I've just heard, or seen on TV, that she—what, did she adopt a wolf?"

"I think the idea was that someone adopted a wolf in her name, then broadcast it from Canyon de Chelly to Stinking Springs," Sandrine said. "She was doing a Science Fair project."

"Some science is not so safe any more," Octavio said.

Alderete added: "Miguel was helping her."

Octavio got his half-frown, half-smirk again. "Nonsense."

"People need to talk with that boy," Sandrine said.

"With an abogado present," Octavio said.

"Not Juan Reilly, please," Sandrine said.

"Don't like Juan? He can be very entertaining. He has some stories," Octavio said.

"Mike and Millie. *The wolf.* Was maybe their excuse to be together," Pete said.

"That would make sense," Octavio said. "Guelito didn't care about wolves. What went wrong?"

"The girl got killed. That's the main thing," Sandrine said. "And we think Miguel knows something about why."

Octavio's demeanor strayed from simpatico to spontaneous combustion.

"They don't believe Miguel killed her," Alderete added.

"That's right," Sandrine said. "They want information."

"There are things that happened in the past that they want Miguel for, however, I believe," Octavio said.

"Fred Archibald," Sandrine said, pausing to look at Alderete, "and Juanito."

Alderete's face turned pale, and he started rubbing his left arm.

"You OK?" Sandrine said.

Pete nodded but said nothing. Pete had made it clear he didn't want this discussed. He did not believe it was something to calmly discuss with the devil himself as though it were a soccer match or a polo game. Sandrine went in without warning.

"Remember? How everybody clammed up. No information about Juanito," Sandrine said.

"Let me get you a glass of water," Octavio said to Pete. "You don't look well. I can have a doctor here in ten minutes. Let me call him."

"No, no," Alderete said. "Let the doctor treat people who need treatment. I need something else, but God doesn't permit it."

"Please don't blame me for what happened to Juanito. Please," Octavio said. "I would never go into that place, the Jalisco."

"You own that place," Pete said.

"Owned," he said. "No more. I had sold that place three, four months before that. Sold it to the Cali. They needed a place. We wanted them off the street, out of the park. You saw where they were, chasing little girls, chasing your Blanquita."

Pete remembered his daughter coming home with stories about torpedoes pulling their big, luminous nine millimeter pistols out and using the cocking spring to pump out unspent rounds that flew into the flower beds in the Rio Santo Parque Central, then handing each little girl an individual bullet as a souvenir. Some of the girls took to wearing them on gold chains around their necks. And then they took to clustering over on the edge of the park near the sidewalk. The torpedoes came by to frighten and excite them.

Blanca told him about those girls, too.

"You brought them into Rio Santo," Alderete said.

"They came in. I didn't bring them. They came on their own. Had to leave Miami. Needed a foothold on the frontera. Look at your fences," he said to Sandrine. "Perfect. They wondered why they hadn't come years earlier."

"You certainly profited," Sandrine said.

Octavio did not like that comment coming from a gringo. But he stayed cool.

"I have seen your ranch," Octavio said. "When Paco Wilson owned it, I was his guest. And I have seen, flying over in my helicopter, the work you have done. You deserve credit, señor."

"Thank you," Sandrine said.

"But you don't live over *here*," Octavio said, slapping the leather arm of his chair. "If you did, you would see what has been necessary and what has not. Just to live, señor."

Alderete got angry. "Don't imagine what you have done was necessary," he said.

Sandrine put his hand on Pete's arm. "Let me answer. He's talking to me. Let me," he said coolly. "I won't criticize you. I didn't intend the comment about profit as criticism. You know the walls of the law and the doors and windows better than I do. You deal with them, not I, but they made you wealthy; your fortunes are entwined."

"I didn't need their money," Octavio said.

"But you accepted it, so now you share responsibility," Sandrine said.

"I most certainly do not!" Octavio said in a whisper, and he slapped his chair again, twice, and doubly hard. It left a hand-shaped impression in the leather.

"That little mining venture," Sandrine said. "Is that for you . . . or for them?"

"It's not going through," Octavio said. "I think I'm going to have a gin and tonic."

He got up and mixed one, then sat down again and sipped it before saying anything more aloud. But Sandrine and Alderete could see the moving finger doing calligraphy inside his skull.

"If this is the price of friendship, I have to pay it," Octavio said. "You remember Miguelito's bodyguard, I believe. Lupe Ramos. He grew up in Santito. His parents were poor. They came to me. 'Please, Don Octavio, can you find a job for our son?' Lupe Ramos cost me millions. Millions. You have no idea. What a monster he was. He supposedly kept Miguelito safe but gave him *guns!* Taught him a most unbecoming swagger. And Lupe on top of it all was a traitor. All of that has led to my boy, my Marianna's boy, having to run away and hide. Like a bandit in the hills."

"The hills of Barcelona, Costa Brava, or Costa del Sol," Sandrine said. "Nice hills."

Octavio smiled grimly. "You Americans."

"You're American, too, Octavio. I know about it. Born in Las Cruces Memorial Hospital. You don't have to live in Santito. You could live in New York if you wanted," Sandrine said. "You're here because you want to be. However, the money—Martin Blye lost forty-thousand dollars worth of cattle last year to smuggle-rustlers. We think you and the Cali should pay that."

"The Cali? That will never happen."

"Martin and I, between us, have thirty-five cattle at the pens in Ascension and another twenty down in Durango. We're getting a load of crap about paying their fees. We think you should pay those bastards off or persuade them to release our cattle. And we think you should give us a letter of introduction to your Spanish lawyer so we can go talk to Miguelito about the Braden case. Just talk."

"I'm sorry, but, gentlemen, surely I am no fool. If I tell you where Miguel is, Mister Hartley and Mister Mann will have warrants of extradition issued within an hour of that moment. Interpol all over the place. And my boy will have to run again."

He got up and turned on the television. Univision. Soccer match. Just beginning.

"Sorry for the distraction," he said. "I'll cut the sound. We can still talk." He pushed the mute button. "I have to see this game. Got some money riding."

Mexico versus Spain.

"Who do you root for when Mexico plays Spain?" Sandrine said.

"It depends."

"Yeah? On what?"

"Who I bet on."

Sandrine nodded.

"We can talk to Miguel without endangering him. Just set a neutral location. You control the place. You control the transportation. Deliver us to and from. Blindfold us if you like. We talk to him a limited amount of time. You set the limit. When we leave, you move him back to wherever he's living."

"Who pays for this?"

"You do, of course," Sandrine said. "I mean, Pete and I will buy our own plane tickets. But the rest is your tab."

"Yes, been meaning to visit la tierra vieja anyhow," Pete said.

"Maybe we should all three go together," Octavio said.

Alderete frowned.

"Nobody can stop anybody from traveling if they want to," Sandrine said. "You can fly on the same plane. That doesn't mean we're traveling together."

"We'd want to talk to Miguel alone," Alderete said.

"That will not happen," Octavio said. "His Barcelona lawyer will be there, I guarantee. Every moment."

"I just meant that *you* will not be in the room," Alderete said.

"Time will come, you'll want me in the room," Octavio said. "When that boy doesn't talk, you will want me to come in, and I will be waiting right outside for you to call. Because you will."

"All right," said Sandrine.

"Why did they postpone the Braden auction?" Octavio said.

"Some problems getting ready, and bidders entered the picture late. Up till the deadline, there was only one," Sandrine said. "Then suddenly they got several bids. Ran out of time preparing. Had to reschedule."

"Why no bids?" Octavio said.

"Nobody wanted to," Alderete said, shrugging. "They were making a statement. They thought they were supporting Sid and Marlie. Then they realized it didn't matter."

"Who are the bidders now?"

"We're trying to find out," Sandrine said. "You, maybe, could be one. Are you?"

Octavio rolled out a warm laugh and patted Sandrine on the arm.

"It's going to be okay," he said. "Don't worry. It will be all right."

As they left, the man in the black suit had matriculated from hose to chamois.

And the soft leather polishing rag squeaked like a rat as he soaked up the last streaks of moisture from the roof of the black Infiniti. Just like Felix's car, Alderete remembered.

It also reminded Alderete that his check to Jack Felix went uncashed for a month.

"Don't you think that's about as odd as a guy washing a car in a tuxedo?" he said.

They walked across the international boundary back into the USA, and Frey stepped out on the porch and waved them through.

"They're OK," he told the checkpoint officers.

"It truly has been a time of odd events," Sandrine acknowledged. "A time to stay home and button down the windows."

"Why do you get carried across and stashed in the Llanos jail?"

"They probably didn't realize you'd rescue us."

"But why take you in the first place? You're not at all entertaining or interesting."

"If we consolidate our border and fortify it, bad for them. They'd want to stop it."

"Maybe. Are you doing that? Something's definitely not right," said Alderete. "Maybe they just wanted a ransom. Maybe they were working a scam, a decoy."

"Mann's looking into it," Sandrine said, "but our border is part of it."

Alderete wondered if Mann could look into what happened to Jackie.

"Don't know if you know it, but Jackie is not entirely a free agent."

"What are you saying?" Sandrine asked.

"He's gainfully employed."

"Yeah, so?"

"By the United States Government."

"In what w—*oh*."

"We need to find him," Pete said.

"If you mean me, I'm contractually bound not to go back into Mexico. By treaty."

"I guess I mean Mann," Pete said, "since Mann did so well the last time."

"Mann's a little preoccupied. The Braden case, the auction, the wolves. Now you want to add Felix and the whole thing with the border, the cartel and Juanito?"

"It's all one case, Guillermo. Surely you can see that. All . . . one . . . case."

So, Mann found himself driving where the dust crossed the road. South of Ascension, in Mexico. The road nearly obscured by sand in numerous places. Amoeba-shaped patches of pavement here and there.

Sergeant Felipe Sanchez rode with him. Behind them a truck with fifteen federales. *Overkill*, Mann believed. But the greater number might reduce the chances of any one person stepping out of line. Too many witnesses. Witnesses falling all over each other, as a matter of fact. *But* . . . Risk you had to take. This falling over one another.

La Clinica del Estado Chihuahua was isolated in the middle of a salt moraine, a few scraggly trees planted around its high adobe perimeter wall. Inside, a quaint nineteenth century hacienda.

And the hardened clay was puddled. Freckled with damp spots. They drove in, the two vehicles creating quite a roar, and the patients fled like a flock of terrified birds that could not get off the ground.

Eyes wide. Arms flapping like gull wings.

The perimeter wall became an asset for Sanchez's men, who deployed around the inner courtyard that surrounded the clinic.

Mann and Sanchez went inside, and Sanchez explained that Mann was Jackie's *father.*

"He do not look like no padre to me," head nurse Pancho Reyes said in an English meant to put the invaders at ease.

They let it pass. They followed Reyes to an inner room with bars, but no windows, bars on a fake window, a former window, and bars on the inside of a door that also had been boarded up. And a cot with a man strapped flat on his back, an IV drip on a chrome pole beside him. And the relentless sound of the electric motor cranking the pump that produced the drip.

"Jackie, *Jackie!*" Mann whispered urgently in his ear. Then he tried it full voice: "Jack Felix!"

One eye opened, then another. They mostly looked at Mann, standing over him in the uniform of the United States Bureau of Land Management, and he thought there's no way this is happening or could ever happen. So he closed his eyes.

"The *BLM*, is that right?" he asked, his eyes still shut.

"I'm just a public servant," Mann said.

"That's what they always say, all of you. But BLM? You're kidding 'em, right?"

"Sergeant Sanchez is actually in charge," Mann said, standing aside.

A doctor came hustling in, demanding: "*¿Qué esta pasando aquí?*"

The sergeant informed the doctor that there had been some kind of mistaken identity and that Jackie was admitted in place of someone else.

"*¿Quién?*" the doctor wanted to know.

The sergeant repeated, simply, directly, emphatically, that Jack was a blunder, and the doc unhitched the leather straps, the tubing, pulled out the needle and helped Jack sit.

It would take Jack about six hours to clear his head of the chemical cobwebs.

He looked at Mann quizzically.

"Pete Alderete was worried about you when his check went uncashed," Mann said. "Sanchez here owed me a favor from when

Pete had to bail old Sandrine out of the Llanos slam. He has a way with red tape."

"I still want that check," Jackie said.

Chapter Nineteen

La Rondita

The sun rose like a dead star, cold, on La Rondita.

Jack Felix was early. All bundled up in his Afghan parka sitting inside a dimple in the hillside out of the wind, waiting for something to go right.

Not much had, up to now.

The hill on the bottom rung of the Black Range, on the boundary between the Bradens' Two Square and the Endicotts' E-Bar-E, was a terraced mound where archaeologists said a slave girl planted crops three thousand years ago. The ancient terraced cultivation, with the passing of three erosive millennia, made the hill rounder, and more fragile, and more protectable, and harder to mine, or even to land on.

Felix planted another kind of seed—money. He'd negotiated a deal months ago for his Juarez client, Octavio Cortes, who claimed he wanted to mine it. Nobody believed him. There was no access. Octavio would have needed to buy more land or a right-of-way to visit the hill in anything but a helicopter or a hot-air balloon. None of the surrounding ranchers would sell. Until now. And now was too late. The deal was dead, the client unmasked, the environmentalists' and preservationists' appeal was filed, and the site all yellow-taped, part of a homicide investigation. More harm could not have been done if they had trucked in explosives and blown it off the map. Felix was up to his neck in it. And the throbbing bits of Vietnam he carried in his leg drove him past distraction. So he found the hammock-shaped foxhole he'd used a month earlier. Back when the trouble started. Eased into it, put feet up. That's better.

Mann wanted a reckoning. Painful but overdue. Felix could handle the pain. Knew where its limits lay. It was the bad luck of the place that worried Felix.

After awhile the men rode in on horseback—Mann, Hartley and father-and-son Cliff and Clay Endicott came from the north. Sid Braden, suddenly old, rode in slowly from the south, Corona along-side him. Fertig was on horseback, too, in city shoes and an FBI windbreaker. They met at La Rondita. Marlie Braden was behind. She'd said she would arrive late—expecting to have it laid out for her with photographic clarity.

Weeks and Alderete were absent and were likely to stay that way awhile.

Alderete was busy elsewhere. Felix had told him: "Stay home and take out the binoculars." *Something worth seeing.* So Pete was ready, focusing his Bushnells as vans pulled up outside Fortress Cortes. Men in flak jackets with *Comandancia* printed in white on their backs swarmed in through the gate, taking cover and setting up defensive positions supporting SWAT. There was no resistance, and Alderete, watching from the balcony overlooking the camposanto saw Octavio being led to a van, his hands braceleted together in front of him.

"Hector! Come here!" he called to his nephew downstairs. "Come up and see."

There was no one else to call. Blanquita, his daughter, was stay-ing with Maya's sister in Denver and ready to attend school there the rest of the year, after the spring recess.

Hector appeared at the bottom of the stairs, looking up: "You called me, *tío?*"

"Come see what happens to someone who cares nothing for law."

"Who?"

"Come see. Hurry. You'll miss it."

Hector took the stairs two at a time. Pete handed him the binocs. He looked out just as Octavio climbed into the van. One of the agents put his hand on Octavio's head, to make sure he did not bump it on the doorframe.

"Who's that old man? Is it Don Octavio?" Hector said. "Is that an ambulance?"

Pete smiled sadly. "Almost," he said. "Kind of like an ambulance. Because I don't think the old man will be coming back."

The wind was cold on Rondita. The men folded their arms to hold the heat.

"Where's Weeks?" Felix said. "I was really hoping to see Weeks."

"He's on his way to Spain," Mann said. "Fixing a loose end."

Corona was skeptical: "*Spain*. We spent twice my budget on this case, grilled half the population of the frontera and got *quesadilla*. Hope you got something for us."

"Oh, yes, I do," Felix said.

The men tied their horses together, and Felix sat in the cavity he called his foxhole, out of the wind, waiting. They'd all heard of Felix, but of those gathered on Rondita that morning, only Mann had worked with him or could say he knew him. But rumors had grown like weeds around Felix the fixer. It was time to mow the weeds.

"Pete hired you?" Corona asked Felix. "For revenge on Octavio—right?"

"No, Pete hired me to find Juanito's body. I did. Then he wanted me to bring Miguel back to Rio Santo, and I couldn't because I already was doing it for Octavio."

"You brought him back," Mann said.

"Yes, but then Octavio, his father, sent him away, right?" Braden said.

"No, it was all lies. *Layers of lies*," Felix said. "We never knew it all, even in the family. Now we find it out. Miguel's real father? Murdered years ago. His mother died not very long afterward. That sealed it all up. In fact, Octavio's being arrested at this moment by the state judicial police in Santito for that killing. I helped them get a warrant of extradition to turn him over to Bob Frey and Dave Belknap in Concha."

Sid Braden sat alone on a low sycamore branch waiting for Marlie to arrive.

Rondita sat in a kind of wind tunnel. Faces were chapping, turning red.

Felix climbed up the slope to the third tier of the terrace and sat down in the furrow, laying his eagle-headed cane across his lap.

"This may take awhile," he said.

His calm voice was faint above the wind. To Marlie Braden, riding over the shoulder of the hill, his words arrived as passengers on the wind. She rode down, dismounted and sat on the furrow below him. Sid Braden walked over and sat next to her. Held her hand.

The words had a flat, rough-edged, raspy feel in the wind. Spinning images. . .

. . . Like the helicopter, blades blurred, descending toward La Rondita, which Cortes already had fitted with pilings for the start of a helipad. No slab yet, though.

La Rondita was flat enough as it was. The chopper settled on top reasonably well. The old man came down the fold-out stairs.

Felix arose. Greeted Octavio. Once, the old man had called him Jackie and had given him candy or money to get lost. The old man would have given him anything today. Felix was leveling more than a mountaintop.

"'Who are you working for?' he asked me," Felix said. "I told him, 'Marianna, who else?'"

"How'd he take that?" Mann asked him.

"He just nodded and smiled. He loved her. But he didn't know how to be a man, how to face reality, how to be a father—or a husband," Felix said. "My poor Aunt Marianna. I knew that household inside-out. It's why I crossed the river."

. . . Like Octavio waiting in the wind for Miguelito to arrive—was that really just forty days ago? The old man wore the woven brimless cap of a Guatemalan peasant, Mayan, with earflaps, to keep his silvery head warm. He was all bundled up in a puffy nylon coat and wore dark glasses, wraparounds, in case the crippled sun burned through.

Rico Ticotin and Ramos, the Fizz, stood by with their Glocks and their Uzis. They had more in the bird, close by, if needed.

Marlie wanted to see it clear as the day, like the bitter things that people need to stay alive. Felix re-enacted, slapped the rim of the foxhole, rose from it as one of the ghosts:

"Hello, uncle," Jack says, eyes on Marlie. She's the one who's got to see it.

"Jackie!" Octavio says with a wide grin. "Something's coming today, I believe."

"It's not here just yet, uncle."

"But it's coming?" Octavio looked for a place out of the wind.

"Yes, it's coming. But you must urge these lads of yours to put up their arsenal. At least the Uzis. They can keep their nines, holstered, please."

"What is all this . . . *fuss?*" Octavio says.

"I'm afraid there's a girl."

"There always is," Octavio laughs. "There always is."

"But she's coming right over this hill, I'm guessing, in about ten or fifteen minutes. Nothing could be done about her coming. She mustn't be harmed. Or even frightened. Or, you know, your *project* here is finished. She's very young, and fine. This must seem exactly as it should—an old man taking a look at a mine."

"Why the fuss?"

"To avoid the fuss, uncle. Why can't you avoid it? You . . . the boys . . . always . . . get . . . into it. Do it my way once and there's no fuss for you to say *'why the fuss?'* about."

"Okay, okay, Jackie. Boys," he gestured the twin tulips to depetal. "Please, please, Uzis in the chopper. Thanks. And keep those *nueves* in their holsters, please. Thank you. But really Jackie, how do we avoid the fuss, eh? That's what I mean by *all the fuss*, don't you see? I mean what's all the fuss *about* a fuss?"

"I just think you ought to try."

"Okay, we'll try. Who knows, maybe our lost boy, our prodigal, will accept our amnesty and come home quietly," Octavio said. "We have sacrificed a few extra calves for him, I believe, to be biblical about it. Where do I draw the line, Felix, eh? Where?"

"We've got to give him the chance," Felix said.

"I hate this," Octavio said, looking at his watch. "Hate waiting. That little *shit!*"

"Easy, easy, uncle. You know you're a little early."

"When did he ever not keep us waiting? God, and it's cold up here, you know that? Why couldn't we have done this at the barn?" Octavio said.

"Because this right here is public land, uncle, and maybe soon it will be yours if you don't screw it up. We haven't trespassed or broken any laws. We've got every right to be here. And when you take him back home, you will be perfectly within your rights."

"You got that court order?"

He pulled the folded paper out of his pocket and waved it at Octavio.

"I wish I knew how you did that," Octavio said.

"They want him out of their country, tío. Real simple."

"Why don't they just deport him?"

"Trouble for them, uncle. This is easier. We're taking a problem off their hands, free."

Sugar was skittish, so Marlie Braden walked over to stroke the horse. Something, maybe a memory, troubled Sugar. Troubled Marlie, too. She stared back at Felix with a bitter, hopeless look.

"You used my Millie as bait," she said softly. There was a dullness to her statement, almost resignation. She went back to Sid and sat down again.

Felix, conjuring with gestures, pointed right at Marlie—right through her—to where her daughter had appeared.

"Millicent comes in, riding her horse, leading a mule packed with cargo that is overlapped by a blue tarp, and she is rounding the base of Rondita. She looks up the hill at us and at the three-bladed Sikorsky. I don't think she sees me at first. My camouflage. But she sees Octavio and the boys, Rico and Lupe. She reads the name on the chopper. It says EightCorp, mining and engineering division.

"The child looks at her pink jelly watch. She's early, too.

"She nudges Sugar up the hill to meet us.

"'Hi, I'm Millie,' she says.

"'How are you, child? How charming,' Octavio says.

"'That is a very nice hat you have, sir. I happen to know it's Guatemalan.'

Octavio's eyes flash with joy. "'Ho-*ho!* You do!'

"'From the north, in the mountains. Mayan,' she says.

"'Right again,' he says. 'Well, we *are* planning a mine.'"

She seems puzzled by the implied connection between the hat and the mine.

"'Do you know anything about mining?' he says. 'This is a sulfide site if I ever saw one.'

"'Copper sulfide, often found with silver,' she said. 'I know a little bit about that. We're in silver country here, and copper country. And with sulfide, the two, copper and silver, are found together.'

"'Perhaps you know then that northern Guatemala is also sulfide country.'

"'I didn't. Are you from Guatemala?'

"'A little bit of everywhere,' Octavio says. 'Some of our boys will be from there, from Guate. We own mines there.'

"'Are you waiting for someone?' the girl asks him.

"'We have a *waiting* look,' he says. 'Yes, we are waiting. For a young man. I believe you know him.' His eyebrows purse, and he hesitates a bit. He's realizing: *This is why the fuss.* He adds: '*Boys, put her in the chopper, please. How would you like a . . .*'

"Instantly she spurs her horse.

"'*Put her in the chopper.*' She reacts to that without hesitation. And she rides straight at Rico, who is unholstering his extra-long, extra-silenced Glock. He has to jump aside before he can break it free.

"Octavio finishes his sentence: 'I wanted to give you a *ride.* A ride, just a ride.'

"He tries to convince himself it was a ride in the chopper. '*I should have said that first*'—a ride. But that's a lie. Needed to control the situation. If he couldn't control her, he couldn't control *it.* Couldn't let her go. That didn't mean he wanted her killed."

Marlie's eyes rolled up. "My poor girl," she whispered into the wind.

"By now, Ramos has fired in her direction—but missed her."

"Who shot her, damn it?" Braden said.

"The one," Felix said, "who tried to save her."

"I could've saved her," Clayton said, almost under his breath.

"You weren't even there," Felix said.

"I heard the shot and saw her die," he said. "Wish I'd tried to save her."

The boy slid down from Whiskey, tossing the reins aside.

"Clay!" His father tried to stop him.

"No, sir, we need to . . . say something here. They need to know. I heard the shot and rode up here." Pointed to the hilltop above them. "Couldn't hear it all, but I saw the helicopter, the men. They took her away. I never told. I was afraid."

Endicott clamped his hand on Clay's shoulder. "Wasn't your doing," he said.

Felix turned to Mann and asked: "Did you know about this?"

Mann nodded. It was Clay he had been following, he knew. The lopsided shoe was still on Whiskey. "I knew the wolves were leading him home, and I'd found his track here on old Rondita. Hard to place the time exactly. You got a bent nail, Clay, in Whiskey's right rear shoe. Track you in a herd of goats. That was you up there on Cerro Verde, too, firing down at me. I'd like you to tell me what that was all about."

Sid Braden stood up and his hands were shaking. He looked like he might explode. But his voice was weak, nearly a whisper. The dry wind made him hoarse.

And he stammered: "Did, does anybody here know how, who killed my Millie?"

Mann sat back down and let Felix answer.

"Miguel Cortes shot her," Felix said. "By accident, by tragic circumstance. A tragedy. Tried to save her. It all went wrong."

Marlie's voice was not quiet. It was clear and shrill. "I thought someone tried to tell me this boy loved her," she said. "Seems like everything you all said was a lie."

Felix nodded. He knew he'd have to cross this run of ghost-white water.

"Yeah, he loved her. He did. But in a very cautious way because she was so young. I watched them. She amazed him. Everything about her, but especially the way *she* loved people, loved life, the land, even wolves," Felix said. "*Even the wolves.* No matter how much hate there was. Either way. She balanced it. She opened his heart. Like letting in sunlight. It changed him. He grew up."

Marlie was still angry, muttering, "Well, that's just fine, just fine, wonderful," and Sid got up and came over to her. "Let's hear all of it," he said. "Let it all be told."

They stood there a moment, rocked by it all over again, then he led her back to the sycamore, and they sat together.

Clay saw his dad slide his rifle back in its saddle sheath, and said to him: "You told me it was war. *We* hated wolves, and *they* hated cows. Simple. Remember?"

"Never hated the wolves," Cliff said, "just the idea."

"I'd ask the other side the same question," Clay said, tears form-ing. "This is where it led."

Marlie looked at Felix, who froze. "Well, get on with it, damn you," she said.

Felix went ahead: "Millicent hit the ground. When Ramos fired, she went down flat on the hillside. Good instinct. Except Miguelito rode in. He was late. Came in at a gallop. Had his own Nine. A bit heavy for him. Heavier than he thought. He caught Ramos aiming, about to take another shot, aiming in that cool way he had. So Miguelito fired at Ramos, but the horse stumbled. He missed. The horse hit the edge of this hole here, my foxhole. Must not have seen it."

Felix sighed. Walked down to the edge of the hole. Dug at it a bit with his toe.

"But, yeah, the shot got fired," he said. "Somebody—the wrong somebody—got killed. Then Miguel wanted to be the one to die. They put him in a doctor's care, too."

"Should've put him in the care of the state prisons," Marlie said. She walked down to Felix's foxhole, looking for the hoof print. Long eroded away. Gone.

"Right about here," Felix said, pointing with his toe.

She thought she saw a little indentation.

"You're *going* to answer," she murmured. "Nobody goes any-where until then."

"What about Octavio?" Mann said.

"Oh, yeah," Marlie said. "The rest of the story. Might as well finish it."

Felix resumed: "Octavio kept saying, 'Just a ride. Just wanted to give her a ride.' Then he got angry at me. Didn't like the way I was looking at him. 'Clean up all this mess,' he growled. 'Those bullet shells. All of them.'

"'You could have offered her the ride *before* ordering her onto the chopper,' I told him.

"'Well, now we've got to move her,' Octavio said. 'Don't look at me that way. This isn't what I wanted.'

"'But uncle, now we've got to move *you*, too.'

"'Such a nice little girl. So shiny bright,' uncle said.

"He wanted me to bury her. I refused. Ramos pulled a gun and hit me with it, hard," Felix said, pointing at his forehead. "I don't remember more. That's all I know."

Mann pointed at Clayton: "You owe me that explanation, son."

Clayton had a chance to think it over and now was not sure he wanted to talk.

He shook his head, and Mann went over to him, tugged his sleeve. "C'mon, tell it."

"Well," he said, "they wanted to bury her up on Cerro Verde, and they looked like they wanted to bury Mister Felix, too. They took her over there in Jackie's trailer, then packed her on the mule. I followed way back. Made sure they never saw me. Agent Mann's the only one figured I was there. Sorry to fire at you. Wasn't goin' to hit you."

Mann nodded: "Just warning shots. I knew that."

Marlie reached out to Clay. He took her hand.

"One other thing I remember," Felix said. "Octavio climbing into the helicopter. He was crying. Had Miguelito with him, arms around him. Had his hands over Miguel's eyes so that the boy could not see what happened to the girl. Then . . . I don't know."

"Ramos hit you," Clayton said. "I saw them put you on that chopper. Thought you were dead, too. Thought I'd be dead, like that other guy, that guy down in Concha."

"So why'd you follow them?" Mann asked. "Why go up on that green ridge?"

"Had to. I could see you coming up the trail. God, it was so close."

Mann nodded. "You had that locket. Had to be you."

"Yeah, had it on me. Was goin' to show her, prove to her. She swore they were just friends, that he was like some big brother, but it wasn't true. She knew. She already knew and didn't care. She knew who he was. Didn't care. I found the locket in Jaime's stuff. In a drawer. That's how I knew."

He was seeing it. Tack drawer. Top drawer under the window, sun streaming in smoky from the grimy window glass. The drawer left open, the gold shining inside.

"It said, 'For our bride.' For Jaime's bride, uh, Miguel's. That's why he had it."

"You placed that locket in her hand?" Mann said. "You did that?"

"Yes, I did. It was hers. But that's not why I was there. What if she was alive?" Clay said. "Then I had to give it to her. Even if she *was* dead, it's hers. Didn't know what else to do. Miguel was gone. I couldn't keep it. Had to give it back."

"Always wondered what happened to that pendant—my aunt Mariana's," Felix said. "Four, five generations of Cortes brides wore it on their wedding day."

"Ramos pawned it, am I right, Tommy?" Mann said.

Hartley seemed surprised, caught off guard like a student who hadn't prepared.

"You investigated that case, right? Ramos pawned that locket?" Mann said.

Marlie was troubled. It showed. "I thought you said . . ."

Hartley then saw it all. Never said a word. Pulled his shoulder gun. Edged toward his horse, which was wedged between Endicott's appaloosa and Mann's gray. "Everybody hold just where you are. No need going off on tangents. I'm not the bad guy here, not the villain."

"Why are you holding that gun, then, Tom?" Mann said. "Just put it down and let us sort this thing out, step by step. That's all we're trying to do here."

Hartley climbed on his horse, but he was stuck. Couldn't back up of the trees. Marlie stepped forward, blocking him, and Tom couldn't bring himself to knock her down. Fertig accepted his pistol. He handed it down, sadly, butt first.

Marlie didn't back off: "I've got a transcript," she told Hartley, "of that briefing where you said Miguel pawned that locket for an automatic rifle. That wasn't true?"

Hartley seemed to consider an answer, but he didn't deliver.

Felix pre-empted: "Right, that wasn't true, ma'am. That was Ramos' gun."

Mann told her: "Ramos pawned the locket if you see the store surveillance tape. Miguel was in another part of the store when the deal was done, right, Tom?"

"He was staying out of the way so he could get his damned Uzi, and Ramos was getting it for him," Hartley said finally. Angrily. Angry with himself.

"I'd like to see that tape," Marlie said.

"Well, sure, we'll do that," Mann said. "So, point is, the boy never got the gun. We ran the clips. Every case where ballistics match is a Ramos case."

Felix added: "Plenty of people in Santito saw Ramos with the gun including me."

Corona remembered: "Yeah, Ramos came across. Came up to Gila Wells. Made a buy. Bought that gun. We found out when the paperwork came through. I checked the store video, sent it to Washington. That's how Mann and Felix got it, I imagine?"

"Something like that," Felix said. "And I can tell you once Ramos owned a gun, he didn't share it. With *anyone*. Let alone a crazy kid who'd probably shoot him."

"Mister Hartley said the boy shot Archibald," Marlie said. "Campesinos agreed."

"That gun shot him," Mann said. "The campesinos changed their story four times. Each time worse for Miguelito. They were caught in the middle of something that scared the hell out of 'em. Eventually, they all disappeared. Right, Tom?"

Marlie still didn't accept it: "Ramos set up Miguel? Why? "

Fertig stepped forward. This was his end of it, and he wanted no doubts left for the Bradens: "That was just the corner Ramos got painted into," he said. "Octavio found out. It was inevitable. People notice stuff like that."

"Stuff like what?" she said.

"Playing both ends. Hard to hide out there with all that surveillance. We saw him. Octavio dumped him over there near the Cali compound, where the Cali mules would find him. Because he belonged to them. But Sandrine found him instead."

"They were trying to move old Octavio out," Braden said.

"Exactly. And not an easy task," Felix said. "Take it from me. I've been trying to move him out for thirteen years, myself. Sometimes you just have to, like they say, work within the system and live with it, and Octavio *was* the system in Santito. But Hartley had a deal—didn't you, Tom—with Ramos. Only Ramos and a couple coyotes knew. The Abeyta brothers. Certain people got across. All that time you thought your deal was with Octavio. Then we ran that scam on you with those two suits from Bogota. They were Cubanos, compadre. From South Florida. You bit on it. Swallowed it."

Mann had one last question: "How does a little piece of antique jewelry migrate from an evidence locker in Concha to the pawn shop in Gila Wells? Tom, any ideas?"

Hartley kept on saying nothing.

Corona had one, too: "And how does an hombre like Octavio go so quiet-like after all these years?" Corona said. "No pistoleros, no siege, no nada."

"He came to us," Fertig said. "After meeting with Mister Alderete and Mister Sandrine, and then after Mister Weeks and Agent Mann did a little more digging. Saw the handwriting. Word from the ramparts was the trees were starting to look like people. Coming for him faster than the federales. It all unraveled for him. Very quickly."

Marlie coughed, and Felix smiled. A gentle, guilt-edged smile.

"I never set up your daughter," he told her.

Sid stood next to her, his arm around her, holding her steady.

"Miguel did that without knowing," Felix said. "After it started, I realized she might ride in. My God, I thought, we've got to stop it. I called you. Remember? *'Your daughter home?' 'No, she's out riding. Who's this?'* I felt Octavio wouldn't harm her. Anyway it couldn't be stopped. Those kids were looking for excuses. It was their day."

"Took you a very long time to report," Sid said to Felix. "Seemed like everybody who knew anything worked overtime to keep it from us."

"I was in a hospital," Felix said. "Strapped to a bed."

"Heavily drugged. They were keeping him quiet," Mann added. "We found Jack down in that so-called hospital. Had to wait a day for him to gather his senses. Brought him back up yesterday. Skull fracture all pretty much healed. But he does have a new ridge on top, which plainly curves around on his forehead. He's permanently reshaped."

"Don't think Uncle Octavio knew what to do with me," Felix said. "Maybe that was part of him quitting, because he knew I wouldn't go away, and he wasn't going to make me go away. Couldn't just give me a quarter and say, 'Shoo.'"

While Fertig took Hartley down the trail, Mann sat on the low bough of the sycamore with Sid and Marlie.

"My fault too," he said, shaking his head. "All my mistakes."

Marlie patted him on the back, and Sid said, no, it was fate.

"That's what it is when so much goes wrong at once. Fate," Sid said. "It was all after the fact, after the damage was done, the only damage that mattered."

"Anyhow, I'm quittin'," Mann said.

Corona overheard.

"You ain't leavin'," he told Mann emphatically, "unless it's to work for me."

"'Fraid I am."

Corona blew a gust of disgust, demanding: "What've you done?"

"Court has it sealed," Mann said. "'Til tomorrow."

"Tomorrow where? I got that Braden auction tomorrow. I can't . . ." Corona said.

Mann shook his head. "Told you. Find out tomorrow."

Then Mann had one last story for Marlie: How the agents found Octavio weeping when they interviewed him last week. After Sandrine's and Alderete's visit.

"Begging his grandson for forgiveness. His grandson wasn't even there."

The story turned tantalizingly in Mann's mind like a Christmas ornament, full of reflected light. He'd held it back, letting it sparkle, letting it rotate. Story a pistolero told him down at La Clinica. Nameless guy. Black suit, black car. Just having a chat.

The story of Ramos behind bars in a basement cell at Fortress Cortes.

. . . Octavio went down to the basement daily and talked to Ramos, who stared back through the bars with cold, watchful eyes. The cell was eight by eight, smaller than Octavio's smallest dog run. Tile floor for easy cleanup. Stone walls, steel bars, cold. Octavio grasped the bars, and just before he spoke his nose would be a quarter-inch from Ramos' nose. Then he would back off a little bit, and he would talk to his prisoner.

"We are the ones that little girls run from, Ramos, no? That bother you? That's not what bothers me," Octavio said. "What bothers me: You don't get it. Why? Because you don't listen. *Hito de la chingada. Somos todos itos de la gran chingada.*"

"He punched Ramos in the face. Right through the bars. A whole lot of times. To where Ramos' face was rearranged—red as hamburger," Mann said. "That happened for two straight days. Third day, Ramos grabbed the old man's arm coming through the bars. Twisted it. Looked like he would rip it off. And Rico shot Ramos."

Ramos is sprawled on the floor, dying. Octavio kneeling, all choked up, says: "Tell me why you did this?" And Ramos replies: "So damn tired of you and . . . all the old . . ." His eyes grew wide, then he died.

Octavio looked up at Rico. "Old *what?* Tell me what in hell, since that's where he is, did he mean by that?"

"Wanted a new life," Rico said. "Said he should be living in your house."

"You couldn't tell me this?"

"Thought he was joking."

"The Cali promised him my house? What'd they promise you, Rico?"

"They couldn't promise me my padrón. I'm nothing without my padrón."

"Your padrón is nothing," Octavio said. "Where does that leave you?"

Octavio was already in a prison. But without the protection of a prison.

On his way out to the highway, Mann stopped to say good-bye to Hartley, locked in the back seat of the squad car way down where the trail meets the road to Gila Wells.

"Time just ran out," Hartley said, staring back at him through the two-inch window slit left open for air.

"You thought you could make something of this mess?" Mann said. "Just needed a little more time?"

"I would have been on a beach in Montenegro," he said. "I would have just disappeared. They'd be looking for me in the City of Rocks."

"Where'd it go wrong for you, Tom?" Mann said. "You could've been great. Could've been anything, a federal prosecutor, a judge, *governor.*"

"They caught me early on," he said. "Showed me I was finished almost before I'd begun. Sent a woman in a red car. Porsche. She wore—almost wore a dress the same color as the car. We, uh. They sent me some photographs later, you know. All they wanted was a small herd of quails to get through, about fifteen head, and all I had to do was spend the appointed hour in Sunflower with ol' Mister Horn. Woman turned out to be fifteen, I think. Sent me a copy of her birth certificate along with the photos. Camera on her hat, which she hung on a peg on the wall. Never saw her again. Wish I had."

"Tell me about Abeyta, Tom."

"Which one?" Hartley said, looking down at his shoes, which Elias Corona had shackled together.

Hartley knew prison for him would be like this: They'd watch him closely until he needed them, then they'd look away.

"I'd settle for the City of Stones," Hartley said. "I think of it as like a graveyard with all those standing stones."

"They sure don't have nothing like it in Montenegro," Corona said, though he had no idea where Montenegro was. He figured maybe it's an island, since it has beaches. Maybe a Caribbean island down there off Nicaragua someplace. Had no idea how far off the mark he was.

Wrong about the rocks, too. Montenegro could be called the Land of Rocks.

Chapter Twenty

Blue Mountain

The sign on the blue van said Blue Mountain, and a young man drove it across the empty reaches of eastern Arizona while an elderly couple sat in back.

The old man wore a straw cowboy hat and a pale blue Western sport coat. The woman had Spanish tortoise shell combs in her gray hair and wore a salmon colored cotton dress. Her name was Esmeralda. Everyone called her Missy.

They drove into New Mexico and across the Zuni Pueblo with its red and gold mesa and its wind-rippled lake. They turned south on the road to Fence Lake, and they stopped at the Navajo trading post in Fence Lake for a cup of coffee.

When Willard Mann the elder stepped from the van, he walked bent at the waist, bowlegged, and he used an oak cane.

White-haired Marbella Tsosie Sarkisian, the eminent Ramah Navajo weaver, was at her loom in the back of the store, and her gray-haired daughter, Maria, was behind the counter, changing a spool of cash-register paper.

Marbella was doing a gray rug. Collectors from Texas and Colorado had already come in and looked at it, even before it was finished. The landlord, Henry Benton, had come in that morning en route to Gila Wells and had agreed: This would pay the rent for the rest of the year.

It was April. The crocuses had given way to daffodils and irises, gold, violet and white, in the garden bordered by railroad ties in front of the store that sat roadside on the edge of their five acres. Their house was back in a grove of sycamores. April. That meant Marbella had eight months' rent tied up in the four by six rug. Figure four thousand for this rug, wholesale. A good deal.

"Mom, we could buy a place with that rug, alone, if we sold it at

Santa Fe Indian Market," Maria said as Benton left.

"We have a lease, and it was tough getting," her mother said. "Buy a place, you still pay taxes on it. What's the diff?"

"The diff is you won't be weaving forever and we'll have nothing."

"You can weave," her mom said.

"Not like you."

Benton tapped the brim of his hat and Mann, the elder, tapped his as they passed each other in front of the Trading Post. Benton did not recognize him, but Mann knew Benton. He said nothing.

Mann held the door open for Missy, and Maria greeted them cheerfully. Missy immediately gravitated toward the loom.

Missy fluttered about the spools of yarn Marbella had for sale and the bolts of cloth Maria had for sale. Missy held a pale tan yarn up against the three-gray rug, just to see.

"I thought about that," Marbella said. "Decided not to. Liked it gray. Just gray."

"Can I tell you something?" Missy said, leaning down.

Marbella nodded.

"That rug is your daughter, gray hair, gray eyes," she whispered.

Maria heard anyway.

"Gray sweats," Maria added, raising her gray arms.

Black Reeboks. Bright red socks.

"The tan is *her*," Missy said.

"Hardly see it for all the gray," her mother whispered.

Maria couldn't quite hear. Mom had mastered volume control.

"What was that?" Maria demanded.

"Gray sells better."

The drive through the west end of the Plain of San Tomas was spattered with raindrops, off and on. Every little cloud seemed intent on liquidation.

But the sun stayed out.

The Manns rode down through the Hidalgo National Forest. They saw elk, deer, cattle, horses, squirrels standing around amid the trees. They saw Bob Marlowe, one of three remaining Wilderness ranchers, down on his knees pulling weeds out of his driveway on the edge of the Apache Wilderness. They were weeds he didn't want his stock to eat. The blue van stopped. The left-rear window behind the driver whirred down.

"Are we on the right road to Redsleeve?" Mann asked.

"Would be if it weren't winter," Marlowe replied.

"It isn't winter; it's spring," Mann said.

"Maybe in Arizona," Marlowe said.

"Is the road blocked?"

"It was, a few days ago. Snow high as a bull elk. Can't say right now."

"We heard it was open—if it's the right road."

"I hope it is," the rancher said.

There were other roads into Redsleeve, but this one was fine. Snow was still piled up along the side of it, and the water looking for the Rio San Francisco was running down the ditches on either side of the highway and overflowing the streams in the little roadside meadows because the beavers had been busy downstream.

The van slowed down some, at Missy's request, because of the sheets of water crossing the road, on both sides, making its way into the ditches. When they pulled into Redsleeve, the brown dried spattered road mud covered the Blue Mountain insignia.

The driver, Abe Martine, stepped into the Green Ways General Store operated by Arlene Woonsocket, a transplanted enviro watchdog from Maine.

"I just want to know where Doc's house is," Martine said.

She looked at him questioningly for several seconds of silence while the other customer slid quietly out the door.

"Doc is a protected person," she said. "We don't give out people's addresses, but you can look her up in the phone book."

She tapped the small book next to the cash register.

"Thanks," Abe said and thumbed through the book. He found Sara Armstrong, address and phone.

"Can you tell me where Frisco Street is?"

"I can," she said. "I won't."

An earlier customer had returned with Undersheriff John Olson, whom he found wandering outside.

"Frisco Street's just south of the crossroads," Olson said. "You hassling people again, Arlene?"

"My constitutional right," she said.

Abe didn't hang around to hear the rest. He drove the Manns south until he saw the shingle swinging from two chains—"University of New Mexico Health Clinics. Sara Armstrong, M.D."

The door was open. Abe went in. The bell overhead rang once.

A nurse stepped out from a room full of files on shelves floor to ceiling. She looked nervously at Abe until she realized: "Oh, you're the driver. Bring 'em in. Sara! Sara-a-a-a!"

Abe went out to get the Manns, and Sara stepped in, seeming to glow in a way that blurred her edges, so that the Manns could not describe her. She wore some kind of radiant dress and Italian shoes that practically weren't there. Her rumpled lab coat hung like prosaic reality on a hook in the room behind her, and she closed the door to it.

"We won't be here today, Abby," she told her nurse, and she stepped out onto the front porch.

Will Senior was letting himself down from the van, and he stopped mid-step, hanging onto the hand-railing, and stared at Sara. Missy, waiting inside the van, finally gave him a shove.

"Don't bother getting down," Sara said. "I'll get in."

She stood a foot above the old man.

He would have none of it. He wouldn't let her in.

"Got to get a hug from this beautiful girl," he said.

She beamed, and Missy decided to climb down after all.

"You're Sara," she said.

"Yep," Sara said.

"So far away from Willy's house," Missy said.

"We call him Will," his father said, "not Willy anymore."

"I might call him Willy now and then," Sara said. "Shall we?"

They all climbed back in the van and Abe followed Sara's directions down a narrow, quarter-mile driveway. Snow clung to the north edges of fenceposts and trees. At the end of the drive was a one-car garage with Will Mann's parked four-wheeler in front.

His dad smiled, face going crinkly. Sitting on the wooden Adirondack lawn chair next to a tree-stump table. Smiling under the backyard aspen because of Sara.

Father and son. Just sharing time. Not saying much, hardly anything at all. But Will, sitting on the edge of the stump table, felt doubly blessed. Because he was.

"Look at *them*," his father said with a sideways nod, pointing his head toward Sara showing Missy the garden.

"Boy, she's something the way she moves in, organizes everything with a swish and a smile. Got you organized in ways you don't even realize."

"Yes, sir," Will said.

"*Really* something."

"Yes, sir."

"And those shoes she's wearing."

"All the way from Italy."

"What?"

"All the way from Italy."

"What, where?"

"Italy."

"Italy?"

"Yep."

"And that dress. That from Italy too?"

"Yep."

"Aren't you a li'l overdressed for an auction?" Dad asked as she came back.

"Not this one," she said, rifling through her handbag.

She pulled out a letter.

"Willy," she said.

Mann the Younger looked up with the oddest look.

Both his parents just stared at him.

"Yes, dear?" he said.

"Would you please drop this in the mailbox?" She handed him the letter.

"For Breitburg at UNM? What's this about?" he demanded.

Breitburg was her supervisor, and their written record was always full of portent.

"I want the board to hire a mediator," she said.

Mann nodded tentatively because he had no clue what she was talking about.

"Labor dispute?" he guessed. "Nurses' strike? Or is this for you and me?"

"Forget about nurses. This is for the town," she said. "I'm asking the university to help mediate this unhappy situation. Discuss problems and differences like grownups, calmly and patiently, with respect. I want a town where families survive, not where I'm X-raying people's mail for bombs. So, speaking of mail, how about you mail it?"

Will trudged down the driveway with it. Slapped it in the mailbox. Raised the little red flag on the side. Trudged back. Auction hour was closing in like a *TGV.*

About half the people were seated on picnic blankets under the cottonwoods. Children trampled the odd-shaped patches of green grass which separated the squares of colored cloth. Closer to the courthouse steps the other half of the crowd was standing. They stood on the grass, on the paths and about ten of them stood on two white metal benches that faced the life-sized statue of Oreste Madrid on horseback, rearing, in the middle of the staircase. The bronze horse stood on a concrete cube that was covered with Spanish tiles. Behind the ill-fated but well-commemorated Madrid, triumphantly defeated, a light standard rose out of the horse's backside like a pole on a carousel.

A few blanketeers had big breakfast baskets with doughnuts and bagels and coffee. The east and west ends of the grassy plaza were choked with people arriving. Police at the corners kept cars out. It was a warm morning, but thunderheads were already building to the west over Arizona.

Two men on the stairs swooped their hats at the new arrivals, trying to scoop them in like water into a tub. One was a short balding federal judge, C. Rowland Pfister. Deputy United States Marshal Tyrone Medvedev was taller but mostly overlooked. The crowd really only noticed the judge, a returning native son. It was as if the judge waved both hats.

After awhile, Medvedev stepped behind the statue and untwirled wires from an amplifier under the hindquarters of Madrid's horse. He attached the wiring to a slim black plastic microphone dating from the nineteen-fifties. Once he had the mike wired, he had to step two stairs down to look Pfister in the eye and hand off the microphone. He tried to caution the judge about mike feedback. The judge didn't like being lectured.

"This ain't my first rodeo," Pfister said, and to his amazement, the words mushroomed back at him from every pillar and wall, and there were several around.

The crowd tittered and applauded a little, and Pfister waved his Stetson at them some more, then set it on his balding head and held the microphone the proper distance away to avoid the deafening shriek of electro-overload. A television camera crew from El Paso captured the spectacle for the evening news.

"Welcome to Gila Wells," said Pfister. Those words also reverberated.

Some of the people seated on blankets rose to join those on foot, and the crowd pushed backward to the middle of the lawn, and some of the blankets had to be moved. About a thousand people standing in the park at nine in the morning was half the town's population. But most were out-of-towners.

The judge, known for lengthy and colorful oratory, was rarely seen anymore. He only came to town on holidays to visit family and about once a year to hear a few federal cases if they could be clustered on a single docket. Otherwise two state judges and three county magistrates were the only ones who used the courthouse.

"This auction . . . is not about you or me," Pfister boomed, pausing every few syllables to let the echoes wane. "Not about cattle . . . wolves or elk . . . or biology or ranching . . . or the environment . . . ideas, values . . . economics . . . hope or disappointment."

"It's about the law," he said. "Our form of government. How we do things." That meant politics, and everybody knew it. They also knew they were trapped by it. By the spin he put on it. Captive right there in the town square.

Murmurs were heard. Some in the crowd hoped to bid if sealed offers were rejected. And some mistakenly thought they'd be able to buy individual items like a tractor or a baler or a prize bull. Some were ready to demonstrate. Girded for just about anything. Most wanted to watch and listen—without conflict if possible—and they looked back and forth at two seething extremes, to see what they would do.

The judge, they thought, was not helping.

Two large loudspeakers stood like sentinels at either end of the staircase. The judge looked at each of them, in turn, as he spoke and determined there was equal noise coming from both. Ten deputy marshals in suits formed a loose phalanx around Pfister, who stood about halfway up the concrete staircase in front of the faux marble pillars of the courthouse entryway.

"If we don't like something, we vote," the judge added.

It occurred to some who had begun to stir that the judge was now trying to bore them back into quiescence.

Deputy Marshals Medvedev and Donald Reims stood beside the judge, on either side, one a little behind and the other a little in front. The sun beat down on them. Pfister's well used Stetson shaded his eyes. It was a sweat-stained cowpoke's hat with a twisted leather hatband.

"Some of you environmental activists may think I'm biased. If I were, it wouldn't matter today."

"Oh, my God, there he goes again," Marlie Braden said as she and Sid waited inside the Billy the Kid Bar and Grill. "Sid, can't you do something?"

The judge looked around to see if any troublemakers wanted to take issue. People who seemed complacent at first now were fidgeting, shifting their weight foot to foot.

Bradens and Selwyn Osteen waited inside the doorway of the saloon, which was next to the courthouse. It was a saloon this judge well knew. His portrait hung in it.

"Known Sid Braden since he wore short pants and rode a pony," Pfister said.

"That's it," Sid said. "I'm putting a stop to this." He started out the door.

The judge grinned, nodded to Sid, whipped off his hat and yelled:Then he put his hat back on and said: "First, the honorable Selwyn Osteen of the law firm of Bracken, Pickett, Wacker, Osteen and Pells, with the list of assets to read. Mister Osteen?"

Osteen followed Sid out of the saloon, parted the crowd, got up on the steps, took the microphone and ran through the manifest as if switched into a higher speed. *Four trucks, two ATVs, three bicycles, a tractor, a dozer, a backhoe, washer-dryer, propane refrigerator, six generators, a baler, a post driver, seven rifles, sixteen pistols, propane stove, juke box, a dozen double bunks, a Cessna airplane, an Aerospatiale helicopter, six ranch houses, eight hundred head of cattle, a furrow plow attachment for the tractor, a road blader, transit-mix cement truck, two snowmobiles, a snowblower, three chainsaws, a dado table saw, ten-inch miter saw, a router, drills, blades, ten cases of whiskey, twenty cases of beer and one hundred fifty thousand acres. That includes one hundred thirty-five thousand federal allotment acres and fifteen thousand acres of deeded land.*

"Forget anything?" Osteen yelled.

"Nope," Braden replied at the bottom of the stairs.

The judge took back the mike and motioned to Medvedev.

"Deputy Marshal Medvedev, I believe, has the bids in a strong box. I would remind you all of the established minimum bid of two-point-four million dollars. And the deputy is only going to read the bids that meet or exceed that minimum. Medvedev," the judge said, nodding to the deputy, who nodded back.

A small metal safe the size of a suitcase, with a suitcase handle on top, was on the stairs beside Medvedev's feet. He picked it up and set it on Colonel Madrid's concrete cube. Just enough room for the suitcase-safe under the raised hooves.

Medvedev opened it, pulled out a white envelope from the top of a small stack, unsealed it and, picking up the microphone, read: "Wild West Coalition, consisting of fourteen national environmental groups, two-point-seven million dollars—and a pledge to remove all cattle from the range."

Cheers and boos arose from the crowd. Several members of the groups in question waved American flags and Green banners. Some of them hoisted the same placards they had used at Sid's last roundup. The ranchers stood with arms folded.

Medvedev returned the envelope to the suitcase and pulled out the next one. It was plain brown manila, and he used a ballpoint pen to tear open the seal. He looked at it, shook his head, tossed it back into the suitcase, and pulled out another. He tore it open, nodded and read it aloud:

"The Neighbors, a coalition of Western ranchers and the Federation of Agriculture and Mining, jointly bid two-point-seven million dollars and promise to comply with any and all federal regulations, continuing the one hundred and sixteen-year tradition of the Two Square."

More cheers and boos. Some of the same folks who waved flags for the environmentalists also waved them for the ranchers, and Henry Benton nodded his acknowledgment and mouthed silent thank-yous to them. Others kept their flags tucked under their arms for one side or the other.

"EightCorp, a Delaware mining corporation, bids two-point-eight million."

Medvedev read through and discarded four underbids, before hitting the bottom of the stack, a bright red and turquoise packet sealed with maroon wax, impressed with an official crest in a language he did not know.

"This is the eighth and final envelope," Medvedev said, breaking the seal.

"Is that from the bank?" Bertie Williams asked Benton, who shrugged.

"Whose bid is that?" Marlie asked Sid.

"Don't know, hon, no idea," he replied.

The crowd had begun a kind of low murmur.

The judge stepped forward and took the partly unsealed envelope and the microphone from Medvedev. "Thank you, Steve," he said, and the deputy stepped back.

"Just a little quiet, please," Pfister intoned, and the crowd fell silent.

An aged, white-haired man with a cane, stepped unsteadily onto the staircase. Willard Mann Junior strode across the stairway to the old man's side and took his arm.

"Who is that old man?" Marlie asked Sid.

"No idea," Sid replied.

The old man rested his weight on Will's arm, and the two stood together at the bottom of the staircase while the judge used a penknife to open the envelope.

He cleared his throat. "Blue Mountain Apache Nation, Arizona, bids three million dollars and pledges compliance with all federal laws, rules and regulations."

There was silence as the old man stepped up to meet the judge.

Pfister took off his hat to shake the old man's hand. Willard stayed a step below him. When the judge handed the old man the microphone, the elder Mann stepped up behind the judge and the three of them faced the crowd.

"My name is Willard Mann, and I am president of the Blue Mountain Apache," the old man said in a breaking voice that boomed out over the loudspeakers.

Only a handful of the people in the crowd had ever heard of him, and they were from Arizona. Benton shook his head in disbelief. He was not one of the handful.

"I wish to thank the United States government for its fairness and this good judge here for his strong spirit," the old man said. "As you see, I am old. My son, here, who many of you know and who does know this land best of all, has been appointed by our tribal council to oversee this ranch and to remain among you until his people call him to higher office." The words were still echoing as the old man handed the mike back to the judge, who put his hat back on and shook the elder Mann's hand once again.

"The Blue Mountain Apache Nation is declared high bidder, and the ranch goes accordingly to the high bidder, concluding this federal auction. God save the United States of America," the judge said.

Medvedev took the microphone as the judge and Willard Mann Senior climbed into a black Lincoln limousine with American flags on the front fenders. Will Mann, still wearing the uniform of a BLM ranger, stood on the stairs and watched them leave.

Marlie Braden found him.

"This couldn't have ended better, you taking care of this legacy," she said.

Mann smiled shyly as Sara Armstrong also scooted up the stairs, two steps at a time, to give him an embrace.

"I hereby resign from the Bureau of Land Management," Mann said with a quiet grin. Only the doc and Marlie Braden heard him. That didn't make him any less resigned.

Henry Benton, dragging Elias Corona, surged forward and jostled Marlie aside.

"This ain't federal," Benton said, his face close enough to Mann's that his breath fogged up Mann's sunglasses. "We're going to assert our rights in state court, where this matter belongs. Ain't no way we're letting some Arizona Indians steal this ranch."

"Henry, shut up," Marlie said, pushing him back down the stairs. He almost fell.

"Did you see that, Elias? She assaulted me," Benton said.

"I saw you assault her," the sheriff said with a smile. "Marlie and me, we go way back. You don't want to mess with her."

"Any help Sid and I can give, just let us know," Marlie told Mann

"Actually, I'd like you to stay through the summer. I'll set up an office in the bunkhouse, and I'll stay out there until the fall," Mann said.

"No, we could never do that," Marlie said.

"I'd hoped to ride alongside Sid for awhile, getting the hang of things," he said. "I heard Sid's going to teach range science in Cruces in the fall. Stay here until then."

"But I don't think Sid's going to Cruces."

Sid, after signing the documents along with three Forest Service officials, finally joined Mann and Marlie on the stairway. He patted Will on the back.

"What about it, Sid, how about a preview of your class this summer?" Mann asked him. "You can try it out on me, test-market it."

"What're you talking about? I'm not teaching."

"He wants us to stay on through—when?"

"Through August, anyhow," Mann said. "I need some help stringing fence."

Braden grinned broadly. "I know some folks can give you some pointers, but I don't string fence any more. That would be my first lesson. No charge. Get some of your young people up here to ride fence. I've got a great job."

"I need you to help me get those trucks running."

"You want Bertie for that. Bertie's a genius with trucks. I'm not," Braden said.

"What about moving cattle?" Mann said.

"They're all gone," Sid said. "I moved 'em all down to the Heel."

"They're coming back," Mann said. "At least four hundred of 'em."

"You're sure? *My* herd?"

"That's right, only it's our herd now," Mann said.

"How do you plan to pay for this?" Braden said.

"We got a sizable credit from the federal government. We agreed to settle much of our BIA claim with land—this land, and some other acreage west of here. Watanabe's place and a couple others. It's a large claim."

Braden shook his head, marveling. "The Apaches rule the Gila . . . again."

"We don't rule anything," Mann said. "We're just permittees like anybody else. The forest ranger's still the boss."

"Well, what are your plans?" Braden said.

"Pick up where you left off. Selling beef, but also farming. We're aiming to feed our people and protect our sacred lands. It's quite a day. *Quite* a day."

"What about your dad?" Marlie said.

"He and Missy are staying with us," Sara said. "We're doing barbecue tonight."

"Where? The Two Square?"

"No, my place," she said.

"Have it at the Two Square," Marlie said. "Everything's all ready to go. We got it all cleaned up, ship shape, party-ready. We'll invite everyone, even Raylinda."

"She's not feeling too well right now," the doctor said. "She's gone home to her mom's in Santa Fe. Don't believe we'll see Raylin for awhile. But I guess we can send someone to pick up that side of beef we've had marinating and bring it down to the ranch."

"Your ranch, too?" Marlie said. "You making plans?"

Sara looked expectantly at Mann for just a split second.

"Yeah, our ranch. Sara's too," Mann said hastily, "if she wants it."

Sara blushed and sputtered, "I, I, we . . ."

Marlie frowned at Mann and gave a strong tug to Sid, dragging him away.

"Come on, Sid," she whispered to him. "Got to let Will alone so he can try again." A little louder she said: "Heard it done a lot of different ways. Not like that."

Mann led Sara up the stairs to the pillars of the courthouse, where nobody could see or hear his lack of artistry.

Sara Armstrong sat on the sofa next to Mann and looked through his scrapbook. There was a boy dressed as a Little Crown Dancer, in his Apache moccasin-boots and his beaded leather skirt, wearing the crown with the ojo in it and carrying a lightning bolt in each hand.

He was a fearsome sight, and doc looked back and forth from the scrapbook to the gray-haired guy in the T-shirt sitting next to her, his polished boots on the floor under the coffee table, his stocking feet propped on top of a pillow sitting on the table.

"You told me you couldn't dance," she said.

"I can't."

"But look at you here," she said, holding the scrapbook up in front of his face so that he couldn't turn away.

"I was eight years old. I was likely to do anything I was told to do, and I was told to imitate the Crown Dancers, and I did the best imitation I could. I had no natural feel for it. It was a mockery in every sense of the word."

"You look bigger than an eight-year-old," she said.

Mann looked more closely at the picture.

"That isn't even me," he said. "That's my older brother."

"Where's he?"

"Right there."

"No, I mean where is he now?"

"Dead," Mann said. "Vietnam."

Then he did turn away and looked out the window. The stars shimmered, and Mann imagined his brother was looking at those stars, too, from a different angle.

"Oh," Sara said finally. She was old enough to remember Vietnam but not to have lost a loved-one. Still, looking at Mann's brother, Kyle, was strange. He wore a mask that nearly covered his face. He wore a costume that did cover his body.

"Zorro," he said. "We used to call Kyle Zorro."

"I can see why."

"Quick as a fox," his brother said proudly, "twice as mean. Now he's buried in one of those walls in Vietnam."

"Walls?"

"Sure. You know. The way they conceal the bodies."

"No, I don't know," Sara said.

"They'd bury them inside the walls."

"Grotesque," she said. "Tell me more about this dancing you did."

"It's all recorded on film," Mann said.

Mann was drowsy because of the wine they had with dinner. The label, he often thought, should caution against operating heavy equipment. Right now, he considered his eyelids heavy equipment.

"C'mon Little Beaver," she said, "let's rock and roll."

She got up to dance.

"Is this where we're going to stay?" she asked twirling around the bunkhouse with her arms flounced out gracelessly.

"What'd'you mean 'we,' white woman?" he asked.

"You and I," she said.

"Oh."

"Assuming you meant what you said under the courthouse atrium."

His clumsiness made him cringe, again.

A new Crown Dancer usually joined the troupe as soon as he could walk steadily. They were a troupe. They moved with purpose, at least Mann did, to cover up his clumsiness.

"They say the Indian's the most coordinated of all humans," Sara said.

"It's a lie."

"Which would you rather have: The truth?" she asked, "Or a cherry tree?"

"I can't handle a cherry tree," Mann said. "Don't have time. Need the firewood."

"The dancing, the dancing. Tell me about the dancing."

"My father taught me when I was three. I remember he cut my lightning bolts out of plywood on his jigsaw."

"Time has carried you through," Sara said, "to me."

The bartender that Sid hired for the evening was finishing putting away the glasses he had just washed and dried.

"Get you something?" the barkeep asked.

"Nah, I don't really drink," Mann said. "But you can get a glass of champagne for my fiancée."

Silently he poured, and the liquid foamed to the rim, edged over and streaked the sides of the vessel.

"Can I have a towel?" Mann asked the 'keep, who slid one across to him.

The barkeep handed Willard Mann, the elder, a beer with lime, and the old man sank his teeth in the lime, then poured beer down his throat after it.

Willard Mann, the younger, carried champagne to his fiancée, and her eyes sparkled like the liquid. Then he turned to his father, who was seated on the second sofa in the downstairs bunk area that their unit had commandeered.

"Hey, dad. Been thinking about you."

"What for?" he said.

"Not sure," Mann said. His father laughed.

"You want us to show off our best dress bead-and-feather," Will said.

"No, I want you to learn from the innocents—they're the way to get through."

Will gave his accord with a blink and a smile, even though his father's message was not getting through, and his father knew it.

"Want you to teach the little ones," his father said, "teach 'em to dance."

Will's smile faded a little with the awareness that life would be different now in every way at every turn, every stroke of the clock and of the pen. The expression on his face carried a much larger question than his father answered.

"That way maybe you'll learn how yourself," the old man said.

"Well, I imagine your office got it. Sure can't still be in the mail."

The patient's smile broadened imperceptibly—only the patient knew it.

Chapter Twenty-One

The Couple

Winter work was spare, cattle gone to the low pastures, the feedlots, railheads. Snow covered most of the grasses throughout the silent Apache Wilderness.

Trees were puffy, fat with snow that spilled off on the passing rider and his hat whenever his horse brushed the branches.

Good time for fixing fences. Good, he thought, working alone at it now in the snow. A crispness the boy could feel on the tip of his nose and the thin edges of his ears. If while singing to himself his tongue met the air, its surface instantly froze, then stuck to the roof of his mouth.

Miguelito carried spools of wire down across a corner of the Wilderness to a place where a mile of Endicott's fence was down, in tatters. The boy had wrapped the spools with an old drop cloth so the barbs wouldn't spook the horse, Darlin'. Good plan. Worked fine at first. But just before Miguelito could mount her for a second trip, a barb cut through to her flank when she rubbed against a fencepost. She started to spin and kick all by herself. The centrifugal force of her spin levitated the spools of wire. Whenever she hit the ground, barbs slapped down like a hammer driving a nail, restarting the spin. Finally she crashed through the fence and was gone.

Cliff Endicott came running out in his thermal underwear, hatless, and watched Darlin' work her way up the trail toward the Navajo-owned Wyler Ranch outside Magdalena.

"Use the mule. Use a pack saddle. Don't put them spools on some poor horse's back," Endicott told him.

"Okay, Mister Endicott," the boy said.

"Thought you knew better, Jim."

False name. Jaime Garza. Miguelito had been here nearly three weeks in the snow-masked Apache Wilderness. Hiding from

Octavio and from the law. Perfect place to hide. It had seemed. But hearing someone say that false name stained it for him.

To the west, clouds bled into the sky and into the frosted trees, blurring the horizon. Then the wind came across the Plain of San Tomas from Arizona, pushing that blur, which was a sleet storm, down onto Miguelito. By the time he recovered Darlin', the day was gone and he was beaded with ice. Too late for his first trip into town, as he had planned. So he rode in next day with the Endicotts in their Suburban. January Twentieth. The day he met Millie.

"If not for that horse they might not have met," Mann said.

Marlie Braden sat next to Mann on her old porch glider underneath the portal at the Two Square. They were having coffee, but it was a reckoning. She'd let a couple days slide by. And the sliding could just keep going if she let it. Mann on his last official day still had the file. Hadn't turned it over yet. Affidavits, hours of tape, a dozen pads of notes. Especially on the Endicotts.

"Miguelito rode in with the Endicotts," Mann told her. "In their Suburban. They all split up when they hit Gila Wells." Ellie to her shopping. Clifford to the livestock auction, Clay making his escape. Seeking release from the gravitational pull of his father, who wanted him to stick close and learn a thing or two. "Clay tends to drift, you know," Mann told her. "When Cliff looked around, Clay was gone."

Clay liked to study the guns in Ron's Sporting Goods in the Gila Emporia shopping center. One roof short of a mall. The horseshoe-shaped strip mall had a commons, a garden with adobe walls and banco-benches where teens congregated. Checked each other out. Had a movie theater, two restaurants, a Wal-Mart, Walgreens, a one-room Sears store with a catalog counter, an insurance office and Ron's place, which had every rod and reel, every set of waders, seventeen kinds of gun, all sorts of ammunition, a fiberglass trolling boat for sale in front, hanging from the portal rafters. Ron wanted two grand. Too much. Pasture was the parking lot.

Across the street and down the block, the pawnshop sat beside the roller rink. And many times what left the Emporia soon entered Simmy's Pawn, where Ramos had unloaded much of the Cortes family jewelry in the past few years. Prominently displayed under shatterproof glass.

Clay feigned a siesta under his sunglasses. Sprawled on a banco. Tracking the girls.

Millie found him there. "You should see yourself," she said with a half-giggle.

"Why—what's wrong?" he said, taking off the shades.

"You need a life," she said.

"You'd rather I was over at the bull auction. Dad wanted me to watch him bid." He raised two fingers. "'Two thousand from the man in the blue hat.' Where'd he ever get a blue hat?"

Millie didn't know how to tell Clay she was giving up on him. But he knew. She just stood there, half turned away from him, watching the cross-currents of commerce, wondering how so many shoppers came from so small a town. Must be from Huntley or the frontera.

Clay put his sunglasses back on. Slumped back against the wall.

Miguelito came across the commons, eating a tamale from a cart with a red umbrella.

Clay took note of him. Millie noted Clay's reaction.

"Who's that?" Millie said.

"New hand. Jaime, or Jimmy. Dad hired him just after New Year's," Clay said, pushing shades up again. Miguelito, using the Jaime papers, spotted Clay and came over.

"Hey," he said.

"Hey," Clay said.

"Hi," Miguelito said to Millie.

She was facing Clay but acknowledged Miguelito sideways with a glance and a nod.

"She talk?" Miguelito asked Clay.

"Sometimes. Depends. Might say somethin' you don't want to hear. That's Millie," Clay said. "Millie, this here's Jimmy."

"Pleasure, ma'am," Miguelito said, taking off an imaginary hat.

"Nice talking to you idiots," Millie said and walked off.

Miguelito went after her when she didn't turn. Took a few steps to catch up.

"Hey, what'd I say?" he said.

"Far as I can tell, below zero," she said, continuing toward the parking lot. "*Does she talk?* If anyone's got a question for *me*, ask me. Don't ask him."

"How old are you?" Miguelito said.

She turned to face him at the edge of the muddy parking lot.

"Old enough to know what's stupid. Not old enough to do anything about it."

"Not for long," he said. "You're pretty smart for a kid. Stand up for yourself. I like that."

She scrunched her face into a mask of disdain. Not real disdain. But it looked real to Miguelito, who backed off.

"Friendly warning," she said, trying to explain. "Dad doesn't like me talking to boys."

"That *is* friendly."

"Mom and dad don't like smart mouths," she said.

"What'll they do about *yours*, then?" he asked, continuing to walk along beside her.

"Can we just walk away in totally different directions?" she said.

"Friends," he said, putting a condition on it.

"Don't know," she said.

"But always a possibility," he said grandly.

She cocked her head at him.

"You're funny," she said. "Bye."

Her father stood beside the pickup as she hopscotched lightly across the lot, stepping only on clumps of grass, mostly missing the mud. She didn't look back at Miguelito, who was trailing her by ten feet. Miguelito gawked at Sid Braden, said "howdy" and then walked off in a completely different direction, as she'd suggested.

Braden looked sternly but silently at him, then at Millie. "What kept you? Been waiting."

"Clayton," she said. "Had those sunglasses. Looking at the girls. Couldn't just pass by."

"No, you couldn't, could you," Sid said with a grin. "That boy."

"Mister Endicott's gone and hired another hand," she said, nodding at Miguelito.

Sid looked at Miguelito, walking decisively away from them.

"Tell me you don't know that boy," Braden said.

"Never laid eyes on him before two minutes ago. Gol-durn, dad," she said. "Next time I'll stay home, let you do the shopping for yourself."

"You just might," he said.

The Endicotts' Suburban slowed at the E-Bar-E turnoff, where the windblown second E hung down and swung in the breeze.

"I could fix that E for you," Miguelito said.

"Okay, Jim," Cliff said. "Clay will get you a ladder. Use the old pickup."

The boy had a funny look.

"What?" Cliff said.

"Just appreciate having this work," the boy said. "I'd like to be a rancher."

"Good you like work, cause you'll get it," Cliff said.

He turned to his son: "How long that E been hangin' down, Clay?"

"Dunno," Clay mumbled.

"Almost a year," Cliff said.

Next day, Millie rode up to see Clay. Knocked the snow off her boots. Set her hat on the end table and told Ellie: "We're gonna do wolves."

"What?" Ellie gasped. "Wolves? Oh, you can't."

"It's just science," Millie said.

Marlie closed her eyes and nodded as Mann read the comment off one of his pocket-sized notebooks. Marlie raised her chin. Set her jaw as the porch glider paused between forward and back. Yeah, Ellie Endicott called Marlie. The wives didn't tell Sid or Cliff. Dads in the dark. Until Clay, bitterly, said: "Hello, *wolf girl.*"

"Millie and Miguelito," Mann began, but Marlie pierced him with a warning look; going too fast; he slowed down, but continued, "went out riding together. *Good,* you thought because it took her mind off the wolves," Mann said. "But you thought the boy was somebody else—and someone Clayton's age."

"Slow down," Marlie said. She was seeing it. His words commingled with her memories. Pictures, some just a flash, or a glimpse, pieced themselves together. Sequenced. Began to flow.

"Hey, kid." The voice floated in from the corral.

Marlie, unfolding a quilt, looked out the bedroom window.

The boy did sit a horse well. Born to it.

Then Millie stepped out of the shadows, and the sun lit her up like a burning bush.

She was all in white—white jeans, white shirt, white hat—carrying her saddle. Almost as big as she. Set the saddle down so she could pull down her brim. Needed to shade her eyes.

"Oh, it's you," she said.

Marlie could hear the surprise—the poor attempt to hide it—in her voice. *Such a little girl.* The child needed practice.

The boy shaded his eyes, too.

Marlie watched as the young man dismounted. Dropped the reins. Crossed the shadow cast by the barn.

"Let me get that," he said, hoisting her saddle up onto his shoulder.

Millie let him. *She let him*, Marlie thought, watching, astonished. That would just never happen. Just wouldn't. And Sugar, the fidget horse, standing *still?*

Marlie couldn't hear, but she saw. The boy was talking to the horse. The saddle blanket was already on her. No problem, far as Sugar was concerned. The boy dropped the saddle right on the marks left on the blanket from a thousand saddlings. Cinched her tight. Did that horse turn and *nuzzle* his boot? *Damn*, Marlie thought. Then they rode out together. Slowly. They were talking. Marlie would have died to hear the words.

"So," the boy said. Let silence finish the thought. Whatever the thought was. In about ten seconds, he added words two through five. "You, uh, ride well."

The girl just smiled.

"Really don't talk much, do you," the boy said after awhile.

"Not much to say," she said, "I guess."

"But there's lots to be said. What a fine day, not too cold, for a change, no sleet," he said.

"Oh," she said. "Weather. Yeah."

"Where are you from, señor?" he asked himself. "Santito. What do you want to be? A rancher. What do *you* want to be?"

The girl clung to her silence.

"That's a question for you," he said finally.

"Oh," she said, but she still didn't answer.

Wasn't so much a hesitation about what she wanted to be. It was leaving behind the person she would not be. Not ready to leave that person behind. Or even think about it. To say *biologist* would be like telling her dad, *No, I won't be running this ranch.* You'll need to find somebody else. That was a cold pang, like riding through a cave where ice never melts. *Someone else.* Dark personage. Dark and distant. Dark and unknown. And she was so much in the light.

The boy seemed to comprehend.

"You don't want to talk about the future; that means you aren't ready to face it," he said.

"What's to talk about?" the girl said. "It isn't even here yet. Doesn't even exist."

"But it sure has a way of getting here," he said. "And getting here fast."

Another thing best left undebated.

"There's a beaver pond up here," she said. "Created by the beavers. But the trout like it, too. And so do I. Want to see?"

"Sure," he said.

They rode over to it. Elk, deer, rabbits, birds all left their tracks in its muddy apron.

"It's a zoo," the boy said.

She shook her head. "No cages."

She gave Sugar some heel, and the horse lurched forward, reluctant to step in the mud; no telling how far she'd sink. "Sugar can't tell how deep or shallow the mud is," she said.

"And you can," he said.

"Sure can, because I've watched this pond get big and then get small again over the last three years. Look at that bedrock over there, that sandstone. This mud sits right on it. It was left there by the water the last time the pond was big. Some of us learn and some of us don't."

"How old are you?" the boy asked her, again.

She looked hard at him. He couldn't tell if she was nodding approval or if Sugar was just compensating for the uneven earth. She rode on. The boy following.

Clay was waiting when Millie and "Jim" got back into the Endicotts' corral. She just wanted to make sure the newcomer made it home OK. Hospitable thing to do. Help a stranger. Clay saw them ride down slowly from the Wilderness, talking, *talking*. Sometimes a flash of impatience. Then it would dissolve. They were plinking each other like toy pianos. Taunting, then laughing at it. Clay shrank down real small inside himself and seemed, to him, to be peering out of much bigger eyes, from a distance. As if Rushmore were hollow and he was trapped inside. Looking out through cave eyes.

"Hello, *wolf girl*," Clay said as they rode in.

"Well, hi, Clay. What've you been up to?" she asked him.

"I can't be helping you with your project," he said.

"I know," she said. "I'm sorry."

Clifford in the barn heard the conversation and came out.

"What d'you mean calling her 'wolf girl,' son? That seems rude," Cliff said.

"Well, that's what she is—riding out with Mister Garza here," Clay said. "Goin' out to look at wolf pens. Goin' out to *volunteer*."

"She's jest bein' a good neighbor, showin' Jim the off-the-beaten so he don't git lost," Cliff said. "Something you or I should've done. But leave it to Miss Millie."

"Ask her," Clay said. "Go ahead and ask her about the wolves."

"Wolf pens?" Miguelito asked. "Like to see that. Really would."

"We don't like wolves much up here, Jim. I'd steer clear," Cliff said. "You, too, Mill."

Millie reverted to her silence. "Well," she said. Turned her horse. Rode south.

Days went by. More silence. Miguelito figured time to have a talk with Sid Braden. Clear up a few things. So he rode down to the Two Square. Found Sid amiable. Helped him cut up a cottonwood.

Chainsaw duet. Slid a sheet of Propanel up onto the shed roof Sid was fixing.

"You don't have time for this, Jim. You have your own work to do," Sid told him.

"I don't mind," Miguelito said. "Figure I'm learning."

Millie would come out of the house, raise a hand, say "Hi," then disappear again, going about her chores, mostly in the stable. Miguelito let it go. Had to. Sid was right. Not much free time. Couldn't drive his car. Risk running into the law. Left it parked under a tarp behind Endicott's barn. Couldn't drive the trail between their ranches, anyway. It crossed a corner of the Wilderness, so cars went the long way around. But one day in February, Millie was back.

"Hear you're stringing fence," she said. "I brought us an extra ratchet."

They rode down together. Finished the fence in a day. Then, Miguelito helped her soap every inch of leather in Braden's stable. Finally, she asked him to ride with her to see the wolves.

"Can't go alone," she said. "Been putting it off, hoping you'd ask. It's getting late."

"Sure, I'll go," Miguelito said. "Don't tell anyone, or it'll get back to the Endicotts."

So then, the big day. Her eyes bright. Hair done up with two little pony-tails sprouting from the top of her head. New brass-framed glasses. New riding pants and boots. She rode Sugar into the Wilderness. Miguelito met her at the crossing. Followed. Not far behind. But every now and then, she'd pull a little farther ahead. Riding that seesaw for a half-hour. In silence.

"How am I supposed to look out for you if this old horse can't keep up?" he asked.

"You have some kind of a little problem there, then, don't you, señor?" she said.

He gave Darlin' more heel. The horse turned around and stared at him.

Another five miles into the great Apache Wilderness they found the release pen where the Fish and Wildlife Service and Wolf USA biologists had their first New Mexico pack set to go.

A woman and two men were camped back of the pen. Separated from it by a wall of aspen cuttings. A blind. Posted land: *Trespassers*

Will Be Prosecuted for Violation of the Federal Wilderness Act, Endangered Species Act and the National Environmental Policy Act.

Millie rode over to Michelle Westover, who wore a sheep coat, her feet firmly planted in large galoshes over worn-out jeans. She took a glove off to shake hands with the horseback girl.

"You know this is trespassing," Westover said. "Whoever you are, you can't be here."

"Sure *can*," Millie said. "We're the Two Square and E-Bar-E. Here to see the wolves."

"No way," Westover said. Spoke into a two-way radio: "Donald! Visitors." To Millie she added: "Got to clear your visit with the federal government. He's on his way."

Donald Badderly, thin and pale, walked down from the mountain behind them shaking his head, which was like waving a flag. Bright red-orange hair.

"It's bad," he said.

"What is?" Westover asked. "These kids want to see the wolves. You want to tell 'em?"

"Oh, sure, fine, no problem," Badderly said. "Hi, I'm Donald. What're your names?"

They introduced themselves again as resident allottees.

"How old are you?" Badderly asked them, looking back and forth between them.

"Is there an age limit?" Millie replied.

"Hmmm. Maybe not," he said. "But why are you here? I thought your ranches were dead set against us, judging by the writs and pleadings and appeals and memoranda that have been filed with the federal judge in this case. We had to get a court order to even be here."

Millie smiled sweetly. Miguelito kept his mouth shut.

"I'm not sure, but I might need a note from your parents," Badderly added.

"He's my escort," Millie said, pointing at Miguelito, who laughed.

"We might be able to accommodate you," Westover said, "if you signed a membership."

"You don't have to join anything," Badderly told the pair. "But . . . what—"

"This would be good," Millie said, pointing at the blind. It was poorly made and fake-looking. Tied together with yellow climbing rope. The wall of leaves had three small openings for observation. Millie pulled out her binoculars. Took a look.

Westover moved to physically stop the child, but Badderly held Westover's arm.

"Do not touch the children," he said quietly. "Let them be our friends."

Miguelito stood back observing and listening and holding the horses.

The biologists' tents were in a clearing up slope about fifty yards from there, and the mountain continued on up to an altitude of more than eight-thousand feet. Miguelito noted the elk trail leading high up on Miller's Mountain.

"I think I see what you were concerned about," Miguelito told Badderly.

"Not about you," Badderly said.

"It's the high ground behind you, so close to the pen," Miguelito said. "Deadly. That's what you meant when you said it was bad."

Badderly looked sharply at the young man.

"Very good. Maybe you'd like to work for us when you're done with school," he said.

Miguelito just shook his head. "Going to be a rancher," he said.

"Oh," Badderly said. "Good luck. Have you considered moving to another country?"

Millie, without turning, waved them over to the wolf blind.

"I see them," she said, still focused through her binocs. "They're down at the bottom of the pen, feeding on a carcass."

"That's an elk they're eating," Badderly told her.

"I know it's an elk," she said. "We have more than two hundred of them on our ranch."

"Wow," Badderly said "Would you consider letting us use an abandoned kill for a feed carcass now and then?"

"Doubt dad would allow it," she said.

Badderly nodded.

"I want to photograph the wolves," Millie said.

"Impossible," Westover said.

"Maybe not," Badderly said. "But you'd have to apply in writing. Say why you need the photos. Specify what sort of equipment you'd bring. Would it be *still* photography?"

"No, video," she said. "I can get a video-cam from school."

"What would you use the images for?"

"My third straight science fair prize," she said.

"Oh, God, a biologist," Badderly said. "You may need to leave the country, too."

She'd already thought about leaving. And now, another trip back from the wolf pens, she was thinking again. The University of London. Oxford. Cambridge. The University of South Wales. Edinburgh. The Sorbonne. The University of Madrid. NYU. Bryn Mawr. Fort Lewis College in Durango, Colorado. Brochures were coming to her from faraway places. Bright, shining places. All collected in a neat pile in the kitchen basket. The egg basket hanging from the ceiling between two ristras of dried red chiles. Next to the phone. Nice concise letters alongside.

"*Dear Miss Braden, Thank you for your early interest in Harvard. Rare it is indeed that one so young takes such precise and detailed interest in our institution. After your fifteenth birthday we shall make a point of inviting you for a visit. Until then, keep those grades up and keep those hopes up. Very truly yours, Albigensia Fourrule, deputy registrar.*" At the top, an embossed red seal: "*Veritas.*"

Sid out back with the ladder. About to scrub out the smokestack with his long-handled chimney-sweep brush. Left it leaning against the eaves. Came around to confront her.

She'd never seen her father so angry, verging on out-of-control, as he was the day he found out about her wolf project. Unpredictable. Scary for her, but she didn't back down.

"It's science. I've got to *see* the wolves," she said. "See them at the moment they're released. It's what scientists do. Doesn't mean I'm the *wolf girl*. I'm not."

"Heck, you *are* just a little girl, Mill. Can't even drive. Barely lift a saddle. What good'll it do? Some small group of—" he broke off. "You want to ruin us. You'll ruin us. Your family."

"Needs to be observed. To be watched. Maybe it won't work. A scientist. A real scientist needs to observe it. If I can be there on that day," she said, "know what that will mean for me? I'll have my choice. Any school. Anywhere in the world. I'm not taking sides. You are, daddy. You're the one taking a stand. Not me."

Right about here, she knew she had him. Up till then, she wasn't sure. But now she was.

"Well, maybe you won't be a scientist at all," Sid snapped. "Maybe you'll just do your chores and be grounded here on the ranch."

"The wolves are on the ranch," she said. "Those are our allotments. I've got to see them, and it's wrong to say I can't because I can and I *will!*"

Sid walked into the house and slammed the door. The first of a few slammed doors.

Westover rose early. Before the rooster outside Watanabe's coop. She hiked quietly back to the ranger station where her car was parked. The car was reluctant in the twelve-degree darkness. Five minutes of revving. Battery running low. The noise wasn't good. Ranger Todd Markie came out of his log residence wearing his ancient buffalo robe.

Westover glared at him as if he personally killed the buffalo.

"Got some jumper cables, Miss," he said. "Happy to get you started so we can sleep."

Westover bit her lower lip. No mention of t'tonka.

"Thanks, Todd, appreciate it. Kind of you to get up and help at this hour," she said.

She hoped Markie would not ask her why she was up and about at this hour, four plus o'clock, too dark to see her watch. Markie almost did ask *why?!!* Finally decided against it. Just more conversation in the cold. Probably a quite long and elaborate explanation. No, thanks.

Markie's jumpstart, aided by his own frigid Jeep, got Westover's Buick Skylark growling. She drove slowly down the ice-patched road to the main highway. Through the dark streets of Gila Wells. Past Elias Corona's palatial brick police headquarters, past the Emporia strip mall, past the historic home of hookers, complete with historic marker, to the Post Office. Westover carried an envelope into the darkened Post Office and came out without the envelope.

In a few weeks, between college brochures, came a letter from Wolf USA, granting Millicent Braden a prize that would pay for her videotape, her editing and her copying.

"And look, mom," Millie said. "This certificate says I went and won their essay contest."

"Didn't know you wrote an essay," Marlie said.

"Neither did I," Millie said. "I never did."

"Must have written something." Marlie said, steaming from the shower, wrapped in her towel, in her closet, in the freezing air. "Wish this cold would quit," she said.

"I just sent a letter, applying to be there with a camera when they release the wolves." Then the wall phone and Marlie's cell phone rang at once. Then Sid's fax machine powered up. Paper fed through. Curled up on the lip of the tray. Fell gracelessly to the floor.

"This is a fax from a TV station in El Paso," Millie said, picking it up and turning on a light. "Who's on the phone?"

"Your Aunt Billie. Saw a story about you on TV," Marlie said. "She *what?* My Gosh."

"What is it, mom?" Millie said. "What's she saying?"

"Shhh. They're calling you the *wolf girl,* dear."

"Oh, my gosh," Millie said. "They can't do that. Can they?"

"They say you defied your father. *Fought* him. Defending the wolves."

"That's not what happened. Not the way it was, or is," she said.

"I'll call the senator," Marlie said.

"Need Miguelito's portion," Mann told Marlie, the porch glider gliding.

"Well, I know what he told her and what he told the Endicotts."

"You'll want to help him. Would be good," Mann said.

"What about the people he killed or hurt?"

"He killed the one person he did not want to kill. Nobody else."

Marlie looked unsure. Frowned. Squinted. Unsure if she wanted to believe him.

"Weeks is heading over to talk to him. You can help," Mann said.

Clayton Endicott and his father arrived, so Marlie got up and went inside. The Endicotts tipped their hats. Sat down on two porch chairs. Both had rifles with them, zipped in their cases.

They stared glumly at Mann, on the glider, who looked down at his notes.

"Clay, you did a brave thing speaking up. And good of you both bringing in your guns. Want to thank you for it. For your cooperation," Mann told him, then raised a hand to stop him responding. "Far as it went," he said.

"Just a minute," Cliff said, half rising.

"Please have a seat," Mann said. "Got a list of things to go through. Your lawyer's invited. He coming?"

"What do I need a lawyer *for?*" Cliff said.

"My last day on the job. Mean to tie up the last loose ends," Mann said.

"You mean me?" Cliff said.

"You and Clay," Mann said.

"Clay hasn't done anything," Clifford said.

"But for a young man who saw so much—saw a wolf get shot, saw a girl get shot—there's a lot he didn't tell. A lot we don't know. And I want it—all of it."

Clay looked at his father, who shook his head.

"First off, I want to see your two-forty-three since I got warrants for the guns," Mann said, picking up Cliff's gun bag and unzipping it. He pulled out a sleek, well-oiled rifle with a three-hundred-X scope. "Where's the magazine?" he said.

"I never carry it loaded in town," Cliff said, handing the clip to him separately. "You're going to find I didn't shoot anybody or any *thing*."

"Where do wolves fit in—as things? Or as something else?" Mann asked. "Wanted to ask about the night of the Neighbors riot in Redsleeve. And Clay was stuck on a mountain."

The boy nodded but said nothing.

"Over by Ojorito hot creek, where Raylinda Wells was swimming, sunning?" Mann said.

Clay looked at his father again.

"Clay hasn't done anything," Clifford repeated. "What are you trying to imply? That Wells woman was not properly clothed. On public land."

"Had to be there to know that, right, Clay? And when that wolf was shot, you said you saw the shooter. Right? You're just a kid, but the law still applies. You got to tell the truth here. How does it feel to look down the barrel of your father's gun?"

Clay looked down at his own bagged gun, leaning against the desk. Shook his head.

"That's something you'll just have to prove, now, ain't it," Cliff growled.

"Won't be hard," he said, patting the two-forty-three. "Easy as a piece of Ellie's pie."

"Well, prove what you can. Don't want to hear about what you can't," Cliff said. "Come on, Clay. We're going."

Clay kept sitting.

"Clay?" his dad said.

"I guess I better sit here for just a little while longer," the boy said. "I guess Agent Mann needs to hear the rest of it. For Millie's sake. I guess I got to, dad. I'm sorry."

Sid Braden watched in anger—as much at himself as anyone—as Millie rode off March Third. Pride mixed with anger. But he wanted to hug the girl and tell her it was okay. It was fine.

But she rode out. Her mind and her mouth set straight.

He waved after her.

She stopped. Smiled at him. Waved back. Headed up the trail. Small in the saddle.

Chapter Twenty-Two

Aragon

The cowboy fussed with his hat. Took it off. Re-dented it. Put it back on. Paced and rocked boot to boot, heel to toe, Stetson in hand. Searching for a hole in the crowd. He'd spent a night over the invisible black Atlantic and was greeting a gray dawn south of Paris. A place called Orly. The only Stetson in the building.

Chaos. A tangle of shuffling people. The serpentine must have stretched a mile within the squared-off customs bottleneck. The velvet cords doubled back on themselves a dozen times before anyone came out the other end. Weeks counted six women with babies ahead of him. Like counting sheep. Elderly men were propped up, one with a cane, another with a foldout stool. Most everyone stood immobile and scuffed their soles on the gritty concrete floor of the converted airline hangar.

Customs Inspector Alexandre Dronne saw the hat and waved Weeks over to his counter to speak cowboy. Weeks' bag tag said New Mexico, a place Dronne wanted to go. He flashed his Spanish. "*¿De donde viene?*" Where from?

"*Los Estados Unidos*, the state of New Mexico."

"*¿Occupación?*"

"Customs—*la aduana*, jest like you," Weeks said.

"How big a port?" the agent said, switching ably to English.

"One man, down in the desert, called Jackrabbit Wells."

"That's it, amigo, stick with me, I get you through. *Me llamo* Alex."

Name tag—A. Dronne. He'd worked a one-man gate, too, at Roncesvalles, where, he said, King Charles the Great re-entered France after battling the Moors in Spain.

Unexpected, inexplicable hospitality made Weeks uneasy. But he thought if you can't trust a fellow aduanero, who can you trust?

"Got a job in Spain. An appointment Monday," Weeks said.

"Where?"

"Barcelona, but I need to get there now. Only got five days, counting the weekend. A witness. He's, um. . ."

"Why not fly into Barcelona?"

"Would've, if there'd been a seat available that moment. I'm better coming through France, anyway. They won't expect it."

"Who?"

"Long story."

"Let's see your papers and tickets."

The documents showed *sleeping car* south to the huge central switching yards at Clermont-Ferrand, where the rail car would be shunted around in the middle of the night and hooked up to a train that would take it down to the Mediterranean, to the border at le Boulou. Switch to Spanish Rail. Fifty miles to Barcelona.

"As it happens, coincidentally," Dronne said, "I'm on the last train tonight heading down to Barcelona. I'll be there tonight. Spain's like home to me. I worked at Boulou three years."

"Great, so we're on the same train," Weeks said.

"No, I'm on the last train. You're on the train ahead of me. But that train won't get there until tomorrow. I get there tonight."

"How's that?"

"My train's faster," Dronne said. "You could probably get changed to my train."

Dronne helped Weeks transfer his ticket, and they boarded the train headed south.

When Dronne looked at Weeks he saw Monument Valley and the mesas and forests of New Mexico, *la grande nature Americaine*, the Wild West. Always wanted to be there. Weeks might be his ticket.

"I suppose everything you're doing is legal," Dronne said as they drank beer in the observation car at sunset near Orleans.

"Hope so," Weeks said.

"Got a warrant?" Dronne asked, watching the last orange cloud fade to gray.

"Letter of introduction," Weeks said, "from the young man's stepfather. His parents are dead."

"Where's the stepfather?" Dronne asked.

"In jail," Weeks said.

With daylight gone, the fields outside flashed past unseen. Moonless night.

"What if this kid, this witness, won't talk to you?" Dronne asked.

"Then maybe he'll at least hear what I have to say. He's in danger," Weeks said.

Weeks sized Dronne up the best he could. Dronne did the same. They'd have to decide quickly. The train was going much faster than clickety-clack. It was a hum.

"There might be trouble," Weeks said finally. "I could use some help."

"I figured," Dronne replied with an unperturbed smile. "Tell me everything."

Sandrine had predicted: France would come through. Sandrine was right.

"I make one big condition," Dronne said. "You give me the Wild West tour."

Weeks tried to straighten out his own crooked grin. Never could.

"Know where this is?" Weeks asked, handing Dronne the lawyer's letter.

Don Septimo de Toledano worked on the Paseo de Colon, named for Columbus, next to the Maritime Museum overlooking Barcelona harbor—the *freight* docks, not the yacht basin, not the beaches, not the classy address that Dronne, for one, would have expected. The burly, hairy Toledano, who looked like a red-headed stevedore, specialized in maritime law, shipping and money-market contracts.

The smell of fish infused the air. A freight train came chugging slowly along the quay and stopped to pick up container cargo from a huge white Greek ship. Two cranes lowered the containers, two by two, onto the train's flatbed cars. Another train pulled out with every flatcar stacked two deep with containers from East Asia from a ship that came through Suez. Two others used their own cranes to set their goods on the rail cars. Down the quay, near the end, where the hillsides are stacked with offices and apartments, cattle were lifted in nets, bellowing as they descended into the bowels of a Japanese ship.

The *noise!* Like a circus. The lawyer slammed his window shut and sat down. It was a nice office, smelling of wood oil. All wood-paneled with silver chandelier over mahogany desk. A brass telescope was mounted eyeball-high on a tripod at the window for watching the comings and goings of the ships and the trains.

Dronne sat exiled in the anteroom studying local tabloids.

Weeks sat across from Toledano, looking at the map for Monday's meeting.

"This meeting's in *France?*" Weeks said. "I was just in France. Why are we here?"

"*Really!*" the lawyer snapped. "You have explicit instructions. Created for security reasons which you'd now want to unilaterally cast aside. *¡Intolerable!*"

"Security's only as good as the willingness, the openness to change," Weeks said. Stood up and went to Toledano's telescope, peering at the trains and boats below.

"They unload those *calamares* down there, do they?" he asked.

"Calamares, yes," the lawyer said. "What about it? I thought this was urgent."

"You've got some bad guys coming for Miguel," Weeks said, panning the scope.

Something peripheral caught his eye. He looked quickly back in that direction.

"Something out there?" Toledano asked.

"Not sure. Thought I saw . . . something odd."

Weeks watched a seiner hoist sling-nets of fish into a refrigerator car with an open roof that was sliding shut now that the fish were captive.

The lawyer's ruddy face drained pale when Weeks pulled out his forty-four magnum revolver and checked the cylinder, double-clicked the safety.

The train began moving even while the last net was being pulled free from the path of the moving door. Maybe a dozen fish fell flapping on the quay. Workers scooped them up and threw them in a large ice tank over in their warehouse, where they could collect them at quitting time and take them home for dinner.

"Where is Miguelito?" Weeks asked, panning slowly with the scope.

"Who knows? You're four days early. He's working over in Aragon, I'd say."

"Any idea how many people died in northern Mexico the last three, four weeks?"

"A few, I'm sure," he said, "but you know that's why we keep Miguelito safe."

"Monday's no longer safe. We should meet at once, if possible," Weeks told him.

The lawyer decided Weeks wasn't going to shoot him. He managed an uneasy laugh, swiveled his chair around again facing his desk, away from the windows.

"Don Octavio said you were impatient."

"No, I'm tellin' you Monday's too late," Weeks said. "Seriously. *Danger*, not impatience. Did you read the letter I just handed you? Octavio is worried about this boy. I'm here to protect him. What happens to *you* if something happens to him?"

"I'm just a lawyer," Toledano said. "You're the cowboy, the one who—"

"Look at this," Weeks said, whistling. "Persistence pays off."

The lawyer swiveled around and they stared out together. Three men in suits trotted down the gangway from one of the trawlers.

"See those goons down there?" Weeks asked him. "The boys in black?"

Toledano nodded, a slowly growing recognition.

"Torpedoes. Two from home," Weeks said. "I know both, but I don't believe they know me—yet. The third one must be local here. Never saw him before."

He rotated the eyepiece over to Toledano.

"The one on the right. Yes, he's ours," Toledano said. "They've been sniffing around. The one gentleman is Colombian. You knew that, I suppose."

"Since they're from a Colombian cartel's staging area on our border, yeah," Weeks said. "They seem pretty open about their movements. Have they been to see you?"

"Not yet. Hadn't realized it, but now I see *you* brought them," he replied.

Weeks shot him back a look, then opened the door and asked Dronne in for a look.

"Smugglers," Dronne said after one quick glance through the scope. "I know the guy on the right. Delacroix, n'est-ce pas? A very nasty man."

"I don't know his *name*," the lawyer said, indignant. "Never met him."

"There they go. Let's take a walk," Weeks said.

Weeks left his Stetson on Toledano's maple hat rack.

The cowboy, the Frenchman and the now-nervous Spaniard walked back up La Rambla to the Calle Fernando, trying to keep the torpedoes in sight. The walking arsenals cut down a stairway into a vaulted subterranean restaurant. Weeks led the pursuit. Now the smell of fish and the noise doubled. There was a steady roar from the hundred twenty people packed into booths separated by planters with ferns and philodendra. The walls were covered with squares of smoky mirror glass. A giant Portuguese tureen with the *fruta de mar* soup of the day sat on a tiled counter. The soup varied daily depending on what came in on the seiners and trawlers. Today it was cod and calamari.

The three torpedoes were seated in a booth at the other end. Weeks picked a spot where he could observe them via mirror. He watched them order drinks and a cup of soup while one of them tapped out a phone number on his cell, which chirped in protest, then he pulled out the retractable antenna with his teeth.

Weeks and Dronne scooped ladles' full of soup into their bowls and sat down opposite the pale, frightened Toledano, who was worrying the torpedoes might notice him. Couldn't eat. But he ordered one sherry, then another. Smiled weakly. He'd eat after all.

"How's the soup?" he asked.

The two customs officers nodded silently.

The lawyer got up and waddled down to the soup counter, ladled himself a bowl, and waddled back. The three of them ate in silence, except for Weeks asking about the weather. It had been raining along the Pyrenees.

Toledano went back for seconds, but when he got back, the pistoleros were on the move again, and Weeks spoke rapidly: "Got to go. Want you to reschedule that meeting. Tonight or tomorrow at the latest. You *will* wait at your office today until I get back?"

Already walking as he said it.

Toledano nodded unhappily. *Americans.* Dropping in as if they owned your country? So *cock-sure,* Toledano grumbled. *Why go along with them?*

"The son of a bitch is probably right is probably why," he sighed.

The afternoon sun was low, beaming on a Zurburan print of geese and dogs on Toledano's wall when Weeks poked his head in and grabbed his hat just after four.

"Well?" he asked the lawyer.

"I've told him you're coming, and I've warned him about the gentlemen in black. I hope he doesn't shoot you by mistake. Tomorrow. At the ranch."

Farga's a little mountain foothill town with stone houses sitting between two rivers, the Segre and the Negurra, beyond the north-eastern corner of the plain of Aragon, near the Basque state of Andorra. The Cortes family had hundreds of square miles of range and olive orchards below the Pyrenees, with cattle grazing among stout olive trees.

The heraldic crest of seashells divided by a diagonal sash marked every fencepost along the highway and along the banks of the Rio Segre.

They picked horses and rode up from the corrals at Farga, next to the hotel where Dronne left the rental car, to the finca northwest of town. Rough country. Scrub foothills and canyons, with the cattle working to stay on the sunny side, the warm side, till they ran up against the fence.

Dronne sat a horse poorly. Weeks led him through the herd that was scattered along the fence for more than two kilometers. The cattle could not remember which end of the line was the front and which was the back. So they stayed strung out there, and down from the foothill came a horseman. To move a herd too dumb to move itself. His face was chapped and leathery from wind and sun, but Weeks recognized him. Miguel wore a Stetson knockoff made in

Mexico. Shirt buttoned all the way up. Kerchief tucked down into the collar. The young man wore a chrome-plated thirty-eight Colt in a Western holster. He sat a silver-studded Mexican parade saddle that made no sense on the range.

"Miguel," Weeks said.

"Mister Weeks. Hear you want to talk."

"In a couple months you change so much? Can that be good?" Weeks said.

"Bein' out in it all day, even after a couple weeks, made a difference. Plus, you know, putting all that shit behind me," he said.

"You seem to like it out here," Weeks said. "Seem to fit."

"Yeah, it's good. My great-greats all come from here, this very spot. It's a better place than Santito. More like up on the Gila. It was why they wanted to settle up there."

"What they got you doin'?"

"Oh, you know. Nothing unordinary. Ridin' fence, running cows, cleanin' barns, just like the Endicotts, except someday this will all be mine," he said.

"Yours? How?"

"Old man said."

"Will you come back and testify at an inquest for Millie?"

"No."

"Her family, they . . ."

"They'd like to see me get the needle," he said. "Them and the Alderetes and the Archibalds. Excuse me just a minute."

The young man rode down to the western end of the line of cattle. The two cows at the end looked at each other as if asking which one was going to move first.

"Hah!" Miguel said to them, slapping his leg with his coil of rope. "Hah. Hah!"

The cattle sort of bumped into each other until they figured which way to go.

One swat to the Numero Uno bull and he was running. Swung his head as he ran. The others followed the bull, and Miguelito rode back to his visitors.

"This here's Alex Dronne," Weeks said. "A French agent. He got me here."

Miguel shook his hand.

"Somewhere we can talk?" Weeks said.

"Up on that rise. Old stone line shack. Built originally by the Romans."

"Can't really wait for you to get these critters moved up the line," Weeks said. "We better all ride up there. Couple things you need to know. The Cali. They found you."

"So the lawyer told me," he said. "And this morning the police called to tell me señor Toledano's body was found along the tracks near Tossa. Shot and dumped."

Weeks' mouth fell open. "We don't have much time," he said.

Miguel looked at Weeks' long-barrel forty-four magnum.

"That cannon will be handy. See you have a holster—finally," the boy said.

"I see *you* have one. And I see my partner's gun in it."

"This guy's gun?" he said, tilting his head at Dronne. "You're crazy."

"Not this guy. My old partner, the cop who died," Weeks said. "The one old Octavio had executed up there by Lordsburg."

"This was *my father's* gun. So I'm told," Miguel said. "Not some cop's."

"That's why I came," Weeks said. "That, and to finish the war, if we can."

"Glad you came," the kid said, tying his horse to an old hitching rail.

He unlocked the coarse wooden door with black iron hinges.

"Come on in." He flicked on the lights. "Solar. Went solar two years ago. Almost the whole ranch, the well pumps. We still use wind, though."

"Very impressive," Dronne said.

Modestly furnished. Sofa, bunk, table, one chair. Tight fit.

"Sit down," the boy said, hanging his hat and slicking back all that hair, which had grown over his ears.

"Best open the window. We're blind in here," Weeks said. "Torpedoes en route."

Miguel threw open the shutters. Light flooded in. A breeze stirred the grasses.

"Well, look down this valley," Miguel said.

Sunlight bounced off the surface of the pond outside the

cottage and from the flowing waters of the Rio Segre down in the draw.

"Anybody coming up this draw, we'll see 'em five miles off," the boy said.

"Any guns besides the ones we're carrying?" Weeks asked him.

"An old rifle."

"Let's see it," Weeks said.

A rifle made in Germany, 1921. The bullets in a rotting leather belt seemed to be intact, but one could not be sure until the trigger was pulled, and then it was too late.

"Civil war?" Weeks asked Miguel, who shrugged.

"Got to be," Dronne said. "The only war Spain's been in since nineteen twenty-one. The Germans sent military advisors."

"It'll have to do," Weeks said.

"We should tell the chief of police down in Farga," Miguel said.

"Toledano was supposed to do that. Now we don't know if he did," Weeks said.

"How much time have we got?" the boy asked, checking his thirty-eight.

"Maybe none," Weeks said.

Dronne put the wood chair by the window and watched.

"Got binoculars?" Dronne wondered.

The boy rummaged in a cupboard beneath the sink. He fished out a captured pair of German field glasses, also left over from the Spanish Civil War. One lens was full of foggy condensation and mold. But the other lens seemed to work fairly well.

They all sat down, Weeks on the bunk, Miguel on the sofa toying with his gun.

"What do you know about your father?" Weeks asked him.

"Octavio? A lot. Why?"

"Know things all your life, then suddenly it all changes," Weeks said. "Be ready."

"He won't change. Bullheaded, dangerous like you, a cop who tends to shoot."

"Well, you're this close, but you're wrong. Your dad was a cop," Weeks told him.

Miguel looked at Dronne. Bizarre situation. It occurred to him suddenly these men might be the real killers. But Weeks was holding out a folded paper. Waving it. Miguel took it. A letter. Octavio's signature at the bottom.

"Well, it says you're trying to protect me but nothing about this cop," Miguel said. "Does Octavio know about this?"

"Oh, yes," Weeks said, pulling out a copy of the indictment. "See, this here tells he's accused of . . . killing a police officer. See this? Michael Samuels. My partner."

Miguel read the indictment. "Nothing about me being some cop's son."

"Read the affidavit. It's at the end."

Miguel looked at Dronne, wondering if the Frenchman would help him if Weeks pulled out that cannon and started blasting.

"You need to listen to this, son. Mike Samuels was his name. Mike was my partner. He and I went to work for Sheriff Corona. Read the affidavit."

"He, Samuels, was a cop?" Miguel said, reading. "Says Octavio killed him. Says my mom . . ." He looked at Weeks in disbelief, then anger.

"See that gun?" Weeks said, pointing at the kid's Colt. "Can I show you?"

The kid looked hard at both men, reluctant to give up his gun.

"That's good," Weeks said. "Good to be cautious. But you need to see this."

"What the hey," Miguel said. "Guess if you were going to shoot me, I'd be dead." He handed the gun butt first to Weeks.

"See this ivory handle?" Weeks said. "It slides forward. Ever notice that?"

The kid took a closer look. The gnarled ivory rotated forward on the set screw.

"Look at the inside of this ivory plate. His name, Mike Samuels."

"So they told me wrong—about this gun," Miguel said.

"They told you right. Understand? Mike Samuels was your father."

"Don't know," he said. "I just don't know . . ." He finished reading the affidavit, the confession: "I did confront Agent Michael Samuels on that night and did shoot him through the window of his patrol unit after learning of his affair with my wife."

It was signed "Octavio Cortes" in that familiar wet-ink flourish.

Miguel looked up at him with eyes a little wider.

"Octavio is not my—*unbelievable!*" the kid said. "Ramos tried to tell me . . . that the Costillas killed my father. He said that, let's see. He told me that right after he shot Fred Archibald. We boosted Fred's car. Kind of a joke. Didn't get very far. Got stuck in the sand. Fred came after us. Wish he wouldn't have. Ramos cut him down, then he says, 'See that, little Miguelito?' That's the way those Costillas killed your daddy.' Octavio had Ramos whipped for that, and Ramos apologized. Told me he'd been lying. Always believed he was lying, anyway."

"Mike was shot pointblank sitting at the wheel—wasn't any Costillas. Now the situation's reversed for old Octavio. He's in a war, and so they're coming for you, too."

"I'm ready for them," Miguel said, patting the old German rifle.

"You're not shooting that. You get my backup," Weeks said, pulling a thirty-eight snub out of his leg holster.

Dronne shook his head: "You brought that through French customs? How?"

"Sorry, amigo," he said. "I won't do it again. Promise."

Miguel grinned, then Weeks grinned. There was too much of his father in the boy's manner, too much to describe. The way the eyebrows moved when he talked. The way his mouth pulled up to the right. The way he tilted his head, and his jaw muscles twitched. And the readiness. Always the brink of mobilization. Mike Samuels. Ghost.

"You crossed into New Mexico," Weeks said, "to get away from Octavio?"

"From Ramos. My bodyguard. What a joke. I was his prisoner."

"You came across after New Year's, after Juanito Alderete was shot."

"Yeah, their whole family blamed me. Even Octavio thought I'd shot him."

"You were with the boys who did it," Weeks said.

"Yeah, trying to stop them. Had a hold of Ramos' arm. But they went ahead anyway. Didn't listen to me. Afterward, Ramos says. 'You come out with us; you go down with us. Just like you pulled the trigger yourself. What you get for messing with our business, Mi-guel-i-to.'"

"So you crossed."

"Yeah, went to work for Endicott. But Ramos and Octavio and my uncle Jackie came 'n got me."

"They took you back, but you broke out again. Came across one more time. That night my gun went off—why'd you do that?"

"Heading for the airport. You scared hell out of me with that Tec-Nine, Mister Weeks, I tell you. Sent me back to Jesus. In that cornfield? I could see you. Sitting there. The whole time. Thought you were plain off your rocker."

"Where were you?" Weeks said.

"Right directly across on the other side of where the car went in. Opposite you."

"How long?" Weeks asked.

"Seemed like hours after you left, but it was about forty minutes.

"Just one question: Why Juanito?"

"Why they shot him? He mouthed off. Said he was blowing the whistle on the Cali. He'd already talked to Hartley, down at J-W. There was a congressman coming to talk to him. Juanito didn't know Octavio would be delighted to see the Cali go."

"Yeah, Hartley set us up," Weeks said. "We never saw. Never imagined Hartley would turn. They got to him. Got him dirty. He figured he had to turn. Lookin' for a way out. But there was no way out. They set us up, son, set us all up. Set up Octavio. Even set Hartley up. And you went up the Gila, up through the wilderness, up to the E-Bar-E. Wolf country. Cliff had a problem. Needed help."

"*Cheap* help. Didn't know me from Adam. While I was *wrangling*, as he called it, he wanted me to scare Millie Braden off the wolves. How could I do that? Cliff told me *steer clear*. Said, 'Jim, you got to convince her before it's too late. She won't listen to us any more. Maybe she'll listen to you. Scare her if you got to, whatever.' But I don't care about the wolves or Cliff's problem with the wolves. The other thing: She didn't scare. Of the whole bunch, she was the only one worth anything. I just cared about her. She'd've been a doctor or something. Was a privilege knowing her. Little kid like that, what, twelve years old, acting like my big sister. She was, she was . . ."

He shook his head, and the tears started to flow.

"See? You'd have had to be blind to miss it," Weeks said.

"She was a little girl," Miguel said, slowing himself down. "Would have come to her senses. I'd never be right for her, y'know? She was too smart to kid herself that way. Got me wrong if you think I'd rob the cradle. But I'd do anything for her. Anything."

"Even make an exception if she grew up and wanted *you*."

"Man, you seen too many movies."

Dronne, keeping watch, was interested in one thing only. The trouble at hand.

"How long would it take the police in Farga to get here?" Dronne asked.

The kid smiled, then laughed. Rubbed his chin. Grinned in that way that caught Weeks completely off guard. His father's grin. His *face*, in fact. Funny he'd never noticed till today as far as he knew, and now it was obvious. The grin transformed him.

"About a month," the kid said. "Why?"

"They're here," Dronne said, pointing at the large yellow thing that had stopped down in the distance. He trained the semi-binoculars on the bus and on the three dark figures that got off, then three more. Spun the lens in search of focus. Finally got them sharply in his sights.

"Delacroix," he said. "From Marseille. Killed an old lady up in Dijon, then crashed the border into Switzerland and disappeared. You got any vehicles up here?"

"No, my uncle Diego took off with the truck three days ago. He's not due back until tomorrow night. Can I look?"

He took the spyglass and found the range. "I know two of those guys," he said. "They work for the cartel. You want a look, Mister Weeks?"

"Just for a second," Weeks said, "then I think we attack."

The assailants worked their way separately up from the highway on either side of the Rio Segre. They had walky-talkies. As they drew closer, Weeks could see they had good mountaineering shoes that they obviously planned to use in their escape, but worse than useless for the sodden fields.

"Rain here lately?" he asked the boy.

"Pretty steady the past four days, why?"

"A hunch." Weeks pointed at his own shoes. Muddy.

"They won't be moving very well out there," he said, "No good at all in the mud."

"What are you suggesting?" Dronne said.

"You mean ride out like cavalry?" Miguel said. "Like Custer?"

"Get ready to ride," Weeks said. "I will cover with this German relic. If the first shot doesn't blow up in my face, you can charge the bastards, and I will pick 'em off as they try to shoot at you."

Like punctuation, Bonifacio's first shot rang out and fell short.

"I'd suggest *now* before they find the range," Weeks said. "Let's see how much the Germans knew about rifles in 1921."

He filled the clip with ammo from the disintegrating belt. He snapped the clip into the rifle. He folded down the gun sight. He lined it up on Bonifacio Gomez's head.

"Get set, and . . ." He pulled off a round that reverberated among the springs in the bunk beds.

Two horses started at a gallop from a dead stop, emerging, rearing angrily from the trees around the stone house. They thundered down the plain at the intruders on either side of the field, using the trees as cover. They had to jump some hedges. Dronne fell behind cutting around them.

Bonifacio was on the ground. The bullet hit him low, between two ribs, and nicked his appendix on its way out. He was in shock. Miguel stopped and picked up Bonifacio's Tec-Nine and his Ruger thirty-eight. Now he had three guns. He put two in the saddle bag. Held onto the Tec-9.

Weeks lined up his sights on Delacroix. The shot exploded, and Delacroix went down. But the barrel of the German gun appeared to have cracked with shot Number Two. Weeks doubted a third shot would be safe or accurate, so he checked the ammunition in his forty-four, then ran out and mounted his horse.

Miguel and Dronne, riding the flanks, pinched back in on old Mariano Holguin, the senior Cali torpedo, who wore glasses, did not drink and put his money in a Colombian bank every Friday. Holguin was a serious weapons technician. Always gunned to the hilt. Always with light weapons. Always deadly.

But now he was alone. And cornered.

Weeks barreled straight down the middle at him like the cavalry of Napoleon, or Custer. Holguin stood up and started shooting. Weeks could hear the bullets missing him, mostly on the right. Then he saw Holguin correct his sights. So Weeks instinctively pulled up, vaulted clear and dropped down behind his horse, which took the round and stumbled forward to the ground. Weeks spread out prone behind the still breathing horse.

"Easy girl," he told her. "Easy."

The horse's breathing was raspy and uneven, and finally it stopped altogether.

Weeks peered over the edge of her carcass, and another bullet sliced into her right below his eyes. It came out of her and hit him in the shoulder holster. Knocked him back on his side, bruised him. And then he heard a couple of shots from the left and one shot from the right, and then silence. When he looked, he saw the other three still running. He rubbed his bruised shoulder, got up and walked out onto the Plain of Farga.

Bonifacio and Delacroix were still breathing, but Holguin was finished.

Miguel had a scratch on his shoulder. Dronne, who fired the final shot, had not a mark on him. Weeks looked under his holster and found the bullet peeking through by about a sixteenth of an inch.

Dronne asked Weeks: "You know best—you think those three will come back? Or send more?"

"Not today. Maybe tomorrow."

Dronne looked worried.

"Just kidding," Weeks said.

Chief of police Daniel Cortez, who disavowed any relationship to the eses, as he called his Cortes cousins, had mobilized his five officers and their antique Mercedes paddywagon. They were parked around the bend south of the Cortes farm.

The last two Colombians and a Spaniard came round the bend and ran *smack* into the wagon.

Weeks, Dronne and Miguel headed down to the tiny Farga jail— a basement basically, that extended back into the hillside. It was a cave. Steel-bar partitions segregated the subterranean cells. Miguel was dumped pretty far back. They weren't allowed to see him. Weeks called Toledano's office and was told they'd already sent Toledano's young partner, Ruy Menendez, who arrived in a matter of minutes.

Then Miguel was free on bail.

Weeks and Dronne sat in the courthouse waiting room. Miguel came out and sat with them.

"Had enough? Ready for some more?" Weeks asked him.

The kid grinned that metamorphosis. "Sure, tell me another one."

"He may be ready. I may not," Dronne said, "but a pleasure meeting you, and I will come visit you soon in America." Dronne left them there and headed for Andorra.

Weeks and Miguelito crossed the street and went into the Santa Cruz Hospital. In an alcove of the surgery waiting room, Weeks and Miguel sat down. Weeks spread documents on the corner lamp table between them.

"The first time we ventured south, Mikey and I, we had visitors' tags like we were going to a convention. The job was to assay prostitution spilling across the border on a daily and nightly outcall basis, they noted the old Jalisco was being redone and would eventually be three stories instead of two. It took a few years.

"We went around to Octavio's fortress. The great wall of Santito encircled him like a prison, and guards with automatic weapons sat around the clock in the corner towers and at the gate. Octavio wanted to lavish luxury on these poor public servants, to give the idea he was on their side somehow. Some took favors from him. Some didn't.

"We, Mike and I, stayed clean. Or thought we did. But when Marianna came down the stairs, and Octavio introduced her to us, our very souls were in danger. Your mother was like Greek sculpture. Such grace. Did you know she was . . ."

Miguel interrupts: "Octavio always told me she was my ma, but then after she was gone he told me she wasn't. One year my sister Felicia came home from school and told me Version Number One again. There's no way Felicia plays along with him. She never comes back there. I get a call from her twice a year. My birthday and Christmas."

Weeks resumes: "That first time. Octavio was talking to us about what he perceived to be the border problems. Anyway, Mike went looking for the bathroom. *He* was gone awhile. Octavio noticed and got nervous. He sent Rico on a search mission."

"Rico didn't really know what happened.

"But he guessed. It went something like: Marianna was *there*. Barefoot.

"'Would you like to see the house? Or the gardens?'

"Both," Mike would've said, Weeks was sure.

Marianna led Mike Samuels upstairs. Paintings. Rugs. Chandeliers. Elegance everywhere. Weeks wished he'd had a script. He found himself stammering, dodging, revising, editing, taming down the story:

. . . How Mike walked with Marianna through the gardens. She invited him back. And he came back. Many, many times. To see her.

One time too often took them past the boundary checkpoint.

Months later, Marianna stood before Mike in an upstairs hallway, a light in her eyes, a distant smile. Mike had only to touch her, and her summer dress, suspended by two single-button straps, fell to the floor with a slight contraction of her shoulder blades. And they made love. Weeks had to sort through what to tell him now and what to save.

There was a garden bench where she sat a certain way, and he was suddenly out of control. And there was a pool, deliberately private, trees thick around it, where they remained locked in a permanent embrace that he carried within him until he died.

Octavio sent Rico, who found them walking together down a path, examining roses and cherry seedlings. Clothed, walking apart. But something about them told Rico everything. Found their wet footprints. Noted the dry clothing. Octavio sent him to check for wet bathing suits in the cabana. "Seeing's believing," Octavio said. There were wet bathing suits, evidence of an innocent swim. But Rico mistrusted that evidence. He trusted rather the ghost images he saw, the walking arm-in-arm, ghosts entwined like smoke from two cigarettes. Rico chose what he saw and believed *that.*

Octavio tried for the longest time to turn us, Mikey and me.

Tried to send us gifts. Even had Marianna call *me.* Could *I* come down for lunch? I went. We had lunch. I left. Octavio met me on the way out. Wanted to know how many new agents were coming in under our appropriation from Congress. I told him five. He wanted to know how they would be deployed. I told him I had no idea. I was working for Corona. The agents were working for Frey.

"But you could find out," he said.

"'Eventually,' I said. 'Right now, I don't think even Frey knows.'"

"Will any of them end up at JW?" Octavio said, meaning the Jackrabbit Wells border crossing outpost.

Weeks had no idea he, himself, would end up at JW.

Mike took to meeting Marianna down at a quaint little bed-and-breakfast in Llanos, south of JW, clearing through Bill Ramacher, Hartley's predecessor, then coming back through him hours later.

Michael was in love. And his wife, busy with two boys, didn't really care that they were drifting apart. She had strong views on boys and guns. The more Mike stayed away, the better. For her boys.

She never found out *why* he was out so much. She was about to, though. And Weeks guessed she'd be worse hurt than when her husband died. He cautioned Miguel about it.

"That's what I want to know—his death—what triggered that?" Miguel said.

"It happened when you were just five. For five years, Octavio had almost convinced himself you were his—and Marianna's. But not quite. He told everyone he was protecting you when he tacked Ramos onto you like a tail on a donkey, but apparently he was mainly thinking he'd keep an eye on you and your mother," Weeks told the boy. "He was deeply suspicious of Marianna. He thought she was going to leave and take you. That hurt his pride. That could not happen."

"Illegitimate—the old man never came out and said it. But I could never please him—or get away from him. I tried. After Millie died, he took me back to Santito and told me I was his heir, that he would protect me. Sent me off to Spain," Miguel said. "Said I would inherit the Farga ranch."

"By then, of course, your real parents were dead. He killed Mike.

Then Marianna died a few years later. Self-fulfilling prophecy," Weeks said.

"Suicide," Miguel said. "They covered it up."

"Called it drugs," Weeks said. "Rico told me. I'm very sorry about that, son."

"They, Ramos, said she was a *whore*," Miguel recalled bitterly. "That she came up through Octavio's organization. The old man did nothing for her, never defended her."

Weeks had Octavio's statement, and Miguel finished reading it. Rico, the old man's most trusted pistolero, it said, had caught Marianna in the cabana with Michael Samuels in a compromising position. In fact, Rico had told Weeks "she was wrapped around him." But Weeks chose less graphic terms for the young son.

"Your father," he said to Miguel. "Michael Samuels, was a fine man and would have been a great father to you."

Rico nearly fell into the pool. Then he went in the cabana and took another look. They never noticed him.

"Rico told me, to this day, he cannot imagine them apart. And of course Octavio never ran any DNA tests. Afraid to see those results. He never let go of the fantasy that you were his son," Weeks said, "in spite of everything.

"Your mother and father are buried on opposite sides of the border, almost within sight of each other—Mike down in Concha Cemetery, Marianna in Rio Santo's."

"Your mother was from a fine family," Weeks said. "She was just a woman in love, and this is what can happen sometimes when people fall in love."

"I know," Miguel said.

"I know you do, son," Weeks said. "Lucky to know it."

"But that had nothing to do with Millie," Miguel said.

"Right. Keep it straight that you were trying to save that child's life. Simple. One clear fact. Forget the rest of it. Let it go. Millie'd want you to have a life. Now, you can."

Weeks sifted through the rest of the papers on the corner table.

"Oh, yeah, and I brought you this from the Bradens," Weeks said, handing Miguel several pages of documents and a bound volume with a small brass lock tab on a leather strap. He also handed him the key they had found in her jewelry box.

"Their daughter's diary," he said, "and all her papers, observations, photographs, taped interviews, on the wolf project and all the other projects."

Miguel seemed moved, and tears filled his eyes again.

"Does this mean they forgive me?" he asked.

"It could," Weeks said. "Might could."

"You read this?" the young man asked.

"No, I haven't read it, except the very last page, which would have been evidence. And a summary prepared by the coroner in assessing the subjective causes of death. It's private stuff. Some of it's meant for you, and nobody else."

"It mentions me?"

"I'd say. But understand: She loved you in a very idealized way. A dream."

The young man stood up over the table and leafed through the papers and photos.

"She knew biology better than most adults," Miguel said, "but I'm not the right one to. . .."

"She was very young," Weeks said. "The young can get obsessive about a thing. Might not know it as well as they might just make you think they know it."

"That wasn't Millie."

"When the subject was you, it was," Weeks said, putting his arm around Miguel's neck. "Two weeks ago I would have gladly snapped this little neck. Now, you're family."

"You want this for a report—for the inquest? My perspective. What if I can't tell it the way you propose?" Miguel asked.

"Don't even mention her death. Okay? Death's a given. Don't refer to it."

Miguel started picking up the papers, one by one, stacking them neatly. "I'll try."

"Sure. Where do I reach you?"

"Tell me where you'll be—I'll reach *you*. Easier that way."

"Tell me where you want me to be. I'll be there."

Miguel nodded. "Back on the Gila, up on the divide," he said, "where we belong." He put all the papers back into the folder, tucked it under his arm and ducked at the door, on his way out.

Weeks watched him walk easily down the hall. Seemed taller. Harder to fit into a small square. Was he America, Mexico, Spain, France—all of the above?

Why not? Weeks thought, then said it aloud. "Why not?"

Chapter Twenty-Three

Smoke

Sugar bent down and pulled up a buttercup. Tasted like dandelion wine, like a potion from a time when magic was essential for people to survive. The Sugar horse munched appreciatively. She loved this part of the forest, where elves and fairies and tribal gods used to skip from blossom to blossom like helicopters carrying contraband. Not much out'n'about these days, certainly not helicopters.

She switched her tail. Couldn't be too careful. Something alit upon her hindquarters, and it might have been a fly. It wasn't. It was a dew drop from a sycamore leaf. Too early in the day, just at dawn, for horMarlie puttered nearby at a pond where beaver had been busy. Looking for sign of elk or deer or cougar. There were tracks from easily thirty elk, a few deer, in the pond's grassy, spongey apron. No cougar. That would be like hitting the lottery . . . unless the lottery hit you. No, she'd expect the few cougars in the forest to be on higher ground at this time of the year, late April.

My God, she thought. Look here. Tracks too big for coyote, too small for a wolf—or at least an alpha wolf. The tracks maybe belonged to a dog, except, she wondered, where did they go? Maybe there were helicopters out here after all. The tracks just came to an end. That ledge had to be ten feet high, right above her, and something scruffed it there on the edge where the buttercups hung down in clusters.

She put one hand on Sugar's neck, and Sugar responded by looking up. She was ready. Marlie swung her right foot over the saddle roll, and she slid perfectly into place on the embossed and polished leather. She looked down at the silver star that shone on top of her saddle horn. A Zuni star, inlaid with cobalt blue cloisonné. She called it her Zuni saddle because of the silver trim, made by a Zuni silversmith.

Not much had changed in the forest since then, the forest that spread from the Rio Grande all the way across to Arizona and then continued on in Arizona with different names. Same forest, though, all the way almost to Kingman, Arizona, almost all the way across from the Rio Grande to the mighty Colorado, one forest. The silver for her saddle came from Chloride, and old Charlie Starr dug it out of the Black Range when he was young, had a stash of it, and made Marlie Williams' saddle back when Marlie was young and single and the world believed she would kick the old globe around like a pelota.

Well, now the world had kicked back. Her daughter and this ranch she believed had been her birthright were gone. This was her last day as owner of the Two Square, and she meant to have it full strength for at least twelve of those hours riding Millie's horse. She started on the west slope of the Blacks, not far from La Rondita, and she meant to ride into Gila Wells by sundown. Had a folded blanket tied on the saddle in case she got slowed by a dammed-up river, where the beaver might have made fording difficult, or a landslide, or some remnant of glacial snow, or wildfire, or if she got throwed.

She nudged Sugar's ribs gently. Sugar went up the switchback to where Marlie believed the wolf tracks led. Had to be. Had to be wolf. Too big a leap for a dog. But not a wolf. Just a scrappy young wolf, probably female, judging by the size of her paws.

Yep, the tracks resumed up there. The scuff marks were made by her hind paws. That's how far she jumped. *Go, girl!* She pointed Sugar at the trees ahead, with the Spanish moss called Saint Joseph's Beard hanging down like filigree and the dewy spider webs glistening in the low sun. She rode an hour with the early sun at her back before she felt its warmth. Then she stopped and listened. She heard Wells River falling from nine thousand to seven thousand feet in just five miles. Sounded like kindergartners at play.

Marlie's bitterness melted away as the sun climbed the sky and the sound of children laughing seemed to grow louder.

And then, with a single turn around a rock outcropping that had been split open by an ever-widening tree, she came face to face with her daughter.

Millie looked fine. She looked healthy. She raised a hand in wistful greeting.

"Hi, mom," she said.

"*Millie?*" her mother gasped. "Millie? Do you live out here now?"

Her daughter nodded her head. Something a little bit wild about her hair, as though she had slept in the buttercups and dandelions, with little stub ends of different grasses sticking out between the curls.

"Are you all right?" her mother said. "Can we come and see you here?"

She nodded again.

"We miss you, dear," she said. "Oh, we miss you so."

"I know, mama. I miss you too, a lot, but I'm not supposed to talk," her girl said.

"Not *supposed* to? Why not?"

"Because I'm a spirit, mama. A spirit of the forest. And that's really all I'm allowed to say. And even then, just to whisper it, so it could be mistaken for the wind."

"But. . ."

Just as quickly the girl was gone.

"Where are you going? Where have you gone? Millie?" she called out. She still heard the children laughing, and she followed that sound down to that silted bedrock table land overlooking the ancient seabed, where the haze filled the basin like the tide.

There ahead she saw the wolf. Collarless. Paused, a paw raised. Waiting. The wolf's eyes met hers. Some kind of communication passed between them. Marlie never could explain, never would try. Whatever it was, whatever it meant, she let it last as long as the wolf wanted. But the wolf finally turned and waded into the smoky morning tide.

Muscle by muscle, hair by hair, the wolf dissolved in the smoke. And when the rider approached the place where the wolf had wisped away, the tracks ended and the hard knots in her heart opened up and the tears finally flowed. The bitter tears that the woman on the horse had hoped for, that she needed, she had found.